More advance praise for

THE TAINTED CUP

"Bennett brilliantly melds genres in this exceptional mystery-fantasy.... The worldbuilding is immediately involving, Bennett's take on a classic detective duo dynamic feels fresh and exciting, and the mystery itself twists and turns delightfully. Readers will be wowed."

—*Publishers Weekly* (starred review)

"Highly recommended ... Introduces readers to a conspiracy of murder and skullduggery as seen through the eyes of a naive junior investigator . . . as his boss and mentor, the rather Sherlockian Ana, threads her way through a complex conspiracy of murders."

—*Library Journal* (starred review)

"Inspired by Nero Wolfe with a bit of Hannibal Lecter added to his prime investigator, Bennett ... kicks off the Shadow of the Leviathan series, which will delight fans of fantasy-infused mysteries."

—*Booklist* (starred review)

"A true fantasy mystery, with a leading duo who stand with Holmes and Watson among the greats ... and Bennett sets it all in a squishy, fascinating, biopunk world I'm dying to find out more about. Bring on the next one!"

—Django Wexler, author of
the Shadow Campaigns series

"A classic murder mystery set against dazzling worldbuilding and sly social commentary . . . Robert Jackson Bennett doesn't miss."
—James L. Sutter, co-creator of
the Pathfinder roleplaying game

"One of the wildest, most original stories I've ever had the privilege to explore . . . I am in awe of Bennett's creativity, the intricate plotting, and this immersive world filled with mushroom air conditioners, killer trees, and giant leviathans that stretches the imagination. I loved every second of it. This is a book that has planted roots in my head for the rest of my life."
—Wesley Chu, #1 *New York Times*
bestselling author of the War Arts Saga

"I loved this. A twisty detective story, a weird fantasy, a thrilling adventure—*The Tainted Cup* is a masterstroke. I want Bennett to write a dozen of these, and send them to me yesterday."
—Max Gladstone, *New York Times*
bestselling co-author of *This Is How You Lose the Time War*

"A riveting murder mystery wrapped in a twisty conspiracy, set in a vivid fantasy world terrorized by eldritch monsters . . . If you love unique, genre-bending, boundary-pushing fantasy as much as I do, look no further than Robert Jackson Bennett."
—Fonda Lee, author of the Green Bone Saga

"Original, imaginative, and suspenseful, *The Tainted Cup* superbly blends mystery and fantasy in this vivid, complex novel. I couldn't put it down. Give me more of this world and these characters ASAP!"
—Meg Gardiner, #1 *New York Times*
bestselling author of the UNSUB series

BY ROBERT JACKSON BENNETT

THE TAINTED CUP

THE
TAINTED
CUP

III

SHADOW OF THE LEVIATHAN:
BOOK 1

ROBERT JACKSON

BENNETT

NEW YORK

Copyright © 2024 by Robert Jackson Bennett
Map and ranking list chart copyright © 2024 by David Lindroth Inc.

Published in the United States by Del Rey, an imprint of Random House,
a division of Penguin Random House LLC, New York.

DEL REY and the CIRCLE colophon are registered trademarks of
Penguin Random House LLC.

Library of Congress Cataloging-in-Publication Data
Names: Bennett, Robert Jackson, author.
Title: The tainted cup: a novel / Robert Jackson Bennett.
Description: First edition. | New York: Del Rey, 2024. |
Series: Shadow of the Leviathan; Book 1
Identifiers: LCCN 2023039782 (print) | LCCN 2023039783 (ebook) |
ISBN 9781984820709 (hardcover acid-free paper) |
ISBN 9781984820723 (e-book)
Subjects: LCGFT: Fantasy fiction. | Detective and mystery fiction. | Novels.
Classification: LCC PS3602.E66455 T35 2024 (print) |
LCC PS3602.E66455 (ebook) | DDC 813/.6—dc23/eng/20230828
LC record available at https://lccn.loc.gov/2023039782
LC ebook record available at https://lccn.loc.gov/2023039783

Printed in the United States of America on acid-free paper

randomhousebooks.com

6 8 9 7

First Edition

Book design by Edwin A. Vazquez

For my mom and nana,

who were the gateway to murder mysteries

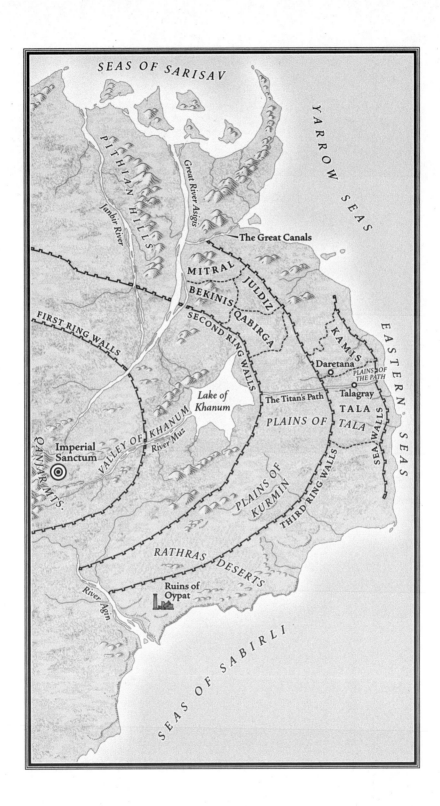

MILITARY RANKS
OF THE
GREAT AND HOLY EMPIRE OF KHANUM

(from highest to lowest)

CONZULATE

PRIFICTO

COMMANDER-PRIFICTO

COMMANDER

IMMUNIS

CAPTAIN

SIGNUM

PRINCEPS

MILITIS

I

III

THE MAN IN THE TREE

CHAPTER 1

|||

THE WALLS OF THE ESTATE EMERGED FROM THE morning fog before me, long and dark and rounded like the skin of some beached sea creature. I walked along them, trying to ignore the flutter of my heart and the trickle of sweat down my neck. A faint blue light glimmered in the mist ahead. With each step it calcified into a mai-lantern hanging above the estate's servants' gate; and there, leaning against the walls beside the gate, was the figure of a uniformed man in a shining steel cap waiting for me.

The princeps watched me approach. He cocked an eyebrow at me, and it climbed higher up his forehead the closer I came to him. By the time I'd finally stopped before him it'd almost joined the hair atop his head.

I cleared my throat in what I hoped was an authoritative manner, and said, "Signum Dinios Kol, assistant to the investigator. I'm here about the body."

The princeps blinked, then looked me up and down. Being as I was nearly a head taller than him, it took him a moment. "I see, sir," he said. He gave me a short bow—a quarter of a full bow, maybe a third—but then did not move.

"You do have a body, yes?" I asked.

"Well, we do, sir," he said slowly. He glanced over my shoulder down the fog-strewn lane behind me.

"Then what seems to be the issue?"

"Well, ah . . ." Again, a glance down the lane behind me. "Pardon, sir, but—where's the other one?"

"I'm sorry?" I asked. "Other one?"

"The investigator? When will she be arriving?"

I suppressed a flicker of worry. I'd dealt with this question when working other matters for my master, but doing so when the situation involved a dead body was another thing entirely. "The investigator isn't able to attend," I said. "I'm here to review the scene, interview the staff and any witnesses, and report back to her."

"The investigator is choosing to proceed with the investigation . . . *without* being present?" he said. "Might I ask why, sir?"

I took him in. His short mail shirt glinted in the low light, each ringlet dabbed with tiny pearls of condensation. Very fancy. Ornate belt at his waist, slightly soft belly hanging over the buckle—a consequence of early middle age. Same for the thread of gray in his beard. Black boots highly polished, trim woven with seaweed-stained leather. The only standard-issue item on his body was the longsword in his scabbard and his dark red cloak, indicating he was an Apothetikal: an imperial officer responsible for managing the Empire's many organic alterations. The rest of it he must've purchased himself, probably for a princely sum.

All this told me that even though I was a signum and thus technically outranked him, this man was not only older and wealthier than me, but he'd probably seen more in his career than I could imagine. I couldn't blame him for wondering why the investigator had sent this twenty-year-old boy in ratty boots to a death scene all on his own.

"The investigator usually is not present at investigations, Princeps," I said. "She sends me to assess the situation and uses my report to make the appropriate conclusions."

"The appropriate conclusions," the princeps echoed.

"Correct," I said.

I waited for him to permit me inside. He just stood there. I wondered if I was going to have to order him to let me into the estate. I'd

never given a direct order to an officer of another imperial administration before and did not entirely know how to go about doing it.

To my relief, he finally said, "Right, sir . . ." and reached into his
pocket. He took out a small bronze disc with a little glass vial set in
the center, which sloshed with black fluid. "You'll need to follow
close, sir. This gate is a bit old. Can be fussy."

He turned to face the servants' gate: a rounded aperture in the
smooth black surface of the estate walls. Hanging on the other side
of the aperture was a veil of curling, furred vines of a greenish-yellow
color. They trembled as the princeps approached—a disquieting,
juddering tremor—and fell back, allowing us to enter.

I kept close to the princeps as we walked through the gate, leaning down so my head didn't scrape the top. The vines smelled sweet
and sickly as they tickled the back of my neck. Likely altered to seek
out flesh, and if the princeps hadn't been carrying his "key"—the
vial of reagents in his hand—then the two of us would have been
paralyzed, or worse.

We emerged into the estate's inner yards. Dozens of mai-lanterns
twinkled in the morning gloom ahead of us, dangling from the gabled roof of the sprawling house set high on the hill beyond. A veran-
dah wrapped around the home, rope nets blooming with bright
decorative moss to shield windows from the morning sun. Floors
wide and smooth, wood polished to a fine shine. A cushioned section
sat on the eastern end—a miniature tea pavilion of a sort, but instead of a tea table there sat some massive animal's skull, its cranium
shaved off to be level. A rather ghoulish adornment for so fine a
place—and it was a fine place, easily the finest house I'd ever seen.

I looked at the princeps. He'd noticed my astonishment and was
smirking.

I adjusted my Iudex coat at the shoulders. They hadn't been able
to find one my size, and I suddenly felt terribly stupid-looking,
packed into this tight blue fabric. "What's your name, Princeps?" I
asked.

"Apologies, sir. Should have mentioned—Otirios."

"Have we identified the deceased, Otirios?" I asked. "I understand there was some issue with that."

"We think so, sir. We believe it is Commander Taqtasa Blas, of the Engineers."

"You believe it is? Why believe?"

This drew a sidelong glance. "You were informed that the nature of his death was an alteration, yes, sir?"

"Yes?"

"Well . . . such things can make it tricky to identify a body, sir." He led me across a small wooden bridge that spanned a trickling stream. "Or even," he added, "to identify it *as* one, sir. That's why we Apoths are here."

He gestured at the fog beyond. I searched the mist and spied figures roving through the gardens, also wearing coats and cloaks of dark red, all carrying what one might mistake to be birdcages; yet each cage contained not a bird, but a delicate fern.

"Checking for contagion," said Otirios. "But so far we've found nothing. No telltale plants have browned or died yet, sir. No sign of contagion on the estate grounds."

He led me to a thin fernpaper door in the estate house. As we approached I thought I heard some long, sustained sound within the mansion. I realized it was screaming.

"What's that?" I asked.

"Probably the servant girls," Otirios said. "They were, ah, the ones who got there first. Still quite agitated, as you can imagine."

"Didn't they find the body hours ago?"

"Yes. But they keep having outbursts. When you see the body, you'll understand why, sir."

I listened to the screams, wild and hysterical. I fought to keep my face clear of emotion.

I told myself to stay controlled and contained. I was an officer for the Iudex, the imperial administration responsible for manag-

ing the high courts and delivering justice throughout the Empire. I
was supposed to be at this fine home, even if it was filled with
screaming.

Otirios opened the door. The sound of the screaming grew far
louder.

I reflected that piss was supposed to stay in my body, but if that
screaming went on for much longer, that might not stay the case.

He led me inside.

THE FIRST THING that struck me was the cleanliness of the
place. Not just the absence of dirt—though there was no dirt, not a
smudge nor smear in sight—but there was a sterility to everything
before me, no matter how elegant: the dining couches were too
smooth and unblemished, and the woven silk mats laid in squares on
the floor were too unspoiled, perhaps having never known the tramp
of a foot. The whole house felt as cozy and comfortable as a surgeon's
knife.

Which wasn't to say it was not opulent. Miniature mai-trees had
been altered to grow down from the ceiling, acting as chandeliers—
something I'd never seen before—their fruits full to bursting with
the glowing little mai-worms, which cast a flickering blue light about
us. I wondered if even the air was expensive in here, then saw it was:
a massive kirpis mushroom had been built into the corner of every
main room—a tall, black fungus built to suck in air, clean it, and ex-
hale it out at a cooler temperature.

The shrieking went on and on from somewhere in the mansion. I
shivered a little, and knew it had nothing to do with the temperature
of the air.

"We've kept all the staff and witnesses here at the house, as the
investigator directed," Otirios said. "I expect you'll want to interview
them, sir."

"Thank you, Princeps. How many are there?"

"Seven total. Four servant girls, the cook, the groundskeeper, and the housekeeper."

"Who owns this estate? I take it not Commander Blas?"

"No, sir. This house is owned by the Haza clan. Did you not see the insignia?" He gestured to a little marking hanging over the entry door: a single feather standing tall between two trees.

That gave me pause. The Hazas were one of the wealthiest families in the Empire and owned a huge amount of land in the inner rings. The staggering luxury of this place began to make a lot of sense, but everything else grew only more confusing.

"What are the Hazas doing owning a house in Daretana?" I asked, genuinely bewildered.

He shrugged. "Dunno, sir. Maybe they ran out of houses to buy everywhere else."

"Is a member of the Haza clan here currently?"

"If they are, sir, they're damned good hiders. The housekeeper should know more."

We continued down a long hallway, which ended in a black stone-wood door.

A faint odor filled the air as we grew close to the door: something musty and sweet, and yet tinged with a rancid aroma.

My stomach trembled. I reminded myself to hold my head high, to keep my expression scowling and stoic, like a real assistant investigator might. Then I had to remind myself that I *was* a real assistant investigator, damn it all.

"Have you worked many death cases before, sir?" asked Otirios.

"Why?" I asked.

"Just curious, given the nature of this one."

"I haven't. Mostly the investigator and I have handled pay fraud among the officers here in Daretana."

"You didn't handle that murder last year? The sotted guard who attacked the fellow at the checkpoint?"

I felt something tighten in my cheek. "The Iudex Investigator position was created here only four months ago."

"Oh, I see, sir. But you didn't work any death inquiries with your investigator at your previous station?"

The muscle in my cheek tightened further. "When the investigator arrived here," I said, "I was selected from the other local Sublimes to serve as her assistant. So. No."

There was the slightest of pauses in Otirios's stride. "So ... you have only worked for an Iudex Investigator for *four months*, sir?"

"What's the point of this, Princeps?" I asked, irritated.

I could see the smirk playing at the edges of Otirios's mouth again. "Well, sir," he said. "Of all the death cases to be your first, I wouldn't much like it being this one."

He opened the door.

THE CHAMBER WITHIN was a bedroom, as grand as the rest of the house, with a wide, soft mossbed in one corner and a fernpaper wall and door separating off what I guessed was the bathing closet—for though I'd never seen a bathing closet inside a house, I knew such things existed. A mai-lantern hung in the corner; in the corner diagonal from it, another kirpis shroom. Beside it were two trunks and a leather satchel. Commander Blas's possessions, I guessed.

But the most remarkable feature of the room was the clutch of leafy trees growing in the center—for it was growing from within a person.

Or rather, *through* a person.

The corpse hung suspended in the center of the bedchamber, speared by the many slender trees, but as Otirios had said it was initially difficult to identify it as a body at all. A bit of torso was visible in the thicket, and some of the left leg. What I could see of them suggested a middle-aged man wearing the purple colors of the Imperial Engineering Iyalet. The right arm was totally lost, and the right leg had been devoured by the swarm of roots pouring out from the trunks of the little trees and eating into the stonewood floor of the chamber.

I stared into the roots. I thought I could identify the pinkish nub of a femur amid all those curling coils.

I looked down. An enormous pool of blood had spread across the floor, as smooth and reflective as a black glass mirror.

A flicker in my stomach, like it held an eel trying to leap out.

I told myself to focus, to breathe. To stay controlled and contained. This was what I did for a living now.

"It's safe to approach, sir," Otirios said, a little too cheerily. "We've inspected the whole of the room. Worry not."

I stepped closer to look at the greenery. They weren't really trees, but some kind of long, flexible grass—a bit like shootstraw, the hollow, woody grass they used to make piping and scaffolding. The thicket of shoots appeared to have emerged from between Blas's shoulder and neck—I spied a hint of vertebrae trapped within them and suppressed another pang of nausea.

Most remarkable was Blas's face. It seemed the shoots had grown multiple branches as they'd emerged from his torso, and one had shot sideways through Blas's skull, bending his head at an awful angle; yet the branch had somehow enveloped his skull above the upper jawline, swallowing his face and his nose and ears. All that was left of Blas's skull was his lower jaw, hanging open in a silent scream; and there, above it in the wood, a half ring of teeth and the roof of a mouth, submerging into the rippling bark.

I stared at his chin. A whisper of steely stubble; a faint scar on the edge from some accident or conflict. I moved on, looked at the rest of him. Left arm furred with light brown hair, fingers calloused and crackling from years of labor. The leggings on the left leg were stained dark with blood, so much so that it had pooled in his boot, filling it like a pot of sotwine.

I felt a drop on my scalp and looked up. The shoots had punched through the roof of the house, and the morning mist was drifting inside in dribs and drabs.

"Sticks out about ten span past the top of the house, if you're curious, sir," said Otirios. "Shot through four span of roofing like it was fish fat. So—a pretty big growth. Never seen anything like it."

"How long did this take?" I asked hoarsely.

"Less than five minutes, sir. According to the servants' testimony, that is. They thought it was a quake, the house shook so."

"Is there anything the Apoths have that can do this?"

"No, sir. The Apothetikal Iyalet has all kinds of grafts and suffusions to control the growth of plants—succus wheat that ripens within a quarter of a season, for example, or fruits that grow to three or four times their conventional size. But we've never made anything that can grow trees within minutes . . . or one that can grow from within a person, of course."

"Have we got any reason to believe it was intended for him?"

"Inconclusive, sir," said Otirios. "He's Engineering, moves around a good bit. Could be he accidentally ingested something during his travels or contaminated himself. There's no way to tell yet."

"Did he visit anyone else in town? Or meet any other infected official, or imperial personnel?"

"Doesn't seem so, sir," said Otirios. "It appears he departed from the next canton over and came straight here without meeting anyone."

"Has there ever been a record of any contagion like this?"

A contemptuous pucker to his lips. "Well. There are contagions all over the Empire, sir. Suffusions and grafts and alterations growing wild . . . Each one is different. I'd have to check."

"If it is contagion, it should spread, correct?"

"That's . . . the nature of contagions, sir?" said Otirios.

"Then how did it happen to this one man, and nothing and no one else?"

"Hard to say at this point, sir. We're checking Blas's movements now. He was on a tour of the outer cantons, including the sea walls, reviewing all the construction. The, ah . . ." He hesitated. ". . . The wet season is coming soon, after all."

I nodded, stone-faced. The coming of the wet season hung over the outer cantons of the Empire so heavily that ignoring it would be like trying to forget the existence of the sun.

"No one visited the room before Blas arrived?" I asked. "Or touched anything?"

"The servants did, of course. We only have their testimony to rely on there."

"And no signs of attempted entry?"

"No, sir. This place has more wardings than the Emperor's Sanctum itself. You've got to have reagents keys just to get close."

I considered this silently, recalling the number of windows and doors in this house.

"It'll be a fine thing if you can explain it, sir," Otirios said.

"What?" I said.

"A fine thing for a career." Another smile, this one somewhat cruel. "That's what you want, right, sir? Advancement? It's what any officer would want, I'd imagine."

"What I want," I said, "is to do my duty."

"Well, of course, sir."

I looked at him for a moment. "Please give me a moment, Princeps," I said. "I will need to engrave the room."

OTIRIOS LEFT ME standing alone before the tree-mangled corpse and shut the door. I reached into my engraver's satchel on my side and opened it up. Within sat row after row of tiny glass vials sealed with corks, each one containing a few drops of fluid: some pale orange, others faintly green. I slid one out, removed the cork, placed it beneath my nose, and inhaled.

The pungent scent of lye filled my nostrils, making my eyes water. I sniffed it once again, ensuring that the aroma lay heavy within my head. Then I shut my eyes and took a breath.

I felt a tickling or a fluttering in the backs of my eyes, like my skull was a bowl of water full of fish flicking about. Then I summoned up a memory.

The voice of my master, the investigator, whispered in my ear: *When you arrive at the scene, Din, observe the room carefully. Check all manners of entry and exit. Look at everything the dead man might have touched. Think of missed places, forgotten places. Places the servants might not think to clean.*

I opened my eyes, looked at the room, and focused, the aroma of lye still loitering in my skull. I studied the walls, the floor, the way every item and every piece of furniture was arranged, the line of every shadow, the bend of every blanket—and as I focused my attention, all of these sights were engraved in my memory.

The great and heavenly Empire of Khanum had long ago perfected the art of shaping life, root and branch and flesh and bone. And just as the kirpis shroom in the corner had been altered to cool and clean air, I, as an Imperial engraver, had been altered to remember everything I experienced, always and forever.

I looked and looked, occasionally sniffing at the vial in my hand. Engravers remembered everything, but later recalling those memories quickly and easily was another thing. Scent was used as a cue: just like ordinary folk, engravers associated memories with an aroma; so later, when I reported to my master, I would uncork this same vial, fill my skull with these same vapors, and use their scent as a gateway to recall all I'd experienced. Hence why some called engravers "glass sniffers."

When I was done with the room I stepped forward and squinted at the clutch of shoots, walking around them in a circle. Then I noticed one shoot had bloomed: a lonely, fragile white bloom, but a bloom nonetheless.

I stepped closer, mindful of the blood on the floor, and studied the bloom. It had a sickly aroma, that of sotwine vomit, perhaps. Inner petals bright purple and dappled with yellow, stamen curling and dark. An ugly little flower, really.

Next I took out all of Blas's belongings one by one and laid them out before me. A bag of talint coins; a small knife; a set of shirts, jerkins, leggings, and belt; his imperial-issued longsword and scabbard, complete with the ornate crossguard for officers; a light mail shirt, probably for emergencies, as real battle armor would be difficult to casually carry about; and, last of all, a small pot of oil.

I sniffed it. It was aromatic, even in this foul-smelling place. Spice, oranje-leaf, wine mullings, maybe incense. My eyes fluttered as I searched my memories for a matching smell—and then I found something similar.

Just over a year ago: Leonie, a friend of mine, had waved a little pot under my nose and said—*Therapy oils. For massage, and other things. Not cheap!*

Yet this was a far fancier pot than that had been. I turned it over in my hand. Then I replaced it with his gear—yet as I did, I noticed something I'd missed: a small book.

My heart fell. I slipped the slender volume out and flipped through the pages. The pages were covered with tiny writing that would have been barely legible to most people—but to my eyes, the letters danced and shook on the page, and I knew I would have great trouble reading them.

I looked over my shoulder at the closed door. I could hear Otirios speaking down the hall. With a grimace, I pocketed the book. It was a major breach of conduct to remove evidence from a death scene, but I had my own way of reading. I just couldn't do it here.

Later, I told myself. And then we'll put it back.

Next I checked the bathing closet. It was a tiny room with a window set above the stonewood bathing basin. The window seemed too small for anyone to climb through, but I made a note to examine the grass below later for any imprints.

I looked at the burnished bronze mirror on the bathing closet wall, tapping it and making sure it was adhered to the wall. I examined the shootstraw pipes, then stepped back and gazed at the wall and ceiling, wondering how they brought hot water in from the distant boiler to fill the stonewood basin. The marvels of the age, I supposed.

Then I glanced backward and did a double take. Mold was blooming along the fernpaper walls, mostly at the top—little blotches of black here and there.

I'd never seen fernpaper walls mold before. I especially wouldn't have expected to find any on these walls, so clean and white and processed. People used fernpaper throughout the Outer Rim of the Empire, partially for their resistance to molds and fungus—and also because when the ground shook out here, and walls came tumbling down, it was better for them to be made of fernpaper than stone.

I studied the mold and sniffed the lye vial again, ensuring that this sight was easily recallable. Then I looked at the body again, this half person frozen in an agonized scream. A drop of water fell from the hole in the ceiling and landed in the lip of his boot, sending a tiny fan of pooled blood dribbling down the leather. The lake of gore on the wooden floor widened by a shred of a smallspan.

A twist in my stomach. I stood and looked at the burnished bronze mirror. Then I froze, staring at the face looking back at me.

A very young man's face, with a thick shock of black hair, dark, worried eyes, and the slightly gray skin of someone who'd undergone significant suffusions and alterations. I studied the face's delicate chin and long nose. Pretty features—not masculine, nor rugged, nor handsome, but *pretty*, and how awkward they looked on a person so large.

Not the face of an Iudex Assistant Investigator. Not someone who was supposed to be here at all. A boy playing dress-up at best, aping authorities he could never hope to command.

And what would happen to this young man if anyone found out how he'd *actually* gotten this position?

My stomach twisted, twirled, danced. I dashed to the bathing closet window, burst through it, and sent a spray of vomit pattering down to the grass below.

A voice said, "Fucking hell!"

Gasping, I looked down. Two Apoth officers were staring up at me from the gardens, shocked looks on their faces.

"Ahh . . ." one said.

"Shit," I spat. I stumbled back in and shut the window behind me.

NOT HAVING A HANDKERCHIEF, I wiped my mouth on the inside of my coat. I sniffed and swallowed three, four, five times, trying to suck the rancid taste and aroma back inside me, bottling it up. Then I stepped carefully around the puddle of blood, went to the bedroom door, and opened it to leave—but then I paused.

Otirios's voice floated down the hall, chatting with another Apoth guard.

". . . stuffy little prick, barely out of puberty," he was saying. "Think I've heard of him, from the other Sublimes. Supposed to be the dumbest one of the lot, nearly failed out a hundred times. I'm surprised to find him working for the investigat—"

I walked forward, fast. "Princeps," I said.

Otirios stumbled to attention as I strode around the corner. "Ah—y-yes, sir?"

"I'm going to review the house and the grounds before I speak to the witnesses," I said. "While I do that, please place the witnesses in separate rooms and then watch them, to ensure they don't talk among themselves. I'd also like your other guards to make sure the exits and entrances are covered—just in case there's an unaccounted reagents key and someone tries to slip in or out."

Otirios blanched, clearly displeased at the idea of managing so many people for so long. He opened his mouth to argue, then grudgingly shut it.

"And Princeps . . ." I looked at him and smiled. "I *do* appreciate all your support."

I was still smiling as I walked out. I had never given such an order before, but I'd enjoyed that one. For while I couldn't really rebuke Otirios—he was part of another Iyalet, a different imperial administration—I could stick him with a shit job and leave him there for a long while.

I walked throughout the mansion, occasionally sniffing my vial as I studied each hallway, each room, the insignia of the Haza clan always hanging over my shoulder at the door—the feather between the trees.

The Hazas were able to afford a kirpis shroom for every major room, it seemed, but the one in the western end by the kitchens was shriveled and dying. Curious. I made a note of it, then kept moving, checking all the windows and doors—mostly fernpaper, I noticed. All milled bright white, and each probably worth more than a month's pay for me.

I crossed through the kitchens, then spied something below the stove: a tiny blot of blood. I touched it with a finger. Still wet, still dark. There might be many reasons for blood to be in a kitchen, of course, but I engraved it in my memory. Then I went outside.

The gardens were very pretty and elaborate: landscaped streams crisscrossing the grounds, little bridges arching over them in picturesque places. A sight from a spirit story for children, perhaps; yet I didn't find anything of interest as I wandered the paths, nodding occasionally at the Apoths still searching for contagion.

I came to the place where I'd vomited out the window and searched the grass for any indentions or marks of a ladder or something similar. Nothing there, either.

The last thing to look at was the groundskeeper's hut. It was a quaint place, made of thin fernpaper walls, the shelves dotted with tiny plants the groundskeeper was apparently nursing along. Lines of merry little blooms, some fresh, some wilting. There was also a clay oven, quite large. I peered inside and noticed the ash in the bottom, then touched the brick there and found it was still slightly warm, like coals had been smoldering overnight.

I made another trip about the grounds to confirm I'd seen all there was to see. Then I glanced around, confirmed I was alone, and slid the commander's book from my pocket.

I opened it, squinted at the shivering, dancing words on the page, and began to read aloud.

"Wall s-segment . . . 3C," I mumbled. "Check d-date the fourth of Egin . . . two t-tons sand, two tons loam . . ."

I read on and on, stuttering through the tiny script, and listened to my voice as I read. I had great trouble reading and memorizing text, but if I read it aloud, and listened to my own words, I could remember them as I could everything else I heard.

I read it all aloud as fast as I could. It was mostly a record of the commander's movements as he did his inspections, with entries like *ck. Paytasız bridges in the north of the Tala canton—6th to 8th of Egin—all pass*, and so on. He'd apparently been very busy just over four weeks ago, during the month of Egin. I had no idea if any of it was pertinent or not, but as an engraver, I was to engrave everything in my memory.

I finished engraving the book, then began crossing the many bridges to return to the house. I had not interviewed anyone as a death witness before, especially not the staff of the house of a gentry family. I wondered how to begin.

I caught a flash of my reflection in the water below, dappled and rippling, and paused. "Let's not fuck this up, yes?" I said to my watery face.

I crossed the last little bridge and entered the house.

I PRESSED THE SERVANT GIRLS FIRST, being as they'd had access to Blas's rooms. I started with the girl who'd been crying so hysterically—a little thing, narrow shoulders, tiny wrists. Small enough to make one wonder how she made it down the hall with all those dishes. It'd been she who'd responded to Blas when he'd started calling for help at eight o'clock, she told me, just before breakfast.

"He called for help?" I asked.

She nodded. A tear wove down her cheek to balance precariously in the crevice above her nostril. "He said he . . . his chest hurt. Said it was hard to breathe. He was coming down for breakfast, and he stopped and went back to his room. I came to him, tried to get him to lie down before . . . before he . . ."

She bowed her head; the balanced tear spilled down her lip; then she started wailing again. "I'm suh-sorry," she sobbed as she tried to regain her composure. "Sh-should have asked . . . W-Would the suh-sir care for some t-tea?"

"Ah . . . No, thank you," I said.

For some reason, this made her sob all the harder. I waited for her to stop. When she didn't, I let her go.

I moved on to the next one, an older servant named Ephinas. She sat down slowly, her movements cautious, controlled. Someone used to being watched, probably. She corroborated the first servant's story: Blas arrived late in the evening, bathed, went to bed; and all had seemed completely normal until he started screaming for help in the morning. She had not gone to him, so she didn't know more than that—but she did come alive when I asked if Blas had stayed here before.

"Yes," she said. "My masters let him stay here often. He is close with them."

"How was this stay different from other stays?" I asked. "Or was it different?"

Hesitation. "It was," she said.

"Then how so?"

More hesitation. "He left us *alone* this time," she said quietly. "Probably because he never got the chance to try."

I coughed, snuffed at my vial, and hoped she could not see me blush. "Tell me more about that, please," I asked.

She did so. From the sound of it, Blas was quite the absolute bastard, pawing at the servants the second he had them alone. She said she wasn't sure if his advances had been reciprocated by any of the other girls, but she didn't think so, though all of them got the same treatment.

"What was the nature of his visit here?" I asked her.

Her eyes dipped down. "He was a friend of the Haza family," she said.

"He's a friend? That's the only reason why he stayed here?"

"Yes."

"Isn't it strange for someone to stay at someone else's house while they're not here?"

This elicited a contemptuous glance. Her eye lingered on my cheap boots and ill-fitting coat. "It is not uncommon for gentryfolk."

Even the servants thought themselves worldlier than I, it seemed. But then, they were probably right.

I asked her more, but she gave me less with every question, withdrawing into herself further and further. I made a note of it and moved on.

I asked the next girls about Blas's advances. While they corroborated the story, all of them claimed they'd never had a relationship with Blas beyond these unpleasant moments, and none of them had much else to say.

"I didn't hear or see anything before he died," said the final girl flatly. She was bolder, louder, angrier than the others. Less willing to quietly suffer servitude, maybe. "Not for the whole night. I know that."

"You're sure?" I asked.

"I am," she said. "Because I didn't sleep much before the guest came."

"Why was that?"

"Because I was hot. Very hot."

I thought about it. "Do you sleep near the kitchens?"

"Yes. Why?"

"Because the kirpis shroom is dying there. Could that be why you were hot?"

She seemed surprised. "Another one's died?"

"They've died before?"

"They're very sensitive to water. Too much and they shrivel up and die."

"What kind of moisture?" I asked.

"Any kind. Rain. Humidity. Leave a window or door open nearby—especially now, when the wet season starts—and they'll get sick right away. They're temperamental as hell."

I leaned back and focused. A fluttering at the backs of my eyes, and I summoned up my memories of searching the house, each image of each room flashing perfectly in my mind like a fly suspended in a drop of honey. No doors or windows had been open that I saw. So how might the kirpis have died?

"Did you or anyone else in the house happen to *close* an open door or window before Blas died?" I asked.

She stared at me. "After seeing what we saw, sir," she said, "we could barely stand, let alone do our work."

I took that as a no, they had not shut any doors or windows, and continued on.

EVENTUALLY I RAN out of servant girls, so I went hard at the cook, asking her about the blood in the kitchen. She was most unimpressed.

"Why do *you* think there might be blood in the kitchen?" she demanded.

"Did you cut yourself?" I asked.

"No. Of course not. I am too old, and too good. If you found blood, I am sure it's from the larfish I cooked for Blas's breakfast—not that he ever got to eat it."

"Larfish?" I asked. I pulled a face. "For breakfast?"

"It's what he likes," she said. "It's hard to get, out close to the walls, where he works." She leaned closer. "If you ask me, he picked up something out there, at the sea walls. Some parasite or another. I mean—think of what the sea walls keep *out*. Sanctum knows what kind of strange things they bring in with them!"

"They don't get in, ma'am," I said. "That's the point of the sea walls."

"But they had a breach years ago," she said, delighted to discuss such grotesqueries. "One got in and wrecked a city south of here, before the Legion brought it down. The trees there bloom now, though they never bloomed before. They weren't trees that *could* grow blooms before."

"If we could get back to the circumstances of last night, ma'am . . ."

"Circumstances!" she scoffed. "The man caught contagion. It's as simple as that."

I pressed her harder, but she gave me nothing more of interest, and I let her go.

THE GROUNDSKEEPER NEXT. Fellow's name was Uxos, and he was apparently more than just a groundskeeper, performing odd jobs about the house, fixing up walls or fernpaper doors. A most timid man, perhaps too old to still be groundskeeper. He seemed terrified at the idea of trying to fix the damage the trees had done to the house.

"I don't even know what kind of tree it is," he said. "I've never seen it before in my life."

"It had a bloom, you know," I said. "A little white one." I described it to him—the inner petals purple and yellow, the sweet and sickly aroma. He just shook his head.

"No, no," he said. "It's not a flower I know. Not a tree I know. I don't know."

I asked him about the kirpis shroom, and he said the same thing as the servant girl: too much water kills them. But how this one had died, he didn't know.

"Someone probably overwatered it," he said. "Dumped a drink in it. It's expensive, but it happens. They're very hard to care for. It's a complex process, cooling the air. They make black fruit in their roots you have to clean out . . ."

Finally I asked him about his oven, and the ashes of the fire out there in the hut.

"I use the fire to clean my tools," Uxos said. "Some plants are very delicate. Can't get fungus from one to the other. So I put them in the fire to clean them."

"Don't they have washes for that?" I said. "Soaps and such for your tools?"

"They're expensive. Fire is cheaper."

"The Hazas don't seem like people who care much about price."

"They care," he said, "if *people* get expensive. Then the people go. I try very hard not to be expensive. I don't want to go."

A worm of worry in his eye. Too old to be groundskeeper by half, I guessed, and he knew it. I pressed him for more, but he had nothing more to give, and I let him go.

LAST WAS THE HOUSEKEEPER—a Madam Gennadios, apparently the boss of the whole place when the Hazas themselves weren't around. An older woman with a lined, heavily painted face. She wore bright green robes of a very expensive make, soft and shimmering—Sazi silk, from the inner rings of the Empire. She paused when she walked in, looked me over with a cold, shrewd eye, then sat down, her posture immaculate—knees together at an angle, hands in her lap, shoulders high and tight—and stared resolutely into the corner.

"Something wrong, ma'am?" I asked.

"A *boy*," she said. Her words were as dry and taut as a bowstring. "They've sent a *boy*."

"I beg your pardon?"

She studied me again out of the corner of her eye. "This is who's trapped us in our house, the house of my masters, and won't let us remove that damned corpse—a great, overgrown *boy*."

A long, icy moment slipped by.

"Someone's died in your house, ma'am," I said. "Potentially of contagion. Something that might have killed you all, too. Don't you want us to investigate?"

"Then where's the investigator?"

"The investigator isn't able to attend," I said. "I'm here to review the scene and report back to her."

Her gaze lingered on me. I was reminded of an eel contemplating a fish flitting before its cave. "Ask me your questions," she said. "I've work to do, a damned ceiling to patch up. Go."

I inhaled at my vial and then asked her about the nature of Blas's stay. She gave what might have been the smallest, least sincere shrug I'd ever seen. "He is a friend of the Haza family."

"One of your servant girls said the same thing," I said.

"Because it's true."

"The *exact* same thing."

"Because it's true."

"And your masters often let their friends stay at their houses?"

"My masters have many houses, and many friends. Sometimes their friends come to stay with us."

"And no one from the Haza clan intended to join him?"

"My masters," she said, "prefer more civilized environs than this canton."

I moved on, asking her about the locations of the staff's reagents keys.

"All the reagents keys are locked up at night," she said. "Only I and Uxos are in constant possession of any during the evening, for emergencies."

I asked about replacing keys, how to duplicate them, and so on, but she was dismissive. The idea was impossible to her.

"What about alterations?" I said. "Have your staff had any imperial grafts applied?"

"Of course," she said. "For immunities, and parasites. We *are* on the rim of the Empire, after all."

"Nothing more advanced than that?"

She shook her head. I felt a heat under the collar of my coat. I didn't like how little she moved, sitting up so ramrod straight, shifting her head only to look at me out of the side of her eye like a damned bird.

"Can you at least tell me the nature of the commander's relationship with the Hazas?" I asked.

A withering stare. "They were *friends*."

"How long have they been friends?"

"I do not know the nature of all my masters' friendships, nor is that for me to know."

"Do they have many friends in Daretana?"

"Yes. In many of the Iyalets, at that." Her eyes glittered at me. "And some of them are above you."

I smiled politely at her, yet the threat seemed very real. I asked her more, but she gave me nothing. I let her go.

THEN IT WAS DONE: all witnesses questioned, all personnel accounted for, all times of departures and arrivals established. The only person who'd arrived in the past day had been Commander Taqtasa Blas, who'd come to the residence at just past eleven on the night of the twenty-ninth of the month of Skalasi. He immediately bathed and went to bed, awoke on the thirtieth, and then paused right before breakfast to die in the most horrifying fashion imaginable. Though I thought I'd made a pretty good job of it—except for my chat with the housekeeper, perhaps—I could make neither head nor tail of the scene: not whether Blas's death was murder, or even suspicious.

Contagion did happen, after all. Especially to those who worked at the sea walls.

I stopped by the bedroom on my way out. To see the corpse one more time, yes, but also to replace Blas's book in his belongings. It felt strange to slip his diary back in his bags, his frozen scream hanging over my shoulder. Despite all the mutilation, the pain of his expression remained striking, like he was still feeling all those shoots threading and coiling through his flesh.

I walked out and thanked Otirios, and he led me across the grounds back to the servants' gate.

"Is it all right for us to remove the corpse for study, sir?" he asked.

"I think so, but please keep all the witnesses here," I said. "I'll report back to the investigator, and she'll likely want to summon some of the witnesses to question herself."

"It was well done, sir," he said.

"What was?"

"Well done. If I might say so. All handled well." He gave me a grin, beaming and big-brotherly. I'd only ever seen such smiles above a fourth pot of sotwine. "Though next time, sir—might want to be a bit friendlier. I've seen undertakers warmer than you."

I paused and looked at him. Then I turned and kept walking, down through the picturesque garden paths and out the vinegate.

"But I've also got to wonder, sir . . ." Otirios asked as we passed through the vines.

"Yes, Princeps?" I said. "What advice do you have now?"

"Might this have been easier if the investigator herself had come?"

I stopped again and looked at him balefully.

"*No*," I said. "I can say with absolute honesty, Princeps, that no, this would *not* have been easier if the investigator had come." I returned to the path, muttering, "You'll have to trust me on that."

CHAPTER 2

|||

THE DARETANA CANTON DIDN'T HAVE A TRUE CITY
in any normal sense of the word, but rather a clutch of Imperial Iyalet
buildings clinging to the main crossroads, along with countless lots
and warehouses and storage barns for all the materials and livestock
constantly being routed to the sea walls. That afternoon it was the
usual morass of mud and men and the press of horseflesh. I danced
south along the corners through the town, pausing for the carts and
wagons, and saw the familiar sights: horses with copper red mud
churned up to their bellies; crawling swarms of thrumming flies;
sweat-drenched officers of the Legion, the Engineers, and the other
Iyalets bellowing names and orders, seemingly indifferent as to
whether they were heard or heeded. I bowed and nodded and bowed
and nodded until I was free of the throng and into the jungle.

The woods were dark and shimmering hot. The sun was in its
descent, spears of its tawny light plunging through the canopy. I
found the narrow jungle path to my master's house and stepped
along it, greeted by the familiar chirrup of frog and beetle. Then the
steam-drenched leaves parted and I glimpsed her little fretvine quarters waiting in the shade.

I picked my way through the tree stumps. The Engineers had cut
all these trees down when my master had first been appointed Iudex
Investigator of this canton, some four months ago now, and then
they'd made her a house from fretvine—the special, altered vine the

Apothetikals had tamed to grow into any shape. Whereas I'd trodden this path so many times I practically walked in my own footprints, she had not left that place since she'd moved in. Not once.

I walked up the steps to her front door and saw a stack of books waiting before the door, tied up with string. Delivery from the Daretana post station, I guessed. I squatted and flipped a few open to read their titles. As always, the letters shook and danced before my eyes, making it hard for me to put them together—the shifting jungle light didn't help—but I made out *Summation of the Transfer of Landed Properties, Qabirga Canton, 1100–1120* and *Theories Related to the Increase in Mass of the Eastern Scuttlecrab Since 800.*

"The hell?" I muttered.

Then I paused, listening. I heard the chirrup of a tossfrog, and the low call of a mika lark; but then I realized I had heard something else: the mutter of a man, within the house.

I pressed my ear to the front door. I could hear one voice within— my master's—but then a second, a man's. One that sounded anxious, even nervous.

"Oh, hell," I said. "She's gone and trapped another one . . ."

I threw the door open and dashed in.

THE MOST REMARKABLE feature of the interior of the little fretvine house, as always, was the sheer number of books: walls and stacks and veritable canyons of tomes, on any number of obscure subjects. My master quite literally lived *between* books, often using them as a desk and nightstand. She even had to carve out a little cavern in them for her bed.

I peered through the valleys of tomes and approached the meeting room at the back of the little house. I could already see the feet of someone sitting in a chair back there—officer's boots, black and shiny—and grimaced. I smoothed back my hair and walked into the meeting room.

The meeting room had gotten worse since yesterday: it was now brimming with tangles of potted plants, many exotic and half-dead, and stringed musical instruments in varying states of disrepair. On the left side of the room sat a small stuffed chair, and today a captain from Engineering occupied it, a thin, middle-aged man who looked absolutely terrified.

The reason for his terror was obvious, for most people found themselves terrified to share a room with my master: Immunis Anagosa Dolabra, Iudex Investigator of the Daretana Canton, who was sitting on the floor facing away from the captain as she worked on yet another one of her projects. It appeared to be some contraption of wires and string I could make no sense of. I guessed she'd taken apart one of her many situr harps—she was an avid if inattentive musician—and was making some kind of loom from its strings.

"I told you, Din," Ana said, "to *knock*. Always."

I stood up straight at attention, hands behind my back, heels shoulder-width apart, knees straight. "Thought I heard voices, ma'am," I said. "Came to check."

"Oh, there's nothing to be worried about." She looked over her shoulder at me, grinning. A strand of her snowy-white hair arched down over her cheek, like the crest feather of some exotic bird. I maintained my stance, but she could not see me, for she was wearing a wide strip of crimson cloth as a blindfold. "The captain and I," she said, "have been having the most *delightful* conversation."

The captain stared at me in naked dread.

"Have you, ma'am," I said.

"Oh, yes," she said. She turned back to her project. "The captain here is in charge of maintaining the irrigation networks about Daretana. During their works they discovered ruins, hundreds of years old, built by some of the folk who lived here before the Empire came. Isn't that right, Captain Tischte?"

The captain looked at me and mouthed—*Help me!*

"Most curiously," Ana continued, "apparently some of the ruins were built using a complex herringbone brick structure, requiring less mortar in their application! Isn't that *fascinating*?"

The captain was now gesturing desperately at me and pointing at the door.

"Very fascinating, ma'am," I said.

"Especially because," she said, "I have long nursed a theory that many of the Kurmini folk in the third ring of the Empire originally migrated from these lands before the Empire was established. And this would offer some confirmation of that, as the herringbone brick pattern is *extremely* common in the Kurmin canton! The people migrated inward, obviously, because . . ." She waved her hand easterly. "I mean, if you wanted to survive, that was what you did."

The captain paused in his gesturing, having noticed a white cloth on a tray beside him. Before I could stop him, he lifted it and stared in horror at the sight underneath: a little jipti sparrow that Ana had caught some weeks ago, then killed, dissected, and preserved in a glass jar. The captain dropped the cloth, his hand trembling.

I rushed to think up a story. "Actually, ma'am," I said, clearing my throat, "I happened to run into some officers from Engineering on the way here."

"Did you?"

"Yes, ma'am. They mentioned they needed Captain Tischte right away."

Ana paused before her contraption, then cocked her head. "Hm. *No.* That is a lie, Din. You're a very bad liar, and I can hear it in your voice. But! I will admit, besides the herringbone discussion, Captain Tischte hasn't really had anything interesting to say, and I'm getting rather bored of him." She turned to him, still blindfolded, still grinning. "You can go, Captain. I do appreciate your time."

Captain Tischte shot to his feet, looking scandalized. He bowed, uttered a single hoarse "M-madam," and then made for the door.

I accompanied him out into the steamy afternoon, wondering how to undo the damage this time.

"I apologize for that, sir," I said. "There's no excuse fo—"

"Apologize!" he squawked once we were outside. "*Apologize!* She sends me a letter to come round with some maps, and when I oblige, she traps me there for *three hours* interrogating me about the whole of my life! She even asked me about the shape of my *feet!*"

"I'm sorry," I said. I bowed, glanced up, saw his furious face, then bowed deeper, until my nose nearly touched my ratty boots. "I would have stopped it if I'd been here, sir, I really would ha—"

"And then . . . then she has the temerity to call me *boring!*" he said. "To think that that madwoman is our Iudex Investigator, I just . . ." He turned and stormed off along the jungle path, back to town.

I watched him go, muttered, "Shit," and reentered the house.

Ana was still coiled before her contraption in the meeting room, posture taut, fingers thoughtfully dancing over the strings.

I said, "You do know . . ." then paused to rethink my words.

"Go on, Din," she said. She tugged off her blindfold. "I almost thought you were about to rebuke me. That would be splendidly entertaining."

"Well, you do know, ma'am," I said, "that . . . that you really can't keep doing that."

"Ordinarily I can't," she said, "but that's because *ordinarily* you're here stopping me, Din."

"I do so, ma'am," I snapped, "because you can't keep cornering these poor people and wringing them of information like juice from an aplilot!"

"I am simply doing my utmost to make this dismal canton a little interesting," she said blithely. She tightened a string on her contraption. "But that requires rather a lot of *work.*"

"Ma'am . . ."

"For example, are you aware, Din, that the southeasternmost water well in Daretana is almost certainly infected with irida?"

"How fascinating, ma'am."

"Indeed. No one was aware. But I gleaned such from the sixty-two folk I've chatted with over the past months. Twelve of them who drank regularly from that well have, unknowingly, described slight aches and insomnia and an unnatural scent to their urine—all symp-

toms commonly associated with the disease. I notified the captain of
this, and recommended he purge the well." Another tweak to the
wires before her. "*That* is what I get from all these chats, Din. I just
need enough information to divine the nature of the pattern."

"Was that why you asked that Legion commander about the smell
of his piss, ma'am?"

"Oh, no, not at all. At the time, I was merely curious."

I allowed a quick glance at her. She was a tall, thin woman in her
late forties or fifties—it was hard to tell with some altered folk—and
though her skin had gray undertones like mine, hers was decidedly
on the paler end. That was mostly because she never went outside,
but part of it was likely because she was Sazi: a lighter-skinned race
from the inner rings of the Empire, whose faces were more angular
and narrower than Tala folk like me. With her bone-white hair, wide
smile, and yellow eyes, she often seemed vaguely feline: a mad house-
cat, perhaps, roving through a home in pursuit of a suitable sunbeam,
though always willing to torture the occasional mouse.

Today she was wearing a long black dress, and on top of this she
had on a smudged, dark blue Iudex Iyalet cloak whose heralds were
all arranged very much against imperial code, organized into perfectly symmetrical groups. Their sorting was different from yesterday's: now organized by color, rather than size.

"Oh!" she said. "Books!"

"Beg pardon, ma'am?" I said.

"Did my *books* arrive, Din?"

"Oh. Yes, ma'am. They're waiting on the porch. I would have taken
them in, but I was distracted by your torture of the captain."

"And now you torture me with your attempt at wit," she said. "But
if you would be so kind . . ."

I bowed, went to the door, and paused to look back with my hand
on the knob.

"Eyes averted!" she said. Her face was turned to the corner of the
meeting room. "My eyes are averted!"

Once I confirmed she would not see out, I opened the door,

snatched up the pile of books, hauled them in, and shut the door. Instantly she was behind me, wriggling one long, pale finger beneath the knot of twine and ripping it apart.

"Took ages this time," she growled. "Two weeks! Can you believe it? Two goddamn weeks to get these to me."

"Must be very hard to go so long without a decent crab book, ma'am."

"You've no idea." She flung them open one after another, shutting her eyes and feeling the pages. Though most of her skin was a pale gray, her fingertips were pink—altered through a graft, I guessed, to be so hypersensitive she could read printed and occasionally handwritten text by touch alone. Which she did quite a bit, since she spent a huge amount of the day blindfolded. *Best to keep the senses limited,* she'd explained once. *And stay indoors. Too much stimulation drives a person mad.*

As I watched her rip through each book, I wondered, not for the first time, how I'd be able to tell in her case. I assumed her afflictions had something to do with her augmentations—even though I had never been told exactly in what manner her mind had been augmented.

"Ahh," Ana said. She rubbed the page of the crab book in a distinctly sensual manner. "This is a book from the Rathras canton. I can tell by the imprints. Their printing presses were first built to publish their holy books, in their language, so some letters slope to the left very slightly . . . Thank you for fetching these, Din. They should keep me occupied for a day or so."

"A day, ma'am?" I said.

"Oh. Do you think it less, Din?" she said, worried.

"Can't say, ma'am."

"Or should I have gotten *more* books, Din?"

"Can't really say, ma'am."

A taut pause.

"Is it possible for you to say a sentence," she said, "that is more than ten words in length, Din?"

I hazarded a glance into her pale yellow gaze and suppressed a smirk. "Could, ma'am," I said.

"I do so admire," she said, "how you can be a flippant shit with a mere handful of syllables. Quite a talent." With a sigh she stood, tottered back to her meeting room, and flopped down in her chair.

I followed, then stood at attention at the doorway. She stared around at the room and all its half-finished projects. A slightly despondent look crept over her face.

"Now that I think about it, Din," she said, "I just might be going a little fucking mad in here."

"Very sorry to hear that, ma'am."

She picked up a small situr harp and absently plucked at it. "*Mostly*," she said, "because nothing ever happens in this dull little canton. And the books take *so* long to arrive."

I was now familiar with these moods. First the elation of a new idea, new problem, new toy; and then, having unraveled it, a crushing melancholy. The only thing to do was give her a new one.

"Well, speaking of which, ma'am," I said, "this morning I—"

"It pains me to say that it's all far more tolerable when you're around," she said. "You're so grim and so *serious* and so dull, Din, that you keep me very grounded."

"I will attempt to take that as a compliment, ma'am," I said. "But that's why I wanted to te—"

"But your position on my standing request," she said, "is still the same?"

I shot her a stern look. "Could you clarify, ma'am?"

"You know damned well what I mean." She leaned forward, grinning. "Will you finally buy me some damned *moodies*? I'd stop interrogating people if you did!"

"The purchase of mood-altering grafts is strictly outlawed among officers of the Imperial Iyalets," I said stolidly. "And I don't break policy, ma'am. Being as I want to keep my position, you see."

"Just a few of the psychedelic ones," she said. "That'd buy me a day away from this boredom."

"Does the imperial code of conduct apply to the psychedelic mood grafts as well, ma'am? For if so, you already have my answer."

She squinted at me and plucked a single harsh chord on the situr. *Here it comes,* I thought.

"When I performed my duties in the *inner* rings of the Empire . . ." she said.

And there it is.

". . . my assistant investigators procured *all kinds* of materials and substances for me!" she finished. "Without question!"

"If you'd like to venture outside, ma'am," I said, "to visit all the graft merchants you'd like, you're free to do so. I can't stop you."

Her glare hardened. "You know that's not going to happen."

"I understand. Too much stimulation for you out there, ma'am."

"Yes," she hissed through gritted teeth. "Titan's taint! Of all the Sublimes who could have been my assistant, why did it have to be the one with a forty-span stick up his ass?"

"Well, technically, you selected me from the list of applicants, ma'am."

"Then I can *unselect* you and get someone else!"

"That seems unlikely, ma'am," I said. "Given that you have interrogated sixty-two officers in Daretana, and most everyone in the canton now thinks you're mad, finding new Sublimes will probably be difficult."

She cast her situr aside. It tumbled onto the floor with a dull *tonk.* "Fuck's sakes. *Fuck's* sakes. How I wish I were back in more civilized lands . . ."

This was a common conflict of ours: to hear Ana tell it, she'd served as investigator in all the deepest, richest enclaves of the Empire of Khanum, and each one had been madder and more depraved than the last. She kept claiming to be confounded when some illicit material or barbarous act was not easily acquired in Daretana, and acted like it was a backwater hole for failing to provide them within an hour.

Which made one ask the question, of course—why *had* Immunis Ana Dolabra been appointed here, to the Outer Rim, of all places?

And the only reasonable answer, as far as I could see, was banishment. The role of Iudex Investigator of the Daretana Canton had not even existed as recently as five months ago. They must have invented it as punishment, presumably because transferring her was easier than dismissing her.

Which made sense. I'd only worked for Ana for four months, but you just had to spend one minute with her to realize she had a gift for inciting outrage. It was easy to imagine some elite imperials getting fed up with her and giving her the boot all the way to my far-flung canton, where she could only get one assistant from the selection of local Sublimes.

But I was that Sublime. Assistant Investigator was the only position I'd managed to get, and I would work it underneath Ana's supervision and receive my dispensation until I was no longer able to collect it. Unless, of course, she got me to do something so illegal that I was discharged straightaway.

"Would you like some tea, ma'am?" I asked.

"No, Din," she muttered, arm cast over her eyes. "Flavorful as it is, no, I do not want any of your goddamn tea."

"Then would you like to discuss the death scene, ma'am?"

She lifted her arm and stared at me for a moment, perplexed. Then her face lit up with delight. "Oh! That dead fucker! Right!"

"Right," I sighed.

"When I got that message from Immunis Irtos," she said, "I had assumed some goddamn idiot had swallowed the wrong graft or something. That seemed about right for this dull little town. But from your demeanor, Din, I gather it was not?"

"No, ma'am," I said. "It was not."

"Then what is interesting about it?"

"A large clutch of trees had spontaneously grown from within the deceased, tearing him apart from the inside, ma'am." I shuddered. "It was . . . it was one of the most horrifying sights I'd ever seen in all my life."

She went totally still. And for the first time that day, all the wild madness in her eyes went dead.

"My goodness gracious," she murmured. "Did you hear that, Din?"

"Hear what, ma'am?"

"That *emotion*," she said.

"Pardon?"

"That was the most emotion I've *ever* heard in anything you've ever said, Din! This must be a real corker of a death if it's cracked your dull demeanor and summoned forth such wild passion."

She pulled on her blindfold, grinning. There was something unsettlingly predatorial about her grin: too many teeth, and all too white.

"Tell me everything," she said. "*Everything* you've engraved within that pretty little skull of yours, Dinios Kol. Go."

I opened my engraver's satchel, slid out the vial of lye aroma, uncorked it, and inhaled deeply. Then I felt a fluttering behind my eyes, and I started talking.

CHAPTER 3

III

WHEN IT CAME TO THE HUMAN BODY, THE IMPE-
rial Apothetikals preferred two methods of alterations: there were
grafts, which applied a single alteration, a short burst of growth—
say, granting a person increased stamina, better immunities, clearer
vision, or stronger bones; and then there were *suffusions*, which were
far more invasive and—most important—changed you permanently
and irreversibly, along with all the children you might have after.
(If your suffusion let you have any, that is. They usually did not.)

This meant the Empire always had better soldiers than most
other fighting forces, certainly. But the beating heart of the Empire
were the Sublimes: the cerebrally suffused and augmented set who
planned, managed, and coordinated everything the many Iyalets of
the Empire did.

Each type of Sublime was different. There were axioms, the people whose minds had been altered to process calculations inhumanly
well; linguas, suffused to be inhumanly skilled at speaking and reading and writing in countless languages; spatiasts, altered to possess
an inhumanly accurate comprehension of space, making them stun-
ningly good drawers and map makers; and then a few other odd sorts
you only saw very rarely.

These suffusions weren't pleasant—many shortened the lives of
those who took them, by years if not decades, and they almost always

rendered people sterile—but Sublimes were irreplaceable. It took every bit of cunning and planning to survive what came from the seas to the east each wet season.

Most sought-after were the engravers, like myself, who had been suffused to remember all they saw, acting as living libraries of information. This was the enhancement I used as I described my investigation to Ana: remembering everything, describing all I'd seen, regurgitating every piece of spoken speech in the exact same tone I'd heard it said to me. Everything I'd captured during my time in that mansion I now gave to Ana, over the course of nearly four hours.

When I was finished talking it was just past sunset. A single mailantern in the corner began to glimmer as the little worms within awoke, began to eat their food pellets at the bottom, and started to glow. There was no sound but the solitary, mournful song of some distant jungle bird.

Ana took a sudden breath, sucking in air like she was waking from a deep sleep, and exhaled. "Right," she said. "Very good. I have a few questions, Din ..."

She asked me many strange things then. How many steps did it take me to cross the entirety of the house? Was Gennadios left- or right-handed? Did Uxos have any prominent scars on his hands? Had I spied any recently disturbed soil at the edges of the estate walls, the moist underside of the mulch churned up by a passing boot, perhaps?

With each question I caught the scent of lye, felt the fluttering in the backs of my eyes, and then the answers fell from my lips with all the grace of a nauseous belch: eighty-nine steps; Gennadios had placed her right hand atop her left in her lap, indicating she was right-handed; Uxos had two thin white scars on the back of his right thumb knuckle, and though his finger knuckles had been bloodied, that had been due to the cracking of calluses there; and no, I'd seen no churned-up mulch except for a bit that had been disturbed by a thrush.

Finally Ana went silent. Then she said, "Thank you for all that, Din." Her fingers flittered in the folds of her dress. "The Haza family . . . You're not familiar with them."

"I know they're rich, ma'am. Know they own a lot of stuff in the inner rings of the Empire. Yet that is the run of it."

"Mm. They are gentryfolk. Which means they own the most valuable thing in all of the Empire." Her hand flashed forward, and she pinched a clod of dried mud off my boot and crumbled it into dust. "*Land.* Takes a lot of dirt to grow all the plants and animals and reagents to make the Empire's many alterations. Just incomprehensibly huge agricultural works, sprawled across the second and third rings of the Empire. This means the ears of the Empire are more attuned to the voice of gentry, and such folk don't necessarily feel like they need to obey all of our laws all of the time—which can make it hard when they're tangled up in suspicious shit like this."

"Did I not meet your expectations in this regard, ma'am?" I asked, worried.

"Oh, no, no. You did fine, Din. I mean, if I'd been in your boots, I'd have found that fucker of a housekeeper's wine cup and dumped in a thimble of ground glass. But really, for your first murder investigation, you did phenomenal—walking up to a Haza estate and interrogating each witness is not something many people would have managed so well."

"Thank you, ma'am," I said, pleased.

"In fact, Din, I'd say you have the *exact* right appetite for bland, bloody-minded drudgery that makes an assistant investigator excel."

"Thank you, ma'am," I said, far less pleased.

"And it's no fault of yours that you're unable to determine the truth of what happened. The Apothetikals of this canton are apparently *so* stupid they must think a pair of trousers to be a fascinating puzzle." She slid her blindfold off. Her eyes were dancing in their sockets so fast that their pupils almost became a blur. "A sweet, sickly bloom . . . white, purple, and yellow, and growing from the flesh of a man . . . Tell me, Din. Do you know the canton of Oypat?"

I summoned the map of the Empire in my mind: a tremendous, spoked wheel within a spoked wheel, with the Empire's curving walls acting as the felloes, and the roads acting as the spokes. But though I'd engraved all the cantons of the Empire within my memory, I didn't know Oypat.

"I . . . do not, ma'am," I said.

"Not surprising," she said. "The canton fell victim to a contagion about eleven years ago. Some clever Apoth there sought to make cheap parchment, and suffused a type of grass to grow very, very quickly . . . It was called *dappleglass*—a simple weed similar to shoot-straw. It grew from tiny, sporelike seeds, and it had a white flower with a yellow and purple interior, and a rather unpleasant aroma. Yet then the dappleglass grew far *too* quickly. It invaded every patch of soil within the canton of Oypat, killing off most of the wildlife, and when it ran out of soil, the grass figured out how to grow within the wood of the homes and structures there, and even on the sides of trees. But the most alarming thing was what happened to the people who happened to bathe in the rivers downstream of this grass."

"Did . . . did it grow *inside* the people, ma'am?" I asked.

"Correct, Din. Very good! Most of the growths could be surgically removed, but others . . . Well. They weren't so lucky. The spores of the plant even tried to grow on fernpaper walls and doors, which, as you accurately noted, are pretty resistant to such things. Mostly they blackened and moldered to prevent the spores from taking root. Just having dappleglass near a fernpaper panel made it grow black dots within hours. But . . ." She stood and began pacing up and down her little house. "I have never heard of dappleglass growing so murder-ously quickly before. Nor being able to destroy ceilings and walls. That is different . . . and much deadlier."

"Have you seen this plant before, ma'am?" I asked.

"Seen it? Absolutely not." She gestured at the books about her. "I read about it, obviously. But I'm sure this is it."

"So . . . what is your conclusion, ma'am?" I asked. "How was Commander Blas exposed to this dappleglass?"

"Oh, intentionally," she said. "That is how."

A taut silence.

"You mean . . ."

"I mean, I am about eighty percent sure that Commander Taqtasa Blas was *assassinated*. Probably not by someone within the house, but with the *help* of someone within the house."

"Truly?" I said. "You think that just from what I told you, ma'am?"

"Certainly," she said. "What you told me is more than enough. In fact, it's so obvious that I'm worried this all might turn out a little boring . . . Can you not see it? The blackened fernpaper, the rotted kirpis shroom, and the insufferable heat?"

"Afraid I can't see a thing, ma'am."

"It's there," she said. She waved a hand, dismissive. "You just have to look at it right. Here are our next steps, Din." She took out a slip of paper and started scribbling on it. "I want you to take this to the Haza house in the morning. This is a formal writ of summons. Use it to bring the oldest servant girl, the housekeeper, and the groundskeeper here, to my quarters, for me to speak to personally. Tell them it's a routine request. And be ready to listen. You're my engraver. You remember what that means, Din? You are the living legal embodiment of our investigation. All that's between your ears is considered actionable evidence within the Iudex of the Empire. So— *listen*. And bring your engraver's bonds."

That gave me pause. An Iudex engraver's bonds were a set of cleverly engineered manacles which came with twenty tiny combination locks that could be quickly set to any sequence. The sequences were so complex that only someone with an enhanced memory could recall them; so, when the manacles were clapped on someone's wrists, only the engraver who'd put them on could easily take them off. Yet I had never had the chance to use mine yet.

"I do wish to ask, ma'am," I said.

"Yes, Din?"

"Well . . . previously all our cases were about pay fraud."

"So?"

"So . . . should I expect anything different here?"

A flippant shrug. "Generally I find the main difference with murder cases is how loud they are. All the screaming, you see. But you should be prepared. There is a very high chance one of those three people you're going to bring here participated in a murder. People under that sort of stress do all kinds of dumb shit. So you'll want to be armed—bring your sword."

"I'm afraid I don't have a sword, ma'am," I said.

"You *don't?*" she said. "Why not?"

"I'm still in my apprenticeship to you."

A stupefied pause. "You *are?*"

"Yes? I've only been working for you for four months, ma'am. I don't get imperial-issued arms until my apprenticeship is up."

"Well . . . hell, I don't know, bring a big fucking stick or something! Do I have to think of everything?"

"I can bring a practice sword, ma'am," I said. "There's no policy against that, and I'm quite familiar with the—"

"Yes, yes, yes," she said, flapping her hand at me. "First in your class at dueling, you wouldn't shut up about that when I interviewed you. Do *that,* then. And search them before they come in. Understood?"

"Yes, ma'am."

"Good." She returned to plucking at her wire contraption. "Good evening, then, Din."

I stood at her doorway, still standing at attention.

"I said *good evening,* Din. But you appear to still be here."

"It's the thirtieth of Skalasi, ma'am," I said. "End of the month."

"Oh." With a sigh, she stood. "Right. Your *dispensation.* Where's the form . . ." She ripped open a drawer, pulled out a piece of parchment, and hurriedly scribbled on it. "There. Another month's good work noted. Dance off to the banks, then, and collect your pay."

I bowed as I took it. "Thank you, ma'am."

She returned to her contraption. "When the hell do I get to stop bothering with those damned forms, Din?"

"When I am no longer your apprentice and become your official assistant."

"Oh, yes." She laughed dully. "When you *graduate*. As if climbing the Daretana bureaucracy was somehow special."

I stood up straight, glaring ahead. She seemed to taste the change in my demeanor: she glanced at me, then sighed.

"Ohh, what is it?" she said. "What have I said now?"

"It *is* special," I said, "to me, ma'am." I looked at her. "And to most of us here in this canton, who have joined the Iyalets to better our position."

She paused. For once there was no hint of a grin playing at her lips.

"Ahh," she said. "Well. Shit. In that case, Din, I . . ." Her jaw flexed, like she had to silently practice the word before saying it; and when she did, she said it grudgingly, like pulling a sour tooth. "I *apologize*."

"Understood, ma'am," I said. "For what it's worth, I do appreciate your being willing t—"

"Shut up!" she snapped.

"What?"

She started waving her hands about. "Just shut up, Din!"

"I mean . . . I . . . what?"

"I mean *shh!* Be quiet!"

She held up a finger, eyes wide, head cocked.

Then I heard it: a soft, eerie chiming sound.

"Are you hearing that, Din," she whispered, "or am I really going mad now?"

"I hear it, ma'am." I looked around for the source of the chiming, bewildered, but Ana whirled to look at her contraption.

"It works? It *works!*" She cackled with glee. "I've read about such instruments, but I wasn't quite sure if I'd be able to pull it off in such a crude environment . . ."

I looked over her shoulder at the contraption. It was a boxlike frame of wires, with a round, heavy weight hanging down from the exact center. The weight had a little metal tip at the end, which rested against a situr string stretched across the bottom of the frame. I realized the weight was moving very slightly, vibrating from some unseen force, so its tip was tapping against the string with a soft chiming.

"What's that, ma'am?" I asked.

"An Engineering quake instrument," she said. "When the earth below moves at all, just shakes the tiniest bit, the weight tries to stay in place, and bounces against the string. It takes a lot to calibrate it right, but if you do it, it can be very sensitive. For example—you can't feel the earth shaking now, can you, Din?"

"The earth is shaking?" I said. "Right now? Truly?"

"You're probably accustomed to it, having been here for so long. But yes. The earth is shaking. Right now."

I watched as the little weight bounced against the string, and felt my skin go cold.

"It's shaking . . ." I said. "It's shaking because . . ."

"Yes," she said quietly. "What we are witnessing, Din, are the quakes from the sea floor about two hundred leagues away, as a leviathan slowly churns its way through the bottom of the ocean, toward the coast."

I stared at the bouncing weight. The atonal chiming suddenly seemed far louder.

"Must be a big one," said Ana, grinning. "Let's hope the sea walls hold, eh?"

CHAPTER 4

|||

IT WAS LATE BY THE TIME I GOT TO THE POST STA-
tion at the edge of town. The Fisher's Hook twinkled high above the
gray treetops, bent slightly to the east, signaling the fading of the
month of Skalasi and the beginning of the month of Kyuz. Though
the post station was deserted except for a few exhausted-looking
mules tied up at the back, Postmaster Stephinos was still leaning
against his counter, arms crossed, a thread of smoke unscrolling
from his tiny pipe. The coal in its bowl danced in the dark as he nodded his head at me.

"Evening, Kol," he said. "Thought I'd be expecting you."

"Evening, Stephinos," I said. "I've a letter to mail."

"I'm sure you do. That time of the month. Hence why I waited for
you."

"Oh. You did?"

He gestured to himself, a flamboyant little flourish—*Obviously, as
I am here.*

"Oh, well. Thank you for that, Steph."

He watched me fumble in my pockets, his black Legionnaire's
cloak half-lost in the dark, his gaze keen but not impatient. The position of Postmaster was close to that of a god in a place like Daretana,
touching nearly everything that mattered to everyone every day. How
lucky we were to have one as benevolent as Stephinos.

I handed over the parchment Ana had given me. Stephinos filed it away and slid another piece of paper over to me: my dispensation, a document I could bring to any imperial bank to collect my monthly pay.

"I'm going to be really indulgent this time," I said, picking it up.

"Are you now," he said.

"Yes. I'm going to hold it for ten seconds rather than the usual five before giving it right back to you, and won't that be a treat."

He grinned. I studied my monthly dispensation, trying to take satisfaction in it. Like every piece of text I saw, the letters quivered and slipped about, but the numbers made sense—though the amount they indicated was very small.

"What a thing it is," I said, "to be rich for a handful of minutes." I sighed, put it back down on the counter, and pushed it over to him. "Or at least slightly less poor."

Stephinos watched me, a sympathetic gleam in his eye. "Need an envelope?" he said around his pipe.

"No," I said. "I've got one." I slid the envelope out of my pocket and handed it over. I'd spent a few minutes yesterday working on the address, sketching parallel lines on its front to make sure the letters touched the lines on the top and bottom. It was difficult for me to write legible text, but if I was patient and careful, I could manage it.

Stephinos appraised my work like I'd made a copy of a holy text. "This one's pretty good!" he said. "Much better than the others."

"Don't need to drown me in compliments, Steph. But I appreciate it."

"You seem in need of them. Is she running you ragged again?"

"If I'm alive, then the answer's yes." I tried to smile, but the chiming of Ana's little contraption echoed in my ears. I glanced eastward, thinking. "Steph—you're Legion, and you know more than anyone about the shape of things around here. Can I ask you something?"

"Knowing the shape of things isn't the same thing as knowing things. But you can try."

"Has there been any word on how the wet season's going to be this year?" I asked. "Any chance we're going to catch a good one?"

A baleful stare. "Ahh. Huh. No such thing as a good wet season, Kol," he said. "But as to whether this one's worse than others . . ." He waved his hand at the warehouses and lots beyond. "Read the mud, boy. Read how it's churned. Read the number of horses, the amount of stone, the crates of bombards headed east. Read those and tell me what you think."

"I guess post my money as fast as you can, then. Sanctum knows if I'll get to send another."

He slipped the dispensation in the envelope and placed it in the pile of outgoing post. "You're a good son, Kol."

I hesitated to respond. My family thought me neither beautiful nor bright, and I mailed my dispensations home out of filial duty rather than love or fondness. "What makes you say that? Half the Sublimes here must be sending their pay home."

"More than half. But I only tell the good ones secrets."

"Oh? Like what?"

He crooked a finger, and I leaned close. "Take the back way to your quarters tonight," he said. "Some route most wouldn't bother taking."

"I see . . . Can you give me more than that?"

"Captain Thalamis came by looking for you. From the Apoths. Asking about something you did today. Didn't like the look of him. I'd avoid him if you can."

"Thalamis?" I said. "Why's he coming after me? I'm not in Sublime training anymore, and he's not my commanding officer anymore."

"Not sure he knows that. Bastard thinks he's commander of all he sees." The coal in his pipe flared hot, and smoke streamed from his nostrils. "Just saying—take the back way home tonight, Kol. And stay safe."

I thanked him and slipped away.

I DID TAKE the back way home, the chimes of Ana's contraption filling my mind and Stephinos's words echoing in my ears—*Read the mud.*

How odd it felt. Commander Blas's death was easily the biggest thing to ever happen to me in my career; yet the chimes and those three words made it seem very small in comparison to what the rest of the Empire did.

Every wet season, the great leviathans rose in the eastern seas and silently, steadily approached the coasts. And every wet season, the bombards and ballistas of the Legions and the great walls of the Engineers kept them back. That was the only reason the people of the cantons tolerated the taxes and drafts and commands of the Empire of Khanum: it was the Empire and the Empire alone that could marshal the resources and maintain the sea walls to keep the leviathans out. Yet when every wet season ended, the folk of the Empire did not breathe easy, but instead asked—*What about the next season? What about then?*

That was what it was like to be a citizen of the Empire of Khanum, especially in the Outer Rim. You lived in endless anxiety, a constant state of crisis.

It often made it a little hard to go about your everyday tasks, frankly. What was the point of fetching food or fixing up your house or caring for your family when a titan could break through the walls and kill you and a thousand others like you in a matter of hours? What was the point of doing anything, really?

Yet the Empire survived because the emperor told us this was not true. Everywhere you saw his effigy, it was accompanied by the words *Sen sez imperiya.* And though this was written in Khanum—an old language almost no one spoke anymore—we all knew what it said: *You are the Empire.*

And, more important, we understood what that meant: *We are all here because of what all of us do.*

Sometimes that made the days a little easier. Even when solving the occasional gruesome murder, I supposed. Yet I had become a

Sublime and labored at my position not simply to support the Empire, but to make enough coin to pay off my father's countless debts and move my family out of the Outer Rim of the Empire—too close to the shores and sea walls of the east—and purchase land within the third ring. Someplace where my family would have more walls between themselves and the titans, where they would be safe.

If there even was such a thing as being safe in the Empire these days.

I WAS EXHAUSTED by the time I got back to my quarters. I'd used the muddiest, worst paths, and always kept an eye to make sure the way ahead and behind was deserted. When I finally approached the apprentices' quarters, I sighed with relief.

Then I heard a sharp voice snap, "*Kol!*"

I stopped short. Captain Alixos Thalamis emerged from the darkness of my quarters entryway, his red Apoth cloak swirling about him.

Son of a bitch, I thought. He'd been waiting for me.

"Stay right where you are, boy!" Thalamis bellowed. "Do not even *think* of moving!"

I stood up straight at attention and waited. He skulked forward, a predator's pace, hands behind his back, the crossguard of his officer's sword winking like a cold star. I avoided meeting his gaze, but he stuck his smooth, handsome, dead-eyed face close to mine.

"I hear," he said, "that you caught yourself some real work today, Kol."

As this wasn't a question, I stayed silent.

"Answer me, damn it!" he snapped. "Is that correct?"

"I was assigned a death scene today, yes, sir," I said.

"Really?" he said. "And how did you manage it, Kol?"

"As my master had directed, sir."

"So why did *I* receive multiple formal complaints," he said, "from some esteemed personages, Kol, indicating that you did not manage it at *all*? Because it sounds like you, as you so often do, fucked it up beyond comprehension!"

The face of Madam Gennadios flashed in my memories.

Friends in the Iyalets, she'd said. Now I knew who she'd meant.

"Keeping the servants of the Hazas held prisoner in their own place of work?" Thalamis said. "Questioning them like they were the plotters of some crime? Do you have any idea what you're doing?"

"There was a death, sir," I said. "A death that could have been caused by contagion."

"Contagion that we Apoths didn't find," he said. "Are you aware that you're still an *apprentice* to the investigator, Signum? You're too damned old for it, but that's what you are. And you do remember your final assignment will need to be approved by the Apoths, including myself. It is we who manage the altered organisms of the Empire. As you are one such organism, your future belongs to me." He stepped closer. I could feel his breath on my cheek, caught the aroma of pepper and the gamy scent of lamb. "Do you understand what it would do to your position to have complaints from the Hazas on your formal record?"

I did not answer. I hated myself only a little for how fast my heart was beating. It'd been months since I'd first trained as a Sublime under Thalamis, but still I remembered all the whippings he had doled out to me. To have him so close now brought memories of the slash of the cane bubbling to the front of my mind.

"Tell me everything that happened at that house," Thalamis said. "Now."

My response was quick and clipped: "It's against policy to discuss investigations with other officers, sir."

"I could give a shit!" he said. "You tell me what happened, you tell me what the investigator is planning, and you tell me *now*!"

I allowed a glance at him. I usually saw malice in Thalamis's eyes, but this time I spied hunger. The man was here on a mission, and not his own. Interesting.

"Sir," I said, "you will be able to review all that when I formally submit my report to the Iudex. But it is against Iudex policy to share investigation information now."

"*What* was that, Signum?" he growled.

"It's the policy, sir," I said. "I cannot discuss it. It might endanger the investigation."

"You little son of a bitch," he said. "If I tell you to brief me on what you've done, you had damned well better do it!"

"But you are not my commanding officer, sir," I said stoically. "Not anymore. The Apoths commanded me after my alteration, but that changed when I was assigned to Immunis Dolabra at the Iudex Iyalet. I am only permitted to discuss the death scene with her."

Thalamis's eyes went cold and dead. "You think," he said, "that because you got to such a position with that . . . with that *lunatic*, you can hide from me. But let me tell you a story, Kol."

He started pacing around me in a tight circle. I was reminded of a wolf waiting out a treed squirrel.

"A student arrives at Daretana to be inducted as a Sublime," he said. "And yet, though he pays his fee for the suffusions, and is granted them, this student remains abysmally, incredibly *stupid*. Reads slow, writes not at all. Applies to all the Iyalets—Legion, Engineering, Apothetikal, Treasury—but fails all his exams, and fails them miserably. It's like a child took his tests for him. Soon it's obvious to everyone that he is the most dunderheaded Sublime to have ever been evaluated, and possibly the dumbest fucking oaf in all of the canton."

The beat of my blood rose. How wonderful it would be to drive a knife into one of Thalamis's squinty little eyes.

"But then," said Thalamis, "the Senate appoints an *Iudex Investigator* to Daretana. And she requests an engraver. A specialized role, requiring an unusually talented Sublime to fill the post. But then . . . why, suddenly out of nowhere, this young Sublime swans in and scores the top marks on his Iudex test. An absolutely phenomenal performance—so much so that he's given another Iudex test, just to confirm it's real. And again, he gets top marks. And so, this investigator picks him. I'd say it's remarkable . . . but that's the wrong word, isn't it? I think a better one is *unbelievable*. Perhaps *impossible*."

I focused on my breath, on my posture, on anything but the face before me.

"I *will* figure out how you cheated, Kol," said Thalamis. "And when that happens, your time here is deader than a butchered hog. And all your dispensation, and any lands you might be rewarded at the end of your service term, are gone. But before you go, I'll have you caned—*again*—just for wasting my time. Is that clear?"

I said nothing.

"Is that *clear*, Signum?"

"I understand, sir," I said grudgingly.

He stepped back. "But maybe I won't need to wait that long, Signum," he said. "Maybe you'll piss off the Hazas so much that they'll find a way to get your apprenticeship terminated."

He walked away. I stood in the dark street, still standing at attention. I could feel my blood beating in my ears and my breath hot in my nostrils. I watched Thalamis go, wishing it had been he, and not Blas, who'd been torn to pieces by those trees.

Yet I remembered the hunger in his eyes, and his very specific questions.

It suddenly felt like Captain Thalamis was working for the Hazas. That seemed valuable to know.

Yet I wondered—how many other officers were friends of the Hazas? What exactly had I gotten myself into this morning? And what did Ana know?

I supposed I'd find out tomorrow. I turned and slinked off to bed.

CHAPTER 5

III

THE NEXT MORNING I LED MY THREE RELUCTANT witnesses to Ana's house, my practice sword swinging at my left side and my engraver's bonds tinkling at my right. The sword was uncomfortable to carry, for the blade was made of lead and wood to build strength, so it was far heavier than a common sword. Gennadios moved the slowest of the three, her painted nose high in the air. Perhaps it was out of protest, but she also wore the platformed wooden sandals associated with high-gentry servants, forcing her to shuffle through the muddy streets. After her came Ephinas, the older servant girl, and then Uxos, the groundskeeper. Both of them seemed utterly terrified.

After what felt like a damned day of walking, we made it to Ana's porch. "I'm going to need to confirm none of you have weapons," I told them.

Gennadios's tiny, glittering eyes widened. "You are not," she said, "laying a finger on me. Or my people."

"I'll touch you only through your robes, ma'am," I said.

"You will *not!*" she said.

"I have to," I said. "It's my duty." I wanted to tell her I certainly wouldn't be enjoying it any, but that didn't seem diplomatic at the moment.

She huffed for a moment. Then she said, "I will pull my robes tight about me, and Ephinas will do the same. Then you will see we have no blades on us. Uxos can do as he pleases, of course."

Ephinas and Gennadios then did so, pulling their clothing tight against their bodies while I looked them over, blushing, for I found this more mortifying than just searching them. Then I cleared my throat and searched Uxos, checking his waist and leggings. Nothing.

"Satisfied?" asked Gennadios.

I ignored her and knocked on Ana's door. I heard a short "Come!" and opened the door.

Ana had redecorated. The books and projects had all been removed from the meeting room. Instead, she had produced a small desk, and she was sitting behind it in her short stuffed chair, waiting for us with her blindfold on her eyes.

She smiled as we trooped in. "Good morning. I am Investigator Dolabra. Please take a seat."

She gestured before her. Two chairs awaited the witnesses, along with a stack of books to serve as the third seat.

The three servants stared at her. I took up a position standing behind Ana, my hand on my practice sword. It seemed unlikely that these anxious people would try anything, but Ana had told me to be ready, so I would be ready.

"Excuse me," said Gennadios. "But—the investigator is *blind*?"

"Only occasionally, Madam Gennadios," said Ana. "I find that reducing one or several senses often makes it far easier to absorb information, and *think*. Please—sit."

They did so, with Uxos taking the seat on the pile of books.

"Thank you for joining me this morning," said Ana. "I know it is unusual—but then, these are unusual circumstances. A man is dead, killed in a most unusual way. I have a few questions for each of you that I thought would be better asked directly."

Gennadios shifted her posture into that same damned position from the house: knees together at an angle, her whole body facing away like Ana wasn't worth looking at. I was surprised to see her treat an Iyalet officer so, but then I remembered what Ana had said of the gentry: *Such folk don't necessarily feel like they need to obey all of our laws all of the time.*

"It would have been easier," Gennadios said, "if you had come yourself."

"Of course," said Ana. "First, Madam Gennadios—I would like to begin by asking you more about why Commander Blas was staying at the estate in the first place."

"He is a friend of the Haza family," Gennadios said. "Surely your boy told you that."

"He did. He repeated what you said—that friends sometimes stay with one another. However, the Hazas were not present. Correct?"

"Obviously."

"And did they have any intention of being present?"

"I am not always informed," said Gennadios, "of my masters' plans."

"Nor were any other Iyalet personnel or imperial officers present."

"No," she said coldly.

"And Blas did not visit any Iyalet personnel or imperial officers in Daretana."

"If you say so."

"So the suggestion seems to be," said Ana, "that Blas was staying totally alone in someone else's mansion with no one but the servants, without any of his colleagues in Daretana being aware of it."

A twitch in the muscle behind the old woman's nose. "It is a very fine residence," she said. "We labor daily to keep it so. I would expect many would travel across the cantons to spend a night there."

"Perhaps so." Ana cocked her head, grinning. "But I do find it curious that Blas, as a commander in the Engineers, also had access to the senior officers' quarters here in Daretana—which is quite a nice accommodation, I understand. Yet he did not stay there, nor even visit."

"A Haza estate," said Gennadios, "is doubtlessly far superior to any Iyalet barracks."

"Of course. But then there is the fact that Commander Blas served in the Engineering Iyalet, on the sea walls. And the wet season is approaching. If such a person were to break away from his duties, I would assume it could only be for official Iyalet reasons. And if *that* were the case, I would assume he would stay at the senior officers' quarters, to discuss his labors with his colleagues. Wouldn't you?"

There was a long silence. The smug look had been wiped off Gennadios's face now. I was so curious where this was going, though, that I didn't have much mind to enjoy it.

"Was there another guest coming to the estate, madam?" asked Ana. "One whose purpose was to *attend* to the commander?"

"My masters' business is their own," said Gennadios. "I . . . I have no need to tell you more."

"You do, though," said Ana. "As this is an official Iudex summons. But I am impatient, so let me cut to it. I will conject that a *woman* was arriving to visit the commander. Possibly more than one. A very courtly retinue, perhaps. After all, it seems like the commander liked women a great deal. He certainly couldn't keep his hands off the servant girls, for example."

Gennadios turned to glare at Ephinas, who was resolutely staring at the floor, and hissed, "What did you tell them?"

"They *all* told Din," said Ana. "Not just her. Perhaps they all hated the commander that much. Allow me to make a conjecture about Blas's relationship to the Hazas . . . The Hazas treat the commander to a good time and provide the girls—even at a critical time like this, the start of the wet season. What I'm wondering is . . . what did the Hazas get out of the relationship?"

Uxos started rocking back and forth on his stack of books.

"I . . . I have nothing to say to you!" Gennadios spat. I saw gaps in the paint on her face. Evidently she didn't often make such hysterical expressions.

"You don't need to," said Ana. "Din here is an engraver and acts as a living legal embodiment of my work. His testimony is considered sacrosanct. As you've said many things in front of him, that's enough."

"Nothing wrong has been done!" Gennadios said. "Amorous arrangements are not illegal in the Empire!"

"But they *do* have political implications," said Ana. "Who is in bed with who—literally or otherwise—can ruin a man's career."

"Then . . . then what reason could I have had for killing the commander?" Gennadios said. "Or any of us? And *how* could we have killed him, anyway? Even the Apoths can't understand it!"

"I'm not suggesting you did," said Ana. "None of the staff, I think, was the true killer." She sat back in her chair, and for a moment the shadows fell across her blindfolded face. "But it is also my job, Gennadios, to figure out *why* he might have been killed. And I must admit, I am *mighty* curious as to why such a powerful family would *ever* *bother* having an estate in the godless backwaters of the Outer Rim. One they don't even visit. Yet . . . I am far more curious to see what will happen when the Hazas find out that their housekeeper not only let a commander get murdered on their property, but then went and chatted about it to the Iudex."

Gennadios now looked positively ill. "You . . . you made me come here! I was *legally* obliged to . . . to . . . to come here, to . . ."

"As anyone who's been past the third-ring wall knows," said Ana, "the Haza clan is not terribly interested in the boundaries of the law."

The three servants sat before Ana, bewildered and terrified. Uxos had stopped rocking and was now frozen on the pile of books.

"What did Commander Blas provide to the Hazas?" Ana asked, every word as percussive as the blow from a hammer.

"I don't know," whispered Gennadios.

"Was it some act? Information?"

"I don't know!" she said. She was panicking now. "I don't! I really don't!"

"I see. Then you, Madam Gennadios, are going to tell me all of the commander's movements before he arrived at the estate," said

Ana. "And the timing of all of his previous visits. I very strongly suspect you know this—it would be *very* useful to have records of when
and where a powerful man had been playing about with prostitutes,
no matter how legal it may be. If you don't give me this, I will make it
known to the Hazas that you have given me far, far worse things. This
would be a lie, but it would be one they'd believe."

Gennadios was trembling. "You wouldn't."

"Of course I would." Again, the predatory grin. "I'm not at all as
morally upstanding as Din here. You give me that, and I'll stay quiet."

"But . . . but just being here," said Gennadios. "Just this happening at all . . . I might be doomed already."

"I think the Hazas may likely forget about that," said Ana. "After
the revelation of how Blas was killed."

A pause.

"You *know* how he was killed?" asked Gennadios.

"Of course I do. He was killed by an assassin." Ana turned her
blindfolded face to Uxos, the groundskeeper. "And you helped them
do it, sir."

"WHAT?" SAID GENNADIOS. "You're suggesting that . . . that
Uxos here . . ."

Uxos shook his head, his beard mopping his collar like a paint-
brush. "N-no. No, I . . ."

"Dappleglass is what killed the commander," said Ana. "A very
powerful contagion. After all, it killed a whole canton. But besides its
murderous, infestatious qualities, it is also known for its odd effect
on fernpaper, causing moldy splotches to grow on its surface—
notable, as fernpaper is so resistant to other blights. This is what Din
saw in the bathing closet—dappleglass stains on the interior of the
fernpaper walls and concentrated at the top. Because, you see, the
contagion was delivered to Blas in the *bath*. I suspect a small length
of the grass was placed in the shootstraw pipes. Blas arrived, bathed
first thing in the evening . . . and as the water steamed, he inhaled it,

lining his lungs with the spores. Yet it also floated *up,* staining the fernpaper walls."

Uxos was now sweating prolifically. "But . . . but I don't do anything with the pipes . . ."

"No," said Ana. "But you do *lots* with fernpaper, don't you? Especially fernpaper doors, and windows. You're the helpful person who replaces them. You let the assassin into the grounds with your reagents key, probably the night before, to tamper with Blas's bath. The assassin then entered and exited the house through a fernpaper door. But it wasn't until after they left that you noticed the door they'd used now had black spots on it—a consequence of either carrying the dappleglass past the door, or perhaps the assassin themselves were unusually dusted with the spores, tainting their very touch."

"But there were no doors stained," said Gennadios.

"True!" said Ana. "But that is because Uxos, being a gardener, realized that the assassin's presence must have stained it. So, he *removed* the door after Blas arrived, replaced it, and then burned the tainted one in his stove."

A stain of sweat was spreading across Uxos's shirt.

"One of the servant girls complained of an intense heat the night before," said Ana. "Because, naturally, the kirpis shroom near the kitchens had died, so it couldn't cool the air. But *how* did it die? Well, they're vulnerable to too much moisture. If someone leaves a door open for too long, and if the air outside is too humid . . ."

"Then the mushrooms wither," said Ephinas quietly.

"Correct," said Ana. "Which is exactly what happened as Uxos— very quietly and stealthily, to his credit—removed the door from its sliding tracks and replaced it. Something he did very commonly, as the groundskeeper. He probably would have replaced the ones in the bathing chamber, too—if Blas himself hadn't been sleeping in there as the poison spread in his body."

There was another tense silence. All eyes slowly turned to look at Uxos, who was still paralyzed, eyes wide, brow blooming with sweat.

"I suspect you were paid well for the job," said Ana. "And you might think that we don't have any evidence. But . . . dappleglass is very resistant even to normal fires. It's a contagion, after all. A normal fire would actually make the spores float about on the smoke, though it does delay their bloom for a little while. But your hut is made of fernpaper as well, isn't it, Mr. Uxos?" She cocked her head, smiling. "So . . . when the two Iudex soldiers I sent to the estate review your hut where you burned those doors, I wonder . . . What colors shall its fernpaper b—"

Then Uxos screamed, stood up, and dove for Ana.

I'D TOLD MYSELF to be prepared, but I had not been ready for this. Uxos had seemed a timid man; yet in one second, he changed into a snarling, furious creature.

I watched as his hand dipped down to his boot; and then, as it came up, there was a glitter of silver in his fingers.

A knife. In his boot. Where I had not searched.

Then I moved.

I hadn't really intended to move. There was no conscious thought: it was like the muscles in my arms and legs had minds of their own, and they all woke up and hauled me along with them. The next thing I knew I was drawing my practice sword—the big, dull blade wrought of lead and wood—then stepping forward in front of Ana and slashing out with it.

My sword cut across him horizontally, smashing into Uxos's arm with the knife, and then clipping his chin and splitting his lip. Out of sheer momentum, he kept hurtling forward and crashed into me.

I fell backward with Uxos on top, landing on the floor beside Ana. I managed to keep my sword up, using it as a barrier between myself and Uxos, who was clearly stunned by the blow but still frenzied. He screamed and raised his knife, intending to plunge it into my throat, perhaps; but I held my practice sword like a stave and shoved the pommel up, smashing him in the face again, this time far harder than the last blow.

He fell backward, stunned, and dropped the knife. The whole room seemed to be screaming: me, Gennadios, Ephinas. Then I was on top of Uxos, grabbing his hair with my left hand and pummeling his face with my right fist, again and again and again.

"Din!" said Ana.

I hit him again, and again, and again.

"*Din!*"

Uxos's eyebrow split. His nose broke. His mouth was brimming with blood. My knuckles were aching, but I couldn't stop hitting him.

Then something struck me on the side of the head—not enough to knock me over, but enough to stun me. I blinked, flustered, and stared stupidly as a copy of *Summation of the Transfer of Landed Properties, Qabirga Canton, 1100–1120* landed on the floor next to me with a *thud.*

I realized Ana had thrown a book at my head—how she'd managed to land the hit despite being blindfolded, I didn't know—and I looked up at her, outraged. "What the *hell?*" I snarled.

"Din, I don't mind your violent appetites," Ana said. "But I would very much prefer it if you *didn't* beat the one man who knows anything about Blas's assassination *to fucking death*! Especially not in my *goddamn house!*"

I looked down. Though I'd barely been cognizant of my actions, I had pulverized Uxos's face to the point of being unrecognizable. He lay on the floor, bloodied and weeping.

My senses returned to me. I grew dimly aware that Ephinas and Gennadios were sobbing in terror.

"You two," said Ana to them. "Outside. *Now.* And stay there. Otherwise I'll send Din after you, and he'll render you as pretty as Uxos." Then she sat back in her chair. "Din—get your sword and get this idiot upright. We've some talking to do."

WEEPING, Uxos gave us the full spill of it.

Someone had approached him two months ago, he said, when he'd gone into town to buy more gardening grafts for the plants. This person had told him that Commander Blas was a traitor to the Empire, and had been slated for assassination, and Uxos could either participate in his assassination or be brought up on charges himself. Uxos had been tempted to walk out on such an outrageous claim— until this person had told him of the reward involved. For if he participated, he would be made a rich man.

"Who was this person?" asked Ana. "They didn't give a name?"

"They didn't," he said, sniffing.

"Didn't mention an Iyalet they worked for? Didn't show you any documentation of their authority?"

Uxos shook his head.

"What did they look like?" asked Ana.

"He had . . . had some kind of disease," said Uxos. "His clothing was very fine, but his face was swollen, disfigured. I could barely understand what he said at first."

"You're sure it was a man, though?"

"I . . . think so. His voice was high. I suppose it might have been a woman."

"Fuck's sakes," snapped Ana. "Can you even tell me what *race* the person was, you fool?"

"I think . . . Tala?" said Uxos, terrified. He gestured to me. "Like him?"

"And no residence? No method of contact information?"

No, Uxos said. All Uxos knew was that he would be paid half of the reward money up front when he agreed to help the assassin; then he was to visit the northwest corner of the grounds first thing each day. If he were to find a yellow wooden ball waiting for him, that would mean the assassination would take place that night, and he should return to that very spot at midnight to help the assassin enter the gates.

"And this assassin," said Ana. "Was it the same person who contacted you?"

"They were all in black," said Uxos. "Even ... even wore a mask, a ... an odd one. With a strange nose ..."

"A warding helm," said Ana quietly. "The kind the Apoths use to prevent themselves from breathing in contagion."

"They didn't even talk to me." Uxos sniffed. "They didn't have a sword or anything. Just a little wooden box in their hands. They walked in, then walked right out. It wasn't until later that I saw the fernpaper rotting from where they'd touched the door. I panicked and ..." He dissolved into tears. "I shouldn't have taken it. Shouldn't have taken the money. But I'm so *old*. They won't keep me forever. And after that I'll ... I'd have nothing." He dissolved into tears, head bowed.

"Din," said Ana quietly. "Your bonds, please. I believe now is the time for their first use."

I fumbled at the bonds at my side, then knelt and placed them on Uxos's hands with a click. He kept weeping, as if unaware of what I did.

Too old to be groundskeeper by half, I'd thought when I'd first seen him. Maybe I should have known then.

AFTER I HAD submitted Uxos to the Arbiters at the Iudex office, I picked up some food and returned to Ana. We lunched in her little house, eating fried bean cakes and sipping aplilot tea.

"Sanctum's sakes," she muttered. "Next time buy *flesh*, Din. I require blood and organs to function, the less cooked the better. Offal. Blood pie. Anything but these roots and legumes ..."

"Noted, ma'am," I said, wrinkling my nose. "How'd you do it, though?"

"Do what?"

"Well. How'd you put it all together so fast, ma'am?"

"Oh, I didn't put it *all* together," she said. She slipped off her blindfold to eat and blinked her yellow eyes in the dim light. "I still don't know who killed Blas, or why. That will take time to figure out. And I still don't know what Blas was giving to the Hazas. Yet you can't predict the madnesses of men. Projecting motives is a fool's game. But *how* they do it—that's a matter of *matter*, moving real things about in real space. The question of how a knife was forged in one place and then traveled across the countryside to be buried in the throat of some dumb bastard entails a lot of tangible, definite facts." She pointed at me. "You get the facts, Din. I do the rest."

I chewed my bean cake. "Yes, but—*how* did you do it, ma'am? What . . ."

"Ahh. What suffusion do I have?" she asked. "What *augmentation*? Is that it?"

"Just curious, ma'am."

"Curious to know what makes me *me*. What keeps me indoors and makes me muck about with my blindfolds and my books. That's the problem with the damned Empire these days . . . All these complacent bastards think the only thing that matters is which tiny beast is dancing in your blood, altering your brain, making you see and feel and think differently. The person an enhancement is paired with is just as important as what enhancement they get. And we get some say in what kind of person we are, Din. We do not pop out of a mold. We change. We self-*assemble*."

I had no idea what that meant, but I sensed she wasn't willing to talk on it further.

"How are we going to pursue this, ma'am?" I asked.

"Well, first off, Blas surely had a secretary," said Ana. "Someone to manage his day-to-day affairs. We need to get ahold of them, whoever they are, and get them in front of me. Then I take them apart." She ripped out a piece of parchment and began writing. "This will take time—I've no doubt his secretary is stationed in the next canton, and it's the wet season, so things must be hectic as fuck-all for the Engineers—but it must be done." She shoved the message in my hands to take to the post station. "Next, I want you to get in touch with the Apoths. Have them check the pipes of the bath. The dapple-glass might have been washed away into a drain. I'll want to confirm that and have them examine it, if so."

"Understood, ma'am."

"I'll also need you to get the materials from Gennadios," she said. "All the dates for Blas's visits. Whoever killed him knew *exactly* when he was coming here, so they've been watching him for some time. The bigger issue being, I bet Blas spent a lot of time at the sea walls in the *next* canton—Tala. A very busy one, with its own Iudex division, and its own investigator. Our abilities to trot over there and start kicking over stones are limited, unless we get something really good."

"Something really good?"

"Yes—something *really* solid indicating this badness with Blas extends to Tala. But I'm guessing it does. Blas was in bed with the Hazas . . . and the Hazas definitely have a foothold in the capital of the canton, in Talagray. If we follow this all the way, it may take us there. I'm just not sure when."

I watched her. There was a queer ferocity in her face now.

"Is there something personal with you and the Haza family, ma'am?" I asked.

"I am decidedly *im*personal with all persons, Din," she said. "Makes it easier when I have to send them to the scaffold. But the Hazas really are a bunch of rotten bastards. I wouldn't mind seeing all their progeny rotting in the ground like a bunch of fucking dead dogs."

"I . . ." I coughed. "I see, ma'am. I was just wondering if that was why you'd asked me to bring Gennadios."

"Oh, partially. I didn't really need her to confirm my hunch. I mostly wanted you to bring her so I could fuck up her day. She sounded like such an *awful* turd."

"Then why did you also ask for the servant girl, ma'am?"

"Dunno. I needed Uxos to feel comfortable coming. And three just feels better than two, doesn't it?"

"And your claim about sending two Iudex guards to check on Uxos's hut? I don't believe you asked me to arrange that."

"Ah, that bit was just a *lie*," she said. "I just wanted him to move. And he did!" She grinned triumphantly. "How fun it is, when things work out!"

AFTER WE FINISHED, I readied to depart to make my formal report to the Iudex Magistry. I noticed that Ana looked very relaxed, and far less manic than she had in the last few weeks, and commented upon it.

"Of course I feel better," she said, slipping on her blindfold to see me out. "Fiddling with something *interesting* is a very elating thing. And this murder is proving quite interesting."

"I thought, ma'am," I said as I stood on her porch, "that our purpose was to deliver justice. The Legion defends the living. The Iudex defends the dead and the wronged."

"Don't be so moralistic, Din, it's boring. And justice is a tricky thing. I mean, Blas sounded like such a *shit*, didn't he?"

"Not so much as to deserve murder, ma'am. Especially like that."

"Not yet, at least. We shall find out more."

I paused on her doorstep. "I did have one more question, ma'am . . ."

She sighed wearily. "Yes, Din?"

"What happened to the canton of Oypat? The one that was destroyed by the dappleglass?"

"Oh, well . . . the Apoths and the Engineers tried to devise a way to save it, if I recall. But they dithered too long. By the time they'd decided upon a plan of action, it was too late. The Apoths applied a burn—not a normal one, but a phalm oil burn. Same thing they use to dispose of the carcasses of the leviathans. The whole canton is now uninhabitable, cordoned off by the Engineers, and the people of the canton became like refugees. They live here and there among us, in pockets and tiny clans. And I suppose they must have some difficult questions on their minds."

"What d'you mean, ma'am?"

"I mean . . . the Empire spends endless amounts of blood and treasure defending a whole continent from sea beasts the size of small mountains. But it can't save a canton from one damned plant?" She cocked her head as a faint chime sounded behind her: her quake instrument was ringing again. "But then, the Empire's only defended us *thus* far. There's always another wet season, Din."

She closed the door with a snap.

CHAPTER 6

|||

I RETURNED TO THE HAZA ESTATE ONE FINAL TIME
to pick up the material from Gennadios. She beckoned me into her
own room to hand it over—a furtive, guilty handoff—and I took it
from her and examined it.

It was a slim little tome with a red leather cover. I opened it up
and squinted hard at the letters. Like every piece of text I saw, the letters tended to wobble and shake and dance around—but I was pretty
sure it was all in shorthand, reading *CV.—4.1127* and the like.

"Is this code?" I asked Gennadios.

"It's dates!" she snapped at me. "If you're too stupid to read it,
your investigator should be able to! She asked me for the book, and
now she has it."

She gave me the boot and I wandered around back. There a whole
swarm of Apoths were draining the boiler and searching the gutters,
all clad in leather warding helms and suits: protective gear their Iyalet
had developed to safeguard them from contagion.

One Apoth saw me from a distance and waved. He lumbered over
and removed his warding helm, revealing the flushed, sweaty face of
Princeps Otirios.

"Found it, sir!" he said. He jerked his head backward toward the
drains. "A slender slip of grass. It'd washed down the drains just as
your investigator suggested."

"How big was it?" I asked.

He held up his hands about eight smallspan apart. "Not big at all. Odd to think such a small thing could kill a man so horribly. But it must be a different breed, perhaps altered or grafted. Dappleglass normally spreads everywhere, and if it does get in people, it only grows in small clumps."

"What are you suggesting?"

"Can't make conclusions yet, sir. But if I were to hazard a guess, I'd say this plant had been altered to release fertile spores only when it encountered hot water—and then those spores would only grow when they entered living tissue, human or otherwise. What's more, the plant that grows *from* that tissue is incapable of creating spores. Otherwise, well, the whole household would have been dead and every bit of fernpaper blackened. It all appears very targeted."

"You're saying someone *weaponized* a contagion?"

"It seems very likely. Made to kill in one swift burst. It wouldn't be the first time such a thing has happened in the Empire. I'll be able to tell you more once we've had a look at it." He stuffed his helmet back on his head. "In the meantime, sir . . . might want to tell anyone you know to give their bath a thorough looking over before hopping in. If you're fond of them, that is."

I left through the side entrance. I passed the groundskeeper's hut as I did so, and tarried to look at its fernpaper walls. All of them were blackened and molded over, the thick, dark clouds of stain splashed across the walls. They seemed to be spreading before my very eyes. I carefully engraved the sight in my memories—one of many unpleasant things now preserved within my head—and departed.

I I

III

THE BREACH

CHAPTER 7

|||

I'D THOUGHT THAT THE CASE OF COMMANDER BLAS would change my life in Daretana, but I was quickly proven wrong. The next thirteen days passed in stupefying torpor.

The rains of the wet season came, bringing intolerable humidity. There was no escape from it, unless you were rich enough to purchase a kirpis shroom and find some insulated place to keep it dry. The only moment of interest was when I finally got an answer back from Commander Blas's secretary.

"Her name is Rona Aristan," I said as I stood in Ana's meeting room. I pretended to read her letter aloud just then, but in truth I'd spent twenty minutes squinting at it and memorizing each word when I'd first gotten it from Stephinos at the post station. "She says she was shocked to hear the news of the commander's murder, that she was aware he had taken personal time to visit Daretana, but claims to be ignorant of the nature of the visit beyond that, ma'am."

A derisive snort. "Indeed," said Ana. "Go on."

"She said she would very much like to come to testify before you regarding his movements, but with the coming wet season . . ."

"All members of the Engineering Iyalet are ordered to stay put," said Ana dully. "Is that the measure of it?"

"Correct, ma'am."

"Typical," she said. "Roads in the Tala canton get so clogged with traffic when the leviathans approach that I'm sure they can't afford anyone unnecessary out there."

"She did send a transcribed copy of the commander's schedule," I said, sliding it out. "It covers the last four months of his movements."

Ana snatched it out of my hand and read it with narrowed eyes. Then she chewed her lip, and spat, "*Shit!*"

"I'd have thought this would be helpful, ma—"

"It's helpful in making this damned complicated!" She held up the small red-leather book we'd gotten from Gennadios. "Because if this book is accurate, then I am almost certain the assassin is located in *Talagray,* or thereabout."

"How so?"

She slapped down Gennadios's book, then held up the secretary's letter like it contained some horrid accusation. "It's as I thought. Blas was staying in Talagray for the past three months before his death. Which makes sense, of course. A commander in the Engineers should be expected to spend a hell of a lot of time in the city that maintains the sea walls before the wet seasons." She stabbed a finger into the heart of Gennadios's open book. "But Blas's visits to the Haza estate were very erratic. The last trip he made here was the thirteenth through the fifteenth of the month of Egin. I'm guessing he just kept slipping away to go frolic with the dainty maidens. This means you definitely couldn't know when he was going to be here unless you were very *close* to him. So the killer must be someone who was observing the commander, in a much larger city that's about sixty miles to the south of here, along roads we probably aren't permitted to travel on—even if our investigation *is* invited to come! Which it might not be! The bastard is clever, I'll tell you that. They made sure to do this before the wet season began properly, so they could move freely along the roads."

"Then what'll we do, ma'am?"

She glowered for a moment. "Well. I guess I better write some damned letters." She grabbed a parchment and a quill.

"To whom?"

"To the Iudex office of the Tala canton," she said. "I'll inform them of what we've found here, and ask permission to come interview all witnesses. Though I probably won't mention Blas playing about with prossies. That would be rather less than tactful. I'll even pay the small fortune to have it sent by scribe-hawk. They'll have to pay attention to it then!"

"You want to send me to Talagray, ma'am?" I said, startled.

"Hell no. For something like this, I'd accompany you. Regardless, I'm not optimistic that we'll get any response for months. The wet season is simply too chaotic. Nobody's going to care about one murder, even if it is a goddamn Engineering commander dying to contagion. Not with leviathans sniffing about the sea walls." She noticed my disappointment. "What's the matter with you, child?"

"I'd thought, ma'am, that being as we solved a murder, at least something might happen."

"What were you expecting? An increase in pay, or a promotion? Or that the emperor himself might send you a nice note, along with a troupe of plaizaiers to come balance atop your delicates?"

"A troupe of . . . of *what*, ma'am?"

"Plaizaiers," she said. "Court dancers. Pheromonally enhanced folk whose mere presence drives people mad with arousal. By Sanctum, is this canton really so uncivilized? Either way, Din, we *haven't* solved a murder. Rather, we are *still* solving a murder. And we won't solve it at all until you send this damned letter!"

She gave me the letter, and I posted it. And that, I thought, would be the end of it for some days.

CHAPTER 8

|||

I WAS LYING IN MY BUNK, DOZING AS I LISTENED TO the half-dozen other Sublimes snoring in their sheets. I didn't know any of them: I was too old to be an apprentice, and thus too old for the Sublimes' quarters, so I didn't associate with them much; but I had grown used to sleeping with strangers about. I almost found the sound comforting.

I listened to the rain pattering on our fretvine roof, and then the sound of distant thunder.

The thunder continued, on and on. It crackled, then snapped curiously. Then more snaps, and more.

I sat up in my bunk, realizing I was not hearing thunder at all.

I stood and shouted, *"Out of bed! Now!"*

"The hell?" muttered one of the boys. "What's the matter with you?"

"That's bombard fire, goddamn it!" I shouted. I ran for the door. "Get outside, now, now!"

I scrambled out into the driving rain to find I wasn't alone: the wet night was filling with figures sprinting from their quarters, all of us making for the earthworks on the eastern side of the town's fortifications. We ran up the sides of the hillocks, grabbing grasses to haul ourselves higher on their slippery slopes, until finally we came to the eastern side and peered south.

I narrowed my eyes. It was hard to see in the glittering, rainy darkness, but I thought I could spy flickers on the southern horizon, flashes of yellow-white light. Bombard fire, bright and brilliant.

"Can't be," said a voice near me. "We're too far out to hear or see bombards . . ."

"Unless it's the big guns," said someone else. "Then who knows?"

"Or they could be firing *in* from the sea walls," said another boy quietly. "But then that would mean . . ."

The rain hammered on us, on and on, pelting our scalps and the puddles at our feet.

"If it's a breach," I said, "we'd see the beacon." I felt a fluttering in my eyes and summoned a map of the region I'd glanced at once. I pointed into a stretch of darkness. "It'd be there."

More flickers of light, more crackles of bombard. We stood on the earthworks listening to the whole of Daretana awaken, the distant orders shouted and screamed, the cry of horses, the slamming of many doors.

And then it appeared, glimmering in the darkness: a single, narrow lick of fluttering yellow flame.

"Beacon's up," I said hoarsely. "A titan's made it past the walls . . ."

Then someone started screaming: "*It's a breach! Breach, breach, it's a breach!*"

The whole world fell to chaos then. The tocsin bells started ringing out, a skull-clattering *clang-clang*. People struggled to light torches or get their mai-lanterns glowing. The engravers among us proved helpful: we remembered the policy for this, where to go and what to do, and soon we had all the other Sublimes and troops and anyone available mustering in the fields north of Daretana, waiting in the pouring rain.

The waiting seemed to go on and on. I heard whispers in the rain, perhaps sobs. I glanced at one Sublime's tall, perfect posture and saw his eyes were shut tight and he'd bitten his lip so hard he bled.

Then a commander of the Legion finally arrived—you could see the shine of his crested helm beneath the glow of a lantern—and the senior officers distributed orders: all Engineering and Legion officers were to pack up and move out south for Talagray immediately. All other soldiers were to help them pack as best they could, then stay behind and prep Daretana for immediate evacuation if needed.

What followed was mad, muddy chaos. The baggage train came rumbling into town and we all swarmed the roads, helping to heave sacks and trunks up onto the towering carts, grabbing gear from Engineers or Legionnaires as they hurried to arrange their personal packs. It was strange to see us all so transformed, so hurried and grim, rushing to prepare these people—acquaintances, friends, lovers, enemies, strangers—to venture out into the darkness and face the unknown. I looked for friends of my own from my first days in Sublime training, but the rain and the half light and the whirl of shouted words made identifying anyone impossible.

Then it was over. We never felt like we finished, but someone told us to stop. We withdrew to the side of the road and watched. Then in the flickering light of the torches, the Engineers and Legionnaires trooped out, this tremendous ribbon of horses and baggage and soaking people, their helmets and caps and armor glinting in the occasional flash of lightning.

We watched them go in silence. Someone shouted something, some order, but I just stood there. How shattering it felt to realize that the order of all our lives could be dashed to pieces in a few frenzied moments by the rumblings in the east.

Then I felt a hand on my arm, its fingers digging into my flesh, and I spun to find the snarling, soaking face of Captain Thalamis.

"Did you hear me, you half-brained idiot?" he bellowed. "Get to your assignment now in case we need to evacuate!" He shoved me, hard, and I slipped backward in the mud. "In *your* case, it means your addle-brained bitch of an investigator! Go!"

I felt my blood flash hot then, and I stood up. He saw the look on my face and tapped the hilt of his sword at his side. "Try it, fool. It'll be faster than failing you out, at least."

I watched him for a moment. Then I turned and trudged away in the rain.

"I thought so!" he called after me.

BY THE TIME I made it to Ana's house the rain had dwindled to a soft patter. I didn't bother knocking, indifferent to what state she was in: I just barged in, fuming and soaking.

"Hello, Din," she called from the meeting room.

I plodded through the house and found her kneeling before her quake contraption, which was chiming and clanking like mad. It was dark within, and I found her mai-lantern and gave it a shake. The little glowing worms within awoke, and their faint blue light slowly filtered throughout the room.

"Ma'am," I said dully. "There's been a breach. We need to get you prepared in case we need to evacuate."

"Thank you, Din," she said softly. "I had gathered as such. But there should be no need for an evacuation."

"What do you mean, ma'am?"

"I have been monitoring the quakes since they began," she said. She nodded to her contraption. "They've grown steadily quieter over the last hour. This indicates that the leviathan has retreated, probably farther to the south, back to the sea walls." She looked up at me, still blindfolded. "It's what they were trained to do."

"Who?"

"The Legion," she said. "They have armaments capable of distracting the leviathans, drawing them away from the cities and towns, and back to the walls—where all the bombards await. They plan to shoot it to death there, I imagine." She took off her blindfold and looked up at me. She must have seen the terror and fury in my face, because she tried to smile, and asked, "Why don't you make me some tea, Din?"

"Pardon, ma'am?" I asked faintly. "Tea?"

"Yes. You make such a good pot of tea, Din. I think that would be quite welcome now."

I went through the motions thoughtlessly, starting the little fire in her stove, setting the kettle to boil atop it. I pulled pinches of dried leaves from the cotton sacks hanging above, moistened them with a few drops of water, and then carefully ground them in the mortar with slow, twisting movements. As the kettle shrieked, I took a few leaves of mint, broke them apart, and added them to the mix, before packing it all into the infuser, which I slotted into the kettle's spout. Then I poured two cups and the air filled with a powerful, complex aroma.

"Smells wonderful," said Ana. She sipped at her cup. "Tastes wonderful."

I bowed my thanks, still unable to speak.

"And I note," said Ana, "that you always make it the *exact* same way. Same twist of the pestle. Same pinches of the leaves. Exactly the same, every time."

"A friend showed me how," I said numbly.

We sat in the blue half light, clutching our cups and listening to the rain and the sound of the tocsin bells in the distance.

"Did you have any friends going out tonight?" she asked.

"A few. In Engineering. Haven't seen much of them recently, since they got their assignments a while ago and I didn't, but . . ." I trailed off, not knowing what to say. "I didn't see them. Didn't get to say goodbye."

"If they're Engineering, they should be safer," said Ana. "Not *safe*, of course, but safer. They don't send the Engineers in until the leviathan itself is dealt with. Then the Engineers take stock of the situation and patch up the fortifications as fast as they can. For that's when things get trickier. They'll relocate the bombards to defend the breach point, but . . . naturally, that makes every other part of the walls harder to defend."

"So my friends won't be in danger now," I said, "but later?"

"Correct, and incorrect," said Ana. "A breach is a terrible thing, Din. We're all in danger now, for the rest of the wet season."

"And what are we to do about that, ma'am?"

She shrugged. "Wait. And see."

I STAYED UP all night with Ana, listening to the chiming of her contraption and her constant babble as she shot around the room, opening up books and massaging their pages with her head at an angle, sometimes reading aloud or voicing some bizarre fact or theory of hers.

"They use seakips in the third ring to pull barges through their canals," she said once, "little swollen dolphin creatures with doglike faces, but apparently there's been some sort of suffusion issue. The Apothetikals bred a new kind of oyster that can grow to great sizes, but the oyster hosts a germ that gets into the water, and this germ makes the seakips *profoundly* aroused, all the time. Apparently they rut themselves to death."

"Is that so, ma'am," I said, exhausted.

"Yes. Many bargemen have taken to castrating their seakips—but this is pretty tricky, Din, as the appropriate anatomy is not terribly accessible. Or identifiable. It takes a trained eye and a steady hand— in case you're ever looking for a new job."

I half smiled at such a gruesome idea. I knew she was trying to keep me distracted from all the horror and the worry, and I appreciated her for it.

Time stretched on. I was about to doze off where I sat—and then I sat up, eyes wide.

"It's . . . gone," I said. "Your chimes. It's quiet."

"Yes," said Ana. She knelt before her contraption, which was now silent. The crackle of bombards in the distance had tapered off as well. "It seems it is."

"Do you think they've really killed it, ma'am?"

"Probably. Hopefully. It's early morning now. We'll know in a day or so if it's really dead."

I RAN BACK to Daretana and found a crowd of fellow soldiers and Sublimes waiting outside of Stephinos's post station. Stephinos made a show of sitting out front on the ground, and when asked he'd only say, "I'd damned well tell you all if I knew something worth telling."

We waited for hours in the muggy air, milling about uselessly. We watched as scribe-hawks sailed overhead—homing birds the Apoths had designed to carry messages long distances—but none came to us, probably because we were already so close to Talagray. No one gave us any duties, nor shouted at us for our aimless loitering. Everyone knew the whole day would change when word arrived.

Then, close to evening, it came: two riders, both in Legion black, mounted atop league-horses—the giant steeds altered to cross huge amounts of land in mere hours. The first rider, a woman, stopped at Stephinos's station; the other, a man, kept going, probably to carry word to the towns beyond.

Everyone hurried to water the messenger's horse and bring her whatever she needed, but all she asked for was a box to stand on. She clambered aboard it and addressed the crowd, shouting, "The leviathan has been felled."

So stern was her face, though, that no one cheered.

"It was felled to the south," she continued. "Just east of the town of Sapfir. It has created a gap in the walls just over a league wide."

A gasp rippled through us. To begin with, Sapfir was near to Talagray, which meant the leviathan had come close to destroying the largest city in the Outer Rim. But far worse was the breach: a gap over a league wide was much larger than any in recent memory.

"As such," said the messenger, "all Legionnaires and Engineers from the ten neighboring cantons will be redirected to Talagray. Daretana will need to expedite their movement as much as possible. You should prepare for a large influx of imperial troops."

The muttering rose among the crowd.

Then the messenger pulled a piece of parchment from her pocket and glanced at it. "Lastly—is anyone here familiar with Iudex Investigator . . . ah, Immunis Anagosa Dolabra?"

The muttering went dead quiet. All eyes slowly turned to look at me. I raised my hand. "Uh . . . I am, ma'am."

"Please tell her she is directed to remain in place and prepare for the arrival of Commander-Prificto Desmi Vashta," she said, "of the Imperial Legion. She will be here by tomorrow evening to brief her. That is all!"

Then she mounted her horse and rode off for the next canton.

"WELL," SAID ANA when I told her the news. "That's a pretty big goddamn surprise, isn't it!" She grinned.

"Apologies, ma'am, but I can't find much to smile about at this moment," I said.

"Oh, you've always got to smile a little, Din," said Ana. "Even during, you know, the abysmally fucking awful times." She cocked her head. "A commander-prificto! That's a high rank indeed . . . and she's coming here for me, personally, during a crisis. Something's amiss."

"I had assumed the same, ma'am. But what, I can't imagine."

"Hm." She sat back in her short stuffed chair, her eyes blindfolded. "Din—you only have the one Iudex coat, don't you?"

"Ah—yes, ma'am?"

"And your boots. They're a bit shit, aren't they? Not to insult you, but . . ."

"They're not as fine as some boots, ma'am," I said curtly. "But they're what I can afford."

"Right . . . I think you're going to need to buy some new clothes, Din. Several coats and new boots, certainly." She stood, walked to one desk, and opened a drawer. "Here." She slid out a small bag of talint coins. "A present for you, given your performance during the Blas murder. Try and get that done before nightfall. Then shower, pack, and be ready."

"Thank you, but—ready for what, ma'am?"

"A very serious conversation," she said. "About something very bad. And then, I think, a departure. But to where, I'm not yet sure."

I WAITED AT the post station, dressed in my fine new blue coat and my shiny black boots. None of my apparel had been broken in yet—the coat chafed my armpits, and the boots pinched my toes—so I kept pacing, hands behind my back.

Then I heard the sound of horses' hooves and peered into the darkness. Two riders emerged from the wet night, both covered in black cloaks, their helmets painted black as well. They slowed to a halt at the post station and dismounted. Stephinos took their horses, exchanged a quick word with them, then pointed to me.

I stood up straight, hands behind my back, face purged of emotion. I'd never spoken to anyone above the rank of captain before— except for Ana, who hardly seemed to count. I had especially never spoken to an elite officer in the Legion, the most demanding and honored of all the Iyalets. I shoved my breast forward at them, ensuring they'd see all my heralds: the flower and the bar, denoting me assistant investigator; and the eye set within a box, indicating I was also an engraver.

The commander-prificto approached me first. I didn't need to see the heralds on her ebony cloak to identify her as such: a glance at her gray face indicated many alterations, and her dark, serious eyes suggested someone who had seen no shortage of horrors in her time. She was a tall woman, shoulders broad, jaw set. Slight twitch to her step, suggesting some chronic tweak in her back. Her helm was ornate, engraved with letters in Old Khanum: the emperor's declaration founding the Legion so many centuries ago. A fine piece of artistry. I wondered if she wore it in such critical moments to command the greatest respect.

She was followed by a Legion captain, a tall, younger man with a handsome, fair face and pale eyes. Though his helm was fine and black, it wasn't engraved like the commander-prificto's. His eyes were dark with fatigue, a dash of stubble clinging to his chin; yet though he was obviously tired, he moved robustly, his big, athletic frame bouncing along merrily. The physical alterations of the Legion, I guessed, could keep a fellow going even after a breach.

I bowed low as they approached. "Welcome to Daretana," I said. "I'm Signum Dinios Kol, Assistant Investigator for Immunis Ana Dolabra."

Both of them gave me the tiniest bows in return. "Thank you for meeting us," said the commander-prificto. Her voice sounded very hoarse, and very tired. "Please take me to the investigator right away."

I led them through Daretana, then to the edge of town and into the dark jungle. They did not talk. I expected them to be surprised by Ana's living quarters, but neither said a thing; either they knew about her situation or they were too tired to care.

I had planned to walk up, knock, and introduce the commander-prificto to Ana; but there appeared to be some unspoken Legion procedure here, for the captain stopped me to talk, while the commander-prificto continued on.

"Beg pardon, Signum," he said. "But has anyone here made inquiries about our meeting tonight?"

"Inquiries?" I said. "No, sir."

"No one has asked about the nature of our visit?"

"No, sir."

"And you have seen no one hanging about your immunis lately? Watchful or paying undue attention?"

He glanced off into the shadows, eyes narrow.

I looked down. His hand was resting close to his sword.

I took a breath, and my eyes fluttered as I summoned up my memories. "I have seen twenty-seven people come near the path to my immunis's house, sir," I said. "Some came several times—nineteen total unique visitors, I should say—but none seemed unusual or malicious."

The captain looked startled. Then he laughed—a rich, merry sound. "Ah! An engraver, of course. I'd forgotten. Very good, then. Thank you." We continued walking, and when we reached the porch he removed his helmet and shook out a startlingly lustrous mane of curly brown hair. As light spilled across his fair face I saw he was not much older than I was.

He gave me a careless grin. "Apologies for all this skullduggery, Signum. I've no talent for it. But perhaps you, in your line of work, are more accustomed."

I had no idea what to say to such a thing, so I bowed.

"Come, then," he said. His smile faded, but he seemed the sort who could never banish all the mirth from his face. "Let us catch up to them."

I OPENED THE DOOR to find Ana had rearranged her quarters into the same manner as when she'd interrogated Gennadios, but with two chairs before her desk rather than three. Ana herself was standing behind the desk, blindfolded as always, and was saying, ". . . hope the journey was well."

"As well as it could be, Immunis." The commander-prificto seemed unsurprised by the blindfold. "Thank you for meeting with me. It's unfortunate that we have to do so under these circumstances. Please sit."

Ana did so, and I took my place behind her. Ana cocked her head, listening to my footsteps, then said, "This is Signum Dinios Kol, ma'am, my engraver. Din, this is Commander-Prificto Desmi Vashta, of the Tala Army of the Imperial Legion."

I bowed again to her. Vashta nodded, sat, and removed her black helmet, revealing hair that was thick, dark, and short. She gestured to the captain beside her. "This is Captain Kepheus Strovi, my second."

The smiling young captain bowed his head to Ana.

"Normally I would inquire about your assignment here, Immunis," said Vashta. "But etiquette is often one of the first casualties during an emergency, so I will cut to it."

"I understand entirely," said Ana.

"You wrote a letter recently to the Iudex office in the Tala canton. About a murder that took place here."

"Yes. Commander Taqtasa Blas."

"You mentioned the nature of the incident. But . . . I was hoping you could summarize it in more depth for me, before we talk further."

"Certainly," said Ana. She gestured to me. "Din can take care of that, naturally."

I blinked, surprised, and looked at her.

She gave me a small, wry smile. "You *are* my engraver, after all," she said.

"Oh. Yes, ma'am." Then I stepped forward and slid out my vial of lye-scent that I'd used the day of the investigation. I sniffed it, focused, and let the queer, tickling sensation flood into the backs of my eyes. Then I started talking.

I kept it short: I listed the dates, the locations, the names of everyone involved, and the nature of the case. Then I detailed Ana's investigation and conclusions, as well as our latest efforts to learn more about Blas and why he might have been targeted for assassination. I was aware as I did so that I couldn't help mimicking Ana's accent and cadence—but that was the nature of engraving someone's speech. You couldn't quite help what you picked up.

I spoke for nearly three quarters of an hour, and when I finished the two Legion officers simply sat there, faces bleak yet unreadable.

"I assume, Immunis," Vashta said finally, "that you are aware of the breach."

"I know a leviathan broke through the walls," said Ana, "but that is the extent of my knowledge."

Vashta was silent, as if debating how best to articulate a question.

"I have speculated that Commander Blas's murder might have weakened our defenses," said Ana. "Or that someone else might have been targeted in the same way. Might that be the case?"

Vashta stared into the distance for a long time. "What I am about to say to you, Immunis," she said slowly, "is a very great secret. One we are still trying to understand ourselves."

"All right, ma'am."

"You and your engraver cannot repeat it to anyone," she said. "For if you did, it could very easily cause a panic. And a panic is *not* what we need right now."

"That is understood, ma'am," said Ana.

Vashta glanced at Strovi, then said, "The leviathan did not single-handedly cause the breach. Rather, the walls were destabilized from *within*. This severely weakened their foundation, leading to a small, contained collapse. This all took place well before the leviathan approached. However, it was this collapse, and this weakening, that the leviathan took advantage of."

"We think it sensed the collapse in the waters, ma'am," said Strovi. "Heard it while it was rising through the sea floor, so it knew where to target."

"We had to remove our bombards from that segment of the walls, fearing further collapse," said Vashta. "As such, the wall was not only weak when the leviathan came, but it had much reduced defenses. It was the perfect circumstances for a breach."

Ana shot forward like a mudsnake striking. "A destabilization from within," she said. "I see!"

Vashta paused, puzzled. "See . . . what, precisely?"

"That it was likely *not* one person who was poisoned," said Ana, "but several, if not many."

I couldn't make any sense of what she'd said, but Vashta and Strovi exchanged another look, this one terribly alarmed.

"What do you mean?" demanded Vashta.

Ana's fingers danced on the edge of the table. "Allow me to make a conjecture, Commander-Prificto," she said.

"Do so."

"Did the destabilization within the walls occur because multiple people within the fortifications—how shall I put this delicately—spontaneously sprouted *trees* from their bodies, damaging the walls?"

Vashta stared at Ana, astonished. "That is so," she said softly. "Yes, that is so."

"I see," said Ana. She nodded, satisfied. Then she sat back in her chair, sniffed, and said, "Well. Fuck."

CHAPTER 9

|||

"IS THIS SOMETHING YOU EXPECTED, IMMUNIS?" demanded Vashta. "Or predicted?"

"Not at all," Ana said. "If I had, I'd have notified you all immediately."

"Then how did you conclude this?"

"Well, I assumed that if you were coming to me, ma'am, then you were here about Blas. And since I'd suspected that Blas's killer was in Talagray, that meant they could kill again with the dappleglass—and thus, I presumed you were here because they had done so. Yet then you said this was about the breach and mentioned something breaking the walls from within. If that was the case, then I presumed—accurately, it seems—that it was not *one* person who underwent such a contagion, but many. Enough to bring the walls down." She leaned forward. I could see it was taking all of her effort not to start grinning like a loon. "Tell me *everything* about what happened."

"W-we're still trying to collect reports," said Vashta, shaken. "We do not have many witnesses. But we are told that the direct cause of the collapse was two senior Engineers working on a critical part of the fortifications."

"A support," said Strovi. "A strut carrying an immense load, as several others had been weakened due to the quakes."

"And when the two Engineers, ah, *sprouted,* let's say," said Ana, "the trees damaged the support, causing the collapse."

Vashta nodded.

"Were they the *only* ones who died in such a fashion?" she asked.

Again, the two Legionnaires exchanged a glance.

"They were not," said Vashta.

"Eight other people throughout the canton underwent a similar transformation, almost at the exact same time," said Strovi.

I was so shocked that I forgot myself. "Ten!" I said aloud. "Sanctum . . . *ten* Engineers were poisoned?"

The two Legionnaires glanced at me. Strovi offered me a tiny, sympathetic smile. "Yes," said Vashta. "This is possibly the worst incident of mass poisoning in all the history of the Empire."

"Four died on the sea walls, including the two who caused the collapse," said Strovi. "Others were in the city of Talagray. One fellow was even on a horse when it happened."

"Oh!" said Ana, interested. "What happened to the horse?"

Strovi coughed. "It, ah, died, ma'am," he said.

"Ohh. Hm." She nodded, a little disappointed, as if she'd expected something more entertaining. "Were there any commonalities to the ten deaths? Did they all use the same bathing facilities? Or visit any site that featured a large amount of steam?"

"They did not," said Vashta. "We've treated this as a contagion so far, reviewing their movements to see what event might have spread this to them all. But so far we can't find any moment when they were even in the same room together in the past month, let alone all inhaling the same steam."

"The only commonality, ma'am," said Strovi, "is that they were all part of the Engineering Iyalet."

"Engineering . . ." said Ana quietly.

"Yes," said Vashta. "The worry is that someone is targeting Engineers for assassination. Perhaps as sabotage. We do not yet know."

"But to do so during the wet season . . ." Strovi shook his head.

"You think," said Ana, "that someone wants to set the titans loose within all of Khanum."

"It would be madness to imagine it," said Vashta. "But these days have been nothing if not mad."

Ana fell silent, her head bowed in thought.

"We need to know how this happened, Dolabra," said Vashta. "To find out who did this and capture them—*before* any other calamities occur. Hundreds if not thousands of people are maimed or dead. The entire canton is at risk, if not the Empire. We cannot repair the breach or battle the titans with confidence until we are sure the threat is resolved. And you are the only person I am aware of, Immunis, who has encountered this phenomenon previously, and it is my understanding that you accurately identified it, and responded to it, within a *day*. We need all the help we can get right now—but I have surmised that we especially need *your* help."

Ana's fingers were drumming wildly on the tabletop now, a frenetic *tatter-tat*. "I can't help you from here, ma'am. I rely a lot on Din for these investigations, but, well, the commute from here to Talagray would be a bit much."

"We had anticipated that," said Vashta. "I have ordered a carriage sent here straightaway, on the hopes that you would consent. It should arrive by morning."

"There are likely some issues of procedure and jurisdiction— yes?" Ana asked. "I am not an Iudex Investigator of that canton. Din is an apprentice, and I believe isn't allowed to leave Daretana until his formal assignment."

"A state of emergency has been declared for the entire Outer Rim," said Vashta. "Policies are being suspended left and right. We can suspend any statute stopping you as well, and the Iudex Investigator of Talagray is all too happy for the help. The only concern anyone has now is to make it through the wet season."

"And . . . what are the prospects of that?" asked Ana.

A bleak smile. "The prospects of that," Vashta said, "are evolving. And will likely depend in no small part on your work in Talagray."

"In that case," said Ana, "how could I possibly say no? Right, Din?"

I said nothing. For there is nothing worth saying when you are being forced into a pit of horrors.

CHAPTER 10

|||

I HAD ONCE THOUGHT TRANSPORT BY CARRIAGE TO be the domain of princes and the gentry. But as I sat in that dank little box for the sixth hour, clutching my seat while the walls and floors bucked and heaved about me, I felt it was the most awful damned punishment I could imagine.

The air was hot and stagnant. There was little to see out the windows except the close, dark, steaming jungle and the occasional flash of a mika lark. Though we traveled along imperial roads, which were bricked and well maintained, the carriage still bumped and banged every few seconds, making sleep or reflection impossible. And Ana, of course, was horrid company, sitting there blindfolded and chattering ceaselessly.

"That bump there!" she'd say to me, excited. "Right *there*! That bump occurs every seventeen seconds when we are on the southern side of the road, and every nineteen seconds when we are on the *northern* side of the road! This indicates to me that it is not a flaw in a wheel of our carriage, but is instead some quirk in the process the Engineers used to build this road, segment by segment! Or perhaps ... perhaps an issue with the land or an effect of the humidity on the stone ..."

She grew most excited when we passed one of the Engineering teams responsible for maintaining the road, and demanded I stick my head out and study the cart of bricks, and the way the dusty, muddy workers dislodged the cracking ones from the road and re-placed them.

"That's the *real* Empire right there, Din," she said, grinning. "The boys and girls who fix the roads."

"Being as we're headed to the sea walls, ma'am," I said, "I might disagree."

"Oh, people love the Legion, with their swords and their walls and their bombards. But though they receive no worship, it's the maintenance folk who keep the Empire going. Someone, after all, must do the undignified labor to keep the grand works of our era from tumbling down."

I shook my head and focused on the maps Ana had gotten for me to engrave in my mind: maps of the city of Talagray, of the Tala canton, of the sea walls, and so on and so on. She'd also procured lists of all senior Engineering officers in Talagray, and asked me to memorize them, hundreds and thousands of names—which I did, haltingly whispering each name as I read them.

Finally we turned a sharp corner in the road. I leaned out the window and tasted the air. A hint of salt on the wind, perhaps, acrid and tangy. I glimpsed a hill to the west, its southern cliff flat and stark. My eyes fluttered, and I summoned the map of the canton in my mind, searching the memory for these landmarks—a kink in the road, and a cliff-carved hill—and calculated where we were.

"Think we're close to the sea walls now, ma'am," I said.

"Already?"

"Yes, ma'am. I should be able to see them out the eastern-facing window soon enough."

"Describe them to me the second you do. I would *much* like to have them in my mind to puzzle over."

The carriage rattled along. The jungle fell back like a curtain, revealing a wide green plain swimming with mist; and there, far in the distance, the shore.

I pulled out a spyglass I'd brought, pressed it to my eye, and peered east.

A towering, slate-gray cliff, running underneath the red-stained sky like a frame below a painting, its stone wet and gleaming and crawling with vines and growth; and there, in one long, vertical seam in the cliff, a hint of movement: some insect, I thought, crawling from base to top in a slow, labored procession.

My eye trembled as I focused on it. I realized it was not an insect but instead a tiny box, wrought of wood, being hauled up on a set of strings. As it reached another notch in the gray cliffs, the box stopped, and even tinier figures emerged.

Horses. Four of them, all hauling a shining steel bombard from the box.

I blinked, staring into the spyglass. The tiny box was not tiny at all: it was a lift, made for hauling troops and armaments up the vast expanse of the sea walls.

I lowered the spyglass and stared at the walls in the distance, dumbfounded.

"Well?" said Ana. "Do you see them? What are they like?"

"The walls," I said slowly, "are very, very big, ma'am."

I described it to her as best I could. I was no spatiast, so I ran out of words for *big* very quickly, trying to express this tremendous spine of stone and earthworks running along the seas. I glassed their tops and spied at least two dozen mammoth bombards arranged there, most pointed out to sea—but some pointed in. Just in case something broke through, I supposed.

"Some of the bombards can be wheeled about by horses," Ana explained. "For the truly giant ones, some segments of walls have rails running along their tops, to make it easier for horses to haul them about."

"How big are those, ma'am?"

"Five to six times as long as you are tall, Din, if you were to stand beside them. The forging of such bombards is immensely difficult.

Like so much of what the Empire does, they are achievements of *complexity*—imagine the systems, the management, the coordination it takes not only to marshal resources and knowledge and facilities to make these remarkable things, but to make them by the *hundreds*, and ship them to the walls every wet season!"

"And . . . how tall are the leviathans, again?"

"Some are as tall as the walls. Most are slightly taller."

I tried to conceive of it, to project an image of such a thing onto the landscape beyond. I began to feel slightly ill at the thought.

"Have you ever seen one, Din?" asked Ana. "Or a piece of one, a bone or a segment of chitin?"

I shook my head.

"Din," she said tersely, "I am blindfolded, so if you've nodded your head, I've no fucking idea."

"No, ma'am, I have not."

"Mm. It's a remarkable experience . . . a tooth as long as two men laid end over end. A claw the size of three carriages. The city of Ashradel actually has a leviathan skull from the old days as part of its citadel. It's about as big as a small fort, I'm told. Quite the sight. How astonishing it is to know that the leviathans grow bigger every wet season."

"I thought that was a rumor."

"They don't like to put numbers to it," she said. "Numbers would make everyone worry."

I stared out the window, shaken. "Have you ever seen a living one, ma'am?" I asked.

"Oh, sadly no. Only bits of dead ones. When the Legion fells them and they sink into the sea, they send ships afterward to try to haul the carcass to ports for study. Chop it up, peel it like an onion. Dangerous work, given their toxic blood, but so many suffusions and grafts are based on their unique abilities. I've had the chance to survey only a few such specimens." She grinned. "I asked the Apoths once if I could eat some of the flesh, but they said no. I've never quite forgiven them for that . . ."

As we approached Talagray the world about us filled up, the fields suddenly swarming with Legionnaires and Engineers and horses, all hauling materials or hastily constructing earthworks on the soaking plains. I even saw slothiks—the altered, giant sloths used for hauling momentously huge loads—which I'd never seen in Daretana. Many of the soldiers were augmented in ways I'd never witnessed: people with large, black eyes, or enormous, curiously pointed ears, or huge, hulking men eight or nine span tall, carrying blocks of stone like they were bales of hay. I described this last sort to Ana as we passed.

"Cracklers," she said. "Or crackle-men. Chaps who've been grafted so they grow so much muscle they need new bones added to their skeletons to support it all. They make odd little clicking sounds as they walk about—hence the name."

"Sounds rather monstrous," I said.

"So might a boy whose brain swims with tiny beasts, making it so he can't forget anything. It's tough being a crackler—most don't live past fifty—but the Empire needs them, and venerates and honors them, and pays them well." Another grin. "That's the nature of Khanum, eh? Safety and security for strangeness. Many are willing to make the deal."

THE CARRIAGE RATTLED ON, and Talagray emerged from the mist ahead. At first the city looked like a long row of low cairns, each one cylindrical and tapered, separated by wide gulfs; but then we rounded a hill and I saw they were not cairns but fretvine towers, with wide bases and narrow tops, like dozens of clay ovens freshly made and set out to dry. Being wrought of fretvine, they bloomed here and there, tiny tufts of sparkling orange or frail green. They were all bedecked in mai-lanterns, rings and rings of glimmering blue lights, so much so that the city looked like some spectral night sky.

Then I noticed the fortifications: though the city had no walls on the western side, the eastern side sported massive ramparts and earthworks, and everywhere they were covered in bombards, all pointed east. I realized that this was where all the soldiers about us were going, adding to the massive artillery placed between the eastern plains and the city.

I described it to Ana.

"Yes . . . it's a utility city, Din," she said. "Run by the Legion and built to service the sea walls, and it in turn is built along its own walls, a city trapped in the shade of ramparts and bombards. The bombards you see won't do much to a titan, mind. They're mostly there to slow it down, give everyone in the city time to escape to the third-ring wall."

"Why's it all so oddly spaced, ma'am?" I asked.

"Quakes. My understanding is they don't build many structures above five or six stories, and almost all are fretvine and fernpaper. When the leviathans emerge from the depths of the seas, the whole city trembles like it's built on the skin of a drum." She leaned her head out the window, smiling as the wind played with her bone-white hair. "A poet once wrote about making love when the earth shook in Talagray . . . It sounded like quite the spectacle."

We rumbled closer and closer, the great wall of the city rising up on our left, the bombards looming overhead. Everywhere I looked there were armored veterans far more experienced than I could ever hope to be—and all of them, and all of the city, existed for one purpose: to do as much damage to a leviathan as possible before it got to the third-ring wall.

"We're getting close, ma'am," I said hoarsely.

"You sound," she said, "a touch shook there, Din."

"I think it'd be mad if I didn't, ma'am. The only comfort I have is knowing you're accustomed to things like this."

She frowned. "Accustomed? Hell, Din, I've no idea what I'm fucking doing."

"I . . . I had thought, ma'am," I said, "that your career in the Iudex had taken you across the Empire?"

"Well, sure, but breaches in the sea walls? Dead leviathans? This is all totally new boots to me, as the old maid says." She pressed her hand against the wall, grinning as she felt the vibrations of the carriage. "We must analyze it for what it is—a new phenomenon, with its own idiosyncrasies and aberrations, all articulating a larger design. And that's your job, Din. To go and *see*. Exciting, isn't it?"

The mammoth gates of Talagray opened, and we trundled through.

CHAPTER 11

|||

I KNEW FROM THE MAPS THAT AT THE CENTER OF the city sat what was called the Trifecta: the offices of the Legion, Iudex, and Engineering Iyalets, around which the other offices gathered like a small constellation. Our Legion driver piloted us toward it, navigating the churning traffic running about the fretvine towers. It was hard to catch the nature of the city from within the carriage, but it felt an improvised place: slapdash fernpaper houses fluttering about us like flocks of fragile moths, with fernpaper signs on leaning poles denoting smithies, boardinghouses, sotbars. The only permanent thing seemed to be the roads and foundations, wrought of stone and brick. All else was impermanent and haphazard. A sketch or a doodle of civilization, perhaps, hastily done on a canvas of soaking stone.

Finally the Trifecta came into view: three tall, conical fretvine towers, each sealed with mossclay and arrayed with the black, blue, or red colors of their Iyalet.

"Keep your eyes open," Ana said to me. She wasn't smiling anymore.

"Trying to take it all in as best I can, ma'am."

"Bother less with the sights," she said, "and more with the *people*. You're going to be with a lot of elite officers soon, Din. They won't ask you to talk much, but you need to watch them. Watch what they look at, what disturbs them, and get it all for me. I want to know who we're working with."

"Is it vialworthy, ma'am?" I said, grabbing my engraver's satchel.

"Of course! Pick a glass and stick it up your damn nose quick!"

We rumbled into the courtyard of the Trifecta. A small group of people were gathering in wait for us before the Iudex building, no more than a half-dozen Engineers, Apoths, and officers in Iudex dark blue.

I studied the Iudex officers most as we pulled up. There were two of them: one a tall, thin, gray-faced man whose breast bore the two bars signifying he was the investigator; and there, beside that heraldry, the eye within a box, indicating he was an engraver, like me. Next to him was a grizzled brick of a man with enormous shoulders, six span tall and six span wide, squinting at us as we pulled up. This man had evidently been altered for strength, so much so he could quite likely cleave a person in two. Upon his breast I spied a twinkle: the bar and the flower, indicating he was an assistant investigator.

I stared at him. This scarred, broad, blunt instrument of a human being was my Talagray equivalent. Even though I was nearly a span taller than him, I had never felt so young and so small in all my life.

When the carriage came to a stop I opened the door, clambered out, and helped Ana climb down. Though the crowd was small, I felt every eye upon me like they were a leaden weight.

The Talagray investigator—the tall, thin man—approached and bowed. "Ana," he said. "It's an honor to see you once more."

"Tuwey Uhad!" Ana said cheerily, grinning like a sharkfish. "By Sanctum, it's been years. Or decades, perhaps?"

"Just years," said Uhad. "Let's not get ahead of ourselves." His face was gaunt, and he looked weary—he probably hadn't slept in days—but he allowed a small smile. He was a reedy, gloomy fellow who looked more like an advocate who argued cases before the magistries of the Iudex than a soldier. But then, I realized, that was probably what most investigators actually looked like.

Uhad's eyes fluttered slightly as he looked upon Ana: a trembling in his pupils, a twitching in his cheek. An engraver indeed, then. "Commander-Prificto Vashta sends her apologies," he said. "She wished to be here, but she has been appointed seneschal of the canton. A grave formality—but a necessary one."

I nodded, for I'd heard of this procedure. In the event of a breach, Talagray anointed one Legion officer as seneschal—essentially a dictator of all domestic matters—until the breach was resolved. This meant that the tall, exhausted-looking woman I'd met in Ana's shack back in Daretana was now judge, jury, and executioner of the canton, and we now operated completely under her purview. If we saw her again, I reckoned, it'd be because things had either gone very right, or very wrong.

"Don't let the size of the group here discourage you, Ana," Uhad continued. "It's far easier to keep a smaller force discreet."

"I've no goddamned idea how big or small it is," said Ana, grinning under her blindfold. "But I appreciate the notice."

He gestured to the broad, grizzled man beside him, and said, "First—this is my assistant investigator, Captain Tazi Miljin."

The broad man bowed deeply to us, but as he rose his eyes lingered on me. He looked every inch the soldier, his shoulders huge, his gray skin sun-darkened and puckered here and there with white scars. His thick white hair fell in a messy mop down to his ears. Nose broad and bent and broken. Beard cut in a manner that made it hard to tell if he was constantly frowning or not. From the look in his eyes, I suspected he was.

Most interesting was the sword at his side: it bore a plain crossguard, yet the handle and the scabbard were uniquely designed, locked together with some complex brass machinery, almost like the clock at the Legion's Iyalet building back in Daretana. Its black leather scabbard was worn but carefully polished and cleaned. However strange the weapon looked, it seemed a beloved thing to him.

I glanced up, and saw he was still watching me. Gaze as cool as the underside of a river rock. No dancing to his pupils. I wondered what alterations he was sporting.

"We're assisted here by representatives from the Apoths and Engineering, naturally," said Uhad. "Immunis Vasiliki Kalista . . ."

A short woman stepped forward and bowed, donned in Engineering purple. She was Tala, like me, thickset and glamorous, with clever, dark eyes and her shiny black hair expertly tied up in an elegant bun. Glittering oysterdust applied to the undersides of her eyes, bronze and ceramic hairsticks winking from the bun on her head. Someone who lived to be seen first and see things second, I felt. "An honor to serve with you," she said.

"And Immunis Itonia Nusis," said Uhad, gesturing to the other. "From the Apoths . . ."

A small, neat, handsome Kurmini woman with short, curly black hair stepped up, pushed back her Apoth red coat with a flourish, and gave a pert bow. "An honor to serve with you, ma'am." She popped up, grinning cheerily. Every piece of her felt cleaned and pressed flat, all angles so adjusted and sharp she felt like a quilt carefully put together piece by piece. Her skin was dark gray, but her eyelids were slightly purpled, the sign of significant grafts. This wasn't unusual for Apoths: being masters at shaping flesh, many of them augmented their own. It was likely the woman could see in the dark better than a jungle cat.

I studied the three immuni, each proud and preening and draped in the colors and heralds of their Iyalets. I suddenly thought of them as birds: Uhad was a blue stork, tall, wavering, watchful, and still; Kalista was a purple courtesan dove, all glamour and gleaming plumage; and Nusis was a little red flicker-thrush, cheerily chirruping and darting from branch to branch. How ostentatious they seemed next to Ana, bent and blindfolded, yet coiled like a predator about to strike.

Ana tapped my chest with a knuckle. "This is Din. My assistant investigator."

All eyes moved to me, then flicked up and down, taking in my height.

"He's new," said Ana, "and big, and I think he lost his sense of humor in some tragic accident. But he helped me solve the Blas issue quick enough." Then, simply, "He is good."

I bowed, but I recognized that, short as it was, that was the highest compliment Ana had paid me yet.

"Ordinarily I'd give you both time to rest and freshen up, Ana," said Uhad, "but given the situation, I thought it'd be best to get to work."

"Absolutely," said Ana. She gripped my arm tight. "Lead the way."

OUR DESTINATION WAS an old Iudex Magistry chamber, one that was normally used for arbitration but had been overtaken by Uhad's investigation. The most striking thing was the sheer filth of the place: the piles of parchments on the big round table, the pots brimming with pipe ash. Every stitch of fabric stank of smoke and sweat and stale clar-tea. It was without a doubt a room people had been holed up in for several days, sleepless and stewing.

Uhad walked up to the round table, eyes fluttering, and plucked out a handful of parchments with his gloved hands—the engraver's gift for remembering where you'd laid things. He stacked them up and placed them before Ana as I helped her into the one clear spot at the table, and she seized upon them like a starving hillcat upon a mouse.

"It goes without saying that all that we show you and all we discuss is of the highest secrecy," Uhad said. "Any who share what we say or review outside of this room will be subject to punishment by the Imperial Legion as an actor of malicious discontent." He gestured as the others settled into their chairs. "The rest of the crew has heard this, too, of course . . ."

Uhad's place at the table, naturally, had no notes or papers, as it was all in his head. Nusis sat on his left, and Kalista on his right, and it was hard to think of two more different people: Nusis nodded pertly before her towers of papers, whereas Kalista lounged and smoked her pipe as she dug through her scattered parchments, like a dozing gentrywoman seeking a piece of jewelry lost in her bedsheets. I sat behind Ana, as per my station. Miljin, however, took a seat beside Uhad, slouching in his chair, the tip of his long scabbard scraping over the floor. He looked more like a gentryman's bodyguard than an investigator, someone whose contributions were strength of arms rather than the cerebral. He crossed his arms and shot a sour eye at the whole crew.

"I'll start with the dead," said Uhad to Ana. "That work?"

"Certainly," said Ana. She cocked her blindfolded head, listening.

I slipped out a new vial—this one scented of grass—and sniffed at it to ensure I captured the whole of the moment.

Uhad's pupils danced until they were a blur. Then he said in a low, solemn voice: "Princeps Atha Lapfir. Signum Misik Jilki. Princeps Keste Pisak. Captain Atos Koris. Captain Kilem Terez. Princeps Donelek Sandik. Princeps Kise Sira. Princeps Alaus Vanduo. Signum Suo Akmuo. And finally, Signum Ginklas Loveh." His eyes stopped fluttering and he looked to Ana. "These are the ten officers whose deaths are confirmed to be attributed to the dappleglass contagion. I have also provided you with all information on their sleeping quarters and movements in the two days before the incident. That is what we've managed to amass thus far."

Ana rocked back and forth in her seat, her hands flittering over the parchments before her like dancers on a stage. "You say these deaths are *confirmed* to be attributed to the dappleglass contagion, Uhad," she said, "because we're unsure if there could be more?"

"Potentially," said Uhad. "It's possible some individuals underwent a similar infestation unnoticed, and then were lost during the breach."

"The term," said Nusis chipperly, "is *bloom*. A dappleglass bloom."

Uhad extended a hand to her. "A bloom, then. Nusis here is something of an expert on the matter. She cut her teeth during Oypat, assisting the Apoths trying to manage the situation there."

"Really?" said Ana. "How intriguing! It must be quite something to bear witness to the death of an entire canton, yes?"

An awkward pause.

Nusis cringed. "Ahh. I suppose, yes?"

Kalista cleared her throat. "I don't think more than these ten succumbed to the bloom, though," she drawled. A lone tangle of pipe smoke slid up her cheek with the final syllable. "Engineers do not work on the walls unaccompanied for this very reason. If someone was harmed and needed help, it wouldn't do to be alone. We keep a very thorough accounting of our dead and injured. I think the list ends with the ten."

"Four of the deceased Engineers died within the sea walls," said Uhad. "Specifically, what is known as the Peak of Khanum. It is one of the thickest and most fortified portions of the entire sea wall, given that it sits close to the mouth of the Titan's Path, leading inland."

"And the other deaths?" asked Ana.

"Two perished while traveling to Talagray from the walls," said Uhad. His eyes danced again as he summoned up his memories. An ugly sight. I couldn't help wonder—did it look so unsettling when I did it? "One died in bed, having retired after a long shift. Another while taking a meal at a mess tent. Another while waiting for a carriage to take her west from Talagray to the third-ring walls. And the final victim died atop a horse while reviewing fortifications. All perished in the same way. A malignant bloom of dappleglass growth within the torso, resulting in an eighteen- to twenty-span growth of shoots over the course of five minutes, weakening whatever was above and below it. Gruesome, really."

Ana's fingers paused as she found some curious phrase in the text, like a tangle in a loom. "But... these manifestations were slightly different from Blas's."

"All shoots emerged from the torso," said Uhad, "but we did notice these tended to emerge lower. From the middle of the back rather than the top near the neck, as with Commander Blas. We're not sure why. Nusis is working on it."

Nusis nodded cheerily, as if examining why plants might burst from someone's back and not their neck was the most exciting thing in the world.

"They didn't die at the exact same time, either," said Uhad. "We're working off of witness reports here, but there appears to have been a nine- or ten-hour window between the first death and the last."

"This *would* suggest," said Nusis, "that they were infected with the dappleglass spores at different times."

"Do we know much about their movements the day before they died?" asked Ana.

"We know enough to know they haven't been all in the same place," said Kalista lazily. "No overlap in station duty, patrols, projects . . . It all makes tracing the point of contagion damned hard."

Ana flipped a page over and moved on to the next, reading it with her fingers. "Do we have lists of their known associates?"

"Not yet," drawled Kalista.

"Have we interviewed any friends or comrades?"

"Not yet," said Kalista. "We haven't interviewed anyone at all. Most of the work we've done in Engineering is to try to predict and stop the next attack."

Ana's brow furrowed. "Next attack?"

"The operating theory," explained Uhad, "is that Engineering officers are being targeted. Perhaps in hopes that their inevitable bloom might damage our fortifications, causing another breach, but . . . after some analysis, we think this somewhat unlikely."

"I assume," said Ana, turning to Nusis, "because *planning* when dappleglass blooms inside someone is utterly fucking mad?"

Nusis's cheery smile dimmed. She glanced at Uhad, who gave the slightest shake of his head—*Ignore it.*

"Ah . . . correct," said Nusis. "It would be impossible to time a bloom with any accuracy. The nature of a body, the person's diet, movement, activity, not to mention the number of spores inhaled . . . these all would affect the growth rate of the dappleglass."

"And the dead didn't all work on the walls," sighed Uhad. "So the idea that someone poisoned ten random Engineers in hopes that some would work in the area where this strut was located—and then, on top of that, that the dappleglass within them would bloom at the *exact* right time to damage this one *exact* strut . . . Well, the idea's a little preposterous."

"But they *were* all Engineers," said Kalista. "And all lower officers—princeps and signums and captains. That's who spends most of their time inside the walls."

"Yet no commanders, like Blas was," said Ana.

"No," said Uhad. "But there seems to be a targeting here, a selection. We just can't see the sense of it yet. Blas was murdered with great intent. We must assume the same for these ten."

Ana was rocking back and forth in her chair very fast now, flipping over page after page of parchment with her fingers, until she came to the very last one. Her face was tight, expressionless. I was reminded of a barge pilot trying to navigate a narrow canal.

"I would like a list of all witnesses to the deaths," she said finally.

"That can be done," said Uhad.

"And I want a list of all the living assignments of the dead going back one year," said Ana. "As well as a list of who was residing in the same facilities at those times."

Kalista snuck a wary glance at Uhad. "That's a tremendous amount of information," she said.

"But you Engineers have it, don't you?" said Ana. "The Empire simply loves to write shit down, and I'd assume the living arrangements of the Iyalets here in Talagray would be well recorded."

"I can get it," said Kalista reluctantly. "But . . . it's a lot. And, as you can expect, the Engineers are overtaxed right now. Might I ask why you need it?"

"To save us all some goddamned time," said Ana, grinning. "We want to talk to everyone who could know something, yes? Seems wise to start with who's been physically around the victims for weeks and months." Then she casually added: "As well as who they might have been fucking. Living arrangements often reveal such relationships—

who's followed who, month after month. Tricky to slip into someone's bedroom through a window. Better to be in the same building. And lovers, of course, are vital sources of information."

Kalista, stunned, removed her pipe from her mouth, leaving a faint indentation in her lip. Nusis's smile was very strained now. I stared fixedly into the back of Ana's chair.

"We'll get you that," said Uhad grimly. "Before the end of the day—yes, Immunis?"

"Certainly," said Kalista. She watched Ana from behind a veil of smoke. "However . . . I *did* think the nature of this relationship was reciprocal, yes? We'd like to get some information from you, too, Immunis, about the previous incident."

"Yes . . ." said Ana. "But I had a question for you all first. Did any of *you* know Commander Blas? Personally?"

The whole room exchanged uncomfortable glances—all except Captain Miljin, who just slouched grumpily in his chair.

"We all did," said Uhad. "He was one of the most prominent Engineers of the Empire. Architect of some of our greatest defensive artifices. Though I, I admit, probably knew him the least, and only cordially at that . . ."

"I never served under him," said Kalista. "But I knew him. I'd met him frequently. Yet that wasn't unusual. He wasn't the type to bottle himself up before a drafting board. He had a way of making himself known."

"I knew him through his activity on the Preservationist Councils," said Nusis.

Ana's head swiveled to her. "Tell me more about that, please."

"Well, ah . . . he was a liaison to many cantons' Preservationist evaluations," Nusis said hesitantly. "Examining whether a new suffusion or alteration, or a new construction project, could impact the natural state of any nearby canton."

"Say more," demanded Ana.

"W-well . . . say you want to apply a suffusion to a riverweed," said Nusis. She was rattled now, a gleam of sweat on her brow. "To make it grow less in a river. But you find the alteration also causes mold in the river to grow *more*, and the mold then turns highly acidic when it washes up on a dam downstream, slowly weakening it, imperiling a town below ... that kind of thing. These changes have to be well thought out. The slightest alteration threatens enormous effects. Apothetikals and Engineers are the most frequent liaisons on these evaluations, and Blas was very active with us."

"But what the hell did he *do*, exactly?" asked Ana, frustrated.

"Well ... he reviewed artifices, infrastructures, and constructions that could either be vulnerable to or might enable the escape of contagion from Talagray," she said. "This is not terribly unusual work, mind ..."

"Hm. I see ..." Ana said, now sounding bored. "And Captain Miljin? Did *you* know Blas?"

Miljin shook his head. "Saw him at a distance, ma'am," he said. His voice was deep and raspy, like his throat was lined with smoking oil. "But never so much as heard the man's voice."

"Fine," said Ana. "So ... would those who had met him please tell me more about the *nature* of the man? I've heard precious little about that aspect."

Uhad shrugged. "He was the image of professionalism. Polite. Studious."

"Very well admired," agreed Kalista. "Especially within my Iyalet. He had no enemies that I was aware of."

"He spoke wisely, and when he spoke, he was listened to," said Nusis.

"I see ..." said Ana. She flapped a hand at me. "Thank you. Now—Din. Do the thing."

I'd tried to make myself inconspicuous thus far, and didn't much like having so many superior officers look at me. I stood up, bowed, but paused. "Ah—what exactly would you like me to tell them, ma'am?" I asked.

"All of it," she said. Another flap of her hand. "The full vomit, boy!"

"Right . . ." I said. "Well. Hold on, then." Again, I took out the vial
of lye-scent, sniffed it, let the memories come pouring into the backs
of my eyes, and started talking.

I GAVE THEM the exact same description of the events as I had to
Commander-Prificto Vashta. I left nothing out. When I finished,
there was a long, lingering silence. I sat back down, replaced the lye
vial, and sniffed at the grass one to make sure I captured the rest of
the present moment accurately.

"So . . ." said Uhad slowly. "The groundskeeper met the assassin.
But . . . their face was swollen?"

"Such was his testimony," said Ana. "I believe there are many dis-
figuring grafts one could apply, with varying levels of permanence . . ."

Captain Miljin rumbled to life, clearing his throat rather extensively. "This is so," he said. "Dernpaste is the preferred one. Swells
the areas you apply it to, makes it so your own mother wouldn't know
you. Skin tone's harder to alter, but . . . Well. They have stuff for that,
too."

"And I suppose if you all had seen some shadowy figure with a
swollen face," said Ana, "skulking around Blas here with a piece of
dappleglass in their hand, you'd have mentioned it by now."

"Of course," said Uhad. "But Blas was very active. He moved
around a great deal. *Many* people knew him."

"What investigatory steps have you taken for him here?" asked
Ana.

"With the wet season approaching," said Uhad, "we've only been
able to do the minimum, unfortunately. The Apoths reviewed Blas's
offices and living quarters. They found nothing of note."

"All right . . ." Then Ana paused. She seemed to be waiting for
something. Her smile slowly retracted, and she swiveled her blindfolded face about the table. "Is that *all*? No one has *anything* else to
say on the matter?"

An uneasy silence followed. Kalista watched Ana, her dark eyes heavily lidded. Nusis stared at the floor, like Ana had just made some embarrassing blunder in etiquette. Uhad watched nobody, his pupils dancing as memories flooded his mind. And Miljin, to my surprise, watched me, arms crossed, his gaze inscrutable.

"Unfortunately," drawled Kalista, "nothing comes to mind."

"I see . . ." said Ana. "Well then. One critical takeaway is that the perpetrator had to be operating here, in Talagray, for weeks if not months. This is the only way they could have known Blas's movements."

"That doesn't necessarily narrow it down," said Uhad. "There's a lot of movement here in the months before the wet season."

"Of course," said Ana. "But there's been one distinct signal that dappleglass gives off. One that even Din here, who'd never heard of it before, noticed right away."

They all looked at me.

"Fernpaper," I said. "It stains it."

"Correct," said Ana. "And I saw quite a *lot* of fernpaper out there in the city. Lots of quakes here, after all. Has any been found stained? For that would likely lead us directly to the killer—or the site of the poisoning."

Uhad gestured to Captain Miljin. "If you please, Miljin," he said, sighing.

Miljin leaned forward, his chair creaking under his bulk. "We read your letter, ma'am," he said. "And we did look for stained fernpaper. Spoke to a few Legion chaps and discreetly sent them out about the city, asking if anyone had seen any fernpaper blackened since the breach. Heard nothing. Then they toured the city from end to end, examining all the fernpaper walls and windows and doors. Saw nothing. Seems to me, ma'am, that either the perpetrator found a way to contain the spores—which seems unlikely, given all we've learned about it—or the poisoning didn't take place in Talagray at all. If so, that puts us in a spot. We can't search the whole of the canton."

I found this news dispiriting—but Ana was just nodding impatiently. "Yes, yes, yes," she said. "But we need to *broaden* our timeline!

How can we find out if any fernpaper was stained *before* the breach? Because apparently some mad fucker was running around the city for a good while with this poison in their pocket, possibly leaving a trail behind!"

Kalista laughed, the sound slightly contemptuous. "Well—we can't! There's no way to find that out."

"I'm inclined to agree . . ." said Uhad.

Ana rubbed her hands together, running her pink fingertips over her knuckles. "Captain Miljin—how many fernpaper millers are there in the city?"

"Dozens, ma'am," he said. "Most of the common structures are made of it, given the quakes."

"Can you ask these suppliers if they'd replaced any stained fernpaper panels in the four weeks *previous* to the breach? Or—better yet—can we get a list of all the orders they delivered in that time?"

Miljin nodded. "We could try that, ma'am. I could ask Captain Strovi of the Legion to help—Vashta's second. He's been assigned to provide support, as needed."

"Then I propose we do so," said Ana. "If we find an unusually big order of panels, that could indicate either the site of the poisoning, or the site where the poison was stored or developed." She turned her blindfolded face to Uhad. "Though, of course, it's not my dance . . ."

Uhad smiled wearily. "How polite of you. Yes, do so, Miljin. While that's going on, Ana—when will you have your nominees for interviewing?"

"If I can get the lists from Engineering soon enough," said Ana, "I should have a good idea of who was intimate with the dead by the morning. Will Miljin do the honors of interviewing? And if so—can Din tag along? He's my eyes and ears."

Miljin looked me over like I was a burden for his pack animal and he was trying to estimate my weight. "Well . . . certainly, ma'am."

"Good. I mean—I could interrogate *you*, Miljin. But I'm not sure you have the patience for it, and definitely not the time."

"And I would save him from the punishment," said Uhad with the tiniest smile. Then he looked to Immunis Nusis. "Though if the young signum is to accompany Miljin outside the city, I believe he will need to have some additional grafts applied, due to contagion ..."

"Oh! Yes," said Nusis, with no small amount of relish. She turned to me and asked, "You're from Daretana, correct? So you should have all the immunity alterations for the Outer Rim, yes?"

"Yes, ma'am," I said.

"Then we'll have to add the Tala canton to them," she said, sighing. "To protect against any wormrot, or neckworm, or wormbone, or fissure-worm you might encounter out there. As well as cheek-worm, of course."

I stared at her as I absorbed the expansive variety of worms waiting in the wilds to devour me.

Miljin spoke up with a sadistic smile: "She don't mean the cheeks on your face, son."

"How ... how might I gain those immunities, ma'am?" I asked.

"Normally you'd make an appointment with the medikkers," said Nusis. "But as we don't have time for that, just come by my offices in the Apoth tower once you're all settled. I'll get you straightened out."

"Good," said Uhad. "Evening falls, I believe. With the canton in a state of emergency, nocturnal passage isn't permitted in the city for anyone except the Legion. Speaking of which ... I doubt if you all know the warning system."

"I've read of it," said Ana. "But Din likely hasn't."

Miljin squinted at me. "You know the flares, Signum?"

I shook my head. "No, sir."

The captain stuck his thumb eastward. "You see green flares in the eastern skies, that means a leviathan's been spotted—so, keep watching the skies. You see red ones after that, means it's come ashore, and is close to the walls, so get ready to evacuate if the worst happens. If yellow flares follow, that means it's made it past the walls—so run like hell."

There was a stark silence.

"Blue flares means it's wandered off or been killed," he said. He grinned mirthlessly. "Don't see those too often."

"On that note..." said Uhad. He stood, wavering slightly. I wondered if his lack of sleep made him light-headed. "I should take you to your quarters, Ana. If I recall correctly, it does take you some time to get acclimated to new environs."

"The problem with being an engraver, Uhad," said Ana, "is that you can't pull any of the 'not sure if I recall' politeness bullshit, because we all know you can damned well recall perfectly." She stood, grinning, and said, "Take me up there. Din can follow with my trunks."

THE IUDEX TOWER was a grand, circular, curling structure, creaking and wheezing as the wind played with its fretvine walls. Frail leaves bloomed at the edges of the ceilings and balconies, and occasionally one spied the odd flower. Yet it was stable, and safe, and I was glad to be in it and not out in the city.

Uhad had put Ana up in a small office on the east side of the Iudex tower, on the third floor, whereas I was on the fifth. I guessed the more senior you were, the fewer stairs you had to run down while escaping a leviathan. The two of them sat in her chambers talking merrily while I hauled Ana's trunks up the stairs, delivering them one after another. When I finished hauling up the final trunk—Ana had apparently brought several loads of books, despite my warnings not to—they were chatting like old friends.

"... never could figure how you lasted so long in the inner rings," Uhad was saying to her as I dragged in the last trunk. He was leaning against a wall and attempting to smile, yet he seemed such a gloomy sort that the effort threatened to sprain something. "Sounded like a viper's nest."

"Though Talagray sounds hardly any better," Ana said. "I wonder how many horrors are trapped in that head of yours, Tuwey."

"More than my fair share, maybe," he admitted. "And though my fits are few, I do have them now and again . . . I have to keep going to Nusis to get grafts to help me manage my headaches."

I paused in my labors as I heard that. Engravers, I knew, tended to experience mental breakdown the more information they engraved in their minds: depressions, fits of rage, moments of dislocation. As an engraver myself, I wondered if this was a glimpse into my future.

"I'd settle for a station in the third ring of the Empire, frankly," sighed Uhad. "Some canton where cow thievery is the greatest crime. And yet . . . the years grow short, yes?"

"Maybe this will be your last parade, Tuwey," Ana said. "Save the Empire, get sent to greener pastures."

I shoved Ana's trunk into the corner, then sat on its top, panting and puffing.

"Maybe," Uhad said. "But you—you'll keep chewing through the world like a crackler's pick-hatchet, yes?"

Ana grinned. "As long as they'll let me."

I wiped sweat from my brow, glaring at them as they laughed. With one final goodbye, Immunis Uhad departed. I bowed and shut the door behind him.

Instantly, the grin melted off Ana's face. "Odd," she said. "Odd, Din! What the *hell* was that?"

"Ahh. Pardon, ma'am?" I said.

"I mean . . . What was your read on that?" asked Ana. "Wasn't something *missing* from all that? Or am I mad?"

I silently reviewed her friendly discussion with Uhad. "Did . . . did you expect your discussion with Immunis Uhad to go . . . *else-where*, ma'am?"

"What?" she said. "No! Not that! I mean that whole goddamned meeting down there! Didn't you notice something wrong with *that*, Din?"

"Besides your consistent use of wildly inappropriate language, ma'am?"

She glared at me from behind her blindfold. "Come, come. Think. Did that meeting *feel* right to you?"

I thought about it. "No."

"Good. Now tell me, honestly—what did you see that felt wrong? This is important."

I thought about it, my eyes fluttering as I summoned each memory of the meeting: each fleeting glance, each gesture, each turn of the head and twist in the seat.

"They were . . . nervous," I said finally. "About the breach, yes. But also about . . . something else."

"Go on," said Ana.

"It was something when you asked if they knew Blas," I said. "They all went quiet. Nusis stared at the floor. Kalista only watched you. Tried to pretend she didn't care what you were saying, but she very clearly did. Uhad was all up in his own head. Looking at memories, trying to figure out something on his own, probably. And Miljin . . . Well. He looked mostly at me, ma'am. Not sure why. But the man stuck his eyes on me and didn't take them off."

"Good," she said. "Well seen, well captured. But you still haven't noticed what was missing. Before your vomit of words, all those people down there testified that Commander Blas was an upstanding, admirable, studious imperial officer. Brilliant and beloved and all that bullshit." She stabbed the air with her index finger. "But then *you*, dear Din, stood up and told them how he'd gotten killed during a fun countryside jaunt to a Haza house to get his prick wet in paid quim! And what did they say about *that*?"

"Oh! Well . . . nothing, ma'am," I said.

"*Nothing!*" she said triumphantly. "None of them seemed shocked, appalled, or even *interested*! They didn't say a damn thing, even when I gave them every chance to do so! Just went on discussing the case! Isn't that terribly strange to you?"

"Yes," I said. I summoned my memories of the last days of Blas's case. "And you didn't include that information in the letter you sent here, so they didn't already know it."

"Hell no. I'm not stupid enough to commit accusations of whoring to parchment. So it should have been a revelation."

"And you don't think they were trying to focus on the breach, ma'am?"

"You hear a sordid tale like that, you at least say *something*. But none of them even reacted to it."

"And what's the significance of this, ma'am?"

"Ohh . . . dunno yet," said Ana. "But nothing good. I shall have to think on it." The breeze played with her white hair, and she turned to the window in her chamber. "Window's open, Din. Please shut it, or I'll never get acclimated to this place."

I went to the window, then paused, watching as the mai-lanterns of the city winked out one after another, the whole of Talagray growing dark like some rising tide was snuffing it out. Soon all I could see was the curve of the towers and the shimmer of the gleaming jungles to the north and the west. I looked east, toward the sea walls, but could see nothing at all through the mist. I closed the shutters and fastened them.

"We need," said Ana behind me, "to get ahold of Blas's secretary. The woman who ran his life for him—Rona Aristan. You remember her address, don't you, Din?"

I did. I'd read it aloud to myself when I'd gotten her letter, and the words still echoed in my ears. "The woman who claimed she knew nothing about Blas's trip to Daretana," I said.

"Yes, but she's obviously full of shit there," said Ana. She ripped her blindfold off and massaged her eyes. "I want to get her and squeeze her like a fucking rimefruit. Something's going on here that no one wants to discuss, and I think she must touch some of it."

I watched Ana glowering into the floor, her face tight like she'd swallowed a lump of sour porridge.

"You say this, ma'am," I said, "like this will be some bit of skullduggery."

"Oh, it is," said Ana, "because we're not going to tell Uhad or the rest of them about her."

"Why not?"

"Because they *should* have brought her up already," said Ana. "In fact, they should have already interviewed her! But all of them seem reluctant to look too much into the dead Commander Blas. And I want to find out why."

A knock at the door. I opened it to find a young Engineering officer, his knees quaking as he held a giant box full of coils of parchments. "Documents for the . . . the investigator," he panted.

I thanked him, took the load, and hauled it inside. "Think this is what you asked Immunis Kalista for, ma'am."

"Good!" She sat down on the floor and dug into them. "Hopefully I can figure out some pattern among all these people and figure out who you need to talk to tomorrow. We have to understand all the locations those dead Engineers visited the days before the breach. Because despite all that we're lacking here, Din, what we *really* need is the place the murder happened. These people were all poisoned somewhere—maybe in more than one place, but I'm betting against it. They all passed through one space in creation, one cursed little spot of this earth—and when they left that space, they were dead. They just didn't know it yet. That's what you and Miljin must find."

"Anything I should know about Captain Miljin, ma'am?" I asked. "If I'm going to be working the interviews with him tomorrow, any advice would be welcome."

"I know he's a war hero. Fought in one rebellion or another. He's a bit like the Empire itself, I suppose. Very well thought of, famously tough—and also *old*. Maybe too old, these days." A flash of a grin. "He was once rumored to be terribly handsome, if I recall. Tell me— does he still have thick wrists, Din? Thick wrists, and big, square, meaty hands?"

"How is that pertinent, ma'am?"

"Just because I blind myself doesn't mean I'm not allowed my indulgences, Din." Her grin grew wider. "Go get your new immunities from Nusis before curfew. Tomorrow, get something good from these interviews—and then, before curfew falls again, get to Blas's secretary and give her this." She hurriedly scribbled out another summons, much like the ones she'd made for Gennadios and the Haza servants. "I want her here and talking about Blas. Because I'm starting to get a very unpleasant feeling about this investigation."

"Beyond what we've already talked about, ma'am?"

"Oh, yes." She pulled open one of the parchments and started reading. "Kalista said Engineers always travel in pairs. That's why we have so firm an idea of who died during the breach."

"So . . ."

"So, the killer's been in Talagray for a while," she said. She tossed the page away and started on another. "What if they've murdered someone besides Engineers, so no one ever noticed?"

CHAPTER 12

|||

"THE THING ABOUT WORMS," SAID NUSIS CHEERILY as she riffled through her shelves, "is how *resourceful* they are. Resourceful, and so very durable."

I glanced about her Apoth office. The place had more of the look of a laboratory, with glass bottles and tanks and bell jars winking from nearly every surface. Some contained furry molds or bulbous fungi or the occasional cross-section of bone, possibly human. In the center of the room sat an operating table made of brass. Though its surface was clean, the floor about it bore faint blooms of old stains. I wondered if the occupants had been alive or dead when those fluids had fallen.

"Worms can figure out how to live in any part of you, and eat any part of you, you know," Nusis said as she searched. "Almost have to admire them, really. I once treated a captain whose legs were so brimming with them you could hear them sloshing about as he sat. Have you ever had an infestation, Kol?"

I eyed a glass cylinder containing a dark yellow fluid. Something long and thin and slimy lay coiled at the bottom, and it nosed the glass, as if smelling me. "Ah—no, ma'am. Not to my knowledge."

"Mm. A pity. You gain a lot of respect for them after . . . Hm. Looks like I'm out of the usual grafts. I'll have to tap into my personal reserves. One moment."

Her red coat fluttered as she darted to a large steel safe behind her desk, one with nearly a dozen little metal doors on the front. She knelt before it, slid a key out of a drawer, and went about unlocking—and occasionally relocking—each lock in what seemed to be a random order, top left, then middle right bottom, then top right, bottom middle, and on and on.

"Do all senior officers keep safes in their rooms, ma'am?" I asked.

"No. Normally I wouldn't have to resort to such measures. But advanced immunity grafts are the preferred targets of thieves—affluent folk are more than eager to pay for protection. That means I have to go through the right sequence of locks *every* time I have to fetch something."

I watched as she plied the key in the many locks. It was a dizzyingly complex combination of movements—and yet, I realized, I was engraving them all in my memory.

"Would you like me to leave the room, ma'am?" I asked.

"Leave the room?"

"I'm an engraver, ma'am. Don't think you'd like me memorizing your system."

"Oh!" she said. "Yes, good point, I always forget. Please, if you'd avert your eyes . . ."

I turned to the wall and listened to the *clinks* and *clanks* as the last locks and tumblers turned.

"There!" she said. "And . . . one moment . . . Yes, here's all you shall need."

I turned. She had retrieved four small pellets of varying colors from a set of boxes inside the safe. One pellet was blue, one white, one yellow, and one brown. Each was about the size of a knuckle.

"I shall muddle these and mix them with milk," Nusis said, bustling about her office. "The proteins and fats will help you digest them. Check yourself in the mirror for an hour after you consume these. Look for any yellow hues to the whites of your eyes, or a rapid retreat where your gums meet your teeth. That would indicate an adverse reaction. In which case, contact the medikkers immediately."

She muddled the pellets with the milk until it was a thick, light brown concoction.

"Will there be any other effects?" I asked. "Psychological ones?"

She slowed the grinding of her pestle. "Psychological . . . Ah. That's right. The last alterations you consumed would have probably been your own engraver's suffusions, yes? To become a Sublime?"

I nodded.

"Did you opt to sleep as they changed your mind, Kol?"

"No, ma'am."

"You stayed awake? Throughout your transmutation?"

"Yes, ma'am."

"How fascinating," she said. "I myself chose sleep when I became an axiom. No, there will be no psychological effects to consuming these grafts. But you must be a tough little bird to have suffered so, Kol." She handed the mixing bowl to me. A smile crinkled her purple-hued face. "Let's hope, at least."

"Why hope, ma'am?"

"Most engravers don't last long in Talagray. Too many bad memories, you see. Especially ones that visit the Plains of the Path. But you're young. It should be all right."

I stared into the milky brown concoction, recalling Immunis Uhad's weary, lined face. Then I tossed the concoction back and swallowed it.

WHEN I WAS done with my treatments I hobbled back to the Iudex tower and climbed the stairs to my rooms. Once there I unpacked my meager belongings: coat and shirt, leggings and underlinens. Standard-issue imperial razor. Wooden practice sword. I arranged them all on the cabinet and waited for the room to feel familiar. The feeling never came.

I rubbed my chin, felt the scrubby friction of stubble. My gaze moved to the burnished bronze mirror on the far wall. I stripped to

the waist, grabbed my razor, and stood before the mirror and attempted to shave.

The night wind played with the fretvine tower, making it shift
and dance; but my hand was steady, and I carefully guided the edge of
the razor, cleanly parting all the scrub from my chin and cheek. How
fine it felt to do something so mundane and ordinary, in this most
abnormal of places. When I finished shaving I looked for any sign of
the reactions Nusis had warned me about, but I could find nothing.
My face was my own.

I stared into my eyes, remembering.

The mixing of my suffusions. The way the medikkers had muddled them in a bowl with a pestle. The splash and coil of the milk.
And then the chalky taste at the back of my throat as I drank, and
drank, and drank.

Then their whisper in my ear: I could take a sleeping draft, and
slumber through what was coming; though this made the transition
longer, and I might dream. Yet I'd told them I wished to stay awake. I
wished to comprehend what was happening to me. To see it, and
know, and remember.

Then came four miserable, awful days of hallucinations and
headaches and insomnia, days and days of wandering in the dreary
dark, time stretching about me like the black plains of an endless
desert. For my mind was being reforged within my skull; and as it
changed, its concept of time changed as well.

And when I emerged from that dark, I was different. My skin was
gray, certainly, but I no longer formed normal memories. For a memory is just a sketch a mind makes of one's experiences, imperfect and
interpretive; yet what my mind made, from that moment on, was perfect, absolute, and endless.

I stood in the Iudex fretvine tower, feeling it dance in the wind. I
stared at my face, my eyes fluttering as I studied the tiny scars and
imperfections here and there. The origin of each minuscule wound
persisted perfectly in my mind.

I turned to look at my back and caught the faint gleam of a handful of scars. Three times Captain Thalamis had caned me during my training, yet he'd always saved his cruelest strokes for the end. The snap and crack of the cane still echoed in my ears.

"You've been through worse," I said to my reflection.

My eyes looked like I was straining to believe it.

Then a quiver in the floor, the faintest reverberation. I went to the window, cracked it, peeked out. The city lay quiet and still, no shouts or cries. A quake, but not one worth troubling over, it seemed.

My eyes lingered on the darkness in the east. I saw no flares, neither green nor any other color. I reflected that, should I fail in my task, and should more Engineers die here, then I might soon see those flares, and the walls in the distance might fall. And then, of course, I would have far more to worry about than sending my dispensations home.

III

III

THREE KEYS AND
TEN DEAD ENGINEERS

CHAPTER 13

|||

TALAGRAY ERUPTED AS DAWN FELL ACROSS THE city, the streets and lanes and corridors swarming with foot traffic like ants tumbling out of a broken anthill. The tides of people were tinted by the various Iyalet colors as they scurried to their duties, rainbows of muddy reds and purples and blacks. The great machinery that made the Empire work was coming to life.

Through this swarming mass of people strode Captain Miljin, stomping along with his long scabbard swinging at his side as I followed behind him, my huge pack rattling on my back. I couldn't see any rhyme nor reason to the movements of the crowds, but somehow the press of flesh always parted for Miljin: the rivers of folk would pause, an arm or two flicking out to hold the rest back; and then came a volley of salutes, the hands of all these strangers rising up to tap their breastbones respectfully as he passed before them. Even the towering cracklers stopped for him, bowing low enough that their chins nearly touched the caps of the people before them.

Miljin, however, took no notice. He just stumped on, yawning occasionally as he discussed the day's tasks, indifferent to the stares and the salutes. "Almost all the poor bastards your master's asked us to press today are in the Forward Engineering Quarters," he said. "Closer to the walls. That's where they prepare their materials and scaffoldry all year long. Shorter haul to the shore."

"Exactly how close to the walls, sir?" I asked.

"Not as close as you're likely worrying. Don't fret. It's a dull shit-hole of a place. Ugly as hell." He yawned again. "Most of the people we're to chat with are injured. Got hurt during the breach. Which means it'll be easy to find them, I guess. Can't run, or can't run far. Did you get your immunities?"

"I did, sir," I said. "I've also packed water, a set of knives, flint and steel, a cook kit, and several graft cures for any wounds, or stings or poisonings from any insects or vermin we encounter along the way."

Miljin stopped, his eye falling upon the pack on my back. "Ahh . . . did you."

"Yes, sir," I said. "I . . . believe it's the standard recommendation when entering the Plains of the Path?"

"That may be," he said. "But we're going to be sticking to the *road*. Which ain't exactly teeming with wild dangers these days. Are you horse friendly, boy?"

"I've ridden before, sir."

"Well, that's something, at least," he grunted. "We'll have to go mounted to get there and back in time." He nodded forward through the rush of soldiers. "Stables are ahead. Won't take a moment."

We were at the eastern edge of the city now, the fernpaper houses clinging to the shallow hills about us like wildflowers. Yet there'd been a change as we'd moved: the fernpaper had grown in quality, shifting from the muddy brown of poor reeds to a luminous white; there was more ornamentation to the buildings—a bronze handle here, an elaborately carved front door there; and there was smoke on the moist air, and steam, and the aroma of oils—a bathing house, or many of them, somewhere nearby. We were in rich country now.

Yet the most striking indication of this area's wealth were the peo-ple on the balconies, looking down at us as we walked by. They were all suffused folk, tall and thin and statuesque, gray-skinned with wide, dark eyes and fine, sculpted faces. Eyes dashed with oysterdust. Lips painted purple, cheeks lined with blue. Many more were ob-scured to me, faces hidden behind rippling veils wrought of silvery fabric, as if their beauty would be tarnished if one such as I beheld them.

Gentryfolk, I realized. I had never seen a member of the gentry before. I asked Miljin about it.

"Ah," he said. He grinned wickedly. "These fine folk have come here to make *friends.*"

"Friends, sir?"

"Yes. It's all politics. Ancient rules and rites. To be eligible for a seat in the Senate of the Sanctum, you've got to serve at least two terms on watch at the sea walls. Can't manage the Empire if you've never faced what it exists to fight." He waved a hand at the motley throngs of soldiers. "Somewhere among these miserable bastards are future governors and senators and Sanctum knows what else. Tax assessors. Some bullshit like that."

"And the gentryfolk . . ."

"Want to get in *early.* Distribute favor and patronage, spy rising stars and ply them with treats. Better lodgings, armor, horses, food. Maybe the odd suffusion. This neighborhood isn't even the fanciest bit, they got estates west of the city where the *truly* nice houses are, owned by the Mishtas, the Kurafs, the Hazas . . ."

My pace slowed slightly as I heard that last name.

Miljin shot a glare at one of the gentryfolk above. "It's like a horse race, boy. They're all here to make their bets. And if they bet right, they can win a lifetime of fortune. Sounds unfair, maybe, but I'm not so sure." He snorted and spat. "Might be the only way the gentry learns what fear is, to live in the shadow of the sea walls."

WE RODE EAST as the sun fought to clear the horizon, wearing straw cone hats to protect us from the sun and rain. The road was rumbling with wagons and carts and cohorts of soldiers all moving out to take their stations in the fortifications. I eyed the fields about me, the legendary Plains of the Titan's Path, aware we now crossed

land that was both sacred and profane: for here countless generations of imperials had fought and bled and died to hold back the titans; including the first imperial race, the blessed Khanum, before
they had died out.

The way ahead was shrouded with fog, but I kept my sight fixed
on the east as we trotted along the muddy path. I wondered what I
might spy there, or what I would do if the horizon suddenly lit up
with yellow or red flares, warning us of a coming titan. My gaze was
only broken when Miljin laughed and swatted my arm.

"You won't be able to see it, lad," he said, chiding me.

"See what, sir?" I asked.

"Anything," he said. "The walls, the dead leviathan. The mist will
cling until midmorn. The walls trap it. Sun has to get high for it to
burn off. The most dangerous things out here, why . . ." He nodded
toward a ditch. "They'll be skulking alongside the roads."

He watched, pleased, as I puzzled over this, before finally explain-
ing, "*Mutineers. Deserters.* Imperials shook by the breach, who want
out. To them, the sight of a young thing like you atop a healthy horse . . .
Well. There's a reason why we still carry these." He patted his mechanical sword hilt. "A sword don't do shit against a titan. But for those
who make it harder to *fight* the titans, why, a blade has many uses."

We trotted along in silence after that, my own sword feeling
heavier at my side—largely because I did not wish to tell the captain
my blade was wood and lead.

ON HORSEBACK WE got to the Forward Engineering Quarters
within two hours. It was perhaps the ugliest place I'd seen since
Daretana, all cranes and ropes and muddy construction yards, or
foundries belching vast rivers of smoke into the sky.

Miljin pulled a face as the air filled up with stinking fumes. "Fuck's
sakes," he growled. "Makes you wonder why the leviathans even want
to come ashore here anymore . . ." He nodded ahead. "There's the
medikkers' wing. How many are we here to question?"

I'd told him this already, of course, but it seemed wise not to mention that. "Eleven people, sir," I said.

"Eleven . . . And they're all, ah, *intimates* with the dead?"

"Most are. Or were. Or rather, my master suspects they were, sir."

"And we're to wring all the stories out of these folk, and try to line them all up to figure out where the hell our ten dead Engineers went that got their guts all full of dappleglass."

"Seems to be the shape of it, sir."

"Best to divvy it up, then. I'll take the last five, you take the top six. Then we compare notes."

After we stabled our horses and entered the medikkers' wing, I gave Miljin his five people to question. He squinted in the light of the lantern at the door, scribbling down the names on a strip of parchment with a length of ashpen. He had me repeat them a few times, then repeat which of the dead people they were associated with. I had never worked directly alongside someone in an investigation before, and Miljin certainly seemed to have a hefty reputation, but the sight of him muttering and shuffling through his papers filled me with unease.

"Are you sure you want to split up the list, sir?" I asked. "Would it be wiser to work together, maybe?"

"I know what I'm doing!" he snapped. Yet another sheaf of parchment slipped out of his hands, and he stooped to grab it. "Or are you suggesting I don't?"

I watched as he shook the mud off his dropped parchment. " 'Course not, sir."

"Then let's get this over with."

MY FIRST INTERVIEW was Princeps Anath Topirak, a medikker with the Apoth Iyalet. I stopped an attendant and asked about her whereabouts and the state of her injuries.

"Hurt in the collapse, sir," the attendant said. "Rather serious. She's recuperating down the hall, last room on the right."

I went to the room and knocked on the closed door. No answer. I turned the knob, walked in—and stopped short.

I'd never been in a true medikkers' bay before. As such, I was unprepared for what I found.

A single mai-lantern glimmered over a large, metal bathing cauldron situated in the center of the dark fretvine room. The cauldron was filled with a curious, whitish fluid that smelled strongly of old milk. Lying in the fluid was a tall Kurmini woman, her head resting back on the lip of the cauldron, her eyes shut, face pale and sweating. Though I couldn't see far into the milky substance in the tub, she was surely naked beneath it.

This was startling enough, but more startling still was the contraption of rope and wires hanging overhead, which suspended her right arm above the waters—yet her arm lacked a hand. In its place was a pale pink stump, and clinging to the stump like barnacles on the hull of a ship were dozens of tiny black snails, greedily sucking away at her open wound.

I stared at the snails, horrified. Then I felt a fluttering in the backs of my eyes, and I remembered something my old dueling teacher Trof had once said in jest: *And if any of you lose an arm or an ear by accident, don't fret, children—the medikkers will slap sangri-snails on the wound until they can grow you a new one.*

Well, I thought. I guess that's what those look like, then. Another memory I'd never be able to get out of my head. I reminded myself to stay controlled and contained.

I opened my engraver's pack, slid out a vial, and smelled it. This one was redolent of smoke and ash. I grimaced, walked to the foot of the tub, and cleared my throat.

Topirak didn't move.

"Princeps?" I said.

Her brow creased ever so faintly. A clean face, handsome and even. Bruises all on one side, now turned the color of old tea. Her skin was gray, much like mine, but her nose was clearly the focus of her alterations: it was purpled and slightly larger than normal, with many veins behind the nostrils. A common grafting in the Apoths, I knew: the ability to smell a concoction or a wound and identify its state was critical in their Iyalet.

"Princeps?" I said, louder.

With a snort and a moan, Topirak awoke. "Wh . . . wha?" She opened her swollen eyes. Their whites were utterly bloodshot. When she saw me, her eyes went even wider and she cried out in alarm, shouting, *"Who the hell are you?"*

"Ahh," I said, bewildered. I looked behind myself, wondering if someone was standing behind me. "I . . . I'm Signum Dinios Kol of the Iudex, Princeps. What's wrong?"

She stared at me for a moment, then sighed in relief. "Oh, thank Sanctum . . . Do you know, when I saw you standing there over me, all dressed in darks and glowering down at me . . ." She laughed wearily. "I thought you were Death himself come for me, sir."

I paused, wondering what to say. I'd been called all kinds of names during my short career with the Iyalets, but no one had ever mistaken me for the Harvester.

"It's the bath, sir," she explained. "There's stuff in these waters that does stuff to your head." She sniffed it. "Murgrass, mostly. A type of algae. Its feces offers many healing properties. That's what makes the water white, you see . . ." She sniffed it again. "Also ceterophins, a sleeping reagent . . . And altias oils. For constipation. Don't want me shitting in here."

"Impressive skill," I said.

She smiled weakly. "Blessed Atir of the Khanum, they say, had altered herself so she could awake and sniff the air, and know the placement of every bird and beast and flower about her for a mile . . . Though I doubt if she ever wound up in a bath like this. I sleep so much . . . I don't even know what day it is anymore."

"It's the eighteenth of the month of Kyuz," I said, "and I'm not from the deadlands, but the Iudex. I'm hoping you can help me with a few questions about the breach."

"Why's the Iudex investigating a breach, sir?" she croaked.

I ignored the question, took a chair from the corner, and sat down beside her. "I need to ask you about Signum Misik Jilki," I said.

A shadow of sorrow crossed her face. "M-Misik's dead, sir," she whispered.

"I know that, Princeps. Did you know her well?"

She shifted in the milky fluid, her expression pained. The white tide sloshed about her torso, revealing a luminous curve of a breast, blackened with storm clouds of bruises. "Yes."

"Very well?"

She glared at me. She was waking up now. "We were lovers, sir. But that's not against policy, being as we're from different Iyalets, is it?"

"I see," I said. I was learning to stop being surprised when Ana's hunches turned out to be right. "How long were you involved with her?"

A slow, sluggish blink as she did the math. "God . . . three years now."

"I'm sorry for your loss, and . . ." I resisted the urge to look down at her missing hand. ". . . and for what happened to you. I'm trying to learn a little more about how Jilki died."

"Why?"

Again, I ignored her question. "Would you have seen her the day before her death?"

Topirak shook her head.

"No?"

"No, sir. She was at the walls," she murmured. "Stayed there overnight, sir."

"She was there all day?" I asked.

"Yes, sir. And the two days before that."

"And she went nowhere besides the walls?"

"Not as far as I'm aware, sir."

"Nowhere with steam, or water, or the like?"

"Don't . . . don't quite know what you're asking, sir. Has something gone wrong?"

I considered what to say. One of the snails trailed across her severed wrist, leaving a stripe of pink flesh behind.

"When was the last time you saw Jilki, Princeps?" I asked.

"I saw her four days before she died, I think, sir?"

"And what were her movements on that day?"

"She went to the walls in the morning, and came back, sir."

"And the day before that?" I asked.

"The same."

I narrowed my eyes as I put this together. "So . . . just to make sure. For the six days previous to her death, the only places she went were here, at these quarters, and to the walls?"

"Yes, sir."

I did not like the feel of this. I knew from Uhad's report that two of the ten dead Engineers had been stationed in Talagray and had not visited either the walls or the Forward Engineering Quarters. Hearing that Jilki had *only* visited these places before her death would mean there was no commonality among the ten, which would make determining where they'd all been poisoned much harder.

"You're asking about contagion," said Topirak. "Aren't you, sir?"

"What makes you say that?" I asked, perhaps too sharply.

"I'm a medikker, sir. I know the questions. Want to figure out where they've been, what they touched, where they got it. Is that the case, sir?"

"Somewhat."

"I thought Misik had died in the collapse. When the walls fell. Why . . . why ask about contagion? And why's the Iudex investigating a contagion, and not the Apoths?"

"We're just trying to understand more. Is there anything you can think of along those lines, Princeps?"

"N-no," she said. "When Misik wasn't at her duties, she was with me." The weak smile again. "That's as I liked it."

She looked to me for sympathy. But I could feel something amiss now, and didn't give her any.

A *drip* as Topirak shifted in her bath. Her eyes searched the ceiling, anxious and fretful. She opened her mouth to speak, then stopped. I waited for it to come.

"Did Misik . . . do something wrong, sir?" she asked.

There it was.

"I don't know," I said honestly. "Do *you* think Jilki did something wrong?"

"No," she said. She stared up at the ceiling again, her pupils darting about. "But on the eighth night before the breach . . ."

"Yes?" I said. "What happened then?"

She swallowed. Tears meandered down her cheeks to drop into the white bath. "She . . . she went back into town, to Talagray. She stayed the night there."

"What for?" I asked.

"She was . . . working on some kind of project. Something to do with the quakes. The walls had been destabilized. She . . . she went back to town for a meeting. Couldn't tell me what it was about. Wasn't allowed, she said."

"Why not?" I asked.

"Something about not wanting to start a panic, sir," she said. "Didn't want people to know how bad the walls were. It felt very secret."

"I see," I said. I let the silence linger, then asked, "Did you believe her?"

"Why wouldn't I?"

I gazed into her face. Eyes wide and fearful, jaw trembling.

"I'm here to prevent other deaths, Princeps," I said. "Other injuries like yours. If something's wrong, I need to know."

"It was just . . . just a feeling," she whispered. "When she went to Talagray for these meetings, she was always quiet after. And there was something she said, both times." She screwed up her face, and said, *"The Engineers make the world. Everyone else just lives in it."*

"This wasn't the first time she went to Talagray for such a meeting?" I asked.

"No. She'd gone once two months before, sir."

"And any time before that?" I asked.

She thought about it, then shook her head.

"When was this previous meeting?" I asked. "The exact date."

"The seventh of the month of Egin, I think."

"And this . . . this feeling you got, after she returned from these meetings. Can you tell me a little more about it?"

She stared into the milky waters before her. "I was worried she had met someone else," she said finally. "And there was a smell about her, each time. She'd washed, I could tell, but . . . but it's hard to hide things like that from me. Oranje-leaf, and bitters. Like the sotwine they make in the cold countries. It was strange. Strange enough to make me think she was seeing someone else. But I wasn't sure, so . . . so I didn't want to ask. I just wanted to keep her."

"I see," I said.

She looked at me pleadingly. "Did she, sir? Do you know? Do you know if she'd been with someone else, sir?"

"I don't. But I have to keep looking. Would you like me to tell you what I find out, Princeps?"

She thought about it, the dark, bruised side of her face bent to the waters. Then she shook her head. "No. I've lost enough. I want to keep the last few days I had with her, at least. I want those to stay mine." A miserable laugh. "I mean—I'm owed that, at least, aren't I?"

CHAPTER 14

|||

I CONDUCTED FOUR OTHER INTERVIEWS AFTER Topirak. All of the people were exhausted and grieving and injured—one man concussed, one woman missing a foot, another with her head and face all bandaged up—and none wished to talk to me. Yet I stayed with them, stalking among the bandages and baths; and as I sniffed my ash-scented vial and pulled words from their battered minds, a pattern began to emerge among the dead Engineers.

Princeps Donelek Sandik had returned to the city of Talagray eight nights before the breach to check on an injured comrade—the same night that Jilki had gone back, the sixth of the month of Kyuz.

Captain Atos Koris had gone to Talagray to arrange a shipment of materials—also on the sixth of Kyuz.

That exact same night, Signum Suo Akmo and Princeps Kise Sira had both returned to the city for reasons they claimed to be high imperial secrets. In fact, after I asked more questions, I discovered this wasn't Sira's first visit: she had *also* gone back to Talagray on the exact same date as Jilki's first visit two months before, the seventh of the month of Egin.

Everything was slowly lining up.

The only outlier was the man I'd been sent to interview about Princeps Atha Lapfir. I went to his healing bay only to find his bath empty and dry, the sole sign of his occupancy a straw cap in the corner. When I asked the medikker, she said simply, "Died last night. We can only do so much."

I stood in the halls of the medikkers' wing afterward, thinking this over. Five of the dead Engineers had visited the city eight nights before the breach, all for reasons either vague or mysterious.

And their reasons all tasted, I thought, rather like bullshit. Jilki hadn't been working on some secret project for the walls, for Kalista would have mentioned it if she had. I began to suspect that if I looked into it, I'd find no shipment of materials that Koris had gone to arrange, nor would I find any injured comrade of Sandik's in the city. They had gone somewhere in Talagray, all of them, and had lied about it to their friends and lovers.

However, only Princeps Sira and Signum Jilki had gone back to Talagray on the seventh of Egin, two months before.

A regular meeting, perhaps—and a curiously secret one. Secret enough for everyone to lie about. And eventually, someone had come to this secret meeting of Engineers, and brought death with them.

WHEN I FINALLY met up with Captain Miljin, he wasn't half as enthused or excited as I was. "By Sanctum, this is awful work," he said, huffing as he walked up. "These poor bastards ... I had to talk to one man with both his legs missing! Bastard was worried the medikkers won't grow the new ones to be the right size ..."

"It is rather deplorable, sir," I said.

"That's a big word for a shit state." He grimaced as one attendant wheeled by a man whose face was obscured by linen bandages. "Honestly, you'd have to be a coldhearted, bastardly fuck to question people like these properly."

I chose not to comment.

"I found fuck-all," he said. He pulled out a parchment and squinted at it. "Only thing of note I got was that Captain Kilem Terez had been worried the last couple of days that he was being followed. By a damned crackler, of all things."

"A crackler was following him?" I said.

"Yeah." He snorted. "It's got to be bullshit. Cracklers are what, ten span tall? Can't think of anyone worse to go sneaking and following folk about. Said the crackler had yellow hair, too. Damn odd. I figure the fellow I talked to had a bruised brain. What did you get, lad?"

I told him what I'd found, and his eyes grew wide with amazement.

"You got *all* that out of them?" Miljin said. "Really? Your bedside manner must be far better than mine, boy."

"Can't say, sir. But that's five out of the ten dead folk who returned to the city—all on the eighth night before they died. What do you think of it?"

"Well." He snorted and ruffled his mustache with a knuckle. "It almost makes sense."

"Almost?"

"Yeah." He consulted his notes, frowning as he flipped through his smudged parchments. "But I have one of the dead ten who hasn't been back to Talagray for weeks. Which breaks your pattern, yeah?"

I felt my heart dribbling down through my ribs and into my boots. "Who, sir?"

"Signum Ginklas Loveh," he said. He wrinkled up his nose as he read. "This is what her, ah . . . hell, I guess her *lover* said, this Signum Sirgdela Vartas I questioned, of the Legion. He said she hasn't been near Talagray for almost a month. And if she didn't go to Talagray at all, then that's not the place of the poisoning, is it?"

"What about the date of the other meeting?" I said. "On the seventh of the month of Egin?"

Miljin consulted his notes. "No, she wasn't in Talagray then, neither."

"Then where was she? Here at the base?"

"No . . . Vartas said that our dead Signum Loveh went to the walls on some trip with Commander Blas himself. That's all else he could give me."

My skin went cold.

"Wait. When? What date in Egin, exactly?" I asked.

He consulted his notes again. "The, ah, seventh and eighth of that month," he said.

I thought this over. Then I slowly slid out my vial of lye-scent and smelled it.

My eyes trembled, and all the details of the Daretana murder filled my mind, like my skull was once again a bubble of water full of leaping fish.

"He just . . . he just volunteered this to you, sir?" I asked.

"Yes . . . why? What's wrong with it, boy?"

"I . . . I think this Signum Vartas lied to you, sir," I said. "No—I *know* he did."

Miljin went stone-faced. "Did he."

"Yes. But I'm not yet sure why. I'd like to find out. Is that all right, sir?"

His jaw worked for a moment. Then he made a fist with his right hand, and all the knuckles of his massive hand crackled all at once. "That," he said, "would be perfectly lovely."

UNLIKE EVERYONE ELSE I'd interviewed, Signum Vartas was out of his healing bath and lying on a cot, with a tray of tea and a slender shootstraw pipe smoking in an ashpot beside him. He wore a set of silk robes that looked brand new, and while his injuries weren't mild by any means—he had haal-paste applied in streaks to his shoulder and neck, probably from gashes he'd gotten during the collapse—he seemed to be recovering much faster than everyone else in the bays here. His room even had a window. None of the others had.

He cocked an eyebrow as Miljin and I walked in—a cold, imperious look—and he put down his pipe. "What's this now?" he asked. "I thought I'd answered all your questions, Captain."

I sat down in front of him, not bothering to bow or salute. "I just had a few more myself, Signum Vartas."

He looked down his nose at me. He was a tall, thin Rathras man, with a high brow and deep-set eyes that looked out at you like you were a household servant he didn't entirely trust yet. "And you are?" he asked.

"Signum Kol, Iudex. Just comparing dates."

"I gave Captain Miljin here all the dates I knew."

"I just wanted to check something. Can you tell me again about Signum Loveh's movements during the days previous to her death?"

"I can confirm all that I told Captain Miljin," he said, bristling slightly. "Or are you doubting his word *and* mine?"

"You told the captain that Loveh had never been to Talagray," I said.

"Yes? Not for weeks before she died."

"Can you remember the last time she'd gone there?"

"No. Could have been months, really. Why?"

"But you were intimate with Signum Loveh, correct?"

His cold gaze danced over my face. He picked back up his shoot-straw pipe and puffed at it. "A shake to your eyes . . ." he said softly. "You're Sublime, like me. You know relationships are tricky for those like us."

"You didn't answer my question," I said.

"Fine. Yes, I was *intimate* with her."

"So you would have known when she went back to Talagray."

"Yes, and she didn't!" he said. Tufts of smoke trickled out of his nostrils. "What's the point of this?"

"And the only other time that you mentioned was one instance, when she went out with Commander Blas."

"Yes!"

"And where did they go?"

"To inspect the walls! I'm sure Miljin told you that!"

Miljin, however, gave Vartas nothing, staring at him with his flat, dark gaze.

"What date was that?" I asked.

"The seventh and eighth," Vartas said. "Of the month of Egin. Just over two months ago."

I watched him. His cold little eyes stared into mine, but I glimpsed a fragile gleam there, a tremble in his pupils.

"That's not true," I said. "And you know it."

"The hell do you mean?" he demanded.

I felt a flutter in my own eyes, and the memory burbled up: me hurrying away into the gardens of the Haza house in Daretana, and reading Blas's records of his inspections aloud, committing the dates to memory. One line in particular now swam up in my skull: *ck. Paytasız bridges in the north of the Tala canton—6th to 8th of Egin—all pass.*

"Because," I said, "Commander Blas wasn't at the walls at all then."

Vartas went very still. "What?" he asked.

"Commander Taqtasa Blas was in the north of the canton, inspecting the bridges, from the sixth to the eighth of that month. I've seen his diary. So that is very wrong, Vartas."

His gaze stayed steady. He slowly replaced his shootstraw pipe in his mouth and puffed at it. "Then I was wrong. She was with Blas during some other day."

"Which days?"

"The fourteenth and fifteenth of Egin. Just a slight mistake."

I shook my head. "That's wrong, too."

"The hell it is!"

"No. Blas was in the Daretana canton then. From the thirteenth through the fifteenth of the month of Egin. I know that, too. I know *all* of his movements for the past three months."

Vartas blinked. The coal of his shootstraw pipe danced as his hand trembled. Miljin slowly rose and came to stand behind me.

"We've two options here," I said. "Either you have no idea where Signum Loveh was during *any* of these days—or, you told the captain here a lie, and she did go to Talagray eight days before the breach. But you didn't want Miljin to know that, and when he didn't ask about it, you didn't speak up. But I'm guessing you got nervous. You wanted to give her an alibi for the *other* time she visited Talagray, on the night of the seventh of Egin—the same meeting that two other of the dead Engineers attended. Just in case. But you misstepped there. Picked the wrong person to put her with. Unlucky for you. You could have just kept quiet, and we'd have never known. But now we do."

"Know what?" Vartas said grudgingly.

"That you know *why* she went to Talagray," I said. "None of the others knew, so none of them tried to lie. But you did."

He lifted his shootstraw pipe back up to his lips. It was positively prancing now. "I don't know," he said softly, "what the hell you're talking abou—"

Then Miljin moved.

I had not been watching him, so I had not been prepared for it. But there was a quick *clack-clack* sound, like someone unlocking a lock; and the next thing I knew his sword was in his hand, spinning around as lightly as if it were a length of straw—and then he was stabbing it down, thrusting it through the cot directly between Vartas's legs up to the hilt, a mere smallspan or two away from the man's crotch.

Vartas screamed, his shootstraw pipe tumbling out of his teeth. He tried to sit up, but Miljin placed a fist on his sternum and shoved him back down.

"Did you lie to *me*, Signum?" Miljin bellowed. "Did you *fucking* lie to me?"

I stared at the sword, mere spans before my face. Its blade was not shining steel, I noticed, but a pale, sickly, whitish green.

Vartas's screams rose into shrieks, and he began slapping at the side of his robe. A small thread of aromatic smoke was gently unscrolling from his clothing above his hip. I darted my hand into the man's robe, found the shootstraw pipe that had slipped to his side, plucked it out, and stuck it in his teacup, where it died with a sputtering hiss.

III

STILL TREMBLING AND QUAKING, Vartas gave us the full
spill of it. I sniffed at my ash-scent vial and listened.

"I . . . I don't know what it was about," he said, sniffing. "I don't
know why Gink went to Talagray. But I knew it had something to do
with her career. With her prospects."

Miljin stood huffing over me like an angry boar. I tried to focus on
Vartas's words.

"How do you know this?" I asked.

"Because after she started going, everything started going right
for her," he said. "Plum projects. Faster promotions. Greater pay. *Far*
greater pay, really, working under Commander Blas."

Every muscle in my body went tight. "Commander Blas? She
worked with him?"

He nodded.

"What did she do for him?"

"Engineering stuff, I suppose. Diagrams and bridges and such. I
just knew she went to Talagray every few months, and the money
came in. And I was told to not ask questions, and keep my mouth
shut. Which I did. Not like she ever thanked me, though."

I took in his fine robes, his tea tray, the aroma of his pipe. Suddenly his living situation didn't seem quite so remarkable.

"How many times did she go to the city for these meetings?" I
asked.

"I don't know. Ten times. Maybe more."

This was noteworthy. Signum Loveh, it seemed, was a much more
regular visitor than all of the other dead Engineers I'd asked about.

"I asked to be let in on the secret," Vartas said resentfully. "To get
to go, too. But she said it wasn't allowed. Said I had to be *chosen*.
What made you chosen, I didn't know. I mean, when I looked at the
rest of her little gang, I couldn't see what made them so special."

Miljin and I glanced at one another, our interest piqued.

"Gang?" I asked. "What gang is this?"

"Dunno if it was a *gang*, precisely," Vartas muttered. "Just . . . just pals, perhaps. Friends. But they all seemed to bear some blessing from above."

"Names," spat Miljin. "Give us their names, damn you."

"D-damn it all," he stammered. "I'm a spatiast, not an engraver! I don't keep this shit behind my eyes!" He grumbled for a moment. "Gink was friendly with three of them. Might have been more, but she and those three hung together tight." One finger probed where his pipe had burned him on his side as he thought. "Vanduo. That was one, I think."

I nodded. Princeps Alaus Vanduo—that was one of the dead.

"And the next . . . I think the name was Lapa? Lapir?"

"Lapfir?" I suggested.

"I think that was it. Maybe, yes. That was it."

Princeps Atha Lapfir, then. Another of the dead ten.

"And the last . . ." Vartas frowned for a moment. "The last was . . . *Jolgalgan*. Right. That was her."

I looked at him blankly. Then I looked at Miljin, who stared blankly back at me. This name was totally new.

"Ah . . . who?" I asked.

"Jolgalgan," said Vartas again. He nodded. "That was her. Captain Kiz Jolgalgan. I remember because she was an Apoth, and no one else was."

My eyes fluttered as I riffled among the many names I'd heard in the past day. Yet Captain Kiz Jolgalgan, I knew, was most certainly not one of the ten dead Engineers.

"You're . . . you're sure about this?" I asked. "You're *sure* this person was grouped in with Loveh and the rest of the Engineers?"

"I am," he said. He'd recovered his pride and stuck his nose in the air. "I told you I remembered, and why. Try listening."

My thoughts danced as I turned this bit of information over. I caught Miljin's eye, and saw a keen, burning look in his face, and knew he was thinking the same thing as me.

We have a survivor. An eleventh member of the group. Someone who went to one of these mysterious meetings—and maybe walked away.

"Describe her, then," said Miljin. "What'd this gal look like?"

"Tall woman," said Vartas. "Broad. Very stern, very serious. Face like she's always sucking on a lemon seed."

"What race was she?" Miljin asked. "Tala? Rathras? Kurmini?"

"You know . . . I couldn't quite tell," admitted Vartas. "She had a Kurmini name, but she didn't *look* Kurmini. She was far too tall, and her hair was pale yellow, and tightly curled. I've never seen a Kurmini with hair like that."

"What assignment did she serve under in the Apoths?" asked Miljin.

"Don't know. I never talked to her in person. I wasn't invited to the party," he said bitterly.

We quizzed him further on this Jolgalgan, but he could give us little. Eventually I gave up and tried a new angle. "Did Signum Loveh bring anything back from these meetings?" I asked.

"No," said Vartas.

"Did she bring anything *to* these meetings?" I asked. "Documents? Money?"

"No, but . . ." He frowned, thinking. "But sometimes she . . . she took something from her quarters on these visits. A little coin thing, it looked like. I caught her putting it in her pocket once. I asked what it was, and she said she couldn't tell me. So I . . ."

"So you reckoned it was part of these meetings," I said.

He nodded. "But that's all I knew. I just knew the meetings, the money, the coin—and not to ask questions. When you came and brought her up, I . . . I worried it was some corruption. I thought she had the right to lie in peace with a clear name, and thought Commander Blas could maybe help give her cover . . ."

I looked him over and didn't see any lie there. Evidently the man didn't know.

"Commander Blas is dead," I said.

"He . . . he what?" said Vartas, shocked.

"Blas is dead," I said. "Along with all these other Engineers who went to these little secret meetings. Probably *because* of these secret meetings. So if there's anything else you know, you need to tell us now."

"I don't know anything more!" said Vartas.

"You sure, boy?" said Miljin.

"I promise, I don't!" Then a faint pout of horror crept into his face. "Why are you two asking about this? Does this have anything to do with the breach?"

There was a long silence. Miljin picked up one of Vartas's unlit shootstraw pipes and sniffed at it. "You keep yourself in this bed, Signum," he said. "You keep your fucking money. And you keep your mouth shut. Otherwise, I am going to come back here—and this?" He pointed to the gash in the bed, between Vartas's legs. "I shall do the same again, but six smallspan higher. And then six again, and six again. Am I clear?"

Beads of sweat came boiling out of Vartas's brow. "As mountain water, sir."

"Good." He pocketed the shootstraw pipe and swatted my shoulder. "Let's get the hell out of here."

MILJIN AND I stood in the medikkers' halls, thinking in silence as the attendants swarmed around us.

"So," he said.

"So, sir," I said.

"We got mysterious meetings of Engineers, meeting about . . . something. Don't know what yet. But all with Commander Blas involved."

"Correct, sir."

"And now we've got an Apoth who might be a part of it," he said. "Except—her name ain't on the list of the dead."

"Yes, sir."

"Got to get ahold of her quick," he said. "And press her to tell us what in hell happened in these damn meetings. I'll tell the Legion lads to start a lookout for her. But maybe she's dead, too. Tree-speared out in the middle of some fucking field somewhere, and we haven't found her yet." He sighed and rubbed the back of his head. "Meanwhile, we've got black-clad assassins in Daretana."

"We do, sir."

"This along with, you know, people sprouting trees from inside theirselves, and all that's brought about."

"Yes, sir."

He snorted and spat on the floor. "Fucking hell. What a mess." Then he chewed his lip, thinking. "You know, if I had some magic coin that could let me into some secret meetings, well . . ."

". . . you wouldn't take it with you to the sea walls, sir?" I suggested.

"Hell no. Sure wouldn't. I'd keep it somewhere safe."

"I agree, sir."

We stood there in contemplative silence. Then two attendants wheeled by a wooden cart, one wheel squeaking wildly. The cart carried a large glass tank, like an aquarium—but as it passed before us, we saw it did not contain any conventional fish. Rather, a massive, rippling, purplish starfish was gripping the bottom of the tank—and growing from its back was a human hand.

The hand's fingers flexed and twitched very slowly as it passed before us, as if exulting in the flow of the water. It had a feminine look to it. Something delicate in the nails and knuckles.

We watched in silence as the tank went by, the one wheel squeaking in protest.

"Looks like Topirak's getting a replacement," said Miljin.

I cleared my throat. "Looks that way, sir," I said hoarsely.

Miljin waited to speak again until its squeak had long faded. Then he grunted.

"Let's go check Loveh's quarters for that fucking coin," he said, "before someone wheels one of them starfish by with a prick growing from its back, and I faint and crack my head open and wind up in one of these goddamn baths."

WE FOUND LOVEH'S quarters on the west side of the building. A small chamber with a single bed, trunk, closet, bookshelf—but if you had the eye for it, the suggestions of wealth could be found all around us. Bedsheets fine and silky. Jar of soapdust on the window-sill, frothy and fragrant. Closet full to bursting with clothing far be-yond what most Iyalets doled out.

I walked across the floorboard, taking in the room. "Such a small coin," I said, "really could be anywhere—"

Then Miljin's green-bladed sword was in his hand, and he went to work.

His sword bit through the bed, the clothes, the walls of the room, chewing through the fretvine, through the planked wood, carving up everything in sight.

"Sir?" I said, alarmed. "What are you doing?"

"Looking," he grunted. His sword slashed open the lock of a trunk, and he dumped clothing from it. "What else?"

"We can't destroy the property of other officers, sir," I said. "Not without due cause, whi—"

"She's dead!" he snapped. "And the damn walls have been breached! And you didn't seem to complain when I nearly put my blade in Vartas's balls! By the Harvester, child, get your head out of your policy book and into the moment!"

Then Miljin stopped and stooped over a rent he'd carved in the floor. With the flick of his sword, he turned the rent into a square hole about three span wide. Then he squatted over it, reached into the hole, and slid out a bronze box.

"Here we go," he said. "Here we go, here we go, here we go . . ." He studied it. "No lock, no graft trips . . ."

"Graft trips?" I asked.

"A fungus or something what grows in the crack, so when it's opened improperly it releases a toxin . . ." He rapped on it. "This is just a box. And what's inside it . . ."

He flicked it open. Inside was a small bed of moss, and lying upon that, a very strange contraption.

It was a small, circular, intricately engraved bronze plate, with five tiny glass vials embedded in it, each one containing fluids of many different colors. Miljin frowned at it, then sniffed it, and grunted, "Well, I'll be fucked."

"What is it, sir?"

"It's a reagents key."

A flutter in my eyes. I recalled Princeps Otirios back in Daretana, taking out a small glass vial sloshing with black fluid and saying— *You'll need to follow close, sir. This gate is a bit old. Can be fussy.*

"For vinegates and the like?" I asked.

"Yeah . . . but I've never seen one like this before. Five different reagents? Whatever portal or path this is for, it must be one of the most secure places on earth." He stood, grimacing. "Let's check another room."

We went to the quarters of Signum Jilki, Topirak's lover. Again, the flicker-flash of the green sword. Another bronze box—this one hidden in a wall—and inside, another reagents key, this one the same as with Loveh.

"Another," Miljin muttered. "*Another.*" He squinted west over his shoulder, like he could see the walls of Talagray just behind him. "Exactly what in the hell," he said slowly, "was going on in my city?"

I waited, watching his brows bristle. Then he made a fist with his hand, all the knuckles crackling again, and he growled, "You keep one, and I keep the other. Got it? Then let's get out of here."

He left, but I tarried behind, thinking of Topirak's testimony. I went through Jilki's wardrobe, sniffing at her garments, wondering if I could catch the strange aroma Topirak had described.

Then I caught something, faint but present on a small scarf: a scent of oranje-leaf and some kind of spice.

My eyes fluttered as I matched the scent to a memory. Suddenly I was in Daretana again, crouched before the mangled corpse of Taqtasa Blas suspended in the trees. I'd held a pot of oil in my hands and sniffed it—and caught the aroma of spice and oranje-leaf and wine mullings and perhaps incense.

That was it. Jilki's scarf smelled just like Blas's pot of oil. Exactly the same.

Then Miljin's voice over my shoulder: "Kol . . . are you smelling that dead woman's clothes?"

I dropped the scarf. "Coming, sir."

CHAPTER 15

|||

WE RODE BACK TO TALAGRAY IN SILENCE. MILJIN'S gruff bravado had vanished. Now he slumped on his horse, glowering ahead, scabbard swinging at his side. It wasn't until we could see the fortifications and the bombards ahead—all pointed toward us—that he finally spoke.

"Didn't use to be like this," he said.

"Pardon, sir?" I asked. "Like what?"

"All this skulking and skullduggery," he said. "Keeping order out here used to mean using this . . ." He patted his sword again. "Until everyone got in line. I mean, it's a goddamned military city. But then the Empire got good at making money, and then they went and got it in everything, even here. Got big, got complex. Now we need boys like you with brains brimming with . . . hell, I've no idea what's in your skull, son."

I glanced at him. "So you, sir . . . You're not . . ."

"I'm no Sublime," he said. "Got grafts and suffusions and the like for strength and reaction speed and recovery. Same shit they use on horses, some tell me. But none of it went toward my mind. Sometimes feel like they keep me around out of some misguided sense of duty."

"Ana did say you're a war hero, sir," I said.

He laughed roughly. "The thing about war, boy, is while it happens, you've no idea what's going on—and when it's over, everyone spends the rest of your life telling you what you did." He gestured at the towers of Talagray ahead. "We don't need war heroes here anyway. We need plotters. Like your Ana. Even if she has pissed off a lot of powerful people."

"She has?"

"Oh, yes. That's the problem with figuring shit out—eventually you run into someone who'd prefer all their shit remained thoroughly unfigured. You know much with a blade, lad?"

"I was first in my swordsmanship class, sir," I said. "About the only class I was ever any good at."

"That doesn't sound right. You were as sharp as a medikker's knife back there. About as cheery and personable, too. But Uhad mentioned you were made for the Iudex."

"He did?" I said, surprised.

"Aye. Said you scored shit on all your other Iyalet exams, except Iudex. Those you were fantastic on."

I looked at him sidelong. The comment seemed genuine, and I did not see any suspicion on Miljin's face. I tried to relax.

"Still, exams are different from serving," he said. "Just as policy and codes of conduct can't guide every goddamn investigation. Ever been in a fight, boy? A real one?"

"No, sir."

"Hum. You'll want to amend that."

I looked at him again. He appeared serious. "Why's that, sir?"

"Ever wonder why Dolabra was transferred to your little canton," he said, "but *without* an assistant?"

I blinked. The idea had not occurred to me. I'd always assumed her previous staff had stayed behind.

"Rumor has it," he said, "Dolabra's previous assistant investigator ran into the wrong end of a sword. Were I in your trousers, boy, I'd learn all I could about fighting, and start growing eyes on all sides of my head." Then he spat and glanced up at the sky. "If you want to see it, now's your chance."

My mind was still spinning from what he'd said. "Wh-what, sir?" I said, startled.

"You were looking east this morning, yeah?" he said. "But the mist was too heavy. Well, now it's burned off. Take your gander if you please, boy."

I looked back over my shoulder. Then I pulled on the reins of my horse and stopped.

The plains of Tala stretched out behind me, brilliant and viridine, yet the landscape was not flat, not everywhere: huge, tufty humps and hills lay here and there, some high, some sunken, and—strangest of all—each was covered with huge, ancient tree stumps like scales on a fish. The largest hill was enormous, almost like a small mountain, shot through with curving rock formations that were a glimmering pale green. The trees that covered its surface were not stumps but newly grown saplings, narrow and stretching into the sky, and their trunks were of many strange colors, violet and blue and a dull yellow.

I stared at the hill and saw something buried in its side. An appendage, perhaps, like a beetle's leg—an enormous one, a quarter of a league long, covered in pale gray chitin and ending in a curious claw. I wondered what was buried in that hill.

And then I realized. The green rock formations in the hill were not rock at all.

They were bones. Ribs.

The leviathan's carcass was not buried in the hill. The leviathan's carcass *was* the hill.

I felt my hands trembling as they gripped the reins of my horse, my eye fixed on the huge, mountainous growth, covered with those strange, shimmering trees.

"Their blood changes all that's about them," said Miljin quietly.

I turned, alarmed, and realized he'd ridden up beside me without my noticing. "P-pardon?" I asked.

"Their blood," he says. "When it hits the soil, it makes the grass grow like mad. Makes trees and plants of all kinds sprout out everywhere. Some start bearing fruit that . . . *does* things to you, if you eat it. Usually the Apoths burn the carcasses. Can't do that now. Not with the breach there. Too many people about, and too many fumes."

I cast my eyes beyond the enormous, grass-covered body of the dead leviathan and spied the wide, rambling black strip of the sea wall in the distance—and there, straight east, a tiny gap, the barest break in the ribbon of stone. Only then did I realize how far the leviathan had rampaged, how much territory it had crossed, and how close it had come to destroying Talagray, which suddenly felt hardly larger than the carcass before me.

How odd it was to meet your maker in this fashion; for all the wonders of the Empire—from Sublimes like myself, to cracklers and fretvines and Miljin's muscles—came from the blood of such beings.

Miljin wheeled his horse back west. "Come on. Sun's getting low. Let's get in before curfew."

My eye lingered on the chitinous limb extending from the hillock. I noted the color of its armor—so gray, and so pale—and reflected that its color was not unlike that of my own skin. Then I turned and left.

MILJIN AND I parted ways at the Trinity in Talagray, though he held me back for a moment. "Here," he said. "You deserve this, after today." He pulled Vartas's shootstraw pipe from his pocket, snapped it in half, and held one half out to me. "Find a hot iron somewhere and enjoy the smoke."

I took it from him, sniffing its end. It was spicy and aromatic. "I will, sir."

"I'll report to Uhad. You grab some grub and get to your master. I've no doubt she'll want to dig all throughout your head." He eyed the darkening sky. "Night'll be here soon, and with it the curfew. So stay indoors and stay safe."

"Understood, sir."

He walked out into the courtyard, then paused midstep as a light rain began to fall. He shot me a look over his shoulder. "A shit end to a shit day!" he barked, half grinning, and strode off.

I smiled after him. Then I waited, counting the seconds and watching as his form receded into the sheets of rain.

I counted out a full two minutes. Then I turned, walked across the Iudex tower entryway, and slipped out into a side street.

All about me the city was closing. Food vendors and inns were bawling out their last calls, the humid air heavy with the scents of fat and spice. Legion patrols roamed the streets, holding their lanterns high and pulling out their curfew bells. Soon tarrying in the street would carry serious penalties—yet I had some final business to conduct.

I summoned the map of Talagray in my memory as I ventured farther into the city. Rona Aristan of the Engineering Iyalet, Secretary Princeps to Commander Blas for going on twelve years. Her address was carved into my skull like it was wrought of molten lead. She lived on the western side of the city, close to the Trinity. And if I hurried, I could make it there and back before curfew.

CHAPTER 16

|||

I FOUND ARISTAN'S NEIGHBORHOOD JUST AS THE rain receded, the stone streets bright and shining wetly as the last light of sunset drained from the sky. It wasn't as fine as the gentry neighborhoods I'd glimpsed this morning, but it was nice enough, fretvine frames and white fernpaper walls. Aristan's house was nestled in the back. I knocked on the door and waited.

Silence. I knocked again, got nothing. Then a third time. Still nothing.

I stepped back from the house and studied it again. All quiet and dark, no light within at all, not even a single mai-lantern. I read the mud in the yard about her house, but I could see no footprints. No one had trodden here at all during this wet day save myself.

I heard the first curfew bells echoing through the city, then scanned the landscape about me. I picked out a half-hidden area that would grant the widest view of the street and took up station there, my coat collar pulled high against the rain. When Aristan returned for curfew, I figured, I'd pounce.

I waited throughout the second warning bells, then the third. Studied the crowds trickling past and engraved their faces, their bearings, their clothes. I did not recognize them, and none came to Aristan's door.

Finally the fourth bells rang. I studied Aristan's house again, frowning. Wherever Commander Blas's secretary was now, she was about to get herself locked up for violating curfew. As was I, probably.

If she was coming home, that was. Or maybe she was home but wouldn't or couldn't answer the door.

My eye lingered on her front door. An idea occurred to me—but a forbidden one. A disadvantage to being an engraver was you remembered every rule you ever heard, along with all the punishments for each violation. But I was bothered now and had to see.

I slipped around to the back of the house, knelt at the back door, and reached up into the sleeve of my coat. Sewn into the lining there were three small, slender lengths of iron I'd bent into different shapes. I hadn't used them in months, but I slid them out now, then eyed the lock in the back door.

I did not really know how to pick locks. Rather, I had memorized the movements required to pick three specific locks I'd experimented with months ago, during my Sublime training. This was very different from knowing how locks actually worked, and how to pick them, but I hoped it was worth the gamble here. Perhaps the lock of this door was similar to the ones I'd worked with before.

I delicately slid my wrench into the lock, followed by the pin. I set my pin, then felt a fluttering in my eyes as I let the memories return to me, and the movements came alive in my fingers.

I turned the pin, then dipped the wrench up and down, the slightest wiggle. With a click, the lock turned.

I glanced around to confirm I was unwatched, and opened the door.

The stench of rot struck me in a thick, staggering wave. I stepped back, coughing with my arm to my nose, then took a deep breath of clear air and returned to the open door, peering inside.

The house within was a wreck. Cupboards all shoved open, their contents poured out onto the floor. Chairs and tables flipped upside down. Cushions slashed to pieces, their moss stuffing ripped out in clumps. Piles of paper lay everywhere, having been torn from many books. The only thing that hadn't been dashed to pieces was the small spyglass set on a stand in the corner—a fancy possession for so modest a home.

Someone, it seemed, had come here looking for something. I wondered if they'd found it.

I looked back at the street, confirming I was unwatched. Then I stepped inside and shut the door behind me.

I MOVED CAREFULLY throughout the reeking house, studying all the refuse on the floor, shattered reagents vials or bowls of tinctures or shredded books. Finally I came to the bedroom, where the stench of rot was so intense I was nearly sick. Clothes had been hauled from the wardrobes and shredded to pieces. The whole of the room was like a stinking rat's nest.

I looked to the mossbed in the corner. There on the floor, peeking just past the drape of the sheets, were the tips of two bare feet, the toes curled and discolored.

I hesitated. Then I walked over and looked at her.

The body was female, somewhat elderly, and had been lying here for some days, her skin darkening in patches from the pooling of her blood within her. She had putrefied so much it was difficult to tell her race, yet she seemed a skinny, frail woman, with a thick shock of gray hair. A pool of black, old blood lay on the floor just beside her head, though I could not see a wound.

I cracked the bedroom shutter, allowing a blade of evening light to cut through the gloom. Then I calmed my mutinous stomach and leaned forward to look at her head. At the base of her skull, hidden among the gray tufts of her hair, was a dark, perfect little hole, about half the width of my little finger. A crackling rill of old dried blood wove away from it down her scalp. I had never seen such a wound in all my life and could not imagine what had felled her.

I stood back, studying the body. Rona Aristan, I guessed. Someone had come calling, looking for something, but she either had not given it to them, or could not.

I glanced around the bedroom, listening to the echoes of the curfew bells. My eye fell on a painting, undamaged but askew. Rendered in thick oil paints on its surface was the somewhat familiar face of a man: only somewhat, however, because the last time I'd seen that face, it'd been shot through with shoots of dappleglass.

I moved to the painting of Commander Taqtasa Blas. It was the first time I'd seen an image of the man whole. His eyes were steely but warm, nose proud with a slight bend from some childhood break. Dark Kurmini complexion overcast with the familiar gray. A handsome, haughty creature, I thought him.

I cocked my head, leaning closer. There was a bruise in the wood, at the frame's corner. Then I saw there were more: another bruise above it, and one more on the bottom. Like this painting had been moved a great deal in its time, and bumped and rubbed up against something.

I thought for a moment. Then I lifted the painting off its nail and turned it around.

A piece of thick parchment had been glued to the canvas's back; yet there, at the top right corner, it had been carefully torn away.

I shook the painting. Something rattled within. I tipped it over, turning its open corner to my palm.

Something small and twinkling slid out from behind the canvas and dropped in my hand: a key.

I held the key up to the fading light in the window. It was a simple thing, made of bright, rosy bronze. A key to a common lock, or a common door. I turned it over in my hand, thinking.

Why hide this key in such a fashion? Was this what the intruder had been looking for?

I looked back at Aristan's corpse, frowning. Then my eye returned to the shuttered bedroom window.

An idea slowly began to congeal in my mind.

I returned to the main room, to where the spyglass was mounted on a stand pointing out the shuttered window there. I pushed open the shutters—pausing to peer out in case I was being watched—then put my eye to the spyglass.

The spyglass had been trained on a set of little houses about a half league up the hill, much smaller than this one. Bland little things that were hardly more than fernpaper, all the shutters of their windows clamped shut.

But one set of shutters—the one in the exact center of the spyglass's lens—was different: a bright blue cloth was wedged in the shutters' crack, dangling down the wall. None of the other houses featured such an adornment.

I drew back from the spyglass and peered at the little house, and the blot of blue hanging from the window.

A signal of some kind, perhaps? One Rona Aristan had once observed, from this very window?

I looked down at the little bronze key in my hand. Then I peered back through the spyglass, moving it a little to study the door of the house.

I spied a wink of rosy bronze there on the door—perhaps the same as the metal of the key now in my hand.

I SLIPPED OUT the back door and returned to the drizzling rain, key clutched in my fingers and the curfew bells still ringing in the distance. I approached the bland little house slowly, eyeing the alleys and windows.

No movement. All was still.

I approached the front door—the make of the knob and lock was indeed the same as the key—and pressed an ear to it to listen. I heard no sound within, so I slid the little bronze key in the lock and turned it. With a click, the door fell open.

Inside it was a stark, miserable little place, barely more than a floor, a ceiling, a wardrobe, and a table and a set of chairs. I shut the door behind me and quietly stepped in, glancing about, wary of any intruders.

Yet there was nothing to see, except perhaps a handful of colored cloths hanging from a hook beside the shuttered window, some red, some blue, some green. My hunch was right, I reckoned: many colors, for many signals, should anyone be watching. Just like the flares of the sea walls, perhaps.

I looked around the bare, empty house. There was no bed—so not a place for living, I guessed. As to what could have happened here that was worth signaling anyone over, I had no idea.

I walked across the floorboards, tapping them with my toe and waiting for a creak or a hollow thump. Nothing. Nor was there anything in the cupboards. Then I looked in the wardrobe.

A small chest sat at the bottom, finely made of pale wood with a bronze top. I tried to open it and found it locked. I reached into my sleeve to produce my lockpicks again, hoping I would get lucky a second time tonight.

My first attempt failed, as did my second. But upon trying the third technique I'd memorized I heard another satisfying click, and slowly lifted the top of the box.

I looked inside.

I stared. Then I shut the box.

I glanced around the tiny house again, confirming I was alone. Then I swallowed, reopened the box, and peered within, struggling to believe I was seeing aright.

Placed in the bottom was a small leather bag, tied shut; and there, beside that, was a stack of oblong, thick silver plates, each bright and shiny and about the size of my palm—and each was carved with the herald of the Iyalet of the Treasury.

I picked one plate up and studied it in the weak light. Its tiny lettering read *ONE THOUSAND TALINTS OF THE GREAT AND HEAVENLY EMPIRE OF KHANUM.*

I set the silver plate down, feeling faint. I had only ever heard of thousand-talint coins but had never seen one. I'd certainly never expected to touch one.

I turned the coin over, thinking. Then I took out my small knife and ran the point along its face, gouging it. The interior was silver as well. A true imperial talint, then.

I took the remainder of the coins out and stacked them on the floor before me. If I was seeing correctly, there were now seven thousand imperial talints here, which was surely more money than I'd ever see in all my days.

I sat on the floor, now weak in the knees, my heart fluttering in my chest. What was this strange little house? And what in hell was going on?

I returned to the box and took out the little leather bag. I untied it gently, worried what improbable thing it might contain. Perhaps a piece of titan bone, I thought, or the keys to the emperor's Sanctum.

But the first item that tumbled out was not nearly so interesting: it was an imperial wall pass, a little leather booklet containing a metal symbol indicating the bearer possessed the right to pass through the third wall of the Empire and to travel from the Outer Rim to the third ring. Written within the front cover in official blue inks was the name *Rona Aristan.* I flipped through the pages, reading the seals from the third-ring cantons she had visited; the third ring was far more rigorous about contagion than the Outer Rim, and tracked all visitors carefully.

Rona Aristan, it seemed, had visited four cantons within the third ring again and again: the Qabirga, Juldiz, Bekinis, and Mitral cantons. She must have traveled to each one at least once per year over the past nine years.

I grunted in surprise and summoned the map of the Empire in my mind. These four cantons were mostly plains country, devoted to growing grain and reagents behind the safety of the walls. What a Talagray Engineering secretary was doing traveling to such places was beyond me. But then, neither could I comprehend how she'd died, nor why she'd hidden seven thousand-talint coins in an empty house mere streets away from where she'd lived.

I set the wall pass down on the table, then reached back into the little leather bag and pulled out the final item within. I paused as I saw it, for this one was more familiar than the rest.

I held it up to the dim light: a small, bronze disc with a little glass vial set in the center, sloshing with black fluid.

A reagents key. Another one, a *third* one, after the two Miljin and I had found. But this key was far less ornate than the one the ten dead Engineers had possessed, and featured only one vial, suggesting it was intended for a much less protected portal.

I studied the three very different valuables placed on the floor before me: the reagents key, the wall pass, and the seven thousand talints.

"Hum," I said aloud.

Not knowing what else to do, I opened up my engraver's satchel and carefully placed them all inside, using a kerchief to cover the silver coins and prevent them from clinking and clanking. Then I buckled my satchel tight, exited and locked the door behind me, and slipped away into the drizzle, sprinting back to the Trinity as the final curfew bells began to ring.

CHAPTER 17

|||

WHEN I FINISHED MY REPORT TO ANA, I WAS SLIGHTLY pleased when she just sat there on the edge of her bed, boggled. She opened her mouth to speak; then paused, rethinking her words; and then she did so again, and again, like she had so many questions for me she wasn't able to get any one of them past her lips.

Finally, she managed to say, "Let me see one of those talints."

I slipped out one of the huge silver coins and handed it over to her. She turned it about in her hands. "So . . . let me get this straight, Din," she said. "You have . . . just been walking around the city . . . with *seven thousand talints* in your bag? Like they were cabbages for the cooking pot?"

"Ah . . . yes, ma'am?"

"By Sanctum," she said. "And people think *I'm* fucking mad! And you didn't slip an extra one in your boot or something, did you?"

"Ah . . . no, ma'am. That seems a good way to invite more hell into my life, when I already have hell aplenty."

"How encouraging it is to see you show wisdom! But . . . but this has been nothing short of an utter vomit of revelations! Secret meetings! A missing survivor! Murdered secretaries making secret journeys across the Empire! And not only a sack containing a goddamn fortune, but *three* reagents keys discovered in one day?" She fumed for a moment. "Well. Well! I shall need to do some *deep immersion* to make sense of all this."

She stood.

"Deep what now?" I asked.

"It's been awhile since I was driven to such means," she grumbled. She walked to one of her enormous trunks full of books, stooped, and began dumping them out by the armload. "But if any situation calls for it, it's this one." She did a double take, glaring at me. "Don't just watch me toil here, boy. Help me!"

I did so, scooping out the books until the trunk was empty. It was one of Ana's few personal possessions, a massive, battered old thing she'd insisted on bringing with her; though now that it was empty, I saw that the interior bottom was not made of wood, but appeared to be cushioned, almost like a bed for some animal.

"Shan't be a moment," said Ana. She slipped on her blindfold. "I just need to meditate on this for a bit before deciding the course of action. The solitude helps me ponder." She climbed into the massive trunk and sat down. "You can wait here. Just don't touch too much of my damned stuff. I *will* know what's been moved!"

"But, ma'am," I said. "What are you going t—"

She snapped the trunk door shut on herself. I stared at it, bewildered. Then came a soft *thump* from within, as if she was making herself comfortable, and all fell to silence.

I looked around, unsure what to do. The silence stretched on.

My eye fell on the sack of talints at my feet, and I reflected that now I really could just walk away with them, if I liked. Yet I decided that the odds of a solitary young criminal with a huge fortune on his person making it through a highly patrolled road that was often pestered with murderous deserters would either be slim to none or none at all. So instead of committing robbery, I made tea.

I opened Ana's window and sat beside it, sipping my tea and drinking in the nightscape of Talagray again. After all I'd discovered today, being in the city felt hardly safer than any of my idle fantasies of theft and escape. This place was meant to be the keystone of all the Empire; and yet, in one day, I'd found it rotten to the core.

Then, with a *snap*, Ana's trunk popped open, and she sat up like a cursed soul from the grave. She paused as she felt the slight breeze in the room. "Shut that damned window!" she barked. "What are you trying to do to me, child? I'm attempting to *think*!"

I fumbled to do so, spilling tea on my Iudex coat, then slammed the shutters closed like there was a torrential rain outside, rather than a peaceful evening. "Apologies, ma'am. Didn't mean t—"

"One needs isolation for the mind to focus," she snapped at me. "If you want to get no work done, get an office with a beautiful view. But if you want to parse all your problems, yo—*fuck*." She slipped on one of her piles of papers as she stepped out, and barely caught herself on the side of the trunk. She then finished climbing out and grumbled for a moment. "Well. Did you make tea, Din?"

"Yes, ma'am."

"Then I'll have a cup."

She sat down on the bed as I poured her one.

"First . . . I have a question." She fixed me in a fearsome glare. "I want answers about something *you* did."

"Ah. Y-yes, ma'am? Did I do something wrong?"

"Yes! Very wrong! Why the *hell* didn't you tell me you knew how to pick locks?"

"Oh," I said sheepishly. "Well. I don't really know how, ma'am. I just memorized the movements to unlock three basic types of locks."

She stared at me, outraged. "That . . . that is basically the goddamn definition of 'knows how to pick locks,' boy! What an absurd thing! What the hell else do you know how to do?"

I handed her the cup. "I do seem to be developing a talent for tolerating verbal abuse and mad questions, ma'am."

She glared at me again. "I wish to know more of your lockpicking, Din . . . But for now, let's start dissecting all this, beginning with this Captain Kiz Jolgalgan. For she is of great interest to me."

"Since she might be our only witness for the poisoning?" I asked.

A long slurp of tea. "No. Because I rather like her for being our murderer."

I stared at her as she dabbed her lips on her cloak.

"Beg pardon?" I asked.

"I mean, who's more experienced than anyone with contagions?" Ana mused. "Apoths. And now you're telling me an Apoth was going to all these secret meetings with the Engineers? And is now possibly the *lone* survivor?"

"You . . . you really think this Jolgalgan might be our poisoner, ma'am?"

"Possibly!" said Ana. "I don't have all the answers yet, of course. Dunno why she'd want to kill all her friends, or why she chose the maddest fucking method ever to do it. Or, indeed, if she also intended to bring down the sea wall and imperil the whole of the goddamn Empire, too! But . . . it hangs! Though it is but a scrap of information, it hangs together, a bit. Captain Miljin has surely notified the Legion to keep an eye out for this Jolgalgan by now. But please get ahold of Nusis tomorrow, Din, and see what the Apoths can dig up on her. They must have files on the woman's alterations. I want to know what Jolgalgan can do, where she's been, what capacities she's served in, and anyone and everyone who might have served alongside her. Let us see if my hunch is right."

"Understood," I said.

"Good. Next—the reagents keys! Show them to me, please."

I slid them both out—the one Miljin and I had found in Jilki's quarters, and the one I'd found in the empty house near Aristan's residence—and gave them to her.

"What an odd thing, to find three in one day . . ." Ana held Jilki's key to her eye. "But Miljin wasn't wrong. This key is for a *highly* warded portal. I believe only Imperial Treasury banks require five or more reagents . . . Fascinating. But this other one . . ." She did the same to the second one, peering through it like a tiny spyglass. "It's not the same at all. So plain, and so simple . . . Sanctum knows what portal it's for." She chewed her lip for a moment, then held up the advanced one I'd found in Jilki's quarters. "But I actually think I know what *this* one goes to—for surely it must unlock the place where all our Engineers were poisoned."

I nodded. "Whatever room or building or chamber where they were all meeting secretly."

"Exactly. Which is quite a find! Good work. If all is going aright, Captain Strovi should be out in Talagray now, collecting all the fernpaper orders for all the millers for the past four weeks. If we find one place that suddenly had to replace all their fernpaper . . . and if that place *also* happens to have a reagents portal, and if this key successfully *opens* it . . ."

My blood began to tick inside my ears. "Then that has to be the place of the poisoning."

"Yes! And you've also gotten us a timeline for all this, dear Din— eight nights before the breach, the sixth of this month. If that all lines up, we can then see if this missing Jolgalgan was present at that place, at that time—and what she did there, and where she's gone. And, perhaps, how she connects to Commander Blas's murder, over two weeks ago now."

My eye wandered back to the sack of talints. "I . . . don't suppose all that money has something to do with it, ma'am?"

"Though it feels obvious, I . . . am unsure," she sighed. "In fact, your discoveries about Blas are so great, they almost make my head a little heavy . . . For suddenly he's not just somewhat corrupt, allowing the Hazas to treat him to lewd holidays at their houses—but is in fact possibly the most corrupt Imperial officer in recent memory! And I worry . . . What if this corruption doesn't stop at Blas?" She turned her blindfolded head toward the closed window. "What if other officials are just as complicit as he is?"

There was a tense silence.

I felt my skin crawl as I realized what she meant. "You mean . . . the investigation team? You're worried about our own colleagues?"

"I am," she said quietly. "The investigation thus far does not seem to have been well managed here. Blas *should* have been looked at. Aristan's body *should* have been discovered before now. But I am reluctant to assume maliciousness when incompetence is a better explanation . . . Hm. Let me see the wall pass."

I handed it over to her as well. She flipped through it rapidly, fingers dancing across the pages. "What a dirty bunch of business! Business that apparently required Blas to store money in a place far less official than, say, a box at an Imperial Treasury bank, where a commander wielding such sums would be noticed. And if Madam Aristan was traveling back and forth between Talagray and these four distant cantons—Qabirga, Juldiz, Bekinis, and Mitral . . . Well." She shut the wall pass with the snap. "She must've been the bag man."

"The . . . the what, ma'am?"

"The courier, the person who carries the money. Blas must have been sending her to the third ring to either pay people off or take payments from them. A better courier you'd never find—for who'd look twice at an elderly Iyalet secretary? Yet—what was Blas paying or getting paid *for*? What the hell was the bastard *doing*? We don't know yet. But it eats at me."

She rocked back and forth for a moment, head cocked, yellow eyes thin. I stayed silent, letting her ponder.

"Well, Din," she said. "I now have another question for you."

"Y-yes, ma'am?"

She pushed up her blindfold until one yellow eye peered at me from beneath it. "What do you think the odds are that Rona Aristan and Commander Blas were killed by the *same* person?"

I considered it, my eyes fluttering as I summoned all my memories. I thought about it for a long while.

"I think . . . I think very low, ma'am?" I said finally.

She nodded, satisfied. "And why is that?"

"One murder was . . . well, more efficient. More typical. They broke in and . . . and did something to the victim's head. Stabbed it, perhaps. And no one even knew anything had happened. But the other was more elaborate and required far more work. Planning well in advance. And a method of murder most unusual. They seem too different."

"Erupting from within due to a sudden vegetal growth is, I concede, pretty fucking unusual," Ana said acidly. "But I think you are right. We now have *two* murderers, Din. Two murderers with two different methods, and two very different sets of interests. The most obvious conclusion for this new murderer is that they are here to *clean up*. Blas is dead, but his connections to all this dirtiness still exist. Thus, they are here to eliminate anything that could connect Blas with this greater corruption . . . including any human beings who are inconveniently alive."

"But . . . we have no idea who this new murderer could be—correct, ma'am?"

Ana went very, very still, her head bowed. "A hole in her head, you told me . . ." she said softly. "Tell me—was it very small?" She held up her fingers about a quarter smallspan across. "This big, say?"

"Yes, ma'am. Thereabout."

"And there were no other bruises or wounding to the body?"

"None that I could see, ma'am."

"How peculiar," she whispered. "Do . . . do you know how difficult it is to pierce the human skull, Din?"

"I, ah, have never attempted it myself, ma'am."

"It is *quite* difficult. It takes abnormal strength and speed to do so. Especially *speed*. The velocity required, and the proper tools . . . It's all rather stunning, you see."

There was another silence, like she'd fallen into a reverie.

"Have you seen deaths like this before, ma'am?" I asked slowly. "Or rather, murders?"

She did not answer for some time. When she spoke again, her voice was low and soft: "Here is what we shall do. First, you're going to take this to Nusis tomorrow." She held up the simple reagents key I'd found in Aristan's safehouse.

I took it from her. "What will she want with this?"

"Well, while I have a good idea what the other key opens, I've no idea for this one at all. And Apoths have arts that can reverse engineer many reagents. We can't learn which exact portal this key opens, but Nusis will be able to tell us what *kind* of portal it opens. The make of the portal, the breed—that may help us narrow the search."

"All right. And the money, ma'am?"

"The money and the wall pass we shall . . . use," she said slowly. "We shall use it to determine if our colleagues on this investigation are true and faithful servants of the Empire. For I still worry, Din— why did they not look into Blas? Why did they not seek out Aristan? These are very common procedural tasks! Did someone on the team *know* Aristan had been murdered? Did they *know* Blas was so wildly corrupt?" She cocked her head. "Could Kalista be false? She seems to have a taste for things rich and fine. Or perhaps it is Nusis? For she worked alongside Blas on the Preservationist Boards. Or is Uhad, so old and feeble, willing to be paid for some comfort in his later days? Or perhaps Miljin? Or is none of it malfeasance, and all of it is simple ineptitude? I do not know."

A tense silence. I felt a terrible sense of dread brewing in me.

"And . . . how shall we use the money to answer any of those questions, ma'am?" I asked.

"Oh, well, Din." She smiled wearily. "You're going to take that money and that wall pass . . . and you're going to stick it with Aristan's corpse. Someplace where it is easily found. Then I shall ask Uhad to investigate . . . and we shall see how much of that money makes it back to us."

I gaped at her in horror. "First you want me to run off on our own investigation—now you want me to *fabricate* a murder scene?"

"Oh, it's not too much fabrication," she said, waving a hand. "I'm not asking you to fucking kill someone, or something! Consider it simply a very unusual method of submitting evidence to the investigation."

"But . . . I mean . . . we've barely been here a day, ma'am," I protested. "And you're already investigating the investigators?"

"Well, yes," she snapped. "Because *we're* the fucking *Iudex*, Din! We're the ones who watch the Empire on *behalf* of the Empire! And something here feels dreadfully wrong! Perhaps it is the breach, perhaps it is incompetence, or . . . perhaps it is something else. But I must know, if we are to move forward."

"And what am I doing for this performance, ma'am?" I asked. "Should I just accompany Miljin to Aristan's house and act surprised at all we see?"

She thought about it. "Good point. You're a bit of a shit liar, Din. Here—I shall tell them I've sent you to see Nusis, have them send Miljin to investigate, and I shall just personally stick close to Uhad and the others to see what happens. It'll be *very* taxing for me—all that small conversation—but this is rather important . . ."

"And if I get caught manipulating a crime scene?" I said angrily. "And am clapped in irons, and stripped of my rank and position?"

"Then I will speak to Vashta," she said simply. "And make my position known."

I stared at her, incredulous, but she seemed quite serious. "You're going to, what, talk down the seneschal? Tell her your mind?"

Ana went very still then. She seemed to turn these words over within her mind, testing how they fit. Then she grinned horribly and leaned forward; and I saw a strange, unsettling light in her eyes that I had not seen before: one I did not wish to look at, let alone challenge.

"I would!" she said cheerily. "I would tell her all I knew. And she would come to agree with our deeds. For who would not, Din? We are here to review the foundations of the Empire's defenses—and that, of course, begins with testing the resolve of its most important officers. Now go, boy, and sleep. If you can."

CHAPTER 18

|||

THE NEXT MORNING I AROSE BEFORE DAWN, DRESSED, picked up the bag containing the thousands of talints and the wall pass—it felt very heavy now—and went downstairs and slipped into the streets.

Once again, Talagray was rumbling to life with countless esteemed and veteran officers beginning their duty. I felt terribly self-conscious as I walked among them, trying to control my gait, my posture, my bearing. Was I walking too fast? Did anyone hear that soft *clink* from my bag? Yet no one had any mind for me at all. There were far more greater things to care about in this place than I.

I'd left the back door to Aristan's house unlocked, so it was a simple thing to open it and slip inside. Once again, I was battered with the awful reek of corpse-stink. I prowled through the house like a common burglar and found Aristan still in her bedroom, the toes of her bare feet still purple and curling.

I stared at her body, heart beating. Then I glanced around the room, wondering where to hide a fortune where Miljin and Uhad might find it. Yet I remembered: I'd seen Miljin search a room just the other day, hadn't I? I knew his methods.

I walked to the other side of the bed, crouched, unsheathed my knife, and pried up a floorboard. There was not much room below but still room enough. I carefully placed the seven thick coins below, along with the wall pass. Then I replaced the board, paced back to the backdoor, cracked it to confirm the lane beyond was empty, and departed, my heart still fluttering in my ribcage.

I made it back to the Iudex tower before midmorning, climbed the steps, and knocked five times on Ana's door—the signal that that job was done. I was met with a lilting "Thank you!" then ran back down the stairs, suddenly worried any one of these officers might stop me.

Yet they did not. I dabbed sweat from my brow as I continued on to the next task.

How queer it suddenly felt: I'd been a model officer for almost all my career, but I had to join the Iudex to become a true criminal.

"ARE YOU ALL RIGHT, SIGNUM?" asked Nusis. "You look a little antsy."

"P-pardon, ma'am?" I said, startled. I wiped more sweat from my brow and glanced around her office, as if worried someone else might have noticed. "Oh. I apologize."

"Oh, don't," Nusis said. "I was just worried it might be a reaction to your new immunities grafts. Or, maybe it might be something you caught out on the Plains of the Path." She leaned forward over her desk, interested. "Have you felt any curious flickering sensations when you defecate, perhaps?"

I wondered what to say to that. "I think it might just be the stress of the job, ma'am," I said honestly.

"I see . . . Well, if you need any stimulants or sedatives, let me know. I've got a variety here, and most are very safe. Now . . . you have a reagents key for me, I think?"

I handed over the plain little bronze disc I'd found in Rona Aristan's empty house. "Yes, ma'am. Found it yesterday among the possessions of the individuals we were investigating. I was hoping you could check it for me." I sweated slightly, though nothing I said was a lie.

Nusis studied the little key. She no longer seemed like the cheery red flicker-thrush as I'd come to think of her, for she moved slower, and she looked like she hadn't slept in some time. The cause was clear: there were piles of parchments mounded on her desk, enough to challenge even Ana's usual seas of texts. It had taken me hours to get in to see her, as well: apparently whatever she was working on was even more important than a visit from the Iudex.

"Hmm," Nusis said, peering at the key. "This one is rather shabbily made. Simple bronze, with tin prongs and a crude bridge. Very amateurish. I don't perceive any gaseous emissions of note . . . though they may be masked by my specimens."

She gestured at the many vials and tanks around her laboratory-like office. I eyed one of the many worms thoughtfully inspecting the seal of its glass prison.

She sniffed the vial. "I can't catch much scent here that I recognize, unfortunately. But then, I am not altered for aromatics, only vision. But I can run it under the usual tests—exposing it to telltale plants and fungi and the like, which will react if there is anything pheromonally interesting. Could that do?"

"Whatever you can do to assist, ma'am," I said.

"Very good. Now . . ." She sighed. "The other business. Captain Kiz Jolgalgan, correct?"

"That's correct, ma'am." I nodded at the papers and said, "I hope this isn't all about her."

"This? Oh, no. These are Preservation Board approvals. The Legion is preparing a new armament to combat the titans after the breach. Lots of grafts and alterations go with it—mostly explosives." She gestured along her back wall, where glass jars containing a dark powder sat in a row. "Some kind of bombard. I'm to review and process the paperwork confirming that none of these alterations can escape the canton and cause havoc." She cast a bleary eye over the remaining parchments. "But paperwork is a task I'm well accustomed to. I manage paper more than reagents these days. Now, I am curious . . . why did you ask about this Jolgalgan?"

I explained the interviews with the Engineers from yesterday, and all I'd learned with Miljin.

Nusis's expression grew somber, so much so that I forgot about my own anxieties. "I see," she said carefully. "Well. I regret to inform you that everyone who knew Captain Jolgalgan is dead."

"Dead? Truly, ma'am?"

"Yes. She was a member of the Twelfth Cohort of the Apoths. And *all* of that cohort died at Sapfir, during the breach. Can't even recover their bodies. Horrid thing. You will have no one to interview, I'm afraid."

"But Jolgalgan," I said. "Is she also . . ."

"Her status is . . . a different matter." Nusis pivoted to her safe, then paused. "Might you avert your eyes again, please, Signum?"

I did so while she again went through the laborious process of unlocking her safe. She popped it open and slid out a scroll of parchment. Then she took the reagents key from her desk and placed it in the safe, next to all her boxes of immunities grafts. "Might as well keep that in here for now . . . I mean, it is evidence, yes? Anyway. I went ahead and fetched Jolgalgan's alteration papers for you . . . She's a Sublime, like you and I. An axiom, inducted and altered some six years ago in the Kurmin canton. Scored very high on her exams. Something else you two have in common, I think."

I coughed and nodded.

"But Jolgalgan always demonstrated—how shall I put this— issues of the psyche," said Nusis delicately.

"Issues?" I asked.

"Anger. Fits of rage. And anxiety, and paranoia. She was a hard worker, but she was hard to work *with*. She has had a pattern of complaints and outbursts throughout her career."

I opened my engraver's satchel. "Is it all right if I . . ."

"Be my guest," said Nusis.

I selected the ash-scented vial again and sniffed at it, anchoring this conversation in my memories. "What was wrong with her?" I said. "Something to do with her alterations?"

"No," she said. "No. It is not that."

I watched her. Eyes still, mouth fixed in a soft frown. She had gone somewhere far away in her mind, I felt. I waited.

"You are aware, Signum," she said, "that I was assigned to be on this investigation team because I served in Oypat."

"Yes, ma'am."

"And what *do* you know of Oypat?"

"I'd never heard of it until Blas. I learned it had been a canton that had been consumed by dappleglass, the same contagion that's been wielded as a weapon here. That is all of it."

"Well . . . I will tell you now, Kol, that what happened in Oypat made many people fear alterations as much as the titans. With good reason. I was a junior officer then, barely out of Sublime training. Axiom," she said, tapping her head. "Figures and mathematics."

"I remember, ma'am."

"Of course you do. I worked on the environmental monitoring team during Oypat, ensuring that no dappleglass escaped the territory. I peered through a spyglass day after day, watching distant hills being eaten by grass. And then in the afternoon, when I served in the medikkers' wards, I saw people having the grass cut from them—tangles in their kidneys, in their lungs, in their uteri. Many more died, of course. Especially after we sealed the whole thing up. They never made it out." She shifted uncomfortably in her seat. "Those that did survive were resettled by the Iudex. And some . . . some of the Oypati say that it wasn't the dappleglass that killed their home. They say it was us. That we imperials killed them with our lethargy. But that isn't so. We tried. It was just too complex. The great and heavenly world is just all too complex, sometimes."

"I see," I said. "But—what's this to do with Jolgalgan, ma'am?"

"You have heard that Jolgalgan has a curious look to her," she said. "Yellow, curly hair. Yes?"

"Yes, ma'am?"

"That is because though she has a Kurmini last name, the captain was not born to a Kurmini family. She was adopted. Her birth name was *Prarasta*. An uncommon name—mostly because all the people who'd normally have such a name are now dispersed or dead." She fixed me in a sad gaze. "Jolgalgan was *Oypati*, you see. She escaped the dying canton when she was a child. Lost her parents. And was resettled. Such a history . . . Well, it's no wonder she displayed afflictions of the psyche."

I felt my skin break out in goosebumps. "I notice, ma'am, that you haven't told me whether Jolgalgan died with her cohort."

"I haven't," she said. "Because Captain Jolgalgan has been missing for weeks." She handed the scroll of parchment out to me. "She vanished just a few days before the assassination of Commander Blas, as a matter of fact. And just before so many Engineers suddenly started dying of the very contagion that killed her canton. Curious—isn't it?"

CHAPTER 19

|||

IT WAS LATE AFTERNOON WHEN I RACED ACROSS THE
Iudex tower atrium, Jolgalgan's parchments rustling in my pocket. I
felt I looked quite a sight, but then I saw Captain Miljin doing the
same, sprinting across the atrium, though he was going out rather
than in.

He skidded to a stop as he passed me. "Kol!" he breathed. "Where
the devil . . ."

I took in his flush face, his wild eyes. Instantly I knew he had
found Aristan.

I fought to keep my voice steady, and asked, "What's going on,
sir?"

"We've just found the *maddest* mess of shit, simply the *maddest*
thing, but . . ." Miljin looked back out the door. "But I have business
to tend to. Go and ask your immunis. She can fill you in!" Then he
dashed away, moving surprisingly fast for a man of his age.

I watched him go. I wondered if Ana's little experiment had
yielded results.

I raced up the stairs for the second time that day, my head spilling
over with thoughts. Yet when I came to Ana's door, I paused.

Voices from inside: hers, then a man's. Soft, not agitated—or at
least not yet.

I knocked. The customary singing "Come!"

I opened the door. Young Captain Kepheus Strovi sat in a chair in the middle of the room, dressed in Legion blacks with his legs crossed—a casual pose, like he was perfectly at home here. He looked over his shoulder and his eyes widened slightly when he saw me.

I stopped short at the sight of him. It took me a moment to recall he was meant to be helping Ana find information on all the fernpaper millers in Talagray.

I looked about for Ana but couldn't find her. Then the overpowering scent of fish struck my nostrils, and I heard her voice: "Din! What good timing. Strovi here has just brought me all those fernpaper orders I'd requested."

I looked down. Ana was lying on the floor on her back at Strovi's feet, half-concealed in a pile of parchments, blindfolded as usual. To her left was a tray containing the remains of a fish, salted and piled with herbs, the flesh so pink it must have never known flame.

"Why are you . . ." I said.

"On the floor?" she said. "I can feel the movements of this tower better from here, Din, reading the wind and the weather with my back." She grinned. "It's marvelous. You ought to try it sometime."

Strovi was watching me with a half smile on his face, amused by the madness of it all. He was not nearly as disheveled as he'd looked that night when he and Vashta had come to Daretana: now he was clean-shaven, his mop of curly dark hair was elegantly clipped back, and his black cloak was pressed and his boots polished. Between his size and his vitality he seemed to take up the whole of the room, even sprawled in a chair with Ana on the floor beside him.

There was a ceramic cup in his lap and a pot of tea on the table beside him. I took off my straw cone hat, bowed to him, and entered. Then I glanced into the teapot—half empty—and laid a finger against its side. It was cool to the touch.

"He's *just* brought you your orders, ma'am?" I asked. "From the shape of things, he's been here awhile. You've been interrogating him, haven't you."

"It, ah . . ." Strovi cleared his throat. "It has been an hour or so, ma'am. Possibly two. Or, ah, three."

Ana waved a hand, indifferent. "Possibly. It's not very often that I get to parley with a Talagray Legion officer."

"So long as he's here with consent," I said. "And you're being civil, ma'am."

"I'm as civil as a magistrate," she said. "Why, I haven't asked the young captain here about the aroma of his piss once."

Strovi's bemused smile flickered out like a candle flame.

"I just passed Captain Miljin on the way in, ma'am," I said pointedly. "He mentioned some discovery that had been made . . ."

She waved a hand. "And I have little update to give you on it. We shall discuss it later."

I narrowed my eyes. Little update? Did she now think our colleagues above suspicion?

"Strovi here was telling me, Din," said Ana languidly, "that the Legion is digging through the old history books for how to get us out of this damned spot. Nearly sixty years ago the Empire suffered a terrible breach, and the only way they plugged it up was by waiting for a *second* leviathan to approach and slaughtering it directly at the breach point, turning its carcass into an impassible obstacle, and plugging the hole! Isn't that *marvelous*?"

"As marvelous as a massive carcass could be, I suppose, ma'am," I said.

"They'll do it a little differently this time about," she said. Her fingers dug in the flesh of the fish, plucked out a thread of pink tissue, and dropped it in her open mouth. "Rather than using thousands of damn soldiers firing hundreds of ballistas, they're putting together some kind of bombard that can—theoretically—drop a leviathan in one shot. A titan-killer."

"I believe Nusis mentioned something about that to me," I said. I looked to Strovi. "Apparently the bombard requires extensive grafts?"

"For the explosive powder," explained Strovi. "It's a new variant. It has to be much more powerful to punch through one of the beasts. But as much as I enjoy answering all your, ah, *extensive* questions about bombards, ma'am, that's not what Commander-Prificto Vashta has assigned me to do here. Rather, I'm to help with your investigation in any way I can."

"Fascinating." Still lying flat on the floor, Ana snatched up a morsel of fish flesh and held it out to me. "Would you care for a bite of tartun, Din? Strovi said no, but it was just caught today."

I eyed the stringy clump of pink meat hanging from her fingers. "Afraid I have to refrain, ma'am."

"Suit yourself," said Ana. She popped it in her mouth. "What else did Nusis have to say, Din? Something useful about this Jolgalgan?"

"I would say *very* useful, ma'am," I said quietly. I placed Jolgalgan's papers in Ana's lap. Ana sat up and began pawing through them, apparently indifferent to the streaks of fish fat she left on the parchments.

"Start talking, child," Ana said sharply. "Now."

I recounted my conversation with Nusis exactly. Captain Strovi's eyes grew wider the more I spoke, and Ana pawed ever faster at the parchments in her lap.

There was a beat of silence as I finished.

Then the captain exclaimed, "You have it, then! You've found her, yes? This Jolgalgan surely is our culprit! What amazing work!"

I nodded to him stiffly. I'd never gotten such a compliment from a senior officer of another Iyalet before, especially not the Legion, and did not quite know how to handle it.

"You know," said Ana thoughtfully, "I am inclined to agree . . ."

"I still have trouble comprehending the why, ma'am," I said. "Why kill so many Engineers in such a fashion?"

"Well, it was the Engineers and the Apoths who were supposed to stop the dappleglass outbreak in Oypat, yes?" said Ana. "And, no offense to our absent colleagues, but they didn't do a very good job, being as the whole fucking canton's dead now. Just as Nusis said, many Oypati hold a bitter grudge. It takes little effort to imagine what horrors a mad Apoth Oypati with a grudge might be capable of. I'm not quite sure what killing a bunch of junior officers might accomplish, but . . . she continues to be an *excellent* suspect, really." She cocked her head. "The only question is . . . why now?"

"What might you mean, ma'am?" said Strovi.

"She's been serving as an Apoth for years. I wonder . . . What set her off? And where is she now?"

"The Legion moves swiftly," said Strovi. "We watch all gates and roads. We shall find her soon enough, of that I am sure."

"Perhaps," said Ana. "But if she really is our killer, she's clever, and skilled at evasion. She used dernpaste to hide her features, and knew how to move across country quickly. And we've no idea where she is now. But we now seem to really be getting somewhere, boys! We possibly have a *who*. Kind of think we have a *how*—for, presumably, Jolgalgan came to one of these secret meetings of Engineers and poisoned them all there. And thanks to your and Miljin's work yesterday, Din, we also have a *when*—the Engineers were poisoned eight days before the breach, the date of their last meeting, the sixth of Kyuz. Now we just need the *where*. And Strovi here has already given us the materials we need to solve the rest!" She turned her blindfolded face to him. "These orders are from every fernpaper miller in the city, correct, Captain?"

"Yes, ma'am," said Strovi. "All we could find."

"And we're looking for *big* orders. All conducted on or about eight days before the breach—the day of the poisoning." She pursed her mouth, chewing on an especially tough piece of gristle, then said, "There are, I think, four options."

Strovi looked startled. "Y-you've already read them all, ma'am?"

"Our conversation was interesting, Captain," she said. "But not so interesting as to occupy the *whole* of my attention . . ." Still blindfolded, she snatched up four different papers, walked over on her knees, fumbled to find Strovi's legs, and then stuffed the papers into his lap. Then she leaned forward to search the top one with her fingers until she pointed to a line. "This mill here—Ostrok's? See it? Order for four panels, nine days before the breach."

Strovi looked positively alarmed to have Ana invade his space so thoroughly, her head hovering over his knees as she pressed her index finger into the papers atop his crotch. "Ahh. Y-yes, ma'am," he said. "I see it."

"And then this one here." She jabbed at the paper, hard. Strovi twitched. "Rakmon. *Six* fernpaper panels, ordered five days before the breach."

"Y-yes, an—"

"And then *this* one." Another jab, this one very hard. Strovi yelped slightly.

"Ana!" I said.

"Mm?" she said. "What is it, Din?"

"I rather think he believes you. Yes, Captain?"

Strovi nodded vigorously. "Y-yes. Very much so. Totally do, ma'am."

"Oh," she said mildly. She slid out from his lap and waved the papers about, yawning. "Anyways. These are the first three options that fit the timeline that Din has so helpfully provided. But I don't think any of them are the best candidates."

"But . . . are you suggesting, ma'am," said Strovi, still shaken, "that you can remember *all* of the fernpaper orders I just gave to you? And you can just summon up any one of them in your memory as you please?"

Ana grinned. "I remember and analyze all things *interesting,* Captain. And this has kept me interested. Thus far, at least."

I smirked, for I was familiar with this line. But I wondered—was Ana actually an engraver? Was that her augmentation? Was she now mentally summoning all the words she'd read with her fingers as she'd lain on that floor? Yet that didn't seem right. Though engravers like myself could instantly recall huge amounts of information, we couldn't make the wild jumps of intuition that Ana seemed so prone to.

"I will say I am more interested in what's *not* on these lists," Ana continued, "than what *is*. There are a few shops, Strovi, that did not respond to your inquiries. Despite you sending some goddamn Legionnaires to their doorstep. Including this shop," she said. A finger stabbed out, nearly piercing one parchment on the floor. "The fernpaper miller Yonas Suberek. This man did *not* answer your summons and was marked absent."

Strovi looked bewildered. "Ah . . . I was not there for that inquiry, ma'am, so I will have to take your word for that. But all we can do is inquire. We can't compel people to be present and answe—"

"And yet!" she said. She ripped another parchment out from the pile and slapped it with the back of her hand. "His neighbor was *another* miller. Fellow by the name of Linz Kestip. Now, *Kestip* dutifully gave you all of his most recent fernpaper orders . . . including one order that actually came from his neighbor, this absent Suberek! A transfer of inventory, in a way, from Kestip to Suberek. For six fernpaper panels! That's *quite* a lot. This is the fourth order I mentioned. And this is our best candidate."

Strovi, mystified by this rush of names and dates and numbers, looked to me for help.

I sighed and asked, "Ma'am . . . What's the significance of all this?"

"The significance, Din, is the *size* of the order," she said. "Kestip sold this now-missing Suberek a lot of fernpaper, and at a high price. Almost as if Suberek had gotten a very, very big order of his own, larger than his own inventory, that he was in a hurry to fill." She turned to me, grinning. "And then there is the date. For this transaction took place *seven days* before the breach."

Comprehension wriggled into my skull. "The day after we think the ten Engineers were poisoned . . ." I said.

"Yes. Suberek was apparently given a very big, frantic fernpaper order from some mysterious person *just* after the Engineers were poisoned. So big was this order, in fact, that he had to buy some panels off of his neighbor to fulfill it! It's rather like how the groundskeeper hurried to replace the fernpaper door just after Commander Blas was poisoned—but far, far larger. And yet now, why . . . Suberek doesn't answer the door, even when the Legion comes knocking."

Strovi sat forward, looking alarmed.

"You think this Suberek might be in danger, ma'am?" I asked.

"I would at least like to discover his whereabouts," she said. "And I would like to find out where this order was *sent* to. For that site is likely either where this Jolgalgan brought her poison, or where the poisoning itself happened." Her blindfolded face turned to Strovi. "It's late afternoon now. We've burned up almost all the day just digging through papers. I shall notify the rest of the investigation team of what we've found—but the curfew extends to everyone in the city except Legion personnel, correct?"

"That's correct, ma'am," he said.

"Then I would like to see if you could escort young Din here to this Suberek's fernpaper mill to check in on him. And bring the Engineers' reagents key as well, Din—just in case you find out where that order went." She raised a finger. "But before you go, Din—a word?"

I WAITED FOR the door to shut before asking, "How went today, ma'am?"

"Inconclusive," she sighed. "Miljin found the corpse, and the money, and the wall pass. He was outraged and shocked. He then brought it to Uhad, who was similarly outraged and shocked. Uhad showed it to Kalista, who was *also* very outraged and shocked. Then Miljin departed to bring Nusis in—I suspect you passed him as he left—and I expect she, too, will be appropriately outraged and shocked. I have done a lot of insipid pretending today, Din, but I have not yet detected a false note from any of our colleagues. All have reacted as they should."

"Then do you trust them now?"

"Oh, no. I continue to feel something is amiss here. I just don't know what it is. Yet still—tonight, stay sharp. We must establish the death scene, and there is most certainly *someone* out there who wishes you not do that. Strovi seems a solid sort, but . . . keep your hand close to your sword."

I paused. "My sword is, ah . . . still made of wood, ma'am."

She frowned and cocked her head. "Oh. Well . . . in that case, make sure your boots are laced up proper, boy, so you can run like hell."

CHAPTER 20

|||

STROVI AND I EXITED THE TOWER JUST AS THE CUR-
few bells stopped ringing. The streets of the city were now silent and
empty, the buildings half lit by a moon shrouded in clouds. There
were no lanterns or lights to be seen, except for the one swinging
from Strovi's hand and those carried by the patrolling Legionnaires.

If I'd not had Strovi striding along with me I'd have been locked
up within twenty paces: each time a Legionnaire spotted us, they'd
hurriedly advance, then pause at the sight of the captain, bow, salute,
and let us proceed. Strovi would often shout a word of encouragement to them, or clap them on the back and bid them farewell. In the
dark of that night, he seemed far older and more at ease than I. I had
to remind myself we were almost the same age.

"Deserters," he said to me at one corner, almost apologetically.

"Beg pardon, sir?" I said.

"That's why there's so many patrols. Streets aren't often safe at
night. Too many mutineers and deserters trickling back from the
walls, trying to make it out of the canton. Captain Miljin might have
acted a bit mad with you yesterday, flashing his sword about, but
he wasn't wrong when he mentioned that. They hide in houses in the
day and move by night."

I tried and failed to suppress a yawn. "I-I . . . I see, sir. I'll take
note."

He smiled sympathetically. "Tired?"

"Somewhat, sir. I'm not used to sleeping so high up in a tower. Especially one that moves with the wind."

"Let us stop at a station, then. I could use a hotfoot myself."

He led me to the next corner, where a huge black canvas tent had been set up in the street. Legion officers in varying states of armor milled about before it, resting, regrouping, or receiving orders. Though I was tall, most of these men were taller, thicker, stronger than I, augmented chaps who could cleave me in two if they so much as tried. Yet they all saluted Strovi as the captain led me through to the back, bowing their heads and tapping their collarbones respectfully.

At the back sat a clay stove, the fire within bright and flickering. Three young boys squatted nearby, tending to the flames and boiling pots of water. Strovi held up two fingers to them, and they poured us two cups of tea, then grabbed a clay cask and dropped in a healthy finger of sotwine to each.

Strovi held his cup up to me. "Hotfoot. Clar-tea and mulled sot. We'll be dancing and prancing for hours now, Kol. Chin to roof."

He tossed his cup back and I did the same. It was hot and acrid and sweet, but not unpleasant. Instantly I felt warmth fill my bones, and then I felt a strange bubbling at the bottom of my brain, as if it were cooking in a pot.

Strovi grinned as he saw my face. "The Apoths have made many amazing alterations, but this strain of clar-herb is my favorite."

We tarried in the warmth of the fire, drinking the dregs of our tea—"The last sip," Strovi commented, "you could practically chew"—while the captain politely inquired about my time in the Iudex, and Daretana, and with Ana. It felt quite strange: I hadn't had such casual conversation with anyone in months—certainly not with Ana—but definitely not with someone like Strovi, who seemed to embody the full bloom of imperial service. The man's movements were easy and graceful, and his face was handsome and noble, with a laugh that never entirely left his pale green eyes.

"Nice to have a bit of civilization, isn't it?" he said as we finished. "The only thing missing is a puff of pipe."

"Oh. Wait a moment, sir," I said. I reached into my pocket and produced the half of a shootstraw pipe Miljin had given me.

Strovi laughed. "What magic! I've half a mind to ask what else you hide in there." He waved to one of the boys, and they brought over a hot iron from the fire. Strovi held it to the tip of the pipe and sucked at it until its end flared hot. Then he drew deeply and savored the smoke, letting it leak out of his nostrils. "I haven't tasted such a fine bit of weed in ages. Where did you get this?"

"From Miljin," I said. Then: "Or, really, from a Signum Vartas, who happily volunteered his pipe after Miljin, ah, threatened castration and disembowelment."

Strovi laughed dully. "The old man hasn't changed, then. The iron fist in the iron glove, about as subtle as six blows from a hammer."

"You might say that, sir."

"Don't have to be so formal, Kol. I mean—I'm following your lead here, a bit, aren't I?"

I didn't know how to answer that. The idea of such a veteran officer following me was baffling.

He held out the pipe to me. "Go on. It's yours, I shouldn't take it."

I took the pipe from him and drew deeply, my lips touching where his had been. I had never smoked before—I couldn't afford such a habit—but I found myself reveling in the taste of the smoke, the way it seemed to twirl in my belly like a dancer.

"This," I said, "is something I could get used to."

He laughed. "You look quite at home here, with your cone hat and your shootstraw pipe!"

"Then I only look it, sir. It's not at all where I expected to be. Last month I was earning my dispensation by chasing down pay fraud."

"It's not so uncommon, though." Strovi looked out at all the Legionnaires, all coming and going in the light of the flickering fire. "So many come here by so many roads, having made deals or signed contracts or bartered away some bit of their life for a bundle of talints. Yet when they're here, standing among one another, and they realize what we hold back . . . That's when they see."

"See what, sir?"

"What the Empire really is." He grinned at me. "Those walls out there—some stretches are four hundred years old. Made back when the Khanum still walked these lands in full force. Planned and wrought and manned by ancient peoples, some of them far stranger than anything the Apoths could brew up now. And since those first stones were laid, no leviathan has ever walked the Titan's Path again, has never made it into the inner recesses of the land. And none has *ever* approached the Valley of Khanum. Because of how we suffer, and labor, and serve." His grin grew rather dreamy. "The Empire is the people next to you, and before you. Bodies in boots on the wall, taking up posts served by the ancients. We are the fulcrum on which the rest of the Empire pivots. And we are all made equal and common in that service, and before its long history." He paused. "Though perhaps I'm being sentimental."

"I'd say Talagray could use some more sentiment," I said honestly. "Especially after all we've discovered, sir."

"Ha! But no need to be so formal." The smile faded from his lips. "I mean, you call your immunis by her first name."

"Ana is . . . different, sir. As you've no doubt seen."

"Yes, but." His smile was gone now. "You're not in my Iyalet. I could be different, too. You could just call me Kepheus, if you liked."

A strangely earnest look stole over his face, and his eyes searched mine. Despite his warm words he suddenly seemed terribly lonely, standing there in the light of the fires, his curls clinging to his temples. I reminded myself to stay controlled and contained.

"Never mind," he said suddenly. "Perhaps I overstepped. Apologies. We should continue on, yes?"

I nodded and followed him into the night.

BY THE TIME we got to Suberek's neighborhood it was fully dark. As Ana had suggested, Suberek's fernpaper mill was one of many in this industrial section of town, which was stacked with tall, narrow wooden structures built next to the canals, all using the water's trickle to power their many wheels and mechanisms. The mills were all quite similar, with stables and large doors at the back for the loading of their wagons. The great wheels hung still and blue and ghostly in the starlight. It must have made a merry scene in the day, but tonight it was strange and spectral.

Strovi pointed into the dark. "That one at the end. That's it."

I studied Suberek's mill carefully. Utterly dark, no trace of light within. Fernpaper walls clean and thick, framed by stonewood posts. A sturdy structure that should withstand the fiercest of quakes.

"I'll knock," said Strovi, as we approached, "but I am empowered by the Legion to enter by force if unanswered. So if we can't get in, I shall break in, to make sure this fellow still lives. That make sense?"

"Yes, sir," I said.

A gleaming grin. "Should be entertaining. I expect this will be the first time you've ever broken into a house."

I chose not to answer that.

Strovi strode up to Suberek's front door, lantern raised high in his hand. As I followed, the mill's stables rose into view. The shadows behind the fence posts flickered and shivered in Strovi's light, making it feel like all the darkness was shifting there. Perhaps it was the clar-tea running through my blood, but I liked it not at all.

Strovi raised a hand to knock as I stared into the stables. Yet then I noticed something and snatched his hand before his knuckles struck the door.

"What is it?" he asked.

I nodded toward the stables, where the gate was standing slightly ajar. Then I gestured to the other mills, whose stable gates were firmly shut.

"Gate's left open," I whispered. "Doesn't seem right."

Strovi looked at them, then at me. He nodded, drew his sword, and together we approached the stables.

The little yard within was utterly abandoned, no pony or mule or hog to pull any cart. A few hints of manure, most of it soft from the rains. I touched the hay piled in the corner and found it soft and mildewed. Smelled it and caught the scent of fungus. Days old at least.

I gestured to Strovi to lower the lantern, and when he did I read the mud at our feet. There I saw the scars and shapes of many footprints, mostly boots, many larger than my own—but no hoofprints of any kind, no animals. And it had just rained today, as my wet clothes could testify.

I looked at the mill again, thinking. Studied the windows, wondering if I might spy some movement within.

Then the wind shifted, rose. I caught an aroma in the air, faint but powerful. As the wind died it vanished, but I recognized it: the scent of rot, and putrefaction.

I kept staring at the house. I felt my blood dancing in my ears, felt sweat trickling on my back, the wooden sword at my side heavy and sagging.

Strovi's face was pale in the lantern light. "Something's wrong," he whispered.

It wasn't a question, but I nodded. Then I crept to the side door, knelt, pressed my nose close to the bottom gap, and inhaled.

The aroma of death was overpowering—a familiar one, after Aristan's house. My eyes watered, and it took all my effort not to cough or gag.

I withdrew from the door and crossed to the corner of the stables.

Strovi followed, lantern held high. "What is it?" he whispered.

"Something is dead inside," I said softly.

His eyes grew wide. "Sanctum . . . You're sure?"

"Yes, sir. And no animal's been in these stables for days. Yet here, many boot prints. It rained mere hours ago. So they are very recent—but the death inside is not."

Strovi turned to the house, head cocked. Then he placed the lantern on the ground and shut its chimney, killing its light.

"They're still in there," he whispered. "Aren't they."

I said nothing.

"I shall go and fetch a Legion patrol," he said. "They'll come and we can round them up."

I looked down at the lantern at our feet, thinking. Panic began unspooling in my belly.

"Wait. Open the light back up," I said.

"What? Damn it all, they'll see the light!"

"They'll have *already* seen the light, from the front windows. They'd have seen us come."

"So?"

"So if the light's suddenly gone out, and they didn't see it leave, then they'll worry, and—"

Then the side door opened, and they came out.

I COUNTED FIVE of them in the dark, large men in light armor, their buckles and buttons winking in the dim light—along with the points of their swords, of course.

Imperial longswords. Bright and glimmering. Finely made tools for quick and easy killing. They offered no shout or cry of warning. They just advanced, swords unsheathed.

Strovi reacted much faster than I, raising his weapon to guard position quickly. His attacker moved in, swinging his sword in a diagonal downward slash, left to right. Strovi caught the blow with his blade and stepped forward into his stance, and I watched him, waiting to see if the gallant captain would live more than a second longer. But then a second attacker was on me, his sword raised high, and all I could think about was the edge of his blade.

I watched the sword approach, unable to comprehend or believe what was happening—and then my eyes shivered and trembled.

Everything slowed down.

I read the swords and the feet and the positions of their shoulders of all those about me. Angles of wrists, of knees, of hips. Grips and crossguards and the tilt of a sword's edge. I read it all, engraved it all . . .

And then I was moved.

This was the only word for it: I did not move, but rather my muscles moved me, like my skeleton was being thoughtlessly shoved about by the flesh around it.

I leapt backward as my attacker approached, mindful of the stable wall behind me. Then I drew my wooden blade, raised it with both hands, and caught the attacker's blow, my right elbow angled high.

My attacker's sword should have cut clean through my practice weapon, yet I had angled it in just such a way that his sword did not cut straight through, but rather at an angle to it, as if trying to shave off the edge. This meant his sword got lodged within my own, trapped inside my wood and leaden blade. My attacker grunted in surprise, evidently not expecting such a thing.

My eyes fluttered. Memories of my training poured into my mind, and my muscles.

Instantly I recalled my old dueling coach Princeps Trof bellowing—*Stop a swing at the right position, children, and you open up the whole of their body. And remember—you don't swordfight with just a fucking sword!*

Old Trof had shown us what to do then.

And I remembered.

I was moved, again.

I stepped forward and shoved my right elbow into where I gauged my attacker's throat to be in the darkness, as hard as I could. My elbow instead met the crunch of cartilage, and the splash of hot blood—his nose.

A howl in the darkness, but I had no attention for it: my muscles were moving me, guiding me mindlessly through the countless dueling steps I'd learned so many months ago. I reached forward with my left hand, grabbed my attacker's wrist, wrenched down, and used my own sword to twist his blade to his left.

His grip broke, and his sword fell free. I snatched the handle as my attacker fell back, wrenched his imperial longsword out of my shabby wooden one, and assumed a two-handed stance.

I had a sword now, a real one, for the first time in my imperial career.

I surveyed the darkened yard before me.

Strovi was still on his feet, engaged with two attackers. The one I'd disarmed was crumpled to my right. A fourth approached me to my left, growling and swinging his longsword across his body from left to right, intending to strike me on the shoulder or neck.

My eyes fluttered. Read the movement, read the position.

His choice, I saw, was a bad one.

Old Trof's voice in my ear—*A fight with blades is all about exposure and leverages! Which swings and slashes and cuts offer your opponent the most openings? Where and when can a movement be stopped? Where shall the sword's path start and end? This is the language of steel, my children!*

My muscles were moving me again, stepping me forward with my sword straight upright to catch my attacker's blade before it could cross their body.

The steels struck, the reverberations dancing up my wrist. Yet because I had stopped the swing so early, the whole of his body was open to me.

Three smallspan, cried Trof's voice in my memories. *Three smallspan, my children! A sword point must only penetrate three smallspan deep on the trunk or neck of a person to disable and kill them. Don't do any more fucking work than you have to!*

I angled my blade to my left, trapping the strong of their sword against my crossguard; and then I jabbed the point left and up, and into their throat.

A cough, a gurgle, and the hot splash of blood in the dark. A salty flavor in my mouth, a stinging in my eyes. I blinked, and the figure fell backward into darkness.

I kept moving.

Another man was coming on my right, screaming, thrusting forward with his sword. If I had been even slightly slower he would have scored a devastating hit; yet I was jittering with clar-tea, and my eyes recognized the movement, and my muscles summoned up the memory of when Trof had forced me to train against such an attack.

I danced to the right, away from the path of his blade. I hacked down hard against the narrow of his blade, putting maximal twist on his grip (*The grip, children,* screamed old Trof in my ears, *is always, always the weakest point of all fights!*), and then I kept moving forward and hacked down again, this time closer to his crossguard, trusting that my destabilizing blow would make it too hard to respond.

I felt the crunch of the bones in his hands, my blade perhaps severing a thumb. He cried out, swung around, and tried to raise his sword with his good hand, but it was too late. My muscles shoved me forward, thrusting my blade into his shoulder; and then, when he turned, into the side of his knee. He collapsed into the mud, shrieking.

A grunt to my right. The man whose nose I'd broken was charging at me, howling. No sword in his hand. I responded instantly, thoughtlessly: a simple jab into his midsection, near the neck, then dancing back. He staggered, tried to turn to see me, and kicked over Strovi's mai-lantern as he did so. Blue light strobed the yard as the lantern fell open, and I saw him clearly: a man of thirty or forty, nose broken and dribbling blood, and blood spurting from the deep gash just below his left collarbone.

He locked eyes with me, mouth working. A piteous, lost look, as if he'd awoken from a bad dream. Then he fell to the side.

I was moving again, being moved, being pulled, dancing through the muddy yard. Strovi was there in the corner, still fighting two men at once, both with their backs to me.

Trof's voice in my mind, screaming, howling—*Rathras cavalry knew that when chasing down fleeing souls, strike at the backs of their knees with a spear! Down them first, then kill them!*

I watched almost helplessly as my sword licked forward, its point diving down to shred the tissue at the back of the man's knee. But then . . .

My left heel met slick mud. My foot slid forward. Instantly, I was sent sprawling in the mud and crashed into one of the attacker's legs.

The man turned, snarling. I saw him raise his blade, its point aimed at my chest.

Then there was a flash of blood from the side of his throat. I felt my face fanned with warmth and wetness. Then he toppled over, stupidly pawing at his neck, and I saw Captain Strovi behind him, his blade black with blood.

I did not see how Strovi felled the final attacker. My eyes were filled with blood, and my head was reeling from where it'd struck the mud. Yet as I sat up, I was aware of only Strovi standing in the yard, his chest heaving as he sucked air into his body, and somewhere the sound of moaning.

I staggered to my feet, then stared around, dazed. The memories of my training withdrew from my body like a veil.

"Who . . . who are these people?" I mumbled.

"Who are they?" said Strovi. "Who are *you*?"

"What?"

"Where the hell did you learn to fight like that?" he demanded. "You killed, what, two men? And disabled another?"

"I . . . I just recalled my training," I said, taken aback.

"You just . . . just *recalled* it? Your *basic* training?"

"Yes. Why?"

He shook his head, stewing for a moment. "These are Legion deserters. You can tell by their uniforms. They must have been holed up in the house. I never would have thought to see a day when an Iudexii could outfight a Legionnaire, let alone three of them, but . . ." Another shake of his head. "Hell. I'll go get a patrol. You stay here. Got it?"

I nodded. Then he sprinted away into the streets.

CHAPTER 21

|||

THE LEGION PATROL CAME TO DEAL WITH THE DE-
serters, and I left the scene in the stables and wandered into the mill,
the smell of rot all about me. It was a cavernous, dark place, with
bundles of fernpaper drooping in great clumps along the posts. Weak
starlight dribbled through a high window, and the skeletons of machinery crouched in the corners. It felt like I was in a tomb, but I was
so stunned I didn't care. I slumped into a chair in the dark and just
sat, listening to the mutterings and calls of the soldiers outside.

My eyes fluttered, shook. I remembered the spray of blood on my
face, the saline taste in my mouth. The way that one man's mouth had
worked stupidly in the lamplight, his eyes so confused and hurt.
Every part of my body was sticky and crackling with drying blood. It
was best to not move at all.

Strovi returned, his mai-lantern held high. He glanced about the
room and set the lantern on the table, his sweat-gleamed face a smear
of light in the dark.

"Did you see a way down, Kol?" he asked.

"A way down?" I said weakly.

"Down into the basement. You haven't looked about?"

I shook my head.

He stared off into the darkness. "I talked to them. They said there
was something there, when they broke in," he said. "The deserters
thought this place abandoned and broke in through a window. But

then they went to the basement, and . . ." He swallowed. "I've sent word to the Iudex. The whole investigation team should be here soon—Uhad and all. For now . . ." He wiped his face with a trembling hand. "I think you should engrave the room. Look at it like your immunis might want you to. Yes?"

I stared ahead. I could hear his words but could not comprehend them.

"Din?" he said. "Din!"

"What?" I said quietly.

"You need to get up and look!" he snapped. "This is a death scene! Get up and . . . Oh, damn it all . . ."

He grabbed me by the front of my shirt and hauled me to my feet. Then he looked into my face, his gaze compassionate yet desperate, and pulled a handkerchief from his pocket.

"That was your first fight, wasn't it?" he said.

I said nothing. Answering such questions seemed pointless.

"By hell, you're a mess." He gently wiped my face of blood, using the cloth to swab my eyes, my nose, my mouth. Then he sighed and said, "Your sword."

"My what?"

"The sword. You need to clean it. It won't do to sheathe it bloody. It's dishonorable."

I looked down and saw the sword still clutched in my bloodied hand. I'd had no idea I still held the thing. I watched as he gingerly took me by the wrist, pulled the sword free from my hand, and wiped down the blade with his bloody handkerchief.

"There," he said. "Not perfect, but . . . It'll do."

I stuck it in my sheath, yet it did not fit: the sheath was too short, leaving at least four smallspan of blade exposed.

"Is . . . is that not your sword, Din?" he asked.

"Had a wooden sword," I said. "Lost it in the fight."

"You *what*?"

"I haven't graduated yet, you see, sir. Still an apprentice."

We both stared at the sword sticking out of the scabbard. Then he burst out laughing.

"By Sanctum!" he cried. "What a thing, what a thing!"

Despite everything, I smiled.

STROVI LEFT ME again to go deal with the bodies, and once I got ahold of myself I studied the mill. It was a strange, complex place, with vats and presses and belts and all sorts of machineries, all for the purpose of boiling, starching, and pressing bundles of parch-ferns until they formed the panels so used in this region of the Empire. Though I knew all this, I had no idea how such a place might actually function.

But I knew what we had come here for: we wished to find out who had placed such a large order of fernpaper just after the night when all the Engineers had likely been poisoned—as well as what had happened to this Suberek who supposedly lived here.

I glanced at a darkened hallway at the end of the room. The stench of rot was very strong there, and blackflies crawled upon the ceiling and walls.

"I'll do you last," I whispered to the dark.

I dug through the counters and cabinets looking for documents or papers, anywhere this Suberek might have written down an order, a name, or an address of a place. I found nothing but tools and materials for millery. Besides this, the machines, and the giant, scarred old worktable in the center of the room, there was nothing.

I searched the side rooms. An old cot and blanket. A rickety stove brimming with ashes. Tools for shaving and the mending of clothes. Suberek, it seemed, had lived alone.

I looked back at the darkened hallway.

The whine of flies. The pounding stink of rot.

I picked up Strovi's lantern, took a deep breath, and walked down the hallway.

The hall narrowed off rapidly, leading to a small hatch, with a ladder leading down. Yet as I approached the ladder, I saw the air was moving.

No, not moving: shimmering and shivering. It was boiling with blackflies, all pouring out of the hatch with the ladder.

I braced myself, looped the lantern over one hand, and descended into the darkness.

The stench of decay grew so awful it made my eyes weep. The world swirled with insects, all furious at my passage. Yet as I reached the bottom of the basement I held the lantern up and looked.

It was a small space for the storage of tools and materials. Scraps of fernpaper to be reprocessed. Wood frames and pieces of presses. And there, at the far end of the basement, a human figure, seated and facing away from me.

I stared at the figure, obscured by a thick veil of flies. Then I steeled myself and walked forward, and the black veil reluctantly parted.

It was a man's body, broad shouldered and thick and roughly dressed. His shoulders and back were black with old blood, though I could see no wound—not yet. I found it all very familiar.

I knelt down and held the lantern up to the corpse's head.

There, at the base of the skull, was a tiny, dark hole. Just like the one I'd found on Aristan's corpse.

I looked at the man's face, engraving what I saw: large nose, broken repeatedly in the past; scanty beard; thick eyebrows; one false tooth the color of pewter. Yonas Suberek, I guessed, our missing miller. I could find nothing more to learn from his body.

I studied the rest of the basement, digging through the junk and the refuse in search of anything else of interest. I found nothing.

A hoarse, harsh voice from above—Miljin's. "Kol!" he bellowed. "You down there, boy?"

"Yes, sir!" I said, popping up.

His gray-maned face appeared in the ladder hatch. "Damn. There's no way I could fit down here . . ." He blinked, waved flies from his face, then narrowed his eyes. "And you're down there with a dead fella, by the stink of it."

"Yes, sir," I said. "This Suberek, I think. Man who owned the mill. He's dead."

"How?"

"Hole in his head, sir. Like someone drilled it."

His eyes narrowed. "Hole in his head . . . Sanctum. That's just like the other."

I nodded, attempting to look solemn. "Aristan, yes. Ana told me about her."

He squinted at me. "Strovi tells me you're the one who put those bodies in the mud out there. That so?"

"Two should be the captain's, sir. The others are . . . mine, I suppose, yes."

His face went strangely shuttered. "Interesting . . . And he said you just remembered. Is that it?"

"Remembered my training. Yes, sir."

"Interesting," he said again. "Hmph. Then let's get you out of there. Whole crew's arriving now. They'll be hollering for answers soon, no doubt."

CHAPTER 22

|||

"IT ALL BEGINS TO SHOW," SAID UHAD WEARILY, "a rather appalling pattern."

I glanced about the room as we listened. All of the primary team was there, standing amid the shadowy machinery of the little mill: Uhad leaned gloomily at the head of the worktable, like a starving blue stork staring into a fishless creek; seated to his right was Ana, blindfolded and bent, her fingers probing the indentations and scars on the worktable surface; across from Ana sat Nusis, still pert and cheery and nodding even at this late hour, her red coat pressed and impeccable; and there at the back of the workshop, half-lost in the bunches of drying parchfern, stood Kalista, somehow glamorous and glittering despite all the gloom about her, her clay pipe clutched in her mouth. She seemed to very much resent being brought here: the courtesan dove sulking in its cage, perhaps.

"We can now safely conclude we are pursuing *two* killers, I think," said Uhad. "One who kills with dappleglass, and one who kills with a spike to the skull. The dappleglass killer has apparently vanished, but this new one appears to still be about . . . and killing quite enthusiastically." He paused, his face grim. "Yet before we speculate further, I would prefer a more experienced eye review this most recent body." He turned to Nusis. "I believe as an Apoth, Immunis, you are somewhat used to the handling of cadavers . . ."

Nusis's cheery smile vanished. She sighed, shrugged off her red

Apoth's coat, carefully folded it, and laid it on her chair. "I shall go see," she said, then retreated into the reeking hallways.

"Won't you need a lantern?" called Miljin after her.

"No," said her voice in answer. "I can see perfectly well in the dark."

There was a surprised silence. Then Miljin scoffed and shook his head. "Damn Apoths . . ."

"Are we *sure* that we have two killers?" asked Kalista. "The first person felled by this spike to the skull was Blas's secretary, yes. And that seems likely related to Blas's own horrid corruption, eliminating anyone who might know things they oughtn't. But why Suberek? Why murder a simple fernpaper miller?"

"I cannot imagine," confessed Uhad. "Unless Blas talked to this fernpaper miller . . . Yet that challenges the imagination."

Ana cocked her head, grinning. "Or we are being too conservative in our estimation of 'cleaning up'!"

All eyes slowly turned to her.

"What might you mean by that?" asked Uhad.

She shrugged. "Perhaps there is someone out there who does not want us finding out how or when or where any of these poisonings took place—for that would lead to yet *more* discoveries of corruption. If we assume that, and also assume Suberek provided fernpaper to help cover up the killings . . . well, then it would make very good sense to kill him!"

There was an uneasy silence.

"If that is so," said Uhad, "we must find the destination of Suberek's last delivery."

"Agreed," said Ana. "Din—before you join the search . . ." She held up a finger. "A word, please."

I moved to her as the others started to dig through the mill. "Yes, ma'am?"

"I would like for you to take me to the stables, if only for a moment."

I held out my arm. She grasped it and I led her outside.

III

THE BODIES WERE gone now. All that was left was mud, blood, and the handful of Legion officers standing at the wall.

Ana stopped in the middle of the yard, face still angled to me, pale and cadaverous in the moonlight. "How are you doing? Are you well?"

"I'm all right, ma'am," I said.

"What? Absurd. People tried to kill you, and you apparently killed them instead. How could you possibly be all right?"

"It was all very fast," I said quietly. "I didn't think at all while it . . . while it happened."

There was a short silence, broken only by the muttering of the Legionnaires just past the gate.

"Well, you aren't limping," she said tersely. "Your pulse in your arm is strong and steady. And you aren't gasping for breath. So you're not hurt."

"I'd have told you if I was, ma'am."

"Yes, but you're the dutiful sort of stupid young man who would hide an injury out of honor," she snapped. "And I wished to be *sure.*"

I looked at her, surprised at the anger in her voice. Her wiry fingers dug into my arm like she was trying to hold me still.

"Have I done something wrong, ma'am?" I asked.

"Miljin said you killed two and disabled one," she said. "Is that correct?"

"Possibly. I . . . I didn't stay to confirm," I said stiffly.

"He also said Strovi claims you fought *remarkably* well. That you said you *remembered* how to fight. Is that correct?"

"Yes, ma'am."

"Describe it," she said sharply. "Describe how that felt."

I did so, struggling to articulate the queer feeling of my muscles remembering the movements, and then moving me about through space like I were furniture being moved in a room.

She nodded when I finished. "And back in Daretana. The way you made tea for me—you did it the *exact* same way, every time. Right down to the turn of the pestle."

"Pardon, ma'am?"

"And then later, when Uxos tried to kill me. You moved quickly and attacked him quickly. Practically without thinking at all."

I said nothing.

"And then there is your lockpicking," she said. "You do not remember how to do it, exactly. You simply remember the *movements*."

"Have I done something wrong, ma'am?" I asked again.

"No. But you've done something *interesting*. And to be honest, of all the things I'd expected to find interesting here, Din, I had not thought you'd be among them. Nor had I wished you to be. Thank Sanctum they were only deserters! When I first heard you'd been attacked at Suberek's, I . . . I thought . . ."

"Thought what?"

She shook her head. Even though she was blindfolded, I could see fear in her face—the first time I'd ever seen any fear in it at all.

"It's nothing," she said.

"Doesn't seem to be nothing, ma'am."

"Well, it is, damn it! And now that I think of it, you *did* do something wrong, Din! You *should* have checked the building *completely* before going down into that basement!"

"Why?" I said.

"Because you didn't know if you were truly alone in the house!" she said. "There could have been someone else in there *with* you, and you might not have known! Another deserter or . . . or something worse. You need to be smarter, child. I don't get on well without an assistant, and I damned sure don't want to lose you now!" She poked me in the chest. "People have been killed in this city for knowing things they shouldn't—like Suberek! And Aristan! Yet it is our job to know things. Act accordingly to make sure you aren't cleaned up as well!"

"You think this new killer is foolish enough to come after an Iudex officer, ma'am?"

"Of course. Of course!"

That flicker of fear to her face again. I remembered what Miljin had told me: *Rumor has it, Dolabra's previous assistant investigator ran into the wrong end of a sword* . . .

"Now focus, boy," said Ana. "Let us search the mill *carefully*. And try not to make it too hard for me to keep you alive!"

WE SEARCHED THE MILL for an hour, all together. We could find almost no writing at all: no documents, no ledgers, no bills of sale, nothing. The only thing of note was Nusis's report as she emerged from the basement of the mill. "A perforation at the base of the skull—and based on the bleeding of the man's left eye, the weapon nearly penetrated straight through. A spike of some kind, I think. For the edges of the perforation are quite smooth."

"Then that would suggest the murderer is physically augmented, yes?" said Uhad. He nodded toward Miljin. "Perhaps like the captain here."

I glanced at Miljin—yet I saw he was staring at Ana, a worried look on his face.

"I would say so, yes," said Nusis. "A very powerful individual— but not a large one. Not if they could fit in that basement. No crackler or augmented Legionnaire could manage that, I think. It's very strange."

"Disturbing . . ." Uhad sighed and rubbed at his eyes. "Yet we still don't know where Suberek sent his last shipment of fernpaper."

"I can't find a damn thing," said Kalista around her pipe. Her breath shivered with smoke as she spoke. "This *is* a professional, surely. They removed everything of note. From the look of it, I almost doubt if Suberek knew how to write."

Ana rocked forward, her hands still probing the workshop table. "No," she said softly. "He knew how to write. And he did a lot of it right here."

There was a long silence as everyone turned to look at her, her hands placed on the slab of wood like a reedwitch telling fortunes at a canton fair.

"You . . ." Kalista laughed, incredulous. "You aren't suggesting you can . . . You can, what, *feel* what was written there?"

"I can feel many things," said Ana quietly. "He was a very hard writer, you see. Pressed his ashpen with tremendous force . . . The tricky thing is identifying what was *recent*." Her index finger paused on one spot of the scarred table. "Here, for example . . . Wrote down an order for two panels . . . Dated sometime in the month of Hajnal. I *think*. Tricky to read this . . ."

Uhad looked to Nusis. "Is this really possible?"

"Of course," said Nusis. "I know some sensitivity grafts help sculptors and surgeons find the weaknesses in many materials."

"If we get a length of ashpen," said Ana, "and a sheet of thin fern-paper, I can discover more."

Miljin and I fetched these for her. Then we watched as Ana carefully ran the length of ashpen over the scarred table, covering its surface with a layer of fine, black powder.

"And now the paper . . ." she said.

Like gentry servants laying down a table spread, we took a thin sheet of fernpaper and slowly placed it on the table. Then Ana took a piece of shootstraw and ran it back and forth, pressing every inch of the paper to the table.

"There," she said. "Now if we take it away . . ."

Miljin and I lifted the paper and turned it over. Everyone gasped quietly—for there on the other side it was all black and gray, yet it was covered in mangled white writings, like the inverse of an imprint.

"Probably looks a mess," said Ana. "The trick is to look for which bit of writing is *clearest*. That will be the most recent one. The last thing Suberek ever wrote in his life, probably . . . And I hope that will tell us where he delivered his order."

I was utterly useless here—normal writing shivered horribly to my eyes, and this was even less clear—but Miljin, Uhad, Nusis, and Kalista crouched over the paper, studying it like it was some holy text, until Nusis, whose eyes were best, pointed to one corner.

"Here . . ." she said quietly. "This looks promising. A good bit of writing, running over all the others . . . Very hard, and very clear. Like what they were writing mattered."

Miljin squinted at it. "Yeah . . . not an address. It almost looks like directions."

"Yes." Nusis held the lantern close. "*North on Ekipti* . . ." she read aloud. "Then this next bit I can't read at all . . . But then here. *West on Petros.* Then a right, and a right . . . And then it seems to stop."

I summoned the map of Talagray in my mind, and found the street quickly. "It's directing us to a long road running north and south on the west end of the city," I said. "It had no names on any maps I've seen. But that must have been where Suberek brought his last shipment."

Uhad turned away, his expression deeply troubled. "I know this road," he said quietly. "That is where the gentryfolk reside."

"And Din," said Ana, "has a *very* expensive reagents key." She looked at me—not a grin, but a small, clever smirk. "Perhaps he and Miljin ought to go to this street and see which door it opens?"

MILJIN AND I trooped off into the streets, rejoined by Strovi, for it was still dark and we needed his privileges to pass. We strode on, following the directions I had engraved in my memory, leaving the fortifications of the east and the fretvine towers behind, and approaching the gentle, rising hills in the west, where the city sprawled out.

"Gentryfolk . . ." Miljin shook his head. "Of all the people to be caught up in this, this puts bad water in my belly."

"Why's that, sir?" I asked.

"You probably don't see too many of their ilk in Daretana," he said. "But gentryfolk wield enormous powers in the Empire. You own a lot of farmland, you get a lot of say with the people who matter." He glanced at Strovi. "Though the captain here knows this better than I, surely."

Strovi said nothing. I gave Miljin a quizzical look.

"Strovi comes from a gentry family," Miljin confided to me. "Very important folk in the west of the Tala canton, y'see."

I turned to Strovi, surprised. He glanced at me sidelong—I noticed he wasn't smiling as he so often did. "I am Legion first and foremost, Miljin," he said stiffly. "Just as you were. And I am proud of it."

"True." Miljin bowed to him theatrically. "Your record and bravery are beyond reproach. But that is why you've no great augmentations—yes, Captain?"

Strovi's face colored slightly. "Miljin . . ."

"Too many augmentations makes it damned hard to engender children," said Miljin to me, offhandedly. "And the Strovi clan has every intention of extending their line, of course."

"Damn it, Miljin," snapped Strovi. "Mind your own affairs!"

I cleared my throat. "Perhaps," I said, "it'd be better if we focused on the case at hand . . ."

Miljin snorted and gazed at the hills before us. "The case, yes . . . Though I grow pessimistic. If the gentry is tangled up in this, Kol, things shall get tricky fast."

Dawn bloomed in the east, and I began to see what he meant: atop the hills before us were many enormous, fine houses, gabled and bedecked with mai-lanterns and encircled by high fretvine walls. Many featured tall bird-perch gates before the houses—ceremonial, double-beamed structures wrought of wood and painted bright red. I had heard of them before, and was aware they indicated gentry-hood, and the emperor's favor. They were so closely entwined with the gentry that the symbol of them was often painted on gentry contracts: two perpendicular lines with two sloping, arched lines running between them. I was frankly awed by the sight of them, and the grand houses behind them.

Miljin spat on the ground. "You can smell the money in the air here. Blow your nose and talints shall come tumbling out."

We continued walking along the gentry road. Tall walls ran on either side of us, fencing off the gentrylands. Each one was paired with a main gate—a common construction of wood and iron—as well as a reagents gate, allowing servants to come and go at any hour. I approached these carefully, my reagents key held out. They were amazing constructions in their own right, often made of twisted roots or flowering fungi or coils of vines, all awaiting the proper key, and the proper signal.

But not the one I bore. Though we walked along the gentry road until the sun broke free of the horizon, none of the reagent gates opened to me.

"Odd to say this failure brightens my mood," muttered Miljin. "I hope we walk this street and find naught at all."

Then Strovi spoke, in a strangled voice: "There is one gate remaining."

Miljin looked at him, puzzled. Then his expression gave way to horror. "Titan's taint. I pray it isn't . . ."

I saw the gate ahead. It was enormous and towering, a huge, curious, coiling root that plugged up the opening in the wall, layered with tendrils of bright yellow vines and dotted with green growths.

I approached it slowly, the Engineers' reagents key held out before me. The vines trickled, twitched. The massive root trembled. And then, as if it were a living knot, the whole thing slowly unwound, falling away, leaving the entry clear, and through the rounded gap I glimpsed dark green hills, and there in the distance a many-gabled house that was nothing short of palatial, standing amid tall, white-trunked trees that shone in the light of the dawning sun.

How familiar it felt. Almost the same as that day in Daretana when I had gone to see Blas's body.

My eye fell upon the bird-perch gate before the house, and the insignia painted there: a feather standing between two tall, white trees.

My eyes fluttered. I had engraved that sight within my memory mere weeks ago.

It felt the same as that day in Daretana, I realized—because in many ways it *was* the same.

"By hell," muttered Strovi. "The halls of the Hazas . . . The Engineers were meeting *there*?"

"Of all the fucking places," Miljin said grimly, "it just had to be this one." He spat on the ground. "That damned house sees more important people than the Senate of the Sanctum. We are about to go dallying in the affairs of the mighty, friends."

But though they seemed surprised, I found I was not. It all felt very obvious, now that I thought of it.

I recalled what Ana had said to me just after arresting Uxos: *Blas was in bed with the Hazas . . . and the Hazas definitely have a foothold in the capital of the canton, in Talagray. If we follow this all the way, it may take us there.*

"She knew," I said.

"What?" said Strovi.

"She knew where it had happened," I said. I turned and strode away, and the reagents gate closed behind me. "She has known all along."

CHAPTER 23

|||

THE INVESTIGATION ROOM IN THE IUDEX TOWER hadn't gotten any cleaner in the last few days. If anything, it had gotten filthier, the reek of pipe smoke overpowering, the very air quaking with the fumes of clar-tea. As I staggered back into the room it hardly felt better than the fernpaper mill, shadowy and swimming with corpse-stink.

Uhad, Nusis, and Kalista all looked up at me as I reentered. Only Ana did not, lounging in her chair with a cup of wine in her lap, her expression brimming with barely restrained satisfaction. I hoped she could feel the glare I gave her.

"Well, Signum?" sighed Uhad. "Did you find anything?" His shivering eyes danced over me, then Miljin, then Strovi, taking in our expressions. "I rather think you did . . ."

I bowed and said, "Would you like the whole testimony, sir?"

"Of course."

I started speaking, summoning up each memory, each turn in the road, each gate we tried—rather slowly, since I had not anchored the experiences with a scent—until I finished my tale.

But as I finished, the atmosphere in the room changed, and the three immuni—red, blue, and purple—all reacted.

Nusis's usual helpful smile flickered, then melted, replaced by a look so grave it was like I was reporting her own death. Uhad put his cup of tea down far too hard, spilling the steaming black fluid over

Kalista's pile of parchments. Kalista herself coughed in the middle of
a puff of her pipe, then spasmed, spilling the smoking weed over the
table, where it died with a hiss in the spilled tea.

Then all was still. The only sound was the drips of tea on the floor.
Ana's triumphant smirk slowly faded as well, and she swiveled her
head around as the silence continued.

She began to look alarmed. So I began to feel alarmed.

"You think . . . you think the Engineers were poisoned at the
home of the *Hazas*?" said Uhad faintly.

He looked aghast. I wondered what to say. I had expected this
news to be taken poorly, but not this poorly.

"And you're sure this took place *eight days* before the breach?" said
Kalista. She looked terrified. "The killer did the poisoning *there*? On
that day? At *that* party?"

"Ahh. Party, ma'am?" I said, confused.

"Kalista . . ." said Nusis quietly.

I glanced at Strovi, who looked baffled. Miljin, however, looked
bleakly amused.

Kalista stood up. "Should . . . should I get tested?" she cried. "*Is*
there a test? I mean . . . Hell, do *I* have those spores growing in me
now?"

"Kalista, if you'd been poisoned at the party, we would have
known by now!" said Nusis.

"You mean I'd be *dead* now!" said Kalista.

"Well, yes, obviously!"

"But we don't know how it works!" squawked Kalista. She
clutched her clay pipe so hard it snapped in two. "We don't know
why it . . . why it took so long with the *other* Engineers! And oh, Sanctum, *I'm* an Engineer! They probably tried to do it to me, too, didn't
they?"

Uhad's eyes shivered. He thoughtlessly lifted his empty cup of tea
with one shaking hand and tried to drink from it. "I can recall . . .
recall no staining of fernpaper during the occasion . . . No steam at
all, surely . . ."

"I feel short of breath!" shouted Kalista.

"Kalista!" snapped Nusis. "Will you *listen?*"

"I feel a . . . a stiffness in my lungs, in my person, I . . ."

Ana stood up and clapped her hands twice, very hard. Everyone fell silent.

Then she stared around at them, turning to each of their faces despite being blindfolded. "So," she said. "I take it there was an *event* of some kind at the halls of the Hazas, on this eighth night before the breach. A *party*. Yes?"

They all nodded.

I cleared my throat and said, "They have nodded, ma'am."

"I see," said Ana. "And . . . and *all three of you* were in attendance at this party? Do I have that correct?"

Kalista was so flustered she descended into frantic mutterings. But Uhad sighed and reluctantly said, "True. Yes. If only for a moment . . ."

"But we didn't see any of those Engineers there!" said Nusis quickly. "If we had, we'd obviously have mentioned it!"

"Correct," said Uhad. "*Many* of the upstanding members of the Iyalets were present at the Haza affair, not just us. And attendance is not uncommon. The gentry hold many events. Officers can decline some, but not all—and especially not those of the Hazas."

"Specifics!" snapped Ana. "How many people came to this party? And during what times?"

"A hundred people or more," said Kalista. "And it lasted hours."

"Yet these Engineers were not present, of that I am sure," said Uhad.

"How are you sure?" demanded Ana.

"We've been studying these people's lives for the past days!" said Uhad with a sniff. "I would know if they'd been there!"

"But are you all even aware, Uhad," she thundered, "of what the dead Engineers *looked* like?"

"I . . . I remember names!" said Uhad, affronted. "And I always make sure to get them, given my role."

"And if they gave *false* names?" said Ana. "What then?"

"What is the nature of your tone here, Ana?" Uhad demanded. "It's not like you think *we* killed those Engineers at this party?"

"I've no idea what to think!" said Ana. "But are you not cognizant, all of you, that you now seem to be *witnesses* to not only the poisoning and murders of ten Engineers, but also the inciting act that caused the greatest calamity of the recent imperial era? Have you not *realized* what this means?"

Another long, baleful silence.

"At the very least," said Ana wearily, "it means we now have to get Commander-Prificto Vashta directly involved."

Everyone looked shocked, myself included. We had not yet encountered something grave enough to call her in from her duties as seneschal of the canton.

"Why?" said Uhad.

"Because as I said, you are witnesses!" said Ana. "You cannot investigate *yourselves*! Nor can you *question* yourselves! Especially not if you all are seen to be in pretty good relations with the owners of the house where these people were originally poisoned!" She looked over her shoulder. "Miljin!"

"Yes, ma'am?" he said.

"Go with young Strovi here to tell Vashta we have urgent news. We will need her input to decide how to move further. Move quickly now! We must form a plan of action as fast as we can."

CHAPTER 24

|||

COMMANDER-PRIFICTO VASHTA SAT IN HER CHAIR at the front of the Iudex adjudication chamber, her gray-peppered hair twinkling in the lamplight. I hadn't seen her since that first night in Daretana, but she looked much as I'd remembered: tall, serious, austere, draped in Legion black, watching us keenly like a scribe-hawk studying a mouse.

But then Ana talked. And talked. And as she did, Vashta seemed to age before my very eyes, so much that her back grew bent and her face appeared to blossom with lines.

Finally Ana finished. A silence stretched on.

"I see," said Vashta softly. "Thank you for your report, Immunis."

No one spoke. The commander-prificto simply sat in her chair, blinking as she tried to process all this.

"This ..." Vashta's eyes searched the seats, then stared out the windows, as if hoping to find someone who could help. "This ... this is nothing short," she proclaimed, "of a fucking *disaster.*"

Her words echoed off the fretvine walls and the wood-paneled seats while Ana, Miljin, and I looked on. This chamber was where the Iudex of the canton determined the sentences of its criminals; and though we had done no wrong, I couldn't help but feel that all three of us were about to be punished.

"Four quakes," said Vashta drearily. "Four quakes we've recorded recently, all over the past week. Do you understand what this indicates? A leviathan approaches. It churns its way now through the mud and soil of the sea deeps. It shall attack in the next seven days, perhaps less."

"Dreadful." Ana's head bobbed up and down like a claydove walking about a town square. "Awful."

"To survive the wet season," said Vashta, "we need the Engineers to be functional. We need *Talagray* to be functional. We need all the complex little behaviors it takes to maintain the walls and the bombards and the Legion to keep on whirring and clunking along. And yet . . . and yet, you tell me now that not only are we no closer to identifying who killed those ten Engineers, but that almost the *entire* investigation team is now compromised. *Because,* the poisoning likely took place in a home of one of the most powerful clans in all the Empire! Right as all my investigators were apparently sipping their sotwine nearby!" A horrified pause. "I mean, I . . . I thought you were tracking the Engineers to some secret meetings, Dolabra, or some such devilry?"

"We were, ma'am," said Ana.

"But now you think the Engineers were having these secret meetings at the *halls of the Hazas*? At their *gentry estate*? And this last secret meeting occurred during some sort of *party*?"

"That is as it seems, ma'am," said Ana. "The dead Engineers possessed reagents keys to the Haza gates. I think they were there that day of the Haza party, and that that is where they were poisoned. But how and why, I'm not sure."

The muscles in Vashta's jaw rippled as she gritted her teeth. "Miljin—I feel stupid asking this, but you *can* testify that you at least weren't there, correct?"

"Wasn't there, ma'am," Miljin said. "Don't get invited to fancy gentry parties. P'rhaps on account I lost my dancing shoes."

"That's a damned blessing, then. You are permitted to keep working this, then." Vashta's hands crawled along the surface of her engraved helm in her lap. "*Sen sez imperiya,*" she muttered. "The workings of the Empire must be honest and straightforward. For if the Empire does not work for one, it does not work for all—and then it cannot work to keep the leviathans back." She glared at Ana. "Well. You've done a very good job here, Immunis!"

The bobbing of Ana's head increased. "Thank you, ma'am."

"You have not only identified the likely time and location of the crime—again, all within a few days—but you have managed to utterly unravel any faith I had in the Iyalets in this canton," she said bitterly. "Quite stunning work! As such, I am hoping you can continue to do stunning work."

Ana's fingers flittered in her dress. She knew what was coming. "Of course, ma'am," she said.

"You shall take over as lead investigator," said Vashta. "You must begin by questioning Uhad, Nusis, and Kalista *immediately*. We must get all their testimony right away."

"Certainly," said Ana.

"Good. And there's nothing else you haven't told me yet, is there?" asked Vashta. "You don't have some *other* magic reagents key that might open . . . hell, I don't know, the emperor's undergarment drawer?"

There was an awkward silence. I glanced back at Miljin, who looked on, uncomprehending.

"Well . . ." said Ana.

"You *don't,*" Vashta said flatly.

"I'm afraid we do, ma'am," said Ana. "We have found a second key."

"I was joking!" cried Vashta. "I'll joke no more, if the gods shall hear them as wishes and make them true! Where did you find it?"

Ana then explained all I'd found in Rona Aristan's safehouse. Vashta grew more and more agog with every word, and Miljin looked first outraged and then resigned to hear that we'd all got to it first.

"I always did hear," he muttered as he shook his head, "that working with Dolabra will drive a man mad . . ."

"Do we have any idea how Blas came into all that money?" demanded Vashta. "And how does that relate to his murder, and the murder of all the other Engineers?"

"We don't yet know, ma'am."

"And you're certain this malign influence doesn't spread to any of the other investigators?"

"At the moment, all their involvement seems ill-advised but coincidental, ma'am."

"And what in hell does this new reagents key open?"

"We don't yet know that either, ma'am," said Ana. "It appears far plainer than the Haza key, so I doubt if it shall open anything quite so controversial, but . . . we have given it to Nusis to analyze. I have not yet heard if she has had time to work on it."

Again, Vashta glowered at us. "Get an update from her when you interrogate her next. We must uncover as much as we can about all of this as quickly as possible."

"Understood, ma'am," said Ana. "But . . . first, of course . . ."

"The Hazas," sighed the commander-prificto. "You would like to go to their home, I assume."

"Yes, ma'am."

"And inspect the residence."

"Yes, ma'am."

"And get lists of all their guests and relations present."

"Yes, ma'am."

"And, surely, talk to all their servants and advisers. Like they were simple country folk."

"That would be most preferable, ma'am."

I almost scoffed. Ana could be quite unctuous when attempting humility.

"I have fought back leviathans for five wet seasons," said Vashta quietly. "But at least the titans are straightforward. Yet the gentry . . ."

That is another matter." She fixed Ana again in a cold, steely gaze. "I will do what I can. But I wish you to know this."

"Yes, ma'am?"

"I am seneschal—but only of *this* canton. The Hazas own some of the most verdant, potent lands in all the Empire, in *many* cantons. Without the reagents grown on their properties, defense of the Empire would be impossible. We would have no grafts for stonewood, for slothiks, for cracklers. For healing grafts, for mending pastes, for any of it. Hell, a full twenty percent of all our fretvine grafts come from the Haza lands! So I will consent to this—but you must, and I mean *must*, step carefully."

"Of course, ma'am."

"Particularly if you happen to actually find yourself in the presence of a member of the family! I think it quite unlikely—the Hazas remain very cloistered, especially here on the Outer Rim, where there is so much contagion—but if by chance you happen to meet one of them, I must insist you be polite, thoughtful, obedient, an—"

Then came a hard knock at the chamber door.

Vashta's rage boiled over. "Damn it all!" she bellowed. "I said we were not to be disturbed! Who the hell is it?"

The door opened, and Strovi poked his head in. His boyish face looked anxious—but I could tell Vashta's anger wasn't the cause of it.

"Strovi?" shouted Vashta. "What in hell?"

"Th-there's someone here to see you, ma'am," he said.

"I told you, Captain, we were to be left alone!"

"I know, ma'am. But I knew you would wish to see this person, ma'am."

"Then who is it? The damned emperor?"

"Ah, no. It is Fayazi Haza, ma'am."

Vashta's fury was wiped clean from her face. She gaped at Strovi, then at Ana, then stood.

There was an awful silence as she considered what to do.

"I see," said Vashta. "Well. Let her in, then."

He bowed and opened the door.

Then she walked in.

SHE LOOKED TO be about my age, and she was as tall as I was, with a long neck, enormous purple eyes, and thick, silvery, straight hair that fell in a shining sheet. Eyelids dashed with blue and purple, traceries of red paints about her ears. Lashes as thick as a stonetree's trunk, her snow-white brow encircled by a gray ribbon threaded with pale green. Her pale skin was so unblemished and luminous it almost appeared to shine, cracks of ethereal white peeking through her robes, which covered nearly the whole of her being from the neck down—except her feet, which carefully shuffled forward on tall platform sandals.

She was without doubt the most beautiful thing I had ever seen. Not the most beautiful woman, nor the most beautiful person, but the most beautiful *thing.* She seemed to emit a silver shimmer simply walking through the adjudication chambers, followed by her retinue of servants and bodyguards, all armed and watchful—but for a while, at least, I had eyes only for her.

Then I noticed something: the point of her nose, the shape of her face . . . She was Sazi. Just like Ana, the only other Sazi person I'd ever met in my life.

I looked to Ana to confirm my suspicion. I saw that not only was I right, but Ana herself showed no reaction at all to the young woman's arrival. Her expression had turned strangely inward, so much so it was hard to tell if she was even awake.

The young gentrywoman came to stand before Vashta, followed by two servants: both Sublimes, judging by the heralds they wore upon their breast, though they carried no imperial insignias with them. Having never met a privately employed Sublime, I found this remarkable. Her six bodyguards clanked along behind her, almost as tall as cracklers, bound up in complex plate armor that was nothing like what they used in the Legion—custom stuff, then, not refurbished or reused. Everything about them seemed expensive.

Fayazi Haza looked up at Vashta and gave a little bow, the barest inclination of her head. Vashta returned it—but reluctantly, I noted. A commander, after all, never enjoys a challenge to their authority.

"Madam Fayazi Haza," said Vashta stiffly. "I am honored to have you before us. What brings you to the city proper?"

Fayazi's amethyst-colored eyes fluttered, her giant lashes beating like a butterfly's wing. When she spoke her words were soft, breathy, and strangely childlike.

"I am here," she said, "with a terrible report."

I glanced at Ana and Miljin, wondering if Fayazi was here to make some accusation against us. Miljin looked bewildered—but Ana did not. Her face had been drained of all emotion, and now she sat there, inscrutable and totally opaque behind her blindfold.

"What report might that be, madam?" asked Vashta.

"I am here," said Fayazi, in tones most tragic, "to report a murder."

I sat forward. Miljin and Vashta looked astonished. Ana continued to sit perfectly still.

"A . . . a murder?" said Vashta. "Of who?"

"The victim," said Fayazi, "is my father. Who fell some thirteen days ago now."

I sat so far forward I nearly fell off the seat. I had only the vaguest of ideas as to who this woman and her father were—but thirteen days ago would be eight nights before the breach: the same night the ten Engineers had been poisoned.

Vashta stared. "K . . . Kaygi Haza? Kaygi Haza is *dead*?"

Fayazi's giant eyelashes fluttered, her brow suddenly creased with a ghost of grief. "We did not know," she said, "that it was murder at the time. He fell to some kind of contagion. But as we have . . . as we have labored to understand it, I have come to believe that it was a poisoning. That it was *murder*. And thus, I now seek your aid in trying to find the killer."

Vashta helplessly looked at Ana and Miljin. Miljin's bafflement had only grown—but then there was a tremor of a muscle in Ana's cheek.

Then I heard her scoff and mutter, ever so softly: "This smug little bitch. Here we fucking go."

IV

HELL AND THE GENTRY

CHAPTER 25

|||

A SPEAR OF WHITE LIGHT STABBED DOWN FROM the high windows, and she sat in a chair in the center of its cold spotlight. Her silver hair was gathered elegantly at her shoulders, her ivory fingers threaded in her lap. Knees and feet kept close together, the very picture of modesty and sorrow. Everything felt like a scene from some great painting: the pale fair maid, grieving at her father's tomb.

"I would have come earlier, of course," said Fayazi. Again, the fluttering of her enormous eyelashes. "But I had no concept that my father's manner of death was malicious. It was not until just today, when a commander of the Apoths mentioned to me that several Engineers had perished from a similar affliction—and that it *was* indeed malicious, a murderous act—that I chose to reach out for aid."

I glanced about. The edges of the chamber were cast in shadow, yet the armor of the guards along the walls glinted like the eyes of cats watching a campfire from the darkness. Fayazi's two Sublimes sat on either side of her. The first, an engraver, was a man, short and pale and rather soft of features, with a coral-painted face and a high collar. Eyes alert and resentful, like a top student worried others might surpass his marks. The other, an axiom, was a woman, tall and rail-thin, with little dark eyes like needles, and a large, smooth brow that gave her face a skeletal suggestion. She moved not at all as Fayazi spoke, but her unblinking gaze shifted about the room, and frequently rested on Ana and me.

"Please describe the manner of his death," said Ana sharply.

Fayazi's amethyst stare floated over to her. There was a twitch at the edge of her tiny mouth—a smirk. Perhaps a sneer.

"I am familiar with the commander-prificto," Fayazi said. "But you, I am afraid, I do not ken."

"This is Immunis Ana Dolabra of the Iudex," said Vashta. "She is commanding the investigation of some recent murders here in Talagray."

"Mm," said Fayazi softly. "This name I know . . . But I cannot place it yet. No matter."

A cold, mirthless smile crossed Ana's face, then vanished.

"My father . . ." A tragic pucker to Fayazi's lips. "My father perished from a *plantlike* growth. It was most strange. It poured out from his body, penetrating him through the breast. We treated it like contagion and locked down the whole of our halls in containment immediately to try to study it. We are often hermetic here in the Outer Rim, you see—the fear of contagion is greatest near the lands where the leviathans fall. Yet we could find nothing, and no one within our halls suffered any more afflictions. It was most mysterious."

"And you did not report this to the Apoths?" said Ana.

"If we had," said Fayazi, "then that would have surely broken our containment—correct? The breath of the words that carry a message might also carry death."

"Then how did you become aware that your father's death might have been malicious?" asked Ana.

"We lifted containment after seven days, for we had experienced no other incidents," said Fayazi, "though we continued trying to discover the nature of my father's death, of course. Just early this morn we received news from . . ." She turned to her engraver. The man's eyes quivered, and he leaned over to whisper in her ear. "From Commander *Hovanes*," she continued, "that there had been other outbreaks like this—ones kept secret from the citizens of the Empire. Yet we had no idea." Though her voice was still breathy and childlike, her last words carried a sharp edge to them.

Vashta narrowed her eyes. "We do as we must, to prevent panic," she said. "For if there's a panic, madam, we will not survive the wet season."

Fayazi nodded, her sheet of silver hair tilting back and forth. "Much may be excused," she conceded, "when we all live under such threats."

Yet I noted this was not precisely an agreement.

"You lifted this containment a week after your father's death," said Ana, "but that would have been nearly a week ago now. So . . . you still did not notify the Apoths of this contagion during *all* this time?"

"No," said Fayazi. "For just after we lifted our containment, the breach occurred. We prepared to evacuate immediately, rather than venture into the city to notify the Iyalets. It was a moment of tremendous confusion and emergency. We simply watched the skies of the east for the flares. I feared for the life of myself and my staff."

Vashta looked somewhat satisfied by this, but Ana was chewing her lip, head bowed.

"Your father's death," Ana said, "however, would have occurred seven days *after* the death of Commander Blas, in Daretana."

The axiom's skeletal gaze was now fixed on Ana. I began to wonder if the woman was even capable of blinking.

Fayazi appeared puzzled. "Commander Blas? Why is that of importance?"

"Are you not aware," Ana asked, "that Commander Blas died in the *same way* as your father?"

"I was told that Commander Blas fell to contagion," said Fayazi, shocked. "This was as it was reported to me. The manner of contagion was not mentioned."

"You were not informed by your own housekeeper, Madam Gennadios," Ana said, "that the groundskeeper at the property had collaborated with an assassin to kill the commander?"

Fayazi's face was the picture of vapid astonishment. "This information would have been referred to my father," she said, "but not to me. I do not even know who this Gennadios is."

"And no one in your household, and none of your clan administrators, informed you that your father and Blas died in the *exact* same fashion?"

"We were in containment," she said. "And I was deep in grief. I did not have the knowledge or the resources to respond, perhaps, as I should have."

I glanced down. Ana's knuckles were white, her fingernails digging into her palms.

She nodded curtly. "Mm-hm. And what is the current state of your father's body?"

"He was cremated, as is our custom," Fayazi said. "His ashes wait in our hall to be returned to our ancestral home, in the first ring. I intend to accompany its return for the funerary rites within a week."

"You burned him. Immediately."

"Of course," she said, blinking sorrowfully. "That is my prerogative as his issue."

Ana's fists were trembling now. "You are now aware, I take it, that several Engineers have perished to this same contagion?"

"I believe," said Fayazi sadly, "that Commander Hovanes suggested such . . ."

"Are you aware that we have evidence suggesting these Engineers were poisoned *at* your estate? Likely on the *same night* as your father? Presumably, now, poisoned at the *same time*?"

"We . . . we had a social event on that evening," said Fayazi, shocked. "Many people attended. But I have heard nothing indicating our guests suffered any sign of contagion. And I had no idea that there had been any other poisonings." She gestured at Vashta. "This was, apparently, kept secret to preserve order."

"Would those guests have included a Signum Misik Jilki?" asked Ana. "Or a Signum Ginklas Loveh?"

Again, the engraver whispered in Fayazi's ear.

"We are unfamiliar with these names," Fayazi said.

Ana listed the rest of the dead Engineers. Fayazi's engraver shook his head to each one—including Jolgalgan's.

"Then perhaps you can tell me, madam," said Ana, "why several of those Engineers possessed reagents keys to your gates?"

Fayazi was appalled. "I've no idea! I . . . I would assume they were stolen. Have you investigated these Engineers? Is it possible it was *they* who snuck in during the night, and killed my father?"

A long silence stretched on, Ana's blindfolded face fixed in an expression of grim frustration, while Fayazi insipidly stared back.

"So," said Ana. "Just to summarize, here—your position is that you were utterly ignorant of Commander Blas's death at one of your properties, so when your father also died of this horrifying contagion, you had no idea that this was the second murder of this sort. You then burned his body and put the whole of your estate into containment, and due to this and the chaos of the breach, you abstained from notifying *any* imperial officials of your father's suspicious death—until now. Nor do you know anything about the Engineers who were likely poisoned at your estate on that very same night, or how they happened to come into possession of reagents keys allowing them access to your properties. Is that the sum of it?"

The two Sublimes stared at Ana coldly. Fayazi's face worked as she tried to process all this. "I . . . believe that is all correct."

"I see!" said Ana, nodding. "I just have one more question."

"Of course."

"What color was the clay?"

Fayazi blinked, confused. "Clay? What clay?"

"The clay you must have stuck in your eyes and ears," said Ana, grinning, "to remain so amazingly fucking ignorant of everything about you."

Fayazi's eyes widened very slightly, but otherwise she did not react.

Vashta jumped to her feet. "*Immunis!*" she bellowed.

"Yes, ma'am?" said Ana politely.

"In there!" snapped Vashta. She pointed at the door to the arbiter's chambers. "*Now!*"

"Of course, ma'am."

She gripped my arm, and we stood.

ONCE THE DOOR WAS SHUT, Vashta let Ana have it. Her lungs were in fine form, and she seemed to have both an enthusiasm and talent for bellowing. I had no doubt that one reason she was being so loud was that she wanted Fayazi to hear the dressing-down that Ana was getting.

Finally, she began to finish: "Was I not clear, Immunis, that all of Talagray *depends* upon those people?" she said. "That we need them about as much as they need us?"

"You were," said Ana. "But she is lying, ma'am. Obviously so. Blatantly so. *Preposterously* so! And when someone lies to the Iudex, they get looked at."

Vashta fumed for a moment, thinking about this. "Do you believe, Immunis, that Fayazi Haza killed her father, and Blas, and those Engineers?"

"I ... think that unlikely, ma'am," admitted Ana.

"And you still think this Jolgalgan is the more likely perpetrator?"

"At the moment, yes, ma'am."

"But to prove any of this, we would need to gain access to the Haza estate to see if Jolgalgan has been present, and in hopes that there is something there that could indicate her current whereabouts. Yes?"

Ana said nothing.

"I do not know why Fayazi is lying," said Vashta. "I do not know her business whatsoever. But I do know that there is someone out there who has killed many Engineers and imperiled all of Talagray, and they could do more damage yet. Finding them is the priority. Not digging up any of your grudges with old enemies!"

Still Ana said nothing.

"You both stay here," Vashta, "while I try to salvage the situation out there, and engineer a way for you to continue your investigation!"

"Understood, ma'am," said Ana.

With one last glare, Vashta turned, flung open the door, charged through, and slammed it behind her.

"WELL, DIN," SAID Ana with a sigh, "I must admit, this . . . is not going well."

"Agreed, ma'am," I said.

"No doubt you would have counseled me to keep my mouth shut."

"Very true, ma'am."

"But I couldn't bear it. I simply could not bear the absurd amount of bullshit being poured at our feet."

My eyes fluttered as I recalled Fayazi's story. "Her explanation seems . . . at least somewhat plausible, yes?"

Ana's face slowly swiveled to me, her mouth open in outrage. "Did you catch a fucking blow to the head during your murderous scuffle, boy? If your father's chest suddenly explodes with greenery, you get up and run screaming for help! What you don't do is sit in total silence—*unless,* of course, you're *hoping* nobody notices your father's dead, because if they do, then people are going to start wondering why he died the exact same way as this other dumb bastard the next canton over! No doubt she hoped we'd never track the poisoning to her home. But then we did, and someone on the investigation must have just happened to mention to a friend, 'Fucking hell, chum, d'you know I almost *died* at this Haza party?' Then word got back to the Hazas, and that tipped them off that we knew the poisoning had taken place in their damned house. And if you can't evade an investigation, you instead work to influence it. And here we are. The noble, famous gentry-clan of the Hazas comes clean—but only to muddy the waters."

"What happens now, ma'am?" I asked.

"No idea. None at fucking all. But I do feel somewhat satisfied. After all, I predicted another murder had occurred before we came here. Don't you recall, engraver?"

My eyes fluttered. I recalled that first night here in Talagray, when

Ana had said—*What if they've murdered someone besides Engineers, so no one ever noticed?*

"Yes, but . . . did you predict the murder of a Haza, ma'am?" I said.

"Oh, hell no. I figured it was likely that the poisoner had killed someone that would connect the dead Engineers to Commander Blas. But I didn't think it would be one of the prime sons of the god-damned Haza clan!"

I shot her a glare. "Why not? You knew *where* the poisoning had taken place, after all. You knew from the start."

"Ohh," she said. "So. You've noticed."

"I have, ma'am."

She sighed and flopped down on the floor. "I wouldn't say I *knew* where the Engineers had been poisoned, Din. I would say I simply possessed a high degree of certainty that this would all eventually lead back to the Hazas. If you want to figure out where everyone got fleas, look no further than the biggest pack of wild cats. Even if they do prowl behind high walls and fancy gates."

I cocked my head, listening. I could hear a little discussion in the chambers beyond. It sounded like Vashta had negotiated things into a better position.

"What do you know about Kaygi Haza, ma'am?" I asked.

"Much," she said. "Maybe too much. I know he was third in line to inherit the whole of the clan. A prime son of the lineage. Besides that, there is—was?—little that made him different from the rest of his greasy brood. He was wealthy, conniving, ambitious, and influential. And *old.* Like a lot of the Hazas, he had access to some *very* pricey vitality suffusions—I think the man must have been about a hundred and thirty when he died. Even Fayazi's partaken, I believe. She should be about sixty, by my reckoning."

"That girl in there is *sixty years old*?"

"Girl . . . Ha! I take it you were smitten by her. Not surprising. Every bit of the woman is altered, and rumor has it some Hazas sport pheromonal grafts—not as advanced as a court plaizaier's, of course, but just below the legal threshold. The scent of the Hazas entrances the minds of those close by, ever so slightly. When Fayazi walks into a room you can practically hear the crinkling of pants as all the pricks stiffen. I'm surprised she's even the one here, actually. She's the daughter of the third son of the lineage—not exactly a position of power within their noxious clan, so to speak . . . Yet now we'll have to work with her to learn why Jolgalgan went to the trouble of killing her father, along with ten Engineers whom she claims weren't there at all!" She snorted. "It will not be easy. If it is Jolgalgan, she does not join exclusive company. The number of people holding a grudge against the Hazas is beyond count."

"Might you also count among that company, ma'am?" I asked.

She raised her eyebrows at me behind her blindfold. "My, my. That's rather insolent of you, isn't it?"

"I would simply note, ma'am, that Vashta just referenced your old grudges with them."

"A rumor," she said dismissively.

"And you also once said of the Hazas—*I wouldn't mind seeing all their progeny rotting in the ground like a bunch of fucking dead dogs.* Which is, I feel, mostly how one talks of one's enemies."

"Oh, yes, well," she said, sighing. "This is why people are so loath to talk before an engraver . . . They never forget a fucking thing you say! One day, Din, when this is all over, I shall tell you many truths, and tales of all that occurred between myself and the Haza clan in the inner rings of the Empire. I've no doubt you've caught rumors of it . . . But today is not the day for my stories."

I glowered at her for a moment. Then I had an idea.

"Are the Hazas responsible for your banishment to Daretana, ma'am?" I asked.

Her smile grew to a grin. "That's not entirely true."

"Did they *kill* your previous assistant?"

To my surprise, her grin didn't flicker one jot. "That's not entirely true, either."

"What's not? That it was the Hazas, or that your assistant was killed?"

"Focus, Din. We are here to figure out how this calamity happened and who is responsible. Follow that thread, and that thread *alone*, and we shall have victory." Then she cocked her head, knelt, and felt the fretvine floor. "Vashta is coming back. I can feel her stride in the very wood . . . And I think Miljin and Strovi are with her. Come. Let us pretend to be professional, you and I, for hell and the gentry await."

"HERE," SAID VASHTA COLDLY, "is what I have been able to salvage. First, Fayazi Haza does not wish to be in the room with *you* anymore, Immunis. To have made such an attack on her character during such a period of grief is beyond toleration. Is that clear?"

Ana shrugged. "That is clear if not welcome, ma'am."

"Secondly . . . Fayazi Haza will permit an inspection of her halls. *Purely* to identify the circumstances of her father's death. We shall pry no more in their affairs than that. This inspection must take place today, immediately. Which means we must postpone interviewing your colleagues about their involvement at this . . . this *party*."

"That is all well," said Ana. "We'll get to them soon enough."

"Lastly, however . . . Fayazi is not comfortable with a large presence from the Iudex. So she has only agreed to open her halls to one officer." Vashta's eyes moved to my face. "That would be you, Signum."

I stared at her, then at Miljin, who looked disgusted, then Strovi, who looked alarmed.

"Me?" I asked. "*Just* me? At the *halls of the Hazas*, ma'am?"

"That is indeed the case," said Vashta.

"It does not feel," sniffed Ana, "that the Hazas should be dictating who can or cannot investigate a murder, even if it did take place in their fancy house."

"We're lucky to send anyone at all!" Vashta snapped. "Though there are ways I can obligate the Hazas to open their doors, that would take time—and the quakes grow ever stronger. We *must* get this resolved quickly. My understanding is that Kol here was your only assistance in Daretana, correct? Then he should suffice once again. Fayazi is even willing to take him in the Haza carriage."

Ana's initial fury now changed to concern. She pivoted her head to me, like she could hear the beat of my heart, and thought for a moment. "I will consent to this," she said, "but I would like a moment to talk it over with Din and Miljin."

"As you wish," said Vashta. We bowed to her, and she departed.

Strovi looked back at me as he departed. He seemed so shaken it was as if it were he who'd been condemned to this task, rather than I. "Go safely, Kol," he said. "The halls are a dangerous place. Not all who walk in return." Then he followed Vashta out.

"WHY . . . WHY'S SHE ASKING FOR ME?" I said. "I mean, out of everyone in Talagray . . ."

"Seems likely they want you there so they can push you around, yeah?" said Miljin. He turned to Ana. "Someone young. New. Pretty. Suspect she thinks the boy'll be putty in her hands." He spat on the floor. "I'd normally begrudge you for fooling about with Aristan's body, boy, but given what's coming now, I've naught but pity."

"But what in hell would Fayazi get out of pushing Din around?" said Ana. "The boy knows fuck-all of anything important!"

"I am standing," I said tersely, "right here."

Ana ignored me, drumming her fingers on the sides of her legs. "The more I consider it, the more I think Fayazi wants to find the killer before us."

"You think she seeks vengeance?" asked Miljin.

"Not quite. I suspect Jolgalgan *knows* something about the Hazas and Blas. Something to make her go to a lot of trouble to kill the two men in such a symbolic fashion. Something I think the Hazas are desperate to keep secret. And then there are the murders of Aristan and Suberek . . ." She fell silent, her face grave. "*That* is what Fayazi will try to weasel out of you, Din. She wants you to give her something that will help her find the killer first and make this all go away before we can dig any further."

"How's she going to do that?" I asked. "Will her bodyguards hold a blade to my throat?"

"Oh, no," she said. She blew a strand of bone-white hair out of her face. "Rather, Din, I'm much more concerned that Fayazi Haza might try to fuck you."

I stared at her, speechless. I looked at Miljin, who stared grimly back.

"I am not sure," I said, "that I heard that correctly, ma'am."

"Oh, you wouldn't be the first," Ana said drily. "You are young and male—and boys are always a lot sillier about these things. And she has several thousand talints of beauty at her disposal, not to mention her pheromonic grafts. Regardless, it is well known that the Hazas use amorous relations, and blackmail, to get what they want. Fayazi likely means to get you under her thumb, Din." She thought about it. "Or under some other part of her person. Or perhaps under a member of her household . . ."

"This metaphor," I snapped, "wears rather thin."

"Yes, yes. But! She might be in for a surprise. For you are not only a curiously focused person, boy, but you're also one of the most emotionally repressed human beings I've ever met. If there is anyone who could resist the allures of the Hazas, it's you. Or, well, I hope it's you."

"Besides fending off unwanted advances," I said, frustrated, "what am I supposed to be doing there?"

Ana thought for a moment. Then she said, "Correspondence!"

"Beg pardon?" I said.

"Correspondence! Communications. Letters. *That* is precisely what we need. News of Blas's murder surely reached her father the second we started investigating in Daretana. So who did he talk to after Blas died? Who did he send messages to? And what did those messages *say*? That's what you must find."

"How am I supposed to do that, ma'am?" I asked.

"The Hazas are known to possess a small fleet of scribe-hawks," she said. "All you need to do is get to their rookery, boy, and look about for anything useful."

I was familiar with scribe-hawks, of course, for the Iyalets used them to carry urgent communications across the whole of the Empire, flying with stunning speed between two fixed locations. The idea of someone privately owning a small fleet of them, however, was nothing short of astonishing to me.

"And . . . how am I supposed to get in their rookery, ma'am?" I asked.

"You're there looking for contagion at a fucking murder scene!" she snapped. "That gets you access to all kinds of places! Make some dumb shit up, improvise, and figure it out, child!"

"Make some dumb shit up," I said sourly. "Very clear orders there. What else, ma'am?"

"Investigate! Go, see, ask—and remain cold and aloof. Find evidence of how the killer did their work, speak little, and glower much. I mean, that's your specialty, isn't it? And remember, this is the *second* time the killer has struck at a Haza house. I suspect they used similar methods. Am I clear?"

"As mountain water, ma'am," I grumbled.

"Good." She grabbed my shoulder. "Eat nothing she gives you, Din. Do not drink any proffered drink. Be mindful of any smokes or fumes you perceive. Do not urinate or defecate on the property, and do your best to leave few hairs behind. Finally, keep your distance from Fayazi—and do not let her touch your face with her bare skin. Understood?"

I thought about it. "I suppose I can't quit, can I?"

"Quit?"

"Yes. Not sure any dispensation could be worth this, ma'am."

She grinned. "Maybe not. But the Hazas know your name, child. If you quit now, they will wonder why, and come asking, and they shall not be as fun to work with as I. Only way out is through. Now clean yourself up and get fucking going!"

CHAPTER 26

|||

WHEREAS THE LEGION'S CARRIAGE HAD BEEN A rattling, rambling, tottering thing, the carriage of the Hazas was sleek, soft, and smooth. I felt not a bump and caught not a bruise as we hurtled along, my backside pressed into the powder-blue cushions.

But this did not mean the ride was comfortable. On either side of me sat two Haza guards, enormous men with wrists as thick as my neck, and nearly twice as broad as I. Their eyes did not leave my figure. Cold gazes, chilly and remote. Fell hands with a sword, surely.

Across from me sat Fayazi's two Sublimes. The engraver looked upon me like a surgeon might a septic limb. The axiom remained totally unreadable, but her dark, needle-like eyes did not move from my person. I felt my skin crawling the more she stared.

Between them sat the woman herself: Fayazi Haza, draped over her cushions like a coat tossed over a chair. She watched me carefully yet inscrutably, her wide amethyst eyes alluring but unreadable. It felt like being watched by an enormous doll.

And yet I was still drawn to her. To the luminous paleness of her skin, to her delicate neck. I had not felt drawn to a woman like this before, and I knew enough to know it was unnatural. Yet I also felt damned silly to be seated before her in my muddy Iudex coat, and my straw cone hat askew upon my head.

"You," Fayazi said finally, "are very tall." She said it in tones of slight offense, like I had chosen an inappropriate piece of wardrobe for the occasion.

I waited for more. When nothing came, I bowed and said, "Thank you, ma'am."

"Is it natural?" she said.

"My height? It is."

"And your face? Your features? Those are natural, too?"

"Ah. They are, ma'am."

"Hum. How audacious."

"Afraid I had little say in the matter, ma'am."

She studied me with that enigmatic doll's gaze. "You have things, Signum," she said, "you wish to ask me."

I looked at her. Then I looked to the right and left, at the guards on either side of me, and then the Sublimes on either side of her. All of them watched me silently. This was not how I'd expected to do the interview.

"I do, ma'am," I said. "But I had thought I'd question you at your home."

She waved a hand, bored. "Ask me now."

I hazarded another glance at our audience. Then I slid open my engraver's satchel, slid out a vial, sniffed it—this one aromatic of mint—and said, "Tell me about the day before your father died, please."

"Mm." She narrowed her eyes very slightly. "We had a party. A big one. We had planned it for some time. Many come to our celebrations. Some wish to, others feel they must. Some of them were colleagues of yours, as you no doubt know."

"How many came?"

She waved her hand at the engraver. His eyes shivered, and he quickly said, "Out of a list of one hundred forty-six invited, we had one hundred twelve attend."

"Can you provide me with a list of all the attendees?" I asked.

"Certainly," said Fayazi. "But not now. I am not going to fill my day listening to two engravers recite memories. But I will make sure you receive the appropriate information, in full." I noticed she seemed a great deal less breathy and innocent now. "It was a rare event, you know. We used to open our halls many times a year—once a month, or more. But contagion has put an end to that. So much is brought in from the Plains of the Path, why, I almost hesitate to breathe the air in Talagray proper."

"What is the purpose of these events, ma'am?"

"What is the purpose of any celebration?"

"Usually to celebrate something, ma'am. A betrothal. A birth. A sacred day."

"Oh, no. Those things—the birth of famous folk, or the dates of their deaths—those are merely *excuses* to celebrate. People celebrate because they are desperate to reaffirm fellowship and remember what it is to be alive. It is at my halls that any officer in Talagray can come and hear the singers tell tales of the first Khanum coming to the Valley of the Titans. Or of the Sublimes Prificto, the first whose minds were altered. Or of the Third Emperor, Ejelgi Daavir, and his march along the Titan's Path." Her eyes shone bright with a queer energy, one I did not find wholesome. "My great-great-grandfather was there, you know. He was among the Legions that slaughtered the beasts and first cleared the path to the sea, and was awarded our first fief. That was before the cantons. Before the building of the third-ring walls."

An uncomfortable beat.

"Very impressive, ma'am," I said. "Can you tell me of your father's movements? During the party?"

A glimmer of resentment in her eyes. Then she waved her hand again, bored. "He moved as one does during such a thing."

"Can you describe that, though?"

"He entered on a palanquin carried by six men," she said, "and waved to the attendees from its window before being taken to his antechamber." She described such grandiose ostentation like I'd asked what size sandals he wore.

"I . . . see. Did he interact with many of your guests?"

"Not many. His time is precious—or . . . or was, I should say. He was very old, and frail. He spent his time carefully and spoke only to the most important folk. Commanders and the like. One or two from the Apoths . . . but none from the Engineers. Not that day."

"And the Legion? Or the Iudex?"

A cold smile. "We rarely see their kind. And when they visit, it is short, and perfunctory. They consider themselves above such entreaties. They govern the world—but it is the Apothetikals and the Engineers who make it."

My eyes fluttered. A voice swam up in my memories: Princeps Topirak, bruised, weeping in the healing tub, and whispering—*The Engineers make the world. Everyone else just lives in it.*

"You just remembered something," said Fayazi's axiom.

It was the first time she'd spoken, and her voice was soft and husky. I found it startling. "Beg pardon?" I asked.

The axiom was watching me carefully now. "You just had a memory—yes? What was it?"

I chose to ignore her question, and instead turned to Fayazi. "Tell me what your father did after his arrival, please, ma'am," I said. "Did he encounter any steam or hot water during the party?"

If my rudeness offended the axiom, I noted, I could not see it in her face.

"Not during," said Fayazi. "But after. He took his steam bath, directly after the party ended in the middle of the afternoon. It's important for his joints."

"Had anyone tampered with his bath?"

"The porters and attendants, surely. But they would have mentioned it if they had seen anything."

"Then what?"

"He went to bed. As I said, he is very old and frail."

I asked her more questions then, about the party and the grounds and the defenses at the gates ("We employed tarsa plants and cloth-seed vines at the entry," her engraver said, "which should have alerted us to any contagion present, be it of the fumic or verdant variety");

about the comings and goings of the attendees ("We had three hundred ewers of mulled sotwine at the start of the event," Fayazi said wryly, "and only sixteen at the end, so things got rather muddled, yes"), and on and on. When I was satisfied, I asked her if anything suspicious had happened at all during the event.

"Nothing suspicious," she said, shrugging. "Not that I can recall."

Her engraver twitched. "There was the fire, ma'am," he said with a slight cough.

"A fire?" I said.

"Oh, that," Fayazi said. She waved her pale hand again—her favorite gesture, apparently. "That seemed as nothing, to me."

"We had blackwood burning in the fireplaces," explained the engraver. "Laced with silverdust, so the fires burned silver and green. One popped and sent an ember onto the carpet."

"And then?" I asked.

"It caused a flare," said the engraver. "A very small fire. Smoke and a stir in the crowd. It is not uncommon. The madam and I attended to it ourselves, and it was quickly dealt with."

"The greater damage was probably done," said Fayazi, "by me showing up with porters and guards and starting everyone's tongues a-wagging."

"When was this?" I asked.

A flicker to the engraver's eyes. "At two in the afternoon."

"And did you account for the presence of all your guests after this?"

"It took time," said Fayazi. "But yes."

"How much time?"

"An hour, perhaps." Her face changed as some thought struck her, a sudden sadness coursing through her eyes: real grief, real sorrow. "You . . . you think that's when they did it, don't you. That's when they . . . they planted the poison."

I studied the gleam of grief in her eyes, surprised by it. "How close were you and your father, ma'am?"

"Why?" she asked. "You don't think *I* am the plotter behind this, do you?"

"I'm obliged by my role to ask about all relationships."

She looked me over. "You are young. And altered recently. Probably for the pay, yes? Sending your dispensations home to your family, like so many Iyalet officers do?"

I did not answer.

"And yet," she said, "you have a fell hand when it comes to battle. Two men I am told you killed, just hours ago, and grievously wounded others. Perhaps beyond the medikkers' mending. Yes?"

Again, I did not answer. But I did not like how she knew such things so quickly. I wondered who in the Iyalets had talked.

"Well. You will likely find it all familiar, then." She gazed out the window as the gentrylands rose around us. "Born into systems beyond our control, into relationships and organizations that obligate us to change, all so our families may prosper . . . That's what the Empire is, isn't it? You wear your colored cloak, and I the vestiges of my station, but we are both compelled to do things we can hardly comprehend."

"Don't say such things, ma'am," whispered her axiom. "It is not as bad as all that."

Fayazi shuddered, as if the woman's words disturbed her. Yet then the emotion was swallowed in her face, and she became as cold and beautiful as polished silver once again.

"My father knew what the Empire was," said Fayazi quietly. "He knew it very well." Then she sat forward. "We are here."

CHAPTER 27

|||

WE EXITED THE CARRIAGE INTO THE BRIGHT MID-day sun. Tall, pale trees lined the road and the hills, their white branches shivering as if listening to a secret. The grass below them was as dark as sable, and only when the rare blades of warm sunlight pierced the canopies and fell upon the tussocks did I see that the grass was a deep, dark green. The Haza lands stretched to the east and west about me, though this tapestry of bucolic beauty ended at a border of dark ribbon: the enclosure's tall fretvine walls, penning us in.

I paused as I looked around, struck by the sight. It was the most beautiful place I'd seen in all the Empire. Even the breeze smelled sweeter here. It wasn't until the guards helped Fayazi exit the carriage, and I caught a glimpse of her bone-white ankle, that I reflected that every blade of grass within this cloistered world might be as altered as its mistress.

"Is it to your liking, Signum?" asked Fayazi.

"It is wonderful, ma'am," I said, and meant it. "How big are the grounds, if I may ask?"

I looked to her axiom, expecting her prompt calculations; but it was the engraver who answered. "It is twenty-three square leagues," he said quickly, his eyes shivering in their sockets.

"And yet," Fayazi said, "this land is worth but a fraction of our farmlands in the inner rings. A strange thing, no?"

We advanced up the main stone stairway, the house hanging before us on the hill like a storm cloud. It was tall and rambling, a complex place with ribs of white columns and huge expanses of glimmering stained glass. Balconies at every level. Copper drainpipes winding around the columns like tree snakes. Yet the higher walls were wrought of fernpaper.

My eye lingered on these. I wondered if any had come through Suberek's mill.

I followed Fayazi's coterie to the top of the stairs, but there I stopped. A sculpture hung over the front landing before us, huge and long and narrow, suspended by cables from rows of tall posts. Yet as I looked closer at it and took in its gray colorings, I realized it was not a sculpture, but a bone.

A claw. An enormous one.

"Two hundred years old, that is," Fayazi remarked. "Cut from one of the final leviathans to freely wander the Path. They were smaller in those days."

I stared at the claw. It was at least three times as long as I was tall. I could not imagine the size of the creature that had once borne it.

"Really," I said. "Do you know how tall it was?"

There was an awkward beat.

"No," Fayazi said, bored. "We do not. Now. What shall you wish to see first?"

I studied her. Eyes cold, watchful. Confident.

I thought of Ana's one command: *Get to their rookery, boy, and look about.* Yet I sensed that to demand to see the Haza rookery now would raise suspicion.

I told myself—wait. Chip away at her confidence. The opportunity may arise soon enough.

I cleared my throat. "Show me where he died, please."

FAYAZI'S COTERIE LED me through vast, vaulted hallways, the walls all wrought of fretvine so finely braided a Legion bombard shot might have bounced off them. Fayazi walked ahead through these yawning spaces like a pale ghost haunting some ruin, and I followed, sniffing my vial all the while. There was little sound besides the clank and rattle of her bodyguard's armor.

The walls were covered by a long silken tapestry that ran the whole length of the building. Now and then a spear of daylight shot down from some hidden window, casting a ray upon the silken tapestry and illuminating a shimmering warrior with a spear, and a chitinous, slavering creature towering over him.

"My ancestry," she said, waving at it. "My lineage is captured there in silk. The engraver can explain it all, if you are curious."

I glanced about as we walked. Partially to capture it all in my memory, but partially to identify the exits and entrances of this strange space, should the worst occur.

Fayazi led me down a side passage leading to a winding stair, and there we climbed up and up, strobed by the lights from the stained glass circling about us, until we came to the fourth floor. We proceeded down another hall, but Fayazi stopped before a tall stonewood door, suddenly troubled.

"It lies there," she said quietly. "I cannot look upon it again."

None of her coterie offered to open the door for me. I approached, grasped the handle, and opened it.

It was dark within, but the smell of old blood was overpowering. I let my eyes adjust until I finally beheld one of the grandest rooms I'd seen in all my life: a huge, sprawling chamber piled up with treasures and fineries—and yet all seemed to fade in the presence of the twisted, towering growth protruding from the side of the room.

I walked to it carefully, yet I was now familiar with the sight of dappleglass: the curl of the roots, the thick clutches of leaves, and the tiny, sickly smells of the blooms. Like in Daretana, the shoots had both burst through the ceiling and eaten into the floor, and the wood flooring was dark and stained around it. Here and there I saw fragments of wood and clumps of dark moss. It had bloomed from old Kaygi Haza while he rested in bed, I guessed, its roots eating through the sheets and the moss and then into the flooring below; and then it had punched up, cracking through the very ceiling.

Fayazi's voice floated in through the open door: "We cannot remove it. It has wound its way into the very fabric of the house. To remove it would mean completely demolishing the room."

I asked her how it all happened, and standing at the door she gave me the full account: her father had been sleeping peacefully during the early morning of the seventh of the month; yet then, just before sunrise, he'd awoken and begun calling for help, saying he was in tremendous pain. His attendants had arrived just in time to witness the inevitable carnage: a trembling column of greenery erupting from just below his left collarbone, growing until the man himself was eaten alive. It was just as Commander Blas had died, then.

I snuffed at the mint vial and glanced around the room, engraving it within my memory. Books and silks and tapestries and paintings were all about me—but so were many casks and barrels of wine, and many silver ewers. One of them glittered at me, encrusted with emeralds and emblazoned with the Haza symbol: a single feather standing tall between two trees.

I returned to the door. Fayazi gazed back at me. "Have you found anything, Signum?" she asked.

"I've seen many things, ma'am," I said, "but I don't know yet if any are significant."

Something in her face twitched strangely. "He didn't ask for me, you know."

"I beg your pardon?"

"When he died. When he was in pain. He rang for his servants, but . . . he did not call for me. I had no idea it'd even happened, until I awoke. They all let me sleep, untroubled, and I awoke to this. Perhaps . . . perhaps it's all still a bad dream."

The axiom reached out and took Fayazi's arm. "Do not speak so, mistress," she said. "He was unwell." She shot me a glare as if I'd provoked these comments. "You can take no lessons from such a death, mistress."

Fayazi nodded, her face smoothing out and returning to its blank, unreadable state. "What next, Signum?" she asked.

"Show me where he bathed, please," I said.

THEY TOOK ME down the hall and out onto a parapet of the main building, where a tall, white bathing house awaited us. I studied it as we approached, eyeing the thick shootstraw pipes running down the main building's walls, which brought water in from somewhere above. A tank mounted on the roof, I guessed.

But most notably, the entire bathing house appeared to be built of fernpaper panels. More than twenty of them, by my count. And all white and pure as snow.

Fayazi's guards opened the door to the bathing house, and I entered. The space within was dominated by a complex bathing apparatus built of brass and bronze pipes. The hot water was fed in from above, I reckoned, and then distributed into a circular set of tall spigots that were accompanied by a small crank. When one turned it, the apparatus would feed water up through the spigots to rain down upon the huge circular, white-tiled tub about them.

"The steam room, he called it," said Fayazi, standing at the door. "It was what soothed his joints. They had many grafts to help him with his age—applied through an awful process, inserted into the bones of his thighs—but he always said hot water helped most."

I touched one of the bronze handles, thinking.

"We considered acquiring some of the more extreme vitality suffusions from the Empire, you know," Fayazi continued behind me. "The ones used by the imperial conzulates, for example. But the side effects seemed unwelcome." She watched me. "Are you familiar with the conzulates, Signum?"

I knew of conzulates—they were the only rank higher than prificto, and essentially directed the Iyalets—but I knew nothing of their nature. I shook my head.

"Conzulates never age, and never stop growing," said Fayazi quietly. "They grow and grow and grow. Some get to be about as big as houses—and just about as mobile—before they're released from their service and given the sword. When taking that into consideration, steam seemed a much more preferable choice . . ." She paused. "You don't think the air in here is *still* tainted, do you?"

I ignored her and walked around the tub, noticing how the edge had been stained here and there with rings of red and yellow. Wine, I supposed, from many cups or casks or ewers placed there during long baths. I traced one ring with my finger.

"Well?" demanded Fayazi. "Do you?"

I walked to the far wall and stooped and studied the lining between the fernpaper panels. The seam was filled with a dark paste—still soft.

"It likely would be dangerous in here still," I said. I looked over my shoulder at her. "Unless the air had been vented out, taking the spores with it."

Fayazi was silent at that.

"Were the fernpaper panels in here replaced, ma'am?" I asked.

"No," she said simply. "Not recently, to my knowledge."

"Are you sure? This seam is soft and new, and removing any panels would allow the air to circulate."

"The lady has spoken her mind," said the axiom sharply. "And she said *no*. You know more of this contagion than we do. How should we comprehend its behaviors?"

"There was a fernpaper miller that fulfilled an order," I said. "His name was Suberek. We have indication that he delivered this fernpaper order here."

"We have no knowledge of this," said the axiom.

I ignored her and looked to Fayazi. "It would be a very large order, ma'am. And being as this fernpaper work appears new, it makes me wonder."

There was another awkward beat. Fayazi glanced at her axiom, then shrugged. "My house and staff are vast," she said. "I do not know everything that occurs here. Perhaps an order was placed. If so,

I do not know where it is now. Do you know all that the Iudex does, or all the Empire, Signum?"

"And you still deny that the ten dead Engineers were ever here at all," I said.

"We do not invite junior officers to our events," the axiom said simply. "Unless it is at special request."

I gazed at the three of them: the gentrywoman, the axiom, and the engraver. Studying their faces was like trying to read emotion in a piece of polished glass. I thought myself contained and controlled, yet these were indisputably masters at it.

"Was the poison delivered here, Signum?" Fayazi asked.

"It was delivered here, yes," I said. "But the agent of contagion isn't here. Because the water isn't heated here, is it?"

"No," she said. "It is not."

"Then take me there, please."

I HAD TO climb a ladder onto the back roof of the halls to access the water tank. It was a huge contraption, bigger than a slothik or a crackler, and its bronzed surface shone like a miniature sun. Fayazi's coterie watched from below as I aligned my eye with the length of its shootstraw pipe, which ran down to the roof of the bathing house.

"How does the water get up here?" I asked.

"The servants bring it up in buckets," called Fayazi. "How else? Then they light the stonewood fires beneath and send it down to the baths."

"And this is what happened after the party, ma'am?"

"Yes. Of course."

I opened the top of the tank and peered in. It was wide and rounded with a small grate in the center.

And there, lying in the middle of the grate, was a small strip of something dark. Though it was hard to see in the shadows within the tank, I had no doubt what it was.

My eyes fluttered, and suddenly I was not leaning down into a water tank: I was back in Daretana, watching as Princeps Otirios held his hands up about eight smallspan apart.

A slender slip of grass . . . not big at all. Odd to think such a small thing could kill a man so horribly.

I swallowed as the memory released me. "That's it," I said hoarsely. "It's still here."

I RETURNED TO the coterie and informed them of what I'd found. "Don't use or tamper with or touch any of the bathing mechanisms," I told Fayazi. "I frankly shouldn't have looked into the water tank. I'll call the Apoths when I return, and they'll dispose of the contagion accordingly."

For the first time, Fayazi looked rattled. "But . . . but how did it get in there at all? We had guards at all the hallways, and . . . and for the love of Sanctum, we had telltales at the entries to the estate! We made all the attendees march past them as they entered! That's how we keep contagion *out*!"

"Calm," said the axiom quietly. "Calm yourself, mistress . . ." Again, her hand returned to Fayazi's arm, gripping her tight.

I considered the situation. The estate was a giant place. And despite what Fayazi had just said, I knew such a giant place would offer many points of entry—but where to start?

I remembered what Ana had told me after catching Uxos: *Projecting motives is a fool's game. But how they do it—that's a matter of* matter, *moving real things about in real space.*

"How do the servants get up here?" I asked. "Do they take the same route we did?"

"They use the servants' passages," said the engraver. He pointed east along the walls. "The entrance is there, out of sight, but it is kept locked."

I went to where he pointed and found a small, bland little door that had been built to blend in with the wall. I tried the knob, but it was locked tight.

"It was locked the day of the party?" I asked.

"Yes," he said.

"And it was only unlocked before Kaygi took his bath?"

"Correct."

"Is this the only servants' door to this part of the house?"

"There is another servants' door inside," he said slowly. "Just past where we entered. But it is not well used."

We crossed the parapet, reentered the hall, and came to the little door, which had been disguised as a stretch of wall. I tried the knob— and the door fell open, revealing a narrow, dark little passageway.

I peered at the knob. The bolt had been broken from its housing, like someone had pried at it with a length of iron.

The axiom stared at the broken knob, then turned to hiss at the engraver, "How did this escape your notice?"

I interrupted as he stammered to answer. "It's possible the poisoner knew this door was little used," I said. "But this must be how they came up. Does this passageway connect to the halls where the party was held?"

"Of course!" the axiom snapped. "How else might the servants move about the house unseen?"

"But much of the passageways are unlit," said the engraver. "Servants and porters usually carry lanterns with them while attending to their duties. I'm sure they would have noticed if one of the guests was running about in the servants' passageways with a lantern."

I gazed into the darkened passageway. "I'd like to see for myself, please."

They had a servant with a lantern lead me through the passageways, which were often tight and cramped. I couldn't imagine how the Haza servants maneuvered within them carrying bundles of linens or trays of food. Yet though I moved slowly, descending always down to where the party had occurred, I could spy no sign of any trespasser's passage—or at least, any sign that was distinguishable from the servants' own.

The servant finally led me to the vast halls on the ground floor, where I found Fayazi and her coterie waiting for me.

She cocked an eyebrow at me as I exited. "Well? Did you find any evidence indicating how this was done? Or how that damned poison was smuggled into our home?"

I dusted myself off and tried to think. It seemed unlikely that the poisoner would have been able to improvise that trip through the passageways—which would mean they'd have to at least have known the passages existed, and where they exited.

"Signum?" Fayazi said. "Are you listening?"

"Still tracing it, ma'am," I said. "Tell me—were these doors locked during the party?"

"Not the ones down here, no. It would have been tremendously awkward if the servants had been forced to lock and unlock doors as they went."

"So anyone could have slipped into one?"

"Yes," said the engraver. "But there were guards stationed in the halls. And the servants, as we've pointed out, would have noticed someone navigating the passageways with a lantern."

I frowned, peering along the long, cavernous halls, studying the near-invisible forms of the servants' doors built into the walls.

"You mentioned a fire occurred during the party," I said. "Please take me to where it happened."

They brought me to yet another of the many halls, this one featuring a tremendous stonewood fireplace that still smelled of old soot. A few square spans of the rug before it were black and crusted, and crunched underfoot as I approached.

I knelt before the fireplace, studying the hearth and the ash pit cover. There were whitish scorch marks all along the back left corner of the firebox. Strangely patterned, almost like pale flower blossoms. I touched them and found they were not residue: the brick itself had been burned.

Then I caught a faint aroma, acrid and unpleasant. I was reminded of horse urine or something similarly foul. I leaned closer to the scorched corner and sniffed again. The scent was much stronger there.

"What is it?" said Fayazi.

"Not sure, ma'am," I said. I clambered back out of the fireplace and sniffed my vial to engrave the memory properly. "But I don't think the ember that popped was natural."

"Meaning someone threw some . . . some device into the fireplace?" asked the engraver.

"Yes. With the intention of causing a diversion. This started the fire, the guards came running—along with you—and someone slipped into the servants' passageways and made it up to the bathhouse and back without anyone noticing."

Fayazi stared at me, shaken. "How could they have maneuvered throughout the servants' quarters without being spotted?"

"Don't know, ma'am."

"And how did they get the damned contagion *in* here in the first place?"

"Calm, mistress," said the axiom quietly. "Calm . . ."

"Don't know, ma'am," I said again.

"There must have been some way!" Fayazi snapped, suddenly riled. "I thought you Iudex people were supposed to be clever!"

"You must be calm!" said the axiom. "Breathe deep the airs of this place and be calm!"

Again, the axiom held her mistress's arm, yet this time she gripped her so tight her fingers disappeared into Fayazi's robes. I could think of no one less calming and reassuring than this needle-eyed creature. Yet I sensed an opportunity.

"I don't think the poison was brought in during your party, ma'am," I said, thinking rapidly.

"Then how?" Fayazi demanded.

"I think it came earlier," I said. "I think it was *already* here, waiting to be used. The murderer simply had to come to the party, pick it

THE TAINTED CUP   263

up, and bring it to the appropriate place. And it wouldn't be hard to sneak something the size of a blade of grass into your estate."

I paused. All I'd said thus far were things I truly believed; but now I would have to lie. And that had never been my greatest talent.

"Then how?" Fayazi demanded again.

"It could have come over the walls somehow," I said slowly, "or, possibly, it was carried in by some small animal."

"Like what?" said the engraver. "The killer used a trained mouse to sneak the blade of grass into the boiler?"

"Or a trained bird," I said. "The estate does have a rookery, doesn't it? For scribe-hawks?"

Fayazi paused, considering this.

"That place," said the axiom softly, "is not for you."

"You . . . you are suggesting," the engraver said slowly, "that someone . . . *posted* the poison to the lady's house? Carried by a scribe-hawk?"

"Possibly. You get a lot of them coming here, I'd expect. And a blade of grass would be a simple thing for such a creature to carry. Do you check your hawks the same way you checked your guests for your party?"

"Do you really think," the engraver said, "that having had this poison carried here upon a scribe-hawk, one of the lady's servants just took it off the bird and . . . what, left it lying about?"

"I would normally think it unlikely," I said coolly, "but then, I would also think someone navigating your servants' passages, breaking the top door open, and then you not noticing either would be very unlikely. And yet, that is evidently what has happened."

A frosty pause. All three of them glared at me.

"Very few are allowed in our rookery," Fayazi said. "Even I was not permitted there, until recently. Only my father and his most trusted servants possessed access."

"I must review all avenues of entry, ma'am," I explained. "The rookery, the walls—everything."

"Would you still wish to see it, Signum," the axiom said, "if you knew that we had *burned* all of the master's correspondence after his death?"

I tried not to let my frustration show in my face. Of course. Of course they'd burned it all. Perhaps for contagion, but also to destroy evidence, surely.

Yet Ana had told me to get into the rookery. Perhaps there might still be something of value there.

"Yes," I said smoothly. "Of course I would."

Fayazi thought about it. "Then I will allow you a moment."

"There is nothing there for him to see, mistress," said the axiom. "We canno—"

"They tell me this boy is the one who investigated Blas's murder," said Fayazi sharply. She glared back at her servant. "Perhaps he can give us assistance." She looked at me. "Five minutes, Signum, and no more."

She turned and began walking, and I and her retinue followed.

CHAPTER 28

|||

AS WE WALKED I PEPPERED FAYAZI AND HER SUB-limes with questions about her father's correspondence. Had there been anything unusual? Any packages that had been laid aside? Any letters or correspondence from unusual places? Part of this was to maintain my story as to why I wished to see the rookery, but I also wanted to learn as much about Kaygi Haza's correspondence as I could, even if it was now burned.

But their responses were short, clipped, and inarguable: "No," or "Certainly not," or "Not that I recall." Nothing useful whatsoever, and the axiom eventually stopped answering altogether.

Finally we came to the rookery, a tall, circular tower built into the northwest side of the estate. I smelled the place before Fayazi's Sub-lime opened the door for me: the musk of straw, the roil of humidity—and, of course, the ripe, acrid scent of birdshit.

The engraver opened the door and beckoned me inside. I looked up as the shadowy tower yawned above me, the sunlight filtering in through the slots along the side of the roof high above. The darkness was rippling with *clicks* and *troks* from the birds, who were nestled in wooden cubbies lining the walls in a spiral.

"There is a desk here," said Fayazi's engraver, gesturing to the cor-ner, where an ornate desk of white wood sat beneath a small roof of green cloth—to prevent it from being shat upon, I guessed. "It was here that the master would read and answer critical letters immediately. But it is empty now. We considered burning the desk as well, but..."

"It is an heirloom," said Fayazi. "From the Khanum days. Older than this very canton, certainly."

I stared at the desk, thinking. If there were no letters here to review, then what was there to see?

I looked up at the birds nestled above. I could not see the birds themselves, but occasionally I caught the gleam of a bright, amber eye peering out between the wooden bars of the doors. The cubbies appeared to have been installed in pairs, little sets of two running up and down the walls, with little bronze plates installed beneath them. Interesting.

"How do they work?" I asked the engraver.

"Work?" said the engraver. "They're altered. That's how they work."

"Yes, but—how do you manage them? What's the process, please?"

He sighed. "They're trained in pairs, one in each location. One for incoming, one for outgoing, as it were. Each bird has been suffused to possess not only great stamina and speed, but also a great memory for the map of the earth. And each pair has exactly one destination they've been trained to fly back and forth to."

"How are they trained to do so?"

"Each bird has a deficit of a compound in its body—one that's necessary for them to live—and each pair is trained to learn that they can only receive those compounds at these two specific locations. Usually in a bit of sukka melon. The bird completes the journey and is then given a sukka melon as a reward. It all becomes very mechanical."

I looked up at the cubbies above, listening to the quiet *troks*.

"The plates underneath each pair of cubbies indicates this fixed destination?" I asked.

"Yes?" said the engraver.

"And the bird devoted to this location ..."

"It is always housed on the cubby on the left."

"So the birds from the other locations—should any arrive with an incoming message—would be housed on the right, before being sent back."

"Correct."

I thought about this. "And if both birds are here, then you've received a message recently," I said. "And if both birds are gone, then you've *sent* a message recently."

The engraver now looked slightly troubled. "Well . . . yes. I suppose that's true."

"And if you locked the estate down after Kaygi Haza's death, then there should have been no new scribe-messages missing *or* arrived."

"Yes . . . ?"

I watched him. The man's face flickered, just a little. A lie, perhaps.

"Then I'll check them for any sign of tampering," I said, approaching the winding stairway up. "And be right back down. It should only take a moment."

I climbed the shit-spattered stairs, my boots crunching with every step, and approached the first pair of cubbies set in the wall.

Fayazi's voice floated up to me: "Go quickly, Signum. I said five minutes, and I meant it. If you wish to see our lands, they are vast, and I did not intend for you to spend the night . . ."

"Understood, ma'am," I called back.

I CAME TO the first set of cubbies. A pair of amber eyes looked back at me. It was difficult to see in the shadows, but the scribe-hawk within was a long, beautiful, slender dark bird, crouched in the straw with rinds of melon curled about it. It *troked*? curiously at me as I knelt before it, as if unsure what I was.

The cubby beside it was empty. This, I reckoned, meant no messages had recently been sent to its destination, nor received.

I looked down at the little bronze plate below the cubbies. It was written in a curving, sloping text that made my eyes ache to look at it.

I furrowed my brow, forcing my eyes to read—the letters kept dancing and shivering before me—and finally I saw that it said:

Llitḍa ñan yarḍaaqñu urkuquna ñanḷana yunḓayḓniyuq kay.

I stared at the intricate text, utterly flummoxed, my mind working
desperately to make sense of what I'd read.

I took my eyes away, then looked back. Instantly, the letters faded
back into meaningless scribbling. I had to focus to get them to make
sense again.

"Ahh," I said aloud. "What . . . what language are these plates in,
please?"

"They are in Sazi," answered Fayazi's voice. "The language of my
people in the first ring of the Empire. Do you know it, Signum? I
rather doubt it . . . It's most tricky to learn, I understand . . ."

I stared off into the tower, trying not to breathe hard.

I did not know this language, of course. I could barely read it, and
some of the letters were wholly alien to me—which meant I certainly
could not read it aloud.

Which meant I could not engrave it in my memory and could not
bring it back to Ana.

I shut my eyes and tried to focus, summoning up the memory of
the words I'd just read. Yet in my memory, all I could see were delicate
scritches and scratches in the plate, a trembling pile of nonsense
where there should have been words.

I opened my eyes and whispered, "Shit."

"Is something wrong, Signum?" drawled Fayazi's voice. "Did you
find something?"

I felt cold sweat breaking out over me and continued climbing the
stairs.

I wondered what to do. I had come here hoping to learn something about the Hazas' communications; and though I hadn't found
what I'd wanted, I could still learn *where* they'd been sending their
communications, and perhaps when; and that might tell us something.

But now I saw I could not. I could not, because I could not read

any of these plates, because of my damned eyes, and my damned brain, which had never been able to learn how to engrave the words I read.

My heart fluttering within me, I mounted the steps. I passed one pair of cubbies with one bird; then another; and then, finally, one pair with no scribe-hawks at all.

A sent message, surely. And there, written on the plate below, was the name of the place the message had been sent to.

I gazed at the plate, trying to focus. I finally got the words to make sense, and saw they read:

Altiŋti yarḍaaqñu urkuquna t'iqramḳanḍkiaqñu chaika.

I gazed into the words, my face trembling, my head pounding. I felt a bright pain behind my eyes. Fayazi Haza said something below, but I ignored her, and tried my hardest to engrave the words in my mind, to keep them, to draw their symbols on my very soul.

I shut my eyes. Instantly, the words were lost, the memory dissolving like sea foam upon the sand.

"Shit, shit, shit," I muttered.

I opened my eyes and tried to whisper the words aloud, fumbling through the mad jumble of consonants.

"What's that?" demanded Fayazi. "What are you saying? What *are* you doing up there, Signum? Your time is nearly up."

"One moment," I said in a strangled voice.

This would not work. I was going to be thrown out of her house if I kept up with this.

I stared at the plate, thinking.

I could not say the sounds, I realized. But perhaps I could draw the words—later.

I took my vial of mint and snuffed at it heavily to ensure this moment was anchored in my mind. Then I placed my finger to the first letter, my fingernail slotting into the engraving in the bronze, and then let the groove guide my finger . . .

"Signum?" called Fayazi angrily.

I traced one letter, then another, then another.

"Signum Kol," snapped Fayazi. "I must insist we go, now."

I finished tracing the letters, hoping that the movements rested heavy in my memories, and moved on to the next pair of cubbies.

"Almost done," I said hoarsely. "Just have to check the rest."

There were four others: three pairs of cubbies with no birds, and one pair of cubbies with two birds—that meant four sent messages in total, and one received. At each pair I sniffed my vial and traced the words on the plate with my finger, praying that my body remembered the movements if nothing else.

As I finished the last one, I felt a hand on my shoulder, the fingers hard as iron. I turned, surprised, to see the axiom standing behind me, her skeletal face staring into my own.

"You are done here," she said softly. "As the lady said."

Shaking, I stood, brushed myself off, and descended the stairs, the axiom following behind me.

What a thing, what a thing, I thought as I trotted back down. What a thing it was, that I had to encrypt this memory and smuggle it within myself, translated into movement so my mind could keep it—though I had no idea if I'd been successful. Perhaps I would return to Ana, try to trace those letters upon some parchment for her, and discover I was drawing utter nonsense.

And then she would know, I realized. She would know of my affliction, and my lies, and I'd be found out and discharged, if not jailed.

My stomach sank as I approached the bottom of the stairs. What had I just gotten myself into?

I came to the door, sweaty and weak from all my attempted reading. Fayazi and her engraver studied me with a look of faint disgust upon their faces.

"Are you all right?" said Fayazi. "Or did you *actually* stumble across any contagion up there?"

"Nothing out of the ordinary," I said hoarsely. "Now—the walls, ma'am?"

Her cold amethyst gaze searched my face. "Yes," she said. "Follow, and we shall take you."

I did so, treading along after the axiom and the engraver—but Fayazi walked behind me, and whenever I glanced over my shoulder, she was watching me very closely.

WE EXITED ONTO the back grounds of the estate, where a wide patio of white stone awaited us. Though I felt weak, I was again stunned by the sights: here huge bright-orange-leafed trees stretched high overhead, shimmering like they were aflame, and all along the edge of the patio stood enormous slender, curved sculptures of pale green. They were nearly forty span high, almost taller than the house—but then I felt a fluttering in my eyes, and I recognized them. I had seen these once, on the Plains of the Titan's Path.

"These are . . . bones, again," I said quietly. "Ribs."

"Correct," said Fayazi. "From a little one. Too hard to move the bigger bits these days—at least over land. Tell me—what do you expect to find at my walls, Signum?"

My eye lingered on the curling arrangement of gleaming ribs. A gruesome sight, I felt. "I don't know, ma'am," I said. "It may be the poisoner has a preference—they prepare early and come early. Last time they communicated to the staff at your household by throwing a yellow ball over the walls." I gazed at the walls in the distance. "That likely won't be the case here, given how tall the ones here are . . . But walls come first in their mind, perhaps."

"Fascinating," she said. She waved a hand to her trailing retinue of servants. "That will take some time, though. You must partake of some refreshments before you examine them, Signum."

A servant strode forward to me, a wide copper plate in her hand. Placed upon it was an assortment of candied fruits, nuts, and dried flesh that had been cunningly spiraled through some artful butchery I'd never seen before.

My stomach reacted instantly to the sight. I had not eaten in hours, and desperately desired to taste these treasures. But I remembered what Ana had told me: take nothing, eat nothing, drink nothing.

"No, thank you, ma'am," I said. I bowed. "I appreciate the effort. But I will not partake."

Fayazi surveyed me coldly. "It is rude to refuse. Are you aware of this?"

"It is rude for me to be here," I said. "My entire presence is rudeness. I can only appreciate your goodwill and apologize."

She looked at me a moment longer; and for a moment I thought I saw a strange expression steal over her face: something akin to pure, mad terror. She glanced sidelong at her two Sublimes, who stood behind her, watching me.

Fayazi Haza, I realized, was very frightened of something. And I did not think it was me.

Yet then the expression faded, and Fayazi laughed, a high sound like pewter bells tinkling. "If you're sure . . . I do think you'll need your energy later. Go off, then, and do your spying about, Signum. I will be most curious to see what you will find."

I bowed again and strode off toward the walls, but her words weighed upon me. Something was wrong with Fayazi Haza, I was sure. But what, I could not yet tell.

|||

CHAPTER 29

I WALKED THE GROUNDS OF THE HAZA ESTATE AS the afternoon shifted into early evening, snuffing at my vial. I was trailed all the while by Fayazi's guards, who followed me like I was some imprisoned gentryman wandering his enclosure, but I ignored them as I studied the high fretvine walls.

The walls were enormous, nearly as high as the house. The idea of anyone trying to climb them or throw anything over was preposterous. The only thing I found of interest was the small stream that ran across the property, entering at the western wall and exiting at the east. I came to where it passed through the western walls first, and found it was protected by a sluice gate: a complex construction of steel and stone that slid up and down in the walls on huge metal tracks. The bottom half of the gate was woven steel, permitting the river water to run through. I crouched and peered at it, studying how the bottom of the gate sank into the muddy riverbed.

I looked over my shoulder at the closest guard trailing at me. He stood atop a small knoll, scowling in my direction.

I whistled at him and waved. "Hey!" I said.

His scowl deepened.

"I've got a question for you."

He didn't move.

"You can stand there and watch me whistle some more," I said, "or you can just come over."

He glared at me for a moment, then stomped over, careful not to get his fine boots in the water. "What?"

"What's this gate for?" I asked.

"For when the river floods after storms, of course," he said.

"Does it always stay like this?"

"No. They raise and set the gates to let the water through, then lower them when the flood's done."

I looked up at the massive sluice gate. "How do they lift it, though?"

"There's a pulley at the top. They run a rope through it, fasten it to a slothik, and have it haul the gate up."

"And when's the last time they had to lift it?"

"How am I supposed to know?" he snapped at me. "Weeks, maybe months. Are you done?"

"No," I said. I turned and walked away eastward, and he swore quietly as he followed.

IT WAS NEAR dark when I got to the eastern sluice gate. It was almost exactly like the first, except its riverbed was rockier, the stones poking through the mud like the backs of beetles sleeping in the soil.

Yet a few seemed different: the stones had been overturned, their stained, muddied sides facing up.

"Hum," I said quietly.

I looked in the direction of the house, thinking. Then I walked in a straight line from the eastern sluice gate, checking the landscape to my left and right for sign of any disturbance.

Then I spotted something: an oval of yellowed grass, there below one of the pale trees.

I walked to it, knelt, and studied it. It was a rounded, oblong patch of dying grass, about five span long, nearly as long as a person was tall. I poked at its center, wriggled my fingers into its soil, and felt something hard below. Then I poked at the edges, found the edge of the hard surface, grabbed it, and pulled it up.

It proved to be an oval piece of stonewood that the turf had simply been placed atop. The sod sloughed off of it like dead skin as I pulled it away. Below was a shallow hole in the ground about five span long and two span deep, yet the soil at the bottom had been pressed flat. I felt the edges, my fingers probing the earth, but I could find nothing here except the soil.

Yet something, once, had surely been hidden here. One wouldn't go to the trouble of making such a length of wood and mounting soil on it for nothing.

The guards rushed up beside me and stared into the hole. "What's that?" demanded one.

I said, "Looks like a hole."

"How'd you find that?" he said.

"I was walking around," I said, "and used my eyes to see it."

They cursed and walked away. I wondered if Ana's insolence was rubbing off on me.

I sat back on the grass, gazing into the hole. I felt something poking me in my coat pocket, and reached in and found the remnants of the shootstraw pipe I'd shared with Captain Strovi.

I turned it over in my hand. How long ago that felt now. I stuck it in my teeth and chewed on it, my mouth flooded with the tingling, numbing warmth of the tobacco. For some reason the taste helped me think.

I was unsure what to make of all this. My study of the rookery had been just short of a total failure. My tour of the walls had produced only a few stones overturned at the sluice gate, and this odd hidden hole here, but nothing else. I still had no idea how the killer—this Jolgalgan, I still assumed—had brought the contagion in, nor did I understand how she had navigated the dark servants' passageways without being found. Nor could I comprehend how the dappleglass in the water tank had managed to kill ten Engineers nearly a week later. Nor did I even know exactly what in hell the ten dead Engineers had been doing at the halls of the Hazas, as Fayazi steadfastly denied they'd ever been here at all.

But the light was dying in the sky now, and I did not wish to stay at this place any longer. The darker it grew in the lands of the Hazas, the more vulnerable I felt.

"Take me back, please," I said to the guards.

WE MADE OUR way back through the queerly manicured forest in the half dark, me chewing on the shootstraw pipe the whole way. Its tip was nearly dissolved now, but it was the only comfort in this strange place, which grew even stranger as night came on, the smooth, rolling hills cheeping with creatures whose sounds I did not recognize.

Yet as we approached the house, Fayazi's engraver crossed the lawn, stopped the guard leading me, and whispered to him. After a quick, furtive discussion, the guard redirected me toward the western side.

"That way," he said, pointing with one thick hand toward the back of the house.

"I thought I was to leave," I said.

"Go that way," he said again.

"What's that way?"

"The lady wishes to speak to you once more," explained the engraver. "In more pleasant environs."

I glared at him, but relented, and walked on, the engraver following behind me.

We walked nearly the perimeter of the halls, the trees about us dancing with glimmering mai-lanterns. Eventually we came to a large ballroom of sorts, built into the back of the house, with small round windows all shuttered, though their cracks shone with golden light.

I heard a voice within the ballroom—slightly raised, as if in argument. I slowed my pace, trying to listen.

It was Fayazi Haza's voice, shrill and angry. She was arguing with someone, but whoever it was spoke so quietly I could not hear them respond. For a good while I could barely comprehend Fayazi; but then I came to one shutter that stood slightly ajar, and I heard her voice leaking through.

I plucked a vial from my satchel—one I had not used, smelling of lavender—and surreptitiously dropped it in the grass.

I stopped walking and turned about, feigning confusion. "I dropped something, sir," I said to the engraver. "My vial. It was right here in my satchel . . ."

He huffed for a moment, then searched the dark grass with me. My search brought me closer to the open shutter; and once I was below it, I paused to listen. Though I could hear Fayazi, the person she was speaking with was still so quiet I could not make them out.

". . . do any of this if you tell me nothing," Fayazi was saying. "A third? Third what? What are they to find? What do they seek? . . . Oh, you keep saying that! I did not ask for any of this, you know. You don't understand what it was like, being here. If he wished me to lead, he would have given me some line. Yet here I stay, tied up like a mad dog . . ."

The engraver's hand flashed out above me, snapping the shutter closed. He glared down at me, then held out my vial. "I found this," he said coldly. "Kindly buckle your bag tighter."

I bowed to him, took the vial, then followed him on about the edge of the house. The voices within, I noticed, had gone silent.

He led me to a door in the back of the house, then opened it and waited for me. He stayed behind as I entered into a long, low, elegant chamber, lit by mai-fruit trees in bronze pots standing here and there. A small table sat in the center of the room, bedecked with food, and on one side sat Fayazi Haza, dining and sipping from a silver goblet of wine. She had changed clothes: whereas before her form had been mostly obscured by her robes, she now wore a dress that tied around her neck, revealing her pale arms and shoulders. Her very image seemed to bend the light about her, making her appear gauzy and surreal.

She looked up at me, and gave me a small, sad smile, and said, "How went the walls, Signum?"

I hesitated, liking this none at all. I glanced around. The room seemed empty except for her guards. I wondered who she'd been talking to.

The guard behind me grew close, ushering me forward. I relented and approached. Fayazi seemed to grow lovelier with each step, until the very air felt like it shimmered about her.

"Well?" she asked. "What did you find at the walls?"

I took the shootstraw pipe out of my mouth, looked down at my feet, and tried to keep my head about me. "Didn't find much, ma'am," I said. "Sorry to say."

"Yet I'm told," she said, "you tarried at our river gates. Did you find something there?"

"I found water, ma'am," I said, "and rocks, and not much else."

A fluttering of her eyes. Yet it felt queerly affected now, like a stage actor playing a role not much rehearsed. Something was wrong.

"And you discovered a *hole* of some kind," she said. "A hidden one. One some interloper must have dug in the grounds. Is that correct?"

"Seems it was hidden. But I don't know who made it. Can't see sense in it yet. I will have to report back first."

I held her gaze—for what I'd said was true, though it was not the whole truth. Finally she took a dainty bite of flesh from the tines of her fork. "Sit. And eat."

"Apologies, ma'am, but I must get back to Talagr—"

"Don't be silly. Sit. And eat."

I glanced around once more and saw that the engraver and the axiom were now sitting in chairs along the wall. Both watched me jealously, as if offended their mistress would deign to give me any attention. I wondered where they had come from—had my senses been so muddled by Fayazi's augmentations that I had not noticed them enter?

I sat at the table, but I decided I would not eat. I couldn't even identify all the food in front of me, neither the fruits nor the flesh, though my belly ached with hunger and it all smelled enchanting. I put my pipe back in my mouth and chewed on it, and the taste of the tobacco dulled my hunger.

Fayazi took a wing of some roasted fowl and delicately sawed off a strip of dark meat. "Do you know," she said, "I think you're going to find this killer, Signum Kol. I really do."

I said nothing.

"None of my other people here put anything together so quickly," she said. "None of them thought to check the servants' passageways." She shot a glare at her Sublimes. "You have a keen mind. A pity, I think, to spend it on such gruesome matters as this. And it's a pity you can view only our halls here in Talagray."

I said nothing.

She drank deeply from her wine. Her lips were crimson now, her teeth a dull purple. "At our halls in the first ring, you know," she said, "we have a *whole skeleton* of a titan. It hangs in our entryway, squatting over our visitors as they pass through our thresholds. Have you ever seen one, Signum Kol?"

"I've seen a carcass at a distance, ma'am. But no more."

"No two are alike, you know. They have different bone structures, different numbers of legs. Different colors. I have spoken much with the Apoths about them." She leaned close. I leaned away. "Did you know that some have the faces of men? Not atop their shoulders— for most leviathans have no shoulders—but hidden away, in their underbellies. Giant visages peering out at the world with wide, blind eyes, their mouths working silently and madly. Like some accidental growth. The Apoths cannot explain it. No one can. Nor does anyone know where the leviathans truly come from, or why they come ashore. Before the Empire they used to wander inland, rampaging here and there in the wet season, before laying down their bodies to rot in the Valley of the Khanum, warping all that grew around them . . ." She set down her goblet, then threaded her ivory fingers like a bridge and rested her sharp chin atop their knuckles. A practiced gesture, I thought—yet it worked, for I found it lovely. "And perhaps that's all they wish to do these days. Perhaps we should let them. Throw down the walls and let them go a-wandering . . ."

She watched me closely. I said nothing.

"It may happen anyway," she said softly. "They grow bigger and bigger every year. Each wet season, the Empire must remake the walls, and design new bombards, and come up with new grafts and suffusions to hold them back. And each year, we barely scrape by. And though no one says it, the Engineers are quietly, quietly remaking the third-ring walls of the Empire, to the west. For if the sea walls fall, and Talagray and the east fail, then, well . . . Then the third-ring walls will become the *new* sea walls, won't they?" She lifted her head off her hands and took another sip of wine. "And when that happens . . . Why, it would be a good thing to have a place to land within the inner rings of the Empire. To have friends in more fertile lands. For then all the Iyalets shall be as motes upon the wind, and there shall be no order."

She waited for me to say something, but I could think of nothing to say to this.

"Does that make sense to you, Signum?" she asked.

"It does, ma'am," I said. For it did, at least, make sense—a cynical sense, but sense it was.

"Then why don't you tell me," she said, slowly and carefully, "what your immunis has found out thus far. Tell me how the investigation goes. For we are friends, are we not?"

I stared into her violet eyes. Took in the way her silver hair piled on her snowy shoulders. How heady the air was here, how strange. All felt perfumed, yet I could smell no scent but the food.

I tore my gaze away and glanced at the two Sublimes, watching me like I was a wounded hind on their hunting lands. "Afraid I can't do that, ma'am," I said.

"Why not?" asked Fayazi.

"It's against policy to discuss investigations with anyone uninvolved, ma'am."

"But are we not friends, Signum Kol?"

I did not answer.

Something went cold in her gaze then: she had made up her mind about something. She held up a finger and bent it, but the meaning of this gesture was baffling to me.

"You are Iyalet for the *money*, yes?" she asked.

I said nothing.

"You became a Sublime to support your family," she said. "To move them farther into the Empire, surely. That's why so many serve. Yet how many months has it been since you've seen them? How long since you've gotten a letter from them? Do they even know how you suffer so? What you've done? What you've become?"

I felt my pulse quicken in my ears. My breath was suddenly hot and quick. I wasn't sure why, but everything felt chilly and tremulous, like I was suffering a fever.

I glanced at the Sublimes, who still watched me. I shifted uncomfortably in my chair. Something was wrong. I wondered if I'd been poisoned, yet I knew I had not tasted of her table.

"There is a path for you," Fayazi said, "that would allow you to walk home, free and unburdened, with all the fortune to save them. I could show you that path. And you would be free to walk it. But in the moment—right now—are you not owed a respite from all this?"

"A . . . a respite?" I said. My voice was barely a whisper.

"Yes," said Fayazi. She smiled. Her face was so sympathetic, so understanding. "You who have suffered indignity after indignity . . . are you not owed the joys of the Empire, too? And there *are* joys, Kol. This I know."

I felt a hot flush in my belly. I was gripping the sides of the table. Sweat was pouring down my temples. Then a throb in my loins, a deep, painful ache, and suddenly I was so aroused it pained me.

I tore my eyes away from Fayazi, ashamed and bewildered.

Then I noticed the shadow on the floor and realized someone stood behind me. I turned to look at them.

It was a girl—or so she seemed to my eyes—watching me with a sad gaze. She was about my age, well-kept and pretty, barefoot with dark eyes and short hair. She wore a silken red scarf about her neck and a red dress hanging from her shoulders; yet it was little more than two sheets of silk cloth, one covering her front and one covering her back, revealing the bare edge of her hip and her breast.

And I desired her. Inexplicably, suddenly, passionately. She was not as beautiful as Fayazi, not so carefully manicured, but there was something in her bearing, her gaze, in her mere presence that made her so alluring to me that I almost felt I might die.

Then I noticed something strange: a swelling at the girl's armpit— a slight, purple-hued nodule from an alteration.

I looked into her face and saw the same violent tint at the corner of her jawline, just above her scarf.

I then knew what she was: a plaizaier, a court dancer. A being pheromonally altered for the delights of others. Ana had mentioned such a thing to me, but I had never thought I'd meet one in all my life.

My body ached for her. I wanted nothing more than to grab her, to taste her, to take her, to know every fold and bend of her. Yet my teeth bit down on the shootstraw pipe in my mouth, and I swallowed, flooding my throat with the hot tickle of tobacco; and then, as if I was pulling my head free of a spider's web, I turned back to face Fayazi.

"I just," I said quietly, "wish to go, ma'am."

"Does she not please you?" asked Fayazi. "We have others. Male, if you wish."

I said nothing. The whole of my body seemed to be boiling over with hot blood.

"What a world it is, Signum," said Fayazi, "where you are forced to change yourself, break yourself, all for a little scrap of money." She leaned forward once more. The smell of her was intoxicating. "Are you not owed respite from this?"

The shadow of the court dancer hung on my shoulder like a leaden weight.

"There can be no wrongdoing," Fayazi said, "in an Empire so broken."

"I just wish to go," I said again.

Fayazi gestured to the plaizaier, who walked closer to me. I turned my face away.

"You were wrong, you know," Fayazi said. "I am a friend to many, Dinios Kol. But never have I met someone so deserving of my friendship as you."

The plaizaier began to use the front of her dress as a fan, raising it and rippling it toward me, washing me in her scent. A strangely sweet musk, I noticed, redolent of oranje-leaf and mulling spice. My heart was racing, and my loins ached so much I wished to scream.

"Have you found something?" demanded Fayazi suddenly. She stood. "Has Dolabra found something?"

I swallowed. I could see the plaizaier raising the front of her dress and fanning it again; and there, amid the flicker of red, a glimpse of her body, and a winking tuft of pubic thatch.

I tried to keep my eyes on Fayazi. That was when I noticed an odd smudge of white on the side of the gentrywoman's dress, almost like paint.

Trembling, I looked at Fayazi's bare arm. Was that paint I spied there? And beneath it, the dark cloud of a bruise—perhaps in the shape of fingertips? Even in that mad moment, I struggled to make note of it.

"What does your immunis know of my father?" said Fayazi, louder. "What has he done?"

Suddenly the axiom was beside her. "Calm, mistress," she hissed. "Calm . . ."

"What does she know about him and Taqtasa Blas?" Fayazi demanded.

All dissolved to chaos then. I ignored it all and bit down on the pipe, furious and confused, incensed to be denied control over my own senses.

And then I felt it—a fluttering in my eyes as a memory awoke.

I knew that smell: oranje-leaf and spice. I had smelled it on the scarf of the dead Princeps Misik Jilki, in the Engineering quarters, the day after I'd first come to Talagray.

And I had smelled it in Daretana, too: from Commander Blas's oil pot.

All three smells were exactly the same.

I gritted my teeth and turned my face to Fayazi Haza. "Y-you l-l-lied to m-me," I said, forcing the words through my clenched mouth.

A furrow in Fayazi's smooth brow. "What?"

"S-Signum M-M-Misik Jilki," I said. "She was h-here. Sm-melled like . . . like this. I know. Oranje-leaf and s-spice. After she'd been t-touched by the same oils and p-perfume as your . . . your court dancers here." I grinned madly. "She f-felt their skin. Knew their flesh. Maybe in . . . in this same r-room. Didn't she? Her along w-with . . . all the others."

The axiom retreated to the walls, dark eyes watching warily like I'd drawn steel.

"What are you talking about?" spat Fayazi.

"D-did they smell j-just like Commander Blas?" I leaned forward. "For he had a taste f-for the aroma, too, didn't he? He c-came to *like* it. That's wh-why he had a . . . p-pot of his own."

Fayazi stared at me, stunned.

"You lied to m-me," I whispered. "They c-came here. Frolicked with y-your court dancers. And th-then they were y-yours. But . . . b-but wh-what did *you* get from them, ma'am? What did *you* get from all those d-dead Engineers?"

Fayazi looked to her Sublimes. When they said nothing, she flicked a hand at her court dancer, who withdrew to the shadows of the room. Then she snapped: "Get him out of here. Get him out of here and get him *gone*!"

Then I was ripped backward out of my seat.

III

MY HEAD SPUN as the two guards marched me through the darkness of the landscape outside. I had never been handled by a person altered for strength, but the second the guards touched me I was like a small child struggling against a parent, my limbs pinned back and my flailing quickly and effortlessly contained. My elbow screamed in pain as one of them bent my arm too far. I cried out, telling them to release me, but they ignored it.

Finally we came to the landing under the claw of the leviathan, and the guards released me. "Down!" one snarled at me. "Down the stairs and into the carriage, damn you!"

I shambled down the steps and crawled into the back of a waiting carriage. The guard slammed it behind me and said to the driver, "Dump him off at the gates, but don't take him any farther." Then the carriage started forward, and we were off.

I peered back at the halls of the Hazas as we took off down the estate road, my head still spinning. Yet I saw someone had come to the top of the steps, and now stood below the massive leviathan's claw: a silvery figure, white and ghostly, looking down on me.

I locked eyes with Fayazi Haza. She seemed utterly transformed in that moment, her eyes wide and terrified and desperate in the dark, like she was a prisoner I was abandoning in her cell. Then her Sublimes ran to her, and her axiom took her by the arm once more, pulling her back, and she was lost in the darkness.

The gates of the Hazas opened, the carriage slid to a stop, and then the door fell open. "Out!" barked the driver.

I did as he bade, but as I stepped down I saw there was a small crowd of people waiting for me: Legionnaires, two of them clutching mai-lanterns; and there, at their front, stood Captain Miljin.

"Easy, boy," he said. He took me by the shoulder. "Are you all right? Are you whole?"

CHAPTER 30

|||

ANA AND MILJIN LISTENED GRIMLY IN HER CHAM-
bers as I recounted what I'd seen in the halls of the Hazas. I sniffed at
my vial of mint aroma and went through every detail, sparing nothing, reciting all I'd seen from the moment I'd stepped into their
carriage—except for my fumbling attempt to review the Hazas' correspondence in their rookery. That I would leave for last.

When I finished we sat in silence in the arbitration chambers of
the Iudex tower. The only sound was the creak and sigh as the building flexed about us in the night breeze.

"You did well, boy," said Ana quietly. "Well to look and see as you
did . . . And well to resist Fayazi's temptations." She shook her head,
disgusted. "What a tool cynicism is to the corrupt, claiming the
whole of the creation is broken and fraudulent, and thus we are all
excused to indulge in whatever sins we wish—for what's a little more
unfairness, in this unfair world? Wise you were, Din, to shut your
ears to it." She went still for a moment, then said, "Now. Repeat Fayazi Haza's first set of questions for me, please."

I took a breath, then echoed: *"Have you found something? Has Dolabra found something? Anything?"*

"I see . . . And the second set of questions?"

Again, I echoed: *"What does your immunis know of my father? What
has he done? What does she know about him and Taqtasa Blas?"*

"Yes . . . and that moment, before you went to see the walls—she offered you food, but you did not take it," said Ana. "Correct? And then she . . ."

I nodded. "She looked terrified. Frightened of something, like she'd done something wrong. But I didn't know what, ma'am. Yet she looked the same when I saw her last, when she came to stand at the top of the stairs."

Ana was silent again for a long, long time. Then she said simply, "And the bit you overheard her saying, Din? To her mysterious visitor, before she tried to tempt you?"

I summoned up some more energy and echoed those as well, mimicking Fayazi's snide cadence: ". . . *do any of this if you tell me nothing. A third? Third what? What are they to find? What do they seek? . . . Oh, you keep saying that! I did not ask for any of this, you know. You don't understand what it was like, being here. If he wished me to lead, he would have given me some line. Yet here I stay, tied up like a mad dog . . .*"

Miljin chuckled morosely. "Your impression of that dreadful woman, boy, is quite something . . ."

"Hm," said Ana. Again her fingers flittered in the folds of her dress. "A third . . . a third what? Third murder? A third poisoner, or poisoning? We do not yet know enough to imagine. But one thing grows apparent . . . I don't think Fayazi Haza knows, either."

I sat there limply, too exhausted to react. But Miljin's brows furrowed until they nearly eclipsed his eyes. "She doesn't know . . . what?" he said.

"Apparently anything!" said Ana. "While it'd be convenient for her to be the spider at the center of this web, I actually don't think Fayazi Haza knows a goddamn thing about what went on between her father and Blas. She might not know any more than we do, in fact."

"Truly, ma'am?" he said. "That seems preposterous. I mean—she's a Haza!"

"She's the daughter of the third prime son of the lineage," said Ana. "Which is not, genealogically speaking, an elite leadership position within the clan. And she's been stuck out here on the Outer Rim, standing in the back rooms while her father ran the show—and it seems he kept many secrets from her. She now suspects we have figured out those secrets, but we have not. Not yet, at least. It's very strange. She sounds so clumsy, so erratic . . . Like she was told to find things out, but was not told enough to comprehend what she found." She chewed on her lip for a moment. "I think Fayazi is a puppet."

"For who?" said Miljin.

"Why, the rest of her family, of course."

"The rest of the Hazas?" asked Miljin. "Aren't they one and the same?"

"Oh, no. The Hazas are a far bigger operation than what we see here in Talagray—and Fayazi is in a rather tough spot within that operation. Her father died, and she was suddenly put into power in his place. However, I suspect she quickly came to realize that her father was running secret little schemes for the family, ones she hadn't been privy to—and, worse *still*, letters then came pouring in from the family proper, deeper in the Empire. Orders. Directives. Commands. Commands that probably told her nothing, other than what to do, not to ask questions . . . and to look for *something* here in the canton. Something important that they're worried we've found. Perhaps this mysterious third. Fayazi is now probably sweating under all those silvery robes—and worried that if this truly goes south, it'll be she who hangs, and none of her illustrious kin."

She allowed a silence as Miljin and I absorbed this.

"This, of course, is only conjecture," she said. "But I feel it's close to the mark, given what you've told us, Din . . ." A savage grin. "The Hazas seek something—an object, or evidence. Perhaps they seek this third. But what it actually is, I don't think Fayazi is permitted to know. Fascinating!"

"Maybe something to do with the ten Engineers," said Miljin. "Being as Fayazi lied to Kol here about that—and he faced down a fucking court plaizaier to prove her wrong."

I wiped sweat from my face as I struggled to free my mind of that memory. "But I still don't understand why the ten Engineers would have been there at all," I said. "Why would Kaygi Haza invite such low officers into his estate?"

Ana laughed gaily. "Oh, that's simple. The answer is *patronage*."

"Patronage?" I said. "As in—giving gifts?"

"Right," grunted Miljin. "Though it sounds like Kaygi Haza was giving them a hell of a lot more than gifts, though . . ."

"Aptly put," said Ana. "The man must've been operating here for years. All these bright young officers coming to Talagray for acclaim and attention . . . and Kaygi gave it to them, putting them on the high road to better positions, better projects. All they had to do was give him information, or do small favors for him . . . or a big one, perhaps." She trailed off, as if struck by a thought.

"Like Blas, ma'am?" I said.

"What?" she said, startled.

"It sounds like the treatment the Hazas gave Blas. But he was far older, and his treatment seemed special."

"Hm. Yes . . ." she said quietly. "It did, didn't it?"

Miljin snorted. "But we're still missing lots of pieces. Patronage ain't exactly illegal—being as it's the gentry who have a lot of say in making the laws. We've also got no real indication of what Kaygi Haza was actually up to, or how Jolgalgan got to him. Unless Uhad, Nusis, and Kalista give us something useful when we interview them tomorrow—which I somewhat doubt they will."

"No . . ." said Ana. "But, Din—there is one thing that's missing. Tell me, were you unable to get into the Haza rookery at all?"

I hesitated, a lump of ice wedged between my ribs. No avoiding it now.

"I did, ma'am," I said. "But the Hazas had burned all of the household's correspondence, claiming a fear of contagion."

"Damn . . ." muttered Miljin.

Yet Ana shot forward. "But you didn't stop there, did you, Din? Surely not."

I took a breath, trying to suppress the dread fluttering in my throat.

"I didn't," I said. "I reviewed all the scribe-hawks of the Hazas, trying to see which locations they were in communication with—as well as which locations had recently sent a message, or received one."

Miljin stared in astonishment, then cackled. "By hell! Finding out which places the Hazas were watching and *listening* to? That's a damn coup, that is!"

Yet Ana cocked her head, sensing the hesitation in my words. "What's the problem?"

"The problem," I said slowly, "is that the locations were all written in Sazi."

"*Sazi?*" said Ana, surprised. Then she sat back, jaw set. "Ah . . ."

"Ah?" said Miljin, puzzled. "Why ah?"

Ana was silent for a moment. "Sazi, Captain," she finally explained, "is one of the trickiest languages to learn—especially in writing. I am Sazi myself, and know the tongue and the letters. But besides Sublime linguas, I've never known a soul who's managed the feat."

"But . . . but if you're Sazi, ma'am," said Miljin, "and if Kol here's an engraver, he can just write the letters out for you to read and translate, yes?"

A heavy silence hung in the air.

I watched Ana anxiously. Her blindfolded face had gone inscrutable, but her posture was tense, like a cat about to spring.

"I mean—right?" said Miljin again.

"Captain," she said suddenly. "Please give me a moment with Din alone."

Again, Miljin's brows furrowed, and he glanced at me. But he nodded, stood, and left.

ANA WAITED UNTIL her door clicked shut.

"So." She turned to me. "What'd you get?"

"S-sorry, ma'am?" I said, surprised.

"What did you get, Din?" she demanded. "I know you came away with *something*. I can hear it in your voice. So—what?"

I thought for a moment, took a breath, and said, "I, ah, found four messages sent to four different locations, and one received, ma'am."

"And?"

"And . . . I struggled with the Sazi, as you suggested, ma'am." I fought to keep my voice from shaking. "So rather than try to memorize the letters or say them aloud, I . . . I traced them with my finger, and tried to memorize the movements to hopefully re-create them here for you."

There was a long, awkward silence. I waited. Any moment now, I knew, Ana would demand to know the reason for this bizarre choice; and then she'd come to know of my afflictions with text, learn of all the work I'd done to hide this secret, and have me discharged from the Iyalet and sent home without a talint in my pocket.

But instead, Ana cheerily said, "Oh! Well. That should do perfectly, yes?"

I blinked. "P-pardon, ma'am?"

"Memorizing the movements should do very well," she said. She took off her blindfold and began puttering around the room, sifting through parchments. "We just need an ink vial and some papers. Should be simple."

I felt myself blushing. "But . . . ma'am. I am unsure if I'll be able to write what I trace—"

"Yes, but you're not going to *write* it, boy. I mean, you didn't write it back there, did you? We just need to duplicate your movements *exactly*. You traced them with your finger, and that is what we shall do again."

She set a sheet of parchment on the table, then opened an inkpot and placed it before me. "Now. Just dip your finger in there, Din— just a bit—and sniff your vial, shut your eyes, and move your finger as you did back in the rookery. Let us see what your movements re-create."

I stayed still, unable to quite comprehend what was going on. Did she really have no questions for me? Did she not find my inability suspicious?

Then she snapped, "Now, Din! *Now!* I've not got all night! Put your damned finger in the damned ink, child!"

Feeling both bewildered and ridiculous, I dipped my finger lightly in the inkpot, placed the nail to the parchment, shut my eyes, and smelled my vial of mint.

Memories unscrolled in my mind.

The rustlings of the birds. The smell of straw and the dappling of slanted light.

I felt my muscles move my arm, my hand, and my finger.

It was queerly like the fight outside Suberek's mill: my body reacted with a will of its own, shifting about as it mimicked the memory. I felt like a man possessed from a fairy story; but rather than being possessed by a spirit, I was possessed by a split second of my own past.

I finished writing and opened my eyes. There upon the page was a very, very messy string of letters—but to my own surprise, they were very close to the string of Sazi text I'd seen below the first pair of scribe-hawk cubbies back at the rookery.

Ana leaned over my shoulder, peering at it. "Fascinating . . ."

"Can you read it, ma'am?" I asked.

"I think so . . ." she said. "It is quite outrageously sloppy, but it looks like it says—*The Engineering Headquarters of the Mitral Canton.*"

I stared at the page, then up at her. "Truly?"

"Truly! You have done your duty, Din. We just need to do a little more. Come now—summon up your other memories of the other plates and bits of text, and let us learn who else the Hazas communicated with after the death of Commander Blas."

I did the others the same way, each time on a new piece of parchment, duplicating the remaining three locations of the sent messages. They were:

The Engineering Headquarters of the Bekinis Canton
The Apothetikal Headquarters of the Qabirga Canton
The Engineering Headquarters of the Juldiz Canton

Together we studied the names of the four places, slightly mystified. Yet then one canton name suddenly sounded very familiar to me.

I summoned up the memory, my eyes fluttering. "Bekinis . . ." I said softly. "And Juldiz."

Ana grinned. "Yes, Din?"

"These . . . these are the cantons Blas's secretary was visiting," I said. "The ones noted in the wall pass I found in that empty house, with all that money."

"Correct, Din! And isn't that *fascinating*?" Her grin grew wider. "It does make one think."

"But what's the connection, ma'am? Why would the Hazas send their letters there?"

"Oh, I have ideas. Many of them. And all of them will require further verification."

There was a tense pause.

"Perhaps the location that *sent* a message to Kaygi Haza will reveal more?" I said.

"Mm, I rather doubt it," she said. "But we should look anyway."

I did the trick again, writing with my finger with my eyes shut, then opening them.

"As I thought," said Ana. She squinted at my writing, then read, *"The Haza Prime Hall, First Ring, Sazi Lands.* In other words, the Hazas' home here in Talagray got a message from the elder brothers of the Haza family very soon after Kaygi Haza's death. Meaning Fayazi's Sublime *lied* to you—they've probably gotten lots of letters from the senior lineage since the old bastard sloughed off his sandals. Not surprising."

"So what does that mean?"

"Isn't it obvious? It means whatever secret Kaygi was rushing to *keep* secret commanded the attention of the senior clan." She grinned wickedly. "So it must be one hell of a big fucking secret, eh, Din?" Then she cocked her head. "Mitral, Bekinis, Qabirga, and Juldiz . . . I wonder what connects them to the Hazas? And Blas, and Oypat, and all those silver coins you found."

WHEN WE WERE DONE, Ana replaced her blindfold and called Miljin back into the room to share these revelations.

"Any chance these cantons mean anything to you?" Ana asked him at the end. "Mitral, Bekinis, Qabirga, or Juldiz?"

Miljin frowned as he thought. "Think I rode through Qabirga once. Lots of farms. And it rained. A lot." He shrugged. " 'S'all I got, ma'am."

"Hm. Rather less than useful . . ." said Ana.

"I note we don't have any conclusions regarding the actual *murder*, though, ma'am," said Miljin. "How Jolgalgan got in to poison Kaygi Haza's bath, or the ten dead Engineers . . . And the fire, and the hole in the ground on the Haza property. Don't have much there, yes?"

"We have more than we think," said Ana. "I believe I have one solid idea, at least. We've been wondering how Jolgalgan snuck poison into the halls of the Hazas, yes? Well—what if she secreted *herself* in with it? For I suspect it's very likely that she infiltrated the Haza grounds and *buried* herself in that little hole for a day, or two, or more, waiting for the party."

There was a short, stunned silence.

"Truly?" said Miljin.

My eyes fluttered as I summoned the image of the little hole up in my mind. "That could work . . ." I whispered. "It was large enough, yes. Then when she heard the music and talking, she could just stand up, slip out, brush herself off, and join the crowd."

"And when the party was done," said Ana, pleased, "she'd just leave with them."

"But how could she navigate the servants' passageways up to the roof?" asked Miljin. "They were close, cramped, and dark."

"Well, Jolgalgan *is* an Apoth," said Ana. "And we know Apoths have a fondness for self-alteration. When Nusis went to go look at Suberek's corpse, remember, you asked if she needed a lantern."

Again, my eyes fluttered as I remembered the moment. "But Nusis said she could see perfectly well in the dark," I said.

"Yes," said Ana. "Admirably simple, isn't it?"

"It's ... interesting," said Miljin. "But not watertight. Still don't know how Jolgalgan got on the grounds in the first place, ma'am."

"We don't!" Ana said chipperly. "But I have a theory, though it will need researching. That's where you come in, Captain. Would you please go about getting a list of recent Talagray Legion personnel, please? I would like especially for you to focus on enhanced individuals. Enhanced for *strength*, specifically—much like yourself."

" 'Course, ma'am," said Miljin.

"Good. I think we have a lot to parse through—but tomorrow, Din, you and I shall get more. For we must interview those we once called colleagues, to hear what they saw at this party. Perhaps they saw our killer in action—and witnessed something that may be useful to us." Then she paused and turned to me. "But Din ... one last thing."

"Yes, ma'am?" I said wearily.

"When you first came to the Hazas' property, you asked how big it was."

"Yes?"

"And then you asked how big the dead titan had been, the one they'd taken the claw from."

"Yes, ma'am?"

"Am I correct in believing that the axiom—the Sublime enhanced to process calculations—said *nothing* to any of this? She voiced *no* numbers at either time?"

"Ah ... no, ma'am. She did not."

Ana's fingers fluttered in her dress. "And on Fayazi's arm. You spied paint there, as if to conceal bruising. Like someone had gripped her arm very tight."

"Yes, ma'am."

"Interesting . . ." whispered Ana. "That is all. I simply wished to confirm. You may go, and sleep."

We thanked her, exited, and departed for our rooms, as it was very late in the evening by now.

It wasn't until I'd undressed and laid my head on my pillow that I realized Ana had not commented at all upon my issues with text. Not once. Before I could think on it further, the tower shifted and creaked below me, my eyes fell shut, and I slept.

CHAPTER 31

III

"*TELL* THE HAZAS?" SAID KALISTA. HER MANICURED eyebrows mounted her forehead. "About the investigation? Of course I didn't."

Ana leaned sideways in her chair in the arbitration room, her blindfolded head bent at an angle as the morning sun crept into the arbitration room. I stood behind her, my face carefully circumspect.

"Why not?" Ana asked politely. "Why wouldn't you?"

Kalista laughed dully, her new clay pipe pinched in her fingers before her mouth. Again, I was reminded of a plump little purple courtesan dove, this one perhaps attempting to smooth its feathers after a fright.

"Well, it's not like I'm a close friend of Fayazi or some such," Kalista said. "Not like we have tea and gossip over which Legionnaire has the shapeliest thighs." Her smile dimmed. "Certainly wouldn't expect them to talk to me during . . . Well. All that's happened."

I glanced at Ana, who did not react. Word of Kaygi Haza's murder had spread quickly throughout the city. It was no surprise that Kalista had caught wind of it.

"But you did mention it to *someone*," said Ana, in tones of tremendous sympathy. "Perhaps there was someone else at the party you wished to contact . . . just to confirm their well-being."

A quiver to Kalista's oysterdusted eyelids. "Well," she said grudgingly. "I was concerned about Commander Hovanes. Of the Apoths."

Ana waited patiently. I stood behind her, hands behind my back, listening and watching.

"He was my . . . companion for that evening," Kalista admitted. "And he is a friend. I did wish to notify him that . . . that we had discovered a potential threat to his health."

"And is he," asked Ana, "acquainted with the Hazas?"

"I was his guest," said Kalista. "He was the one invited to the affair. So, yes. I would say so. More than I, at least."

Ana nodded, plainly pleased to have determined the source that had tipped off the Hazas to all our discoveries. "I see. Now! Why don't you describe the party, Kalista?" Ana said. "Your movements, who you saw, and when you saw them."

Kalista began to speak. I listened, sniffing the vial scented of mint, engraving every word.

She arrived at midday, she said, and had been searched at the gates by the guards and exposed to the estate's many telltale plants. Having proven unarmed and untouched by all contagion, she and Commander Hovanes had been permitted to enter the grounds, pass through the winding walkway between the white trees and the bird-perch gate, and approach the party.

"Yet to call it a party," Kalista said, smiling, "is to call a war a spat!" This hadn't been a convivial gathering over wine and mussels, she told us: it was akin to a high imperial ceremony, an almost celestial orchestration of art, food, music, and company, like something out of the ancient days.

Pipers placed at the front steps, their music low and sultry. Banners and ribbons waving at the doorways. Fires of green and silver flickering in every hearth. "And then there was the food," she sighed. "And the wine. And the air . . . For some chambers held moodblooms. Just tarrying in the smokes of those plants for a moment made the very feeling of time change . . . If the Khanum still walked these lands, they'd have expected to be greeted similarly."

"Very nice," said Ana dryly. "But the *people*, Kalista. Did you see many people?"

"Oh, of course!"

She gave us the names of the people she saw. Most of her testimony consisted of gossip she'd heard; a parade of half-remembered, half-sotted conversations that had been half drowned out by the pipers. She only saw Nusis and Uhad fleetingly.

"Uhad, being insufferably supercilious," Kalista said, "was there but a moment. Stayed long enough to be polite, and no longer. Nusis attended with some of the Apoth folk. If I recall, several of the younger, rather sotted men tried to chat with her—it was quite late in the day by then—but she dissuaded them all, claiming she was bound to another." A rather cruel smirk. "First I've heard of that."

"You didn't see anyone who didn't seem to belong there? Perhaps a tall, stern woman with pale yellow hair?" asked Ana.

"You mean Jolgalgan? No, I saw no one resembling her."

"Nor anyone looking, say, slightly *dirty*?" asked Ana. "No one with a bit of soil on their sleeve?"

"Dirty?" echoed Kalista. "I . . . No, not that I recall."

"Did anything of note happen?" asked Ana, growing impatient.

"I *did* hear a commotion before I left. There had been a fire in the second-floor hall. A small one. Some spark had escaped its hearth and alighted on a rug. I didn't see it, but I passed by the area, and saw nothing awry. There *was* a smell in the air, though."

"Describe it, please."

"Oh, well . . . I'm not sure how." She wrinkled her nose. "Smelled like goat's piss, if you ask me. A powerful aroma. Thought it odd. Though . . ." A nervous smile. "Though I'm *not* the sort of person to often handle goats, of course."

"I'd never dare suggest so," said Ana, grinning. "Did you see anyone about this fireplace beforehand?"

"No. As I said, I didn't see it."

"And you didn't see anyone unusual entering the party from the gardens?"

Kalista stared at Ana placidly and blinked. "I'm afraid," she said,

"I'd had a bit too much fumes and wine by that point to be, ah, reliable."

"You mean you were sotted enough to piss your trousers," said Ana, "and never know it."

"Well," said Kalista, scandalized, "I . . . I wouldn't quite say tha—"

"You know now of Kaygi's death, yes?" demanded Ana.

Kalista stopped and nodded nervously.

"And you likely know of the nature of the death."

"Dappleglass. Again. Yes."

"Do you know of *any* connection between Kaygi Haza and Commander Blas?"

"I know they were friendly," said Kalista. "But Blas was known by man—"

"By many people, yes, yes, yes," said Ana. "But you are not aware of any *special* relationship between the two?"

"No. I am not privy to such things, of course."

Ana nodded slowly. "And are you aware of any connection between Commander Blas, and Kaygi Haza, and the canton of *Oypat*?"

There was a long silence.

"Beyond . . ." Kalista said slowly. "Beyond that all three were apparently killed by the same contagion?"

"Yes. Is there anything else that could connect the three?"

"No. But why should there be? As far as I am aware, Blas has never served in Oypat."

Ana nodded, her smile retracting very slightly. "I see . . . Then thank you, Immunis Kalista. I believe that is all we need from you."

NEXT CAME IMMUNIS UHAD, entering slowly in his storklike gait, his blue Iudex cloak swirling about him. He looked exhausted and beleaguered as usual, like a piece of vellum worn so thin you could see the cloudy sun through it. He sat down in the chair, his fingers threaded together, and sighed and said, "So . . . Kaygi Haza is dead."

"Correct!" said Ana.

"In fact," he said balefully, "the man has been dead for over two weeks."

"So it seems."

A taut silence.

"They're going to come at you, you know, Ana," said Uhad.

"I beg your pardon?" she said.

"I've worked as Iudex investigator here for too long to think otherwise. The Hazas will find a way to attack you. You might think this is their key play—coming in and announcing this hidden murder, starting off this bit from the negotiator's chair—but they will have other designs, surely."

"Do you really need to tell *me*, Uhad," said Ana, "of all people, that the Hazas are prone to schemes and plots?"

"A fair point. Now. Do you want the . . . how did you put it for young Kol here . . . the *full vomit*? I did not anchor the experience with an aroma, so what I offer may seem disjointed."

"Whatever you give us would be lovely."

"Fine."

He sniffed. Sat up. Then his face trembled, and he began talking.

What came forth was a blistering, startling rush of words and descriptions, snippets of sentences and bursts of clauses, all capturing the simple experience of walking through the Haza gates, up the path, and into the party within. Some of the things he said were so abrupt, or so stark and spare, that it was difficult to glean any meaning from them. He would rapidly utter things like, "Immunis Eskim, male, short, west of the thirdmost column, Apoth colors, shirt untucked on the left"; or, "Wine lukewarm, freshly mulled, six spice pods floating at rim, spoon rattling in the ewer," and you'd have to struggle to conceive what he was relating.

More startling was Uhad's demeanor as he spoke: he trembled, spasmed, tremored, and twisted as his memories poured out of him. Fingers twitching, knees shaking. Eyes dancing horribly, pulled about by some mad muscle in his skull. He seemed like a man in a vision, overcome with divine revelation.

I listened to all he said, sniffing my vial and engraving all the names and times and details in my memory—but it was difficult to focus. I had never seen another engraver give such a thorough recounting before. I realized I must look the same, during all the times I gave my reports to Ana, and found the prospect horrifying.

An odd pair we were then, like two insects from some bizarre species, with one forcefully inseminating another—yet he was filling up my mind with facts, data, information. And almost all of it was unimportant, or so it seemed to me, just names, dates, times, people; and none felt terribly critical.

He stopped talking. Then he sat back in his chair, panting.

"Good," said Ana. "Very thorough. Thank you, Uhad."

He mumbled a welcome.

"From the sound of it," said Ana, "you weren't at the event long!"

"I wasn't," muttered Uhad. He pushed back his graying hair. "I am not as young as I once was. I must spend my time judiciously. Social events force me to absorb a great deal of information . . ." His eye lingered on her blindfold. ". . . surely something you can sympathize with, Ana. I saw few people and departed."

She then asked him the same questions she'd asked the others: what connection could there be between Blas and Kaygi Haza, and the canton of Oypat?

"Well," said Uhad. He smiled bleakly. "Two of them were murdered. But the canton of Oypat merely *died*, correct? Eaten by contagion. Beyond that, I know no more."

Ana asked him more questions then—about the Hazas, about their schedule of events and parties, about their relations with the Iudex, about Jolgalgan—but she got nothing more. She thanked him and let him go, and I walked him to the door.

"Have you felt the displacements yet, Signum?" he asked me.

"Beg pardon, sir?" I said.

"The displacements," he said. "A psychological affliction. You might spy some object, or catch some scent—and suddenly you are *displaced*. It reminds you of something, and pulls a memory forward, or the object itself literally speaks to you in your mind. The memory describing itself to you, like it was a person living in your head. Have you had one yet?"

"N-no, sir," I said, startled.

"You will," he said grimly. "When they start, it is best to begin living ascetically. Fewer things to remind you of anything, you see. It's something I wished they'd told me when I was your age."

Then he turned and left. I stared after him, bewildered by his comments. I looked to Ana, who merely shrugged.

LAST CAME IMMUNIS NUSIS. "I'm afraid," she said as she sat, "that I haven't made much progress with the reagents key you gave me, Dolabra." Despite the abashed look in her eye, her dark red Apoth's coat was clean and starched, and she wore a bright coppery scarf about her throat—still the cheery little flicker-thrush, despite all the recent sorrows.

"What seems to be the issue?" asked Ana.

"Well, I've exposed it to the usual pheromonic telltales," Nusis said. "Plants that should wither or react upon being placed close to it. These should let me know what kind of reagents portal the key is designed for—but thus far, I've had little luck. It is most unusual." She coughed into her hand. "Though I don't mean to begin the discussion with bad news, of course . . . Where should you like me to start?"

Ana asked Nusis the usual then: had she seen anyone unusual at the party, anyone dirty, or strange, or someone loitering near the fire?

"No," said Nusis. "No, no. I saw nothing like that. If I had, I would have told you already."

"Thank you . . . Next, I wish to inquire about a potential graft," said Ana. "Are you aware there was a fire at the party?"

"Yes . . . I did hear about that. Something about a rug?"

"Correct." She waved a hand at me. "Din here saw the fireplace and spied white scorch marks in the corner of the firebox. They had a curious aroma, yes, Din? A rather *urinal* tang?"

I cleared my throat. "Aptly put, ma'am."

"And Kalista noted the smell was much stronger," said Ana. "She said the whole hall smelled of goat's piss after the flare—her words. I believe the woman is surprisingly well acquainted with goats, you know." She grinned. "Are these phenomena in any way familiar to you, Immunis?"

Nusis sat up, and some of her perk returned to her, as if pleased to be back on known territory. "A urinal tang . . . That sounds like blackperch mushrooms."

"And what are those?"

"They were a fire starter, suffused by the Apoths in the Rathras canton. They build up highly flammable deposits in their inner cores. They were eventually abandoned as fire starters and kindling, being as their fires were so unreliable. Some would create bursts and flares of heat. And the smell afterward was in no way desirable, of course . . ."

Ana went very still. "How long would it take for them to flare?"

"Oh, not long. Many would flare the second they touched flame. Another reason why they were unpopular fire starters—people would place them within a little nest of flaming kindling, and the next thing they knew their whole hand was alight."

"So it would be immediate. An *immediate* reaction."

"More or less, yes."

Ana's bearing was grave now, as if Nusis had just given her dreadful news. "I see," she said quietly.

"Was this . . . this information not welcome, Immunis?" asked Nusis.

Ana was silent for a long while, before finally saying, "It was *unexpected*, I should say."

"I see. But that is all I know. Is there any other way I can assist?"

"Actually, there is," said Ana, coming alive again. "I've been wanting to talk to you about Oypat."

Nusis balked, surprised. "Oh. Oypat? I thought I had talked of this to Signum Kol ..."

"You did. But I wanted to ask you a very simple question."

"Yes?"

"Why did the canton *die*, Nusis?"

"Oh. Well ... the canton of Oypat perished," she said slowly, "because the dappleglass spread too quickly for the Apoths and the Engineers to intervene. But that's well known, of course."

"But too quickly for *what*?" asked Ana. "What was the Empire doing to *stop* it?"

Nusis cleared her throat. "Well ... here. I only know all this from a distance, mind, as I was a very junior officer at the time. But we Apoths sought to make a cure for the spread of dappleglass, to treat the contagion like it was a disease, neutralizing its ability to bloom within flesh or soil. We had to formulate this cure within weeks."

"It must have been a preposterous task."

"It was. The very idea was ridiculous, frankly. But then—rather miraculously—we appeared to be successful."

Ana's mouth fell open in shock. "Wait. You *were*? You mean you actually made a *cure for dappleglass*?"

"Possibly," said Nusis, somewhat reluctantly. "That is a question of some controversy. The senior Apoths created a graft that held promising capabilities of neutralizing the contagion. Twenty little vials, all ready for testing and review. We simply had to get approval to scale it up and begin deploying it within Oypat."

"Then why didn't you?" asked Ana.

"Because, as I said, we needed *approval*. Namely, by all the Preservation Boards. The first rule of the Engineers and the Apoths— outside of Talagray, of course—is to *do no harm*. If you wish to intervene in the Empire, you must first prove that what you do will not damage anything *else* in the Empire. This is where the Preservation Boards step in, ensuring that the status quo will never be threatened."

"And . . . what did the Preservation Boards do regarding Oypat?"

"They moved quickly. Or . . . they *tried* to. But the cantons that would have to grow the reagents for the cure . . . Well, they brought many concerns. They protested how creating these new reagents could lead to environmental issues with all their *other* reagents and agriculture. They demanded tests and studies, wanting to ensure that there was no commingling or mutagenic possibilities."

"I see . . ." said Ana softly. "Then what happened?"

"The process simply took too long. The dappleglass reached a critical point. It had devoured too much land. Too long a border for it to ever be properly neutralized. Like a tumor infecting the bone, or the tissue of the heart, it was too late. So we evacuated the canton, and then . . . then we applied a phalm oil burn."

"Usually reserved for disposing of titans, yes?"

"For destroying their carcasses, correct," said Nusis. "It burns hot enough to destroy anything organic. We burned everything within a half mile of the walls of the canton of Oypat. All the trees, fields, homes . . . everything. And . . . then we sealed it up. Like a tomb. And let it lie." She swallowed. "And that was that. The Empire was saved. And the fertile fields and little towns of Oypat are no more."

There was an awkward silence.

"It might have happened anyway," admitted Nusis. "Years after Oypat, I personally led a team to retest the twenty little vials of cure we'd produced—just in case dappleglass ever infected another part of the Empire. Three of the vials had degraded until they were little more than water. So perhaps the cure might have been ultimately ineffective. We shall never know, unfortunately."

Ana cocked her head. "Strange . . . Was Commander Blas ever involved in Oypat? Did he *ever* assist with containing the contagion there, or perhaps in his work with the Preservation Boards?"

"Blas?" said Nusis. She seemed surprised. "No. No, not that I was aware of. Why?"

"Just a question," said Ana. She smiled wearily. "Yet there is one more thing I'm curious about . . . You mentioned that several cantons had curiously *prepared* protests about the dappleglass cure."

"Yes?" said Nusis.

"Might you recall which ones those were?"

"Oh! Hm. Off the top of my head . . ." Nusis thought about it. "The Juldiz, Bekinis, Qabirga, and Mitral cantons, I believe."

There was a long silence.

"You're sure," said Ana. "You're sure it was those four?"

"I believe so, yes."

"I see," said Ana softly. "Then you may go, Immunis Nusis. Do keep me updated on that reagents key."

I WAITED FOR the door to shut.

"Those cantons," I said. "Those same four cantons again."

"Yes," said Ana quietly.

"The ones Blas's secretary was traveling to, with the money. And the ones Kaygi Haza sent his scribe-hawks to."

"Yes."

"But . . . what's it all mean, ma'am?"

"I am not yet entirely certain, Din," said Ana. She smiled dreamily. "But it's very interesting, isn't it? Very interesting indeed."

CHAPTER 32

|||

AS AFTERNOON TURNED TO EVENING, ANA, CAPTAIN
Miljin, and I lounged in the courtyard of the Iudex tower, sipping
clar-tea and listening to the troops filing in and out of the city.
Miljin had brought Ana her list of Legionnaires altered for strength,
and while she read I related the interviews to him, one after another.

He shook his head when I finished. "Poor old Uhad . . . They
should have transferred him out of here years ago. Can't take too
many wet seasons, the engravers. They don't age well. But I can't find
nary a thing in what you've told me that helps me make sense of
what's going on."

"It's all very tangled, yes," said Ana quietly. She sat back and lifted
her face to the cloudy skies. "There are, I think, three different crimes
we are now investigating." She raised a finger. "There are the
poisonings—Blas, Kaygi Haza, and the ten Engineers. For this, we
have a likely candidate—Jolgalgan—and though she may have involved more accomplices in her works, it is she that we are the closest
to catching now."

"We are?" I said, surprised.

Her finger swiveled to me. "Wait! Wait. I am not done yet." She
extended a second finger. "Then there is Kaygi Haza. He has committed some foul deed, something to do with Blas and Oypat. But I can't
yet see the shape or the why of it. Regarding this, all I have are suspi-

cions, and very little proof at all. We are not helped that these events took place over a decade ago."

"We don't think the Hazas ... well ... introduced the contagion to Oypat, do we?" I asked. "That they poisoned the canton like one might a person?"

Miljin shook his head. "The shit with Oypat is well-documented. The idiot who brewed up dappleglass to make paper was drummed out of the Apoth Iyalet, and nearly got tossed in prison. The Hazas' touch doesn't lie there."

"No," said Ana. "But there is *something* there. Something they wish to hide, which touches all these other murders." Then she extended a third pale finger. "And then there is the fernpaper miller, Suberek, and Blas's secretary, Rona Aristan. Both with holes in their heads—and, increasingly, evidence that connects them to the Haza clan." She dropped her fingers. "Ironically, for these murders, I am *most* certain of the motive, *and* the nature of the killer. But, unfortunately, I think we have the least chance of catching this culprit."

I looked back and forth between Miljin and Ana. Miljin did not look surprised at all, and though both of them appeared troubled, they did not say any more.

"You are?" I said. "You *know* who killed Suberek and Aristan, ma'am?"

"Somewhat. As does Captain Miljin, I believe."

I glanced at Miljin, who had a somber look on his face.

"Then ... who is it?" I asked.

"That answer is complex," she sighed. "Before we get into it, I would like to test out a theory I have ..."

"About what, ma'am?"

"About *you*, Din." She turned to Miljin. "Would you be ready, Captain?"

Miljin looked surprised. Then he sighed. "Are you sure about this, ma'am?"

"Very," said Ana. "I am most curious. Are you ready, Captain?"

"Hell. I guess. Stand up, boy," he said. He began unbuckling his scabbard from his side. "And take my sword." He handed the sheathed blade out to me.

Ana cocked her head. "I thought you were going to see what he could do in combat?"

"Figured this was safer, ma'am," said Miljin. "Less chance we accidentally cut our own heads off. Take it, boy."

I eyed the scabbard. "For . . . for what, sir?"

"For a test. Gonna see how easy it is for you to remember how to get this sword out."

I hesitantly took the scabbard from him. I was shocked at how light it felt. The blade within must have weighed hardly more than a feather.

He saw the look on my face and grinned. "Made from the core of a titan's bone," he said. "Hard as hell to craft such material. It's strong, yet light—something to do with the pressure of the water, or some shit. Yet it holds its edge longer than the finest steel." He tapped the locking mechanism. "It's valuable enough that I had to get this fancy scabbard made for it. Have to move it right to unsheathe it. I memorized the way, though it took me damned long, but . . . Let's see. You take the grip, shut your eyes, and I'll show you the movements. And we'll see what you retain."

He took my hands and guided them through slowly unlocking his sword, the half turns and quarter turns and eighth turns this way and that. I could feel the mechanisms of the sword hilt click with each turn, the little pins sliding in and out. It was monstrously complicated. How Miljin had managed to memorize it, I couldn't fathom.

"Now," he said. He locked the blade in place and stepped back. "Open your eyes, and let's see if you can get it out. Now, Kol. Fast as you can."

"But you only showed me the once," I said.

"So? Try."

I frowned. Then I took the grip in my right hand and held the scabbard in my left; and then my eyes fluttered, and it was like someone breathed air through the muscles in my arm and my hand. I turned the sword, once this way, then the other, and then . . .

In the flash of a second I had the naked blade before me, pale green like the buds of new leaves upon the tree. I stared at it, shocked by my own success.

"Good job," Miljin said, but he did not seem at all pleased. He looked to Ana. "He has it, then."

"He does, it seems," said Ana.

"I . . . I have what?" I asked. "What are you all talking about, please?"

"*Memory in the muscles,*" explained Miljin. "You learn how to move and you remember it, Kol, so you can do it again. Perfectly, every time."

He said this with some awe, but it sounded more or less in line with all the rest of my alterations. "But . . . that's because I'm an en-graver, sir," I said. "Yes?"

"Hell no," said Ana. "Most engravers capture experiences—sights, sounds, and especially smells—but not movement. They can duplicate speech and words, but they can't make their bodies act out something complex. That's much harder. But if you are taught how to move in a way once, Din, then it seems you can move *exactly* that way again, and again, and again."

I was thunderstruck for a moment. "That . . . that can't be so," I said finally.

"Oh, yes?" said Ana. "And how did you learn to pick locks? Or duplicate Sazi text? And how did you cut down three men with al-most no combat experience? Your muscles *remembered.* They remem-bered movements, remembered your training, from long ago. They saw the dangers and moved you about."

Miljin took his sword back from me and sheathed it. "And though I don't know who trained you, boy, they must've done a proper job."

I listened to this in quiet shock. Memories of the fight outside the miller's flooded my mind: the way I'd been pulled, the way my eyes had read the soldiers' movements, the way my hands and feet had acted as if another had been controlling them. And in a way, I realized they had been: they had been obeying a different Dinios Kol, one from many months ago, when he'd acted out those very motions in training.

"They never tested me for this," I said.

"That's because it's rare as all hell," Ana said. "So rare even I've never seen someone with the knack."

"But I have," said Miljin. He gaze grew distant. "I once knew a man who was one of the greatest duelists I'd ever seen. Could parry and dance and fight like no other. And though his arms were corded and strong, he was no crackler—yet almost none could defeat him. I wondered how he'd learned his trade ... Though now and again, I noticed that as he fought, his eyes seemed to shimmer. To vibrate in his very skull. An engraver, with the knack. Just like you."

"So ... why is it we wished to confirm this about me?" I said. I returned to sit at the table. "Do you wish me to become some kind of bladesman like that, ma'am?"

Ana turned to Miljin. "Perhaps not a bladesman—but someone capable of defeating the threats we now face?"

Miljin stared at her. "What? No. *Hell* no. Even with his knack, we can't manage such a thing in a day, ma'am."

Ana frowned. "No? Why not?"

"Well ... I don't wish to be impertinent, ma'am, but you can't just memorize combat as if it were a country jig," said Miljin. "The boy here almost got killed at the miller's on account he put his foot in the wrong bit of mud! There's all kinds of bits you have to learn just by doing. Reading the landscape, the look in the other man's eye, the type of blade he has. Those aren't purely movement, so I doubt he can memorize it. If he trains, he can learn quick—but it'd still take time."

"Damn it all, Miljin," she snapped. "Then what *can* you give the boy in the time we have that would actually keep him alive?"

"Beg pardon," I said, "but—keep me alive?"

They both looked at me, then away. There was an awkward silence.

"Why are you so worried about me, ma'am?" I said. I recalled what we'd been discussing before their little test. "Does this have anything to do with the person who killed Aristan and Suberek?"

Another silence. Ana waved a hand at Miljin as if to say—*Well, go on, then.*

Miljin stared off into the courtyard for a moment. Then he asked: "You ever heard of a twitch, boy?"

"A twitch? No, sir."

"Hmph. Wouldn't expect you to. It's an altered being. A soldier, suffused for combat. Or they used to be." He leaned forward conspiratorially, the bench creaking under his girth. "See—a twitch is suffused to possess superhuman *explosiveness.* Not just strength, for that's different. Rather, twitches can move faster than most human beings, leaping forward like a mantis snapping a moth from a flower."

"What might you mean by 'used to be' soldiers, sir?" I asked.

"Well, it's one thing to have strength," said Miljin. He tapped his arm. "You can alter muscles and ligaments to support that pretty good. But speed ... that wears you down. And that's what happened to twitches. The more they moved, the more their very joints and bones dissolved, their flesh unraveling like a shoddy scarecrow in the wind. Apoths put some kind of healing graft in them to try to keep them upright, but there was some kind of problem with that, too ..."

"Contagion," said Ana. "Most healing augmentations, ironically, are quite susceptible to contagion. Very active blood is good for healing, but also for spreading mold or fungi throughout the whole of your body, apparently."

"That was it," said Miljin. "Anyways, Apoths figured that it wasn't worth it. Not when they had folks like me who were easier and cheaper to make and maintain. But the Hazas ... Rumor had it that the Hazas employed a twitch or two. Ones that looked like ordinary folk but could be called upon at a moment's notice, when the Hazas had a problem."

"A problem," I echoed. "You mean ... when the Hazas needed someone dead."

"One way of putting it," he said.

"You're saying . . . You're truly saying the Hazas use some kind of immensely altered *assassins*?" I said. "All across the Empire?"

"It's a rumor," he said. "The Iudex could never find evidence of it. So a rumor it stayed." He shot a glance at Ana. "But I also heard there was a series of killings in the Sazi lands a few months back. Folk found with holes drilled in their heads. Folk on the wrong end of the Hazas. No one could figure who could have done the deed and vanished in such a fashion . . . except, maybe, a twitch."

I glanced at Ana as well. Her face stayed turned to the sky, and she said nothing.

"And . . . that's what you wanted to train me for, ma'am?" I said. "In case I meet this twitch?"

"You meet a twitch, there's no training I can offer that'd save you, even if we had months and years to do it," said Miljin. "They were supposed to be unbeatable in combat—for about a minute a day, mind. After that, their muscles wore out and they had to recover." He shrugged. "If you last that long, maybe you can stand a chance. But my best advice is stay the hell away from them—if a twitch really is here."

"And I suspect one is," said Ana. "For there are many people the Hazas would likely want dead here in Talagray. Namely, anyone who could link them with the deaths of Blas and the ten Engineers, and the breach."

"Like Aristan," I said. "But what about Suberek?"

"Well, there I have conjecture," said Ana. "But pretty solid conjecture. My guess is—when Fayazi Haza took over after her father, she panicked. First thing she did was try to get rid of the evidence. That meant burning her father's corpse—but also getting rid of all the stained fernpaper. She ordered new panels from Suberek, then replaced all the ones in the bath house. But then the prime sons of the clan sent in the heavy to take over and clean up—the twitch. The twitch identified Suberek as a link, so they promptly took care of him."

I listened to this, thinking. "So . . . where is this twitch? And what does he look like?"

"No one knows," said Miljin. "It could look like any regular fella. They don't appear augmented at all, really."

Then my skin went cold. "Wait. Could the twitch have been in the halls of the Hazas while *I* was there?"

Ana shrugged. "It's entirely possible."

"And . . . you knew, ma'am? You knew I was going to be in the company of an assassin? And you didn't warn me?"

"If I'd warned you," said Ana, "you'd have acted paranoid, like any reasonable soul would. And *that* could have put you in real peril—if the twitch was there. Which I am not yet convinced of." She turned her face east. "They could be here, in Talagray, masquerading as an Iyalet officer. Or perhaps a simple miller, like Suberek. We do not yet know. I'd hoped to give you an advantage, Din, should you cross paths with such a being—but perhaps simply knowing what you can do can help."

"AS LURID AS ALL THIS SHIT IS," said Miljin, "I'm most interested in one bit you mentioned, ma'am . . . namely, that we're close to catching Jolgalgan. Which is, frankly, news to me."

"Oh, but we are," sighed Ana. She returned to parsing through the papers before her. "I just have one last bit of information to figure out . . ."

I eyed the papers. "And you'll find it in lists of Legionnaires augmented for strength, ma'am?"

"Naturally. Have neither of you arrived at it? Captain Miljin here ought to know, at least," she said, grinning. "Being as it was his damned interview that tipped me off. Don't you recall?"

Miljin stared at her blankly. "No . . . ?"

"When you went to the medikkers' bay and did your interrogations," she said, "you were told the dead Captain Kilem Terez had been worried someone *very unusual* had been following him."

"Why ... yes," said Miljin, startled. "A ... a crackler. That was what he'd said."

"And you thought the idea mad at the time—but what if it wasn't?" asked Ana.

My mouth opened in surprise—yet Miljin remained unmoved. "A man ten span tall was following this Engineer," he said. "Around the streets of Talagray. We are to take this seriously?"

"It's very simple," said Ana. "Jolgalgan got onto the grounds, made a hole, and secreted herself away until the party. But how did she get *past* the walls? Well, Din's reports, and our interviews with our witnesses, have forced me to conclude that the only way our poisoner got onto the estate grounds was through the sluice gates."

I nodded as I began to understand. "But the sluice gates are heavy ..."

"Right! Yet someone very, very *strong* might have lifted the sluice gate just enough to allow Jolgalgan inside. And, Miljin, you were told that Terez said he'd been seeing a rather suspicious crackler about— one with *yellow hair*. And who else has yellow hair?"

"Jolgalgan," I said. "She has pale yellow hair ..."

"She does!" said Ana. "Because she is from *Oypat*. As is, I think we can now assume, this mysterious crackler who helped her break in. Two Oypatis, taking apart the Empire from within Talagray ... The theory that Jolgalgan is out for some kind of bloody revenge for the death of her canton grows ever stronger!" She turned a page. "And thus, I now look through the list of all the folk in Talagray augmented for strength. We find an *Oypati crackler*, then we find Jolgalgan." She paused, very briefly. "Along with any other collabora- tor she might be working with. I just need a name. Just one name to hunt down ..." She grimaced, and her stomach growled noisily. "By hell, what time is it? I'm so damned famished I can hardly think!"

I beckoned to a porter standing at attention across the courtyard, waving him over.

"We need a meal here," I told him.

"What might you prefer, sir?" the porter asked.

"Flesh. Beef or fish, preferably, and as recently slaughtered as possible. It doesn't have to have been cooked, just oiled and salted and sliced thinly."

Ana paused as she turned the page, a smile playing at the edges of her mouth. "You're beginning to know me well, boy. But have it brought to my rooms, please. I will need to study this list in a place with a little less stimulation..."

I dropped a few talints into the porter's hand, and he bowed and trotted off.

Ana began messily piling her papers. "I shall finish my work and find a name. But pursuing this crackler will not be simple. An Apoth like Jolgalgan will have many invisible ways of murdering you, possibly beyond dappleglass. Thus, once I have a name, I shall contact the Apoths to ready a contagion crew."

Miljin's face darkened. "A contagion crew... By the Harvester, I never wished to ride out with one of them."

"We have no choice. I'll not have you or Din choking on your own blood because Jolgalgan set graft trips in your path." She stood. "Come to me in the morning, and I will give you your orders. Perhaps we eliminate one of our three mysteries tomorrow. But Miljin..." She lifted her blindfolded face. "Unless I'm mistaken, we do have an hour or so of light left..."

He rolled his eyes. "I'll show the boy a few tricks, ma'am."

"Very good. Thank you. But one last thing... Din? Come here."

I did so, extending my arm to her as I was accustomed. Yet her fingers pawed up my shoulder, then to my head, where she plucked out three of my black hairs.

I winced. "Ma'am! What was that fo—"

"Oh, relax," she said. "I need some black hairs. And my and Miljin's hair is too pale. Only yours could do."

"Do for what, ma'am?"

"To keep me alive, of course. For I'm relatively sure someone shall try to poison me as well, and that right soon—yet these shall protect me." She grinned. "Good night!"

III

AS THE EVENING grew full dark, Miljin showed me a few ugly little moves of his; not really fighting techniques as much as dirty tricks, ways to hobble or hamper your opponent. My particular favorite was one where, if you had time to identify a thrust, you could deflect the blow and angle your blade in such a manner that you trapped their sword with your crossguard, and they impaled their shoulder upon its point. I did it so well that Miljin had to stop himself from piercing his flesh. "That's enough of that one, then!" he said, shuddering.

And as he guided me through the movements, I began to see what they had been trying to show me: every gesture, every position, every shift, and every turn seemed to sink into my very bones, engraved in my body and flesh—but the knack was as limited as it was comprehensive, for I could only duplicate those *exact* movements. If the fight called for something I hadn't memorized, then I was instantly vulnerable.

"Good," said Miljin, sweating mightily after a few minutes of sparring. "But don't let this swell your ego. None of these dirty tricks will do you any good against a twitch, or a crackler. Try and spar with him tomorrow and the fella will rip you apart. Now let us sup, and to bed. There are many ways to an early grave in this canton, and pairing a hungry belly with a tired mind is surely one of them."

He walked me back to the Iudex tower entrance, the Fisher's Hook twinkling and glimmering far above.

"Do you think she meant it, sir?" I said. "That someone will try to poison her?"

"At this point, if your immunis claimed all the world were an aplilot and a giant leviathan was about to take a bite out of it, I'd fucking believe her," he said. He squinted up at the Iudex tower. "In fact, I wonder if she knows the truth of all that's happened. Or if she even *planned* to be here."

"What do you mean, sir?"

"An Iudex officer with such a history with the Hazas? Popping up right when Kaygi Haza gets murdered? She knows more than she's telling. Question is when she tells us."

"As well as if we survive," I said. "That question bothers me a bit more now, sir."

"True," he said. "But that's as Talagray is. The fields of these lands are wet with the blood of many officers. And though we keep hoping the Empire grows more civilized, somehow it finds clever new ways to stay savage. Yet you've an advantage, Kol."

"Because of my knack?"

"No. Because Dolabra's decided to look out for you. Though she's mad, count yourself lucky to be in her shadow."

"I'm in danger *because* I'm in her shadow, sir."

He laughed. "Suppose that's a good point!"

We walked on. It was a queer thing, to know I had this knack; but any excitement I had was drowned in dread of all the threats before us. It was all too easy to imagine some shadowy figure lifting a stiletto to my skull and drilling a hole behind my ear, leaving a tiny, trickling spring of dark blood.

Finally we came to the tower entrance.

"It's a defect as much as it is an advantage, you know," Miljin said, "or they used to say so."

"Pardon, sir?"

"Memory in the muscles, I mean." He squinted at me. "Apparently it only happens to engravers who have trouble engraving other shit—or so I'm told. The duelist I mentioned, he couldn't remember songs at all. Not a bit of them. They were like a big blank space in his mind. Couldn't whistle or tap his foot, neither. I guess it's like everything else in the Empire—there's always a trade-off."

He waited for me to say something, but I did not speak.

"But you seem a keen sort," he said. "Suppose you just got lucky, Kol."

Then he told me good night, turned, and stomped off to his quarters.

CHAPTER 33

|||

THE NEXT MORNING MILJIN AND I MET THE APOTHS'
contagion crew at the Talagray stables. There were six of them—four
women, two men—all wearing curious armor of leather and glue-like
grass that appeared to seal off their whole beings from the air, except
for the heads. The leader of the group, a tall woman with a steely gaze,
shook Miljin's hand and introduced herself. "Signum Kitlan. Told
we're here to deal with contagion, possibly out in the Plains of the
Path—that right, sir?"

"That's right, Signum," Miljin said.

"Can you tell me more about this contagion?"

"It's a plant being used by an Apoth and a crackler. A spore, I'm
told. Breathable. Similar to dappleglass."

None of them seemed surprised or even intimidated by this. They
just nodded, eyes flinty. They were so altered their faces were more
purple than gray, and some of them bore strange scars on their faces
and necks, patches of puckered white from some injury or another.
They were easily the hardest-looking officers I'd ever seen.

"Where are we starting, sir?" Kitlan asked Miljin.

Miljin waved to me. My eyes fluttered as I recalled Ana's briefing
from early this morning, her teeth gleaming in a grin as she'd pro-
nounced: *One! There is only one crackler in service to the Legion stationed
here in Talagray who hails from Oypat. A Militis Drolis Ditelus, stationed*

at a forward outpost close to the walls. And he's had quite a lot of demerits recently. Can you guess what for?

I assume not for poisoning various imperial peoples with dappleglass, ma'am, I'd said.

To which she'd responded: *Don't be smug. No. He's apparently been wandering off to do fuck knows what out in the Plains of the Path when he's supposed to be at the wall. Fellow's in deep shit, really! He has to be our man.*

I relayed this information to the Apoths as we geared up to ride out, along with how dappleglass functioned: fertile and infectious when exposed to steaming water, but after its horrid bloom, it was safe. Again, they did not react.

"We find this crackler, this Drolis Ditelus," said Kitlan. "He takes us to this traitor Apothetikal, and we find the contagion there and destroy it—that it, sir?"

"If it proves that simple," Miljin said, "I'll be overjoyed. But yes."

She spat so profusely on the ground that Miljin looked impressed. "We'll make it simple."

We mounted up and started east, across the Plains of the Path, the same road we took to the medikkers' bay just a few days ago. Our progress was soon blocked, however, for the road east was suddenly packed with teams of beasts—horses, oxen, and giant slothiks—all hauling something toward the walls. Or rather pieces of something, something enormous. At first I thought it was perhaps some kind of piping, huge and curving and carried on massive carts, but then I realized I was wrong.

It was a bombard. Segments of a bombard, slowly making its way toward the distant sea walls. A bombard so huge and so complex my mind could hardly grasp it.

"Huh," I said aloud. "A titan-killer. Just like Captain Strovi said."

"It'll be devilish hard to get to this crackler with all that ahead," growled Miljin. "We'll have to cut across country. Come on."

Our horses were none too pleased with the change in terrain, which made the going much slower. But as midmorning changed to midday we finally approached the forward Legion outpost, which much like the road was crawling with movement.

I studied the scene as we arrived. Panic hung heavy in the air. Legionnaires darted about with hurried, fraught movements, like people readying for some desperate escape. We reined our horses at the front gate and stalked inside, and after a few moments of Miljin's hollering we were brought to the princeps of the outpost.

"Ditelus, sir?" she said. "You're looking for him? Hell, get in line. I'd love to find him, too."

"He's missing?" asked Miljin.

"Yes. Again! With the quakes so hard that the mud dances at our feet, and the titan-killer churning up the road out there. I shall behead the bastard when I find him again." The princeps paused to look us over. "If Iudex is looking for him, though, then he's done something serious . . ." She looked back at Kitlan and her people, impatiently waiting behind us. "And you've a contagion crew with you?"

"We need to know where he is immediately," Miljin said to her. "Is there anyone who worked with him who might know?"

She shook her head. "Everyone's off to assist with the bombard. Engineers say the titan'll be here in a matter of days, maybe hours. Ditelus's whole cohort is long gone."

I looked at the princeps, thinking. It had been weeks since I'd last interrogated a princeps—the smirking Otirios, back in Daretana—but it suddenly came to me easier now, with death and madness rumbling past the horizon.

"You're Ditelus's commanding officer?" I asked.

"I'm the operating officer of this outpost, yes, sir," she said.

"So you would have been the one to write up his demerits?"

"Ah—yes? The Iudex manages demerits now?"

"He was marked for absences, correct?" I said. "Did you ever catch him coming back to the outpost after his absence?"

"I did, a couple of times."

"What direction might he have been coming *from*?" I asked. "And is there anything out there?"

She fetched a map and pointed to the spot. "He was coming from the west, back toward Talagray. There used to be an old Legion fortress that way, decades ago, but it got destroyed during a breach. Killed a titan and it fell right on top of it. Some Legionnaires used to sneak out to the ruins to get sotted back in my day. You think he's there?"

"Much thanks, Princeps," said Miljin curtly.

We left, mounted our horses, and departed, pausing only for Miljin to give me the tiniest nod—*Well done.*

"WE'RE IN A BAD STRETCH OF LAND NOW," warned Kitlan as we rode. "You see anything moving that isn't grass or leaves, don't go near. The Plains are rife with contagion. Worm pits and nests and hives abound. This whole bit of world wishes to eat you."

"Are we allowed to be here?" I wondered aloud.

"Allowed?" Kitlan snorted contemptuously. "No one bothers to fence off these lands, Signum. You'd have to be a fool to traipse in thoughtlessly."

I didn't argue. We'd entered a strange part of the Plains, with giant hills rising on either side of us covered in tussocks of thick, yellow grass—the remains of dead leviathans, surely, felled by the Legion decades if not centuries ago. There were so many hills that I began to wonder why we still called it the "Plains of the Path" at all. Much of this place had to be of higher elevation than the rest of the canton.

More disturbing still were the flowers on the ground about us. None were alike. There were blooms shaped like cups and funnels and rosettes and bells; some were huge and pendulous, others tiny as fleas; and in the deeper parts of the hills, where the rainwater gathered, the blooms grew as thick as the stars, yet all were of different colors, whorls of pink and orange and purple.

The sights did not cheer me, for I knew the ground here had long soaked in the otherworldly blood of the leviathans. Dappleglass no longer seemed such an uncommon threat.

I started glancing over my shoulder toward the east every few miles, looking up at the sky.

"What you looking for, Kol?" asked Miljin.

"Flares, sir," I said. "Just in case."

He laughed roughly. "Warning flares? That won't matter, lad."

"How might you mean, sir?"

"I mean, if we see red or yellow in the sky, it won't matter. We're too close to run. We'll just be dead. So look forward, boy, and not back."

I did as he asked, counting the hills about us as we passed. I'd memorized the princeps's map, but it hadn't been totally accurate regarding the number of carcasses about. Yet I knew we were getting close to the ruins of the fort.

Then one of the Apoths cried out: "Scent! Got scent!"

Kitlan wheeled her horse around to him and demanded, "What kind?"

"Blood, ma'am." The Apoth raised his face and sniffed the air again—his nose was large and violet-hued—and pointed south. "That way."

We followed the Apoth until he stopped at what appeared to be an undistinguished patch of meadow. But he pointed down, and I saw a large splotch of blood resting among the rocks.

"Wet," said Miljin. "And fresh. But is it Ditelus's?"

"Don't know, as we don't have his scent," said the tracker Apoth. He pointed south. "But I smell more that way."

We wheeled about and headed south.

WE FOUND HIM within an hour.

He was easy to spy, a huge, shambling, shifting form just on the horizon, trudging south. Yet even though we were still so far from him, I could see there was something amiss.

The figure in the distance didn't move right. He limped. Staggered. Hobbled along, like he'd broken many bones in his feet, perhaps.

Miljin sensed it, too. "Don't like this," he muttered. "Something's wrong. Is that really him? Where's he going? And what's he running to?"

"Could have worms," mused Kitlan.

"You goddamned Apoths always think it's worms."

"That's because so many people have so many fucking worms."

Kitlan and Miljin led the way, spurring their horses on but pursuing the figure carefully. When we were a quarter of a league away, Kitlan raised a hand for us to stop. Then she and her people pulled bizarre, complex helmets from their packs: the helms had glass bubbles for eyes and were conical in shape, giving them a wasplike appearance, and they ended in what looked like a small brass grate that was packed with moss.

"Warding helms?" I asked.

"Yes," Kitlan said. "Uses suffused mosses and materials to filter out contagion. It will keep us safe as we approach." Then she tossed one to me. "It buckles about the neck."

I pulled mine on and buckled it. The world grew muffled and hot and dark immediately, and I had to squint through the glass bubbles to see. I hoped I didn't wander off blindly and get lost out here among all the horrors about me.

Kitlan waved a hand and we proceeded, gaining on the distant figure hobbling across the wretched wilderness. As we grew closer I came to comprehend the size of the person we were following. He was enormous, nearly as tall as one and a half of me, and as wide as three of me standing shoulder to shoulder—and I was no small person. His black-clad back was as broad as a carriage, and his feet made tremendous *thumps* as he staggered across the Plains, his giant boots churning up the grass and mud before him.

And he was bleeding. From something on his front. I could see the blood dribbling down from between his knees, rills of dark red threading over his thighs.

We rode on until we were within fifty span of him. Then Miljin bellowed through his mask: "Ditelus! Hold!"

The crackler didn't stop moving. He just kept hobbling on.

"Stop where you are, damn you!" said Miljin. "By order of the Imperial Iudex, I command you to stop!"

He did not stop.

"Militis," said Kitlan in a warning voice. "We are here from the contagion crew. If you don't comply, and if we can't determine your state, we will have to set you alight. It's up to you if you're alive or dead while you burn."

Still, he did not stop.

We all looked at one another. Then we spurred our horses on until we were alongside Ditelus, though we rode at a safe distance.

Unlike his body, the crackler's face was surprisingly normal. His pale gold hair was cropped close to his dark, sun-tanned scalp, and his eyes were small and sad. Blood poured from his lips down his chin and his neck, soaking through his black shirt and dribbling between his legs. He wheezed and gasped as he walked, his massive lungs gurgling and clicking with each breath. Every now and again his face spasmed with pain, like he was putting weight on some bone broken within his foot.

"Ditelus! Where is Captain Kiz Jolgalgan?" demanded Miljin. "Is she here?"

The crackler said nothing. He just shambled on, his giant boots making a *thump-thump.*

"Where have you been? What have you done?"

He said nothing.

"Did you help her break into the halls of the Hazas?"

Still nothing.

Then, sighing, Miljin asked, "Ditelus ... where are you going, man?"

For a while Ditelus kept hobbling on. Yet then he answered in a soft, curious, high-pitched voice, whispering, "H-home."

"You're going home?"

"Yes," he gasped. Blood flew from his lips with the word.

Miljin looked ahead. "There's naught but wall in this direction, son."

"I . . . I am going home," whispered Ditelus. His face shook with pain. "To the g-green fields of beans, and . . . and yellow fields of wheat I once knew." He blinked hard, and tears began running down his cheeks, carving cloudy lines through the blood. "Air hazy with pollen in early spring. And th-the forests thick with leaves just after, and then heavy with d-dark fruit." As he limped on, his body began to shake, and he wept. "I shall be there soon."

"The hell is he talking about?" said Kitlan.

"Oypat," I said quietly. "I think he's describing Oypat."

"Y-yes," whispered Ditelus. "It was my home. Yet it is dead, and . . . and I go to join it. I will wander those lands in this next world. And w-what . . . what a joyous thing that will be."

Then he stopped, arms limp at his side. His whole body was quaking now.

"Captain Miljin," said Kitlan lowly. "Get away. Get clear."

"They took it from us," wept Ditelus. "Let it die. Made it die."

"What do you mean?" Miljin demanded. "Who did?"

"And then her . . . He did it to her, I . . . I . . . He did it to her, didn't he?" Ditelus said helplessly. "Didn't he?"

"Who?" demanded Miljin. "Jolgalgan? Is that who you mean? What's happened?"

"Miljin!" said Kitlan, louder. "Get away! Something's wrong!"

She was right. Something was moving at Ditelus's breastbone. Something twitching and curling, under his shirt.

"You . . . you Iudex," screamed Ditelus. "You say you want justice. You always say that! You *always say that!*"

Miljin saw what was happening now. He wheeled his horse away, looking back over his shoulder as something within Ditelus began to . . .

Sprout.

"To see these walls!" roared Ditelus. *"To see what men have made! And know that they could have saved us, but ... but ... "*

Then came a horrid sound, akin to thick fabric ripping, followed by an awful crackling, crinkling sound; and then, like a moth breaking free of its pupa, the dappleglass emerged, a thick, vibrant, undulating shock of bright iridescent green splitting his flesh and rising into the air. It burst from his collarbone, parting him along the side and boiling forth from the edge of his rib cage. Blood poured from his throat in a sudden splash, and then his face was concealed, lost in the shivering coils of roots and the quaking, dark leaves; but the crackling sound continued, as if the vegetation was breaking every length of his bones, crushing them to powder. Then the crackling stopped, yet the column of dappleglass kept silently rising, stretching into the sky in a dark, shimmering column.

I watched as the dappleglass consumed him, until he was little more than a giant puppet held aloft in the towering shoots. I heard the cries and the calls of the Apoths about me, but I had no mind to listen. There between two slender shoots I could spy a sliver of his face, his sad eyes staring into shadow.

"Must have been infected for some time," Kitlan said. "His crackler's body contained it until it ... it ..."

I kept staring at his tears. Watched how they gathered at his chin, growing into a pregnant pink drop, before tumbling off into the leaves.

"From where?" said Miljin's voice beside me.

"Wh-what, sir?" I said dully. I turned to see his furious eyes watching me through the glass bubbles of his helm.

"He was coming from somewhere," bellowed Miljin, "but from *where?*"

I looked north, in the direction Ditelus had been walking from. With a flutter to my eyes, I summoned the image of the map we'd seen at the Legion outpost.

"The old fortress," I said. "It's that way."

"Then come on!" said Miljin. He turned his horse about and started north.

"We have to burn the contagion, sir!" said Kitlan. "It's protocol!"

"Then leave some boys to follow protocol and fucking *come on!*" he bellowed over his shoulder.

KITLAN LEFT TWO APOTHS to burn the body. Then we rode north with her and the rest until we finally spied it: a little clutch of structures leaning against one of the giant hills, just west of an open stretch of yellow-grassed fields.

We approached it slowly and quietly. The place was hardly more than a ruin, the fretvine and stonewood fortifications blasted apart or upended nearly everywhere, its many tottering towers and structures leaning about like a jaw full of broken teeth. There were curious ripples and crests in the soil about it, all radiating from the giant hill behind. I guessed that when the leviathan had fallen however many decades ago it had broken all the world below, before finally being eaten by grasses and trees like the other carcasses.

We entered the ruins on the western side. It felt like riding through a giant child's broken toys, or some stretch of coast where shipwrecks were washed ashore. Nothing I saw seemed whole, except for a tall, crooked tower that leaned in the center of the wreckage.

Miljin caught my gaze and nodded. We led Kitlan and the three other Apoths through the maze of tumbledown structures until we finally approached the tower. It was tall, and whole—but the door, unlike everything else in this place, was well-maintained. Wood solid and dark, the rope handle white and new. Iron hinges free of rust.

I stared at the door, wondering what, or who, was behind it.

"Kitlan," said Miljin quietly. "You want me to open that door or you?"

She didn't answer. She just dismounted, tossed the reins of her horse to one of the other Apoths, and advanced. She placed a hand on the rope, took a deep breath, and pulled the door open.

I couldn't see inside, but Kitlan stared through the doorway. Then she turned away, disgusted.

The door fell open, I glimpsed within.

A clutch of shoots nearly filled the interior tall tower. Leaves slender and dark green, dappled with blooms of white and purple. And there, suspended in the clutch of shoots, a figure: a woman, dead and rotting, her eyes dark and her yellow hair gleaming in the midday sun.

MILJIN AND I stood aside and watched as the Apoths came and went from the crooked tower. They were taking samples, they said, cataloging all the reagents and specimens found within, along with all the Apoth's tools.

"She had quite the array," said Kitlan, taking stock. "Fermentation chamber. Purification dome. Casks of suspension fluids. Suffusion feedstock. Phalm oil for any reagents gone awry. And tank after tank of plants . . . All of them the same kind."

"Dappleglass," I said.

She nodded her helmeted head. "This is where it happened. This is where they made it. Secreted out all this gear and got to work brewing up her poisons."

"And we're sure it's her?" said Miljin. "That body in there is Jolgalgan?"

Kitlan walked to the pile of cataloged material, sorted through it, and returned with a sheaf of paper. It was a wall pass, like Aristan's, permitting the bearer to pass from the Outer Rim of the Empire into the third ring. Though it was hard for my accursed eyes to read through the glass bubbles of the helmet, I could still barely make out the name *JOLGALGAN* written in the corner.

"There's more," said Kitlan. "More documents. Some in her name, some counterfeit and falsified. Seems she was hoarding up to run. But it's her."

Miljin stared in at the corpse suspended in the darkness. "And she just . . ."

"Had an accident, by the look of it," said Kitlan. "My guess is something didn't seal right. There's a bottle in the back that's burned dark and still warm. That was likely the source, boiling a bit of water that's now evaporated, but the steam leaked out, carrying the spores. She's been dead about a day or two. I suspect the crackler came to check on her and was exposed as well. If we didn't have our helmets on right now, we'd be dead, too."

I felt my heart quaking as I realized how close I'd come to meeting the same horrid fate as Ditelus. "How . . . how likely is such a mistake to actually happen, though?" I asked.

"Very," said Kitlan. "This is an improvised laboratory. None of this is to Apoth code. And they were handling a very, very dangerous contagion. There's a reason why we built walls around Oypat, after all."

I gazed in at the tower. "How much dappleglass could she have brewed in there?"

Kitlan shrugged. "Lots."

"Is there any way to know if there's more out there? Planted among the canton, waiting to bloom?"

"No way to tell here, I'm afraid."

She returned to the tower. We watched her in silence.

"So—the second we get close to Jolgalgan," said Miljin quietly, "she goes and fucks up and gets herself and her sole collaborator killed."

Wind ripped through the barren ruins. The corpse within the tower danced and shivered in the trees.

"That feel right to you?" Miljin asked me.

I said nothing.

V

III

THE SHADOW
OF THE LEVIATHAN

CHAPTER 34

|||

I FINISHED SPEAKING, MY VOICE HOARSE, MY EYE-lids aching from the fluttering. My last few words echoed in the adjudication chamber until they finally faded.

Commander-Prificto Vashta peered down at us from the high bench. "So," she said slowly. "It's . . . done?"

Ana shifted in her seat like she'd sat in something wet. "Partially," she conceded. "Possibly."

Vashta frowned. Though her Legion's cuirass was bright and polished and her cloak dark and clean, the commander-prificto's face looked more beleaguered than ever, so much so that I found myself worrying about the state of the sea walls.

"Immunis," said Vashta, "could you kindly clarify what in hell you mean by that?"

"I mean, it is possible that the case is solved," said Ana. "Or that it is partially solved. Or perhaps it is only possibly partially solved, ma'am."

There was a long silence. I stared down at my new boots, which were now no longer identifiably new, being so caked with mud and stained from the Plains. Miljin, sitting beside me, suppressed a yawn. I sympathized: though this moment felt fraught, we were both exhausted from our ride back and our many debriefings with Ana and Vashta.

"To review, Dolabra," Vashta said, "Jolgalgan was who you *always* believed to be the primary poisoner."

"Yes, ma'am," said Ana.

"And she is now dead."

"True, ma'am."

"And the laboratory where she'd been brewing this horrid contagion is now destroyed."

"Burned with phalm oil, ma'am, whose heat even dappleglass spores cannot resist."

"And her collaborator is dead as well—killed by the same accident?"

"Yes," said Ana. "But there is still little we *actually* know about her. Did Jolgalgan truly wish to kill those ten Engineers? If so, we know neither how she accomplished this, nor why. We have great reason to believe she killed Kaygi Haza—but we've no true idea why there, either. For if this is indeed part of her desire to avenge Oypat, why pursue this one ancient gentryman?"

"The Hazas are one of the greatest clans of the Empire," said Vashta. "They provide incalculable reagents that maintain our very civilization. Surely killing a prime son of the clan would have many ill effects."

"Perhaps it is so simple. But if so, ma'am, why would the Hazas hide his murder? Why deny the presence of the ten Engineers at their halls? Why deny all knowledge about Commander Blas? We do not know. And then there is Rona Aristan, and Suberek, the secretary and the miller. They are both dead—and not by Jolgalgan."

"What are you suggesting?"

"That they were killed by someone else. And judging by the nature of their deaths—a tiny puncture to the skull for both of them—it was someone very augmented, ma'am."

Vashta stewed for a moment. "Do you have a suspect?"

"Nothing firm, ma'am."

"Do you have a motive for their killings?"

"Not a clear one, ma'am—not yet. But all we've learned continues to point toward the Hazas."

"And yet, you have surely heard all I've said already about the Hazas. Though I am seneschal, if you wish me to haul the owners of the most valuable land in the Empire into this tower like a pack of jackals, I cannot do it during the wet season, when a leviathan grows so near—and especially not after a breach."

There was a tense silence. Ana's fist was clenched, her knuckles white and trembling—just like the day she'd interviewed Fayazi Haza in this very chamber.

"I am here to protect the Empire, Immunis," said Vashta quietly. "Not deliver justice. That is not the purview of my Iyalet, and justice is not always easy to come by in such times."

"I see, ma'am," said Ana. "Yet there is one last question that troubles me most of all."

"And what might that be?"

"The blackperch mushrooms," said Ana.

Vashta blinked. "The . . . the what?"

"Well, presumably, Jolgalgan used blackperch mushrooms as a distraction at the halls of the Hazas—causing a fire to flare up immensely, drawing eyes as she slipped into a servants' door."

"So?" said Vashta.

"So, Nusis testified that blackperch mushrooms flare *immediately* when exposed to flame. Which means that Jolgalgan would have to have been present when the flare occurred."

"*So?*"

"So, such a thing would not do for a distraction. She would be drawing eyes *to* her, rather than away."

"Can you get to where you're going with this, please, Immunis?"

"The likeliest explanation, ma'am," said Ana, "is that there was a *third*. A third person, a third collaborator. Someone *inside* the party who tossed the mushrooms into the fire for her, to act as a distraction, while Jolgalgan slipped into the servants' passages."

Vashta frowned, troubled. "Do you have any evidence or testimony for this?"

"Again, nothing firm, ma'am. But being as I also wonder how Jolgalgan knew so much about Commander Blas's movements—a knowledge that neither she nor Ditelus should have been privy to—I find my dissatisfied thoughts bending in this direction. There is, I think, a third poisoner out there."

"And what," Vashta asked, "would ameliorate your dissatisfied thoughts, Immunis?"

"I would like to request a week to review all evidence and perform any additional interviews, ma'am. Jolgalgan surely saw many people before her apparent disappearance. So did Ditelus, and Blas. I want to talk to them all, and then we shall find our third, if they exist."

Vashta silently debated all this. "Do you expect any more Engineering deaths?"

"To dappleglass? I doubt it."

"And no more bits of the sea wall shall come down."

"I don't believe so, no."

"And your investigation won't interfere at all with our preparations for the approaching titan."

"No, ma'am."

"Then I can give you a week," she said. "But I cannot promise it will actually be given."

"Because of the leviathan?" said Ana.

Vashta smiled—a cold, jaded expression. "This is Talagray, Immunis. Nothing is ever certain here. Still, I must say . . . you have performed your duty. Even if we don't fully comprehend this crime, you have identified the killers and found them out within a matter of days, when we needed it most. You have done well."

Ana bowed. "Thank you, ma'am."

"And although I agree this end doesn't satisfy, I will congratulate you. Many officers shall sleep far more soundly tonigh—"

The ground shook below us. This quake was much stronger than some of the others I'd felt in the past days. I glanced out the window, worried I might spy green flares rising on the horizon, warning us of a leviathan's approach.

"Well," said Vashta. "As soundly as they can, I suppose." She rubbed her tired eyes and sniffed. "Will you and your signum be at the banquet tonight?"

"Ah—possibly, ma'am," said Ana.

"I'd encourage it. The conclusion of your investigation will no doubt be interpreted as a good omen, and your presence will boost morale. Which we need now, of course. *Very* much."

"Understood."

Vashta sighed once more. "Captain Strovi has volunteered for the firing crew of the massive bombard. I tried to talk him out of it, but he wouldn't listen, of course . . . He is valiant to excess, I find. Perhaps you all can grant him a blessing of your own at the banquet."

"I shall go, of course," said Miljin. He yawned yet again. "Though I should like to find a bed first."

"And Din will be there," said Ana. She bowed her blindfolded head low. "I thank you for your approval, ma'am. We shall leave you to attend to more important affairs."

"BANQUET?" I asked Ana as we crossed the central atrium of the Iudex tower.

"The Banquet of Blessings," Ana said, gripping my arm. "An old religious rite practiced before facing a titan. They haven't done one in years—usually the wall and our artillery are enough—but this time is different. The Legion must wait for a titan to come to the breach, fire the giant bombard, and kill it dead in one shot, plugging the gap. All hands that touch the bombard must be blessed, then. It should be a very interesting affair. Ritual celebration. Lots of smokes. Lots of animal bloods, and wine and chanting. You will go in my stead."

"Afraid I don't feel much like banqueting after that, ma'am," I said.

"Ahh . . . you don't feel any of this satisfies, either, Din?"

"No," I said.

We started up the stairs. The sight of Jolgalgan's corpse swaying in the dappleglass lingered in my mind.

"Suberek and Aristan, ma'am," I said, "have not found justice."

"No," she said. "They have not."

"The ten Engineers have not found justice."

"That is so."

"And the canton can't spare a care for it, it seems. Not with the leviathan coming. Feels wrong."

"It feels wrong because it *is* wrong, Din," she said. "Civilization is often a task that is only barely managed. But harden your heart and slow your blood. The towers of justice are built one brick at a time. We have more to build yet."

I helped her up the last steps. "You don't think it's really over?"

"Hell no," said Ana. "I *don't* think Jolgalgan was looking to damage the Empire. I think her killing of Blas and Kaygi Haza was personal. I just don't yet know why. And then there's what Ditelus said . . . '*He did it to her, didn't he?*'"

I opened the door for her. "I take it you don't think it was the twitch who poisoned Jolgalgan, ma'am."

"Of course not. The twitch doesn't kill with dappleglass. So Jolgalgan's death either really was an accident—something I consider unlikely—or it was someone else. Possibly this third poisoner, whom I worry about. Fearing they were to be caught, they sabotaged Jolgalgan's lab, and when she fired up all her brewing kits, she poisoned herself—and then Ditelus, when he came to check on her. And they left us a neat little story." She sat at the open window, blindfolded, and tilted her head, listening to the churning city below. It was the one time I'd ever seen her expose herself to such stimulation. "The city awakes, and empties . . . with some going east, to fight, but many more going west, to flee. Yet you and I shall stay here, Din. We shall stay until the work is done. And it is very nearly done. Yet I must now think." Fumbling, she shut the window, and the room was veiled in darkness. "A third . . ." she whispered.

"Pardon?"

"A third—that was what you overheard Fayazi Haza saying as well. Someone from her clan was looking for a third . . . For a long while, I thought they meant the third poisoner, the one I now suspects exists. But now I am unsure."

"Then . . . what are we to do, ma'am?"

"I . . . I will do what I do best." She sat on the bed. "I will *think*. But you—you should go to the banquet, Din."

"Beg pardon, ma'am. But I don't—"

"Yes, yes, don't feel like banqueting. But a Banquet of Blessings is a profoundly rare occurrence. More so, Vashta has *specifically* requested we be there. Since she's basically the dictator of the canton, it would be wise to keep her on our side. I will have use of her soon. And besides, you've had a horrid few days, and I think you need reminding of what the Empire is even for."

I cocked an eyebrow at her, puzzled.

"It's not all this!" she said. She waved her hand at the shuttered window. "It's not all walls and death and plotting! Nor is it dreary dispensations and bureaucracy! We do these ugly, dull things for a *reason*—to make a space where folk can live, celebrate, and know joy and love. So. Go to the banquet, Dinios. Otherwise, I'll find some truly dreadful shit for you to do."

CHAPTER 35

‖‖

THE SUN HUNG LOW IN THE SKY AS I APPROACHED the Legion tower. The streets about it were already filling up with Iyalet officers, most in Legion black, but many in Engineering purple and Apoth red, and the occasional flash of Iudex blue. As we lined up to enter the Legion courtyard a singing began from within, a high, ululating, solemn song in a language I did not recognize.

The ceremony had begun, I realized. The line moved faster, and soon I passed under the black-bannered arches, took my place among the crowds gathering along the circular courtyard walls, and looked to see.

In the center of the courtyard were two lines of people, bluely lit by the lanterns: one line composed of some two dozen Legionnaires, all kneeling, heads bowed; and there, standing over them, was a line of people of a sort I had never seen before. They were all from many different races—Tala, Sazi, Kurmini, Rathras, Pithian—and each was arrayed in strikingly different raiment, all swirling dark robes and fine gold chains, or veils of silver and high, peaked hats.

They were holy folk, I realized: priests and clerics and rectors and curates from all the imperial cults. I struggled with this for a moment, wrestling with the idea of an Empire so vast it could accommodate such wildly different cultures. Yet all of them intended to make their blessings known here, it seemed, invoking their pantheons to stem back the titans of the deeps.

I glanced about the courtyard. The front area seemed to have been reserved for the senior officers: I spied Vashta sitting among them, her breast covered with so many heralds and tributes that her whole front twinkled like the night sky. When she wasn't solemnly watching the ritual she studied the crowd, marking who had and had not attended, I guessed. When her keen eye fell on me, she smiled tightly and nodded. I bowed in return.

The holy folk sang aloud from their texts and swung their thuribles before the kneeling Legionnaires, bathing them in incense and sacred smokes. Then they wrapped the soldiers in holy cloths and anointed their brows with paints and the bloods of pheasants and calves, slowly layering them with prayers, with hopes, with calls to the divine.

Among this sea of strangeness I saw something I recognized: a round, gold effigy mounted high behind the holy men, depicting a long, gaunt face that was both sympathetic and stern, with words written below in an ancient, half-forgotten language—*Sen sez imperiya.*

I stared back at the face of the emperor. I tried to make his words mean something to me, knowing that the twitch and the Hazas had killed two people at least, and perhaps ten Engineers and countless others as well; and not only might they go unpunished for it, but Ana and I might never comprehend what had really happened here. Blas, the breach, the party—all of it might be washed away like footprints in a rainstorm.

The more I thought on it, the more I wished to leave this holy rite. The emperor offered many blessings to the Legion, it seemed, but precious few for the Iudex. How simple the titans seemed, and how impossible justice felt.

The ceremony appeared to be drawing to a close: three holy men touched the brow of the kneeling Legionnaire at the very front. Then they proclaimed something in ancient Khanum and kissed him upon the head, bowed, and drew back. All the Legionnaires stood and bowed in return; and that seemed to be the end of it, for the courtyard then filled up with mutterings and quiet conversation.

The scent of incense was pushed away by the aromas of fats and spices and wine. Food arrived, the tables suddenly piling high with sliced meat and pickled vegetables, and cask after cask of sotwine. I had no idea what else I was to do at such a ceremony, so I ambled forward to fill my bowl.

A voice behind me: "It's a pleasure to see you triumphant, Signum."

I turned. Immunis Uhad emerged from the crowd in his stiff, storklike gait, his blue Iudex cloak swirling behind him, his face still as gaunt and bleak as ever.

"Good evening, sir," I said, bowing.

"I've heard the news," he said to me, "and all the details of all your victories. You and Ana have handled things marvelously. No, no, don't bow again. Be merry. This is the time for such things, after all."

I filled my cup and raised it to him. "I've never been to such a ceremony before, sir. I wish them luck and fortune." Yet I noticed Uhad bore neither wine nor bowl.

"Can't indulge myself much these days, Signum," he admitted. "Too much wine leads to too many, ah, afflictions. And social events cause no end of headaches." A weary smile. "Enjoy it now, while you have it."

"Do you mind me asking, sir . . . When did you start having afflictions?" I asked.

"Oh, when I was about fifteen or twenty years older than you. So you have some time still. Though it's moments like these that make it worthwhile. Engrave this victory deeply, boy. It will be a treasure to you."

I said nothing.

"But . . . I suspect you are likely pained by the way it ended." His tired eyes lingered on me. "Not all who perpetrated injustice have met justice, after all."

"No, sir," I said. "They have not."

"No." Uhad sighed. "But righteousness rarely finds ones so powerful. They are critical to the Empire, and use their importance to gain more power, and grow all the more unassailable. It irks me. It always has. But I shall let it irk me no more." He smiled wearily. "My time as a Sublime is finally at an end."

"You're being relinquished from duty, sir?" I asked.

"Oh, yes. This was my last investigation. I shall retreat to a small plot of land in the first ring of the Empire and spend my last few days partaking in what peace I can find there."

I was surprised he could afford such a place. The first ring of the Empire was the most protected enclave of all of Khanum. To hear that Uhad could buy his way into such a paradise was quite startling.

"Though I do wish I could keep serving, frankly," he confessed. "Anyway . . . Ana tells me you are remarkably skilled at making tea. Is that so?"

"Oh. Somewhat, sir."

"Have you even had the chance for a cup during all this madness?"

"Not in a while. Though we did bring the kettle, of course."

"What a pity. You and Ana are both owed some reprieve. Though you must make me a cup before I go." He bowed. "I will pester you no more and shall leave you to form some more pleasant memories than these tonight, Signum. I suspect many will wish to congratulate you." He glanced over my shoulder. "And some come right soon."

Commander-Prificto Vashta then swept through the crowd, flanked by a half-dozen officers so elite I felt my whole body go stiff with shock. "Here he is," she said, smiling a smile that didn't quite meet her eyes. "Here is our victorious Iudex signum, who helped end our rash of horrid poisonings . . . Signum Kol, we've many here who'd like to learn how you managed this miracle!"

The many officers looked at me expectantly. I glanced back at Uhad, only to find he was already gone.

THE NIGHT WENT ON, dripping by in the humid, spice-soaked air. Vashta wielded me about like a lucky talisman, introducing me to

Engineering and Legion officers, proclaiming my accomplishments, eager to assuage everyone's anxieties after the breach. The officers all bowed low and offered me thanks, and blessings, and wine, shaking my hand and claiming my victory was full of good portent. Their praise did not hang easily on me, and eventually I began bowing low so they couldn't see the strained smile on my face.

Finally a Legionnaire approached Vashta, whispering news from the walls. She thanked me for my attendance and released me. It was late by now. The crowd was thinning out around me, and the lanterns growing dark. I was exhausted, and felt a liar after such merriment and congratulations. I moved to leave, then stopped.

One Legionnaire stood alone below the visage of the emperor: the one whose brow had been touched and kissed by the three holy men. He stood with a somber expression on his face, staring out at the dwindling crowd, his face streaked with holy blood and oils and paints, his shoulders streaming with colored ribbons and cloths.

Then he looked at me, and I realized it was Captain Strovi.

He went still at the sight of me. I looked back. It was not until that moment, stripped of all the signals of rank and status, that I realized how Strovi looked at me, and perhaps had looked at me all this time.

I smiled at him. He returned the smile, faintly relieved. He gestured to himself and shrugged, as if to say—*Can you believe what they've put me in?*

I laughed. I gazed back at the lingering crowd. Then I set down my sotwine and walked over to him.

Strovi grinned ashamedly as I approached. "You know, they tell us all about the sacred ways of getting into this gear," he said. "But never how to get out of it."

I studied him. The blood on his face was now dry and crackling. Yet he was still handsome, even under all that.

"You look quite the sight, sir," I said.

"I look quite the sight," he said, nodding.

"Do you know what all those are for?" I asked. I gestured to my face. "As in—what each thing they did to you means?"

"Some," he said. "But most, ah—absolutely not. I don't even know all the cults that just blessed me. It's all a bit mad."

"They said you're firing the cannon. Is that true?"

"That is a little like assigning the death of a titan to one Legionnaire. I am part of the *team* that will be firing the cannon. It is monstrously complicated to do. But yes."

"Then I wish you the emperor's blessing, and all the luck of all the gods."

"And I thank you," he said, bowing, "but I admit, I am about as tired of hearing that as you're likely tired of being congratulated on your success."

I said nothing.

"Are you enjoying yourself?" he asked.

I thought about it. "No," I said.

"No?" he said. "I thought I saw about two dozen officers walk up to shake your hand. And three were commanders, to my eye."

"You must have been watching me closely then, sir."

He smirked and let the comment hang. Then he said, "Why aren't you enjoying yourself?"

Again, I considered what to say. "They all shook my hand," I said finally. "Like we'd won. But we didn't win. It all just fizzled as we got close. And many dirty folk who wrought so much death still go free. And . . . and everyone seems to know. Old Uhad walked up and chatted with me about it. Like it was dinner conversation. And I'm supposed to keep doing my duty. As if it wasn't there, atop all I do."

He watched me closely, his face sympathetic. "In the Legion they tell us to ask—do the walls still stand? Does the Empire persist? And if I can say yes to that, then I should feel satisfied with the day, and call it victory. We have to, I think. Otherwise, it'll grind you down, Dinios."

"All I feel," I said, "is alone."

The last few officers lingered at the gates of the courtyard, speaking in loud, drunken tones.

"You don't have to feel alone," said Strovi.

I looked at him. The moment stretched on. He tried to smile again, yet there was a desperation to it. I remembered then that whatever trials vexed me, Strovi's were far greater. I felt suddenly ashamed, and hated the sight of such worry in his face and wished I could wipe it away like I might the oils and paints upon his brow and cheeks.

"There's a bathing basin in my chamber," I said.

He blinked at me, puzzled.

"I could get all that off for you," I said. "I'd just be repaying a favor. I mean, you did it for me, once, in the mill. Sir."

He blinked again, this time in surprise. "Oh," he said.

Again, the moment stretched on. I felt mortified, suddenly convinced I'd overstepped. If the ground had cracked open before me I'd have gladly jumped into the chasm to hide from the shame.

Then, after a moment, Strovi said, "Are . . . are you sure?"

Relieved, I nodded, laughing faintly.

"Well . . ." He glanced around the courtyard and grinned. "Then lead on. And hurry, before someone else stops you to shake your ha—"

Then the drunken voices at the courtyard entrance went silent, replaced by the sound of the tramp of many boots.

Together we turned and saw a half-dozen Legion officers pouring in, their steel caps glinting as they looked about. I glanced at Strovi, thinking they were surely here for him.

"Ohh, what's this?" said Strovi. "What's happened now?"

One Legionnaire cupped a hand to his mouth and called, "*Signum Dinios Kol! Is Signum Kol present?*"

I sighed deeply. "Shit," I said.

Strovi shut his eyes and sighed as well. "Ah . . . yes. Shit. Shit indeed."

"Some other time?" I said.

He gestured at the dark skies. "If the fates will, certainly."

I quietly cursed this day and this evening, then raised my hand and called, "I'm Kol."

The Legionnaires trooped over to us. "You're needed at the Apoth tower, sir," the lead one said breathlessly. "Right away. Your immunis is already there waiting for you."

"Ana's out of her rooms?" I said. "What's happened?"

"Don't quite know, sir," she said. "But . . . Immunis Nusis has been injured. Not responding. Could . . . could be dead." She touched the back of her scalp. "Something to do with her head."

I looked at Strovi, alarmed. He nodded back, his face sad. Then I followed them into the night.

CHAPTER 36

|||

THE APOTH TOWER WAS ABUZZ WITH OFFICERS AS I ran up the steps. The Legionnaires cleared the way for me, ordering folk to step aside, and soon I was back in Nusis's office, the walls stacked with tanks and jars and pots, the throngs of worms writhing behind so many glass walls, though now all was shadowy and silent, and the air reeked with the copperish scent of blood.

"Come in, Din," said Ana's voice from the far darkness. "I need you to see for me."

I took a lantern from a Legionnaire and moved closer. Ana sat before Nusis's desk, I saw, blindfolded, head bowed. Sitting behind the desk was Nusis.

She was bent forward, her head resting on the desk with her arms on either side like she'd been working and decided to take a short nap. Spreading from the base of her neck was a pool of blood, smooth and dark and mirrorlike. It dripped off the edge with a slow *pat-pat*.

I could not see her face. For that, I found myself glad.

"No," I murmured. "No, I . . . It can't truly be her, can it?"

"Din," said Ana. "Focus. The base of the skull. Please look."

Trembling, I walked around the corner of the desk. Her hair was thick and took some work to part; but there, behind Nusis's ear, was a small, dark purplish hole, slowly leaking blood.

"The Hazas' twitch?" I asked. "They . . . they did this?"

"The wound looks the same as the others?" Ana said sharply. "Not a mimicry? Because, if so . . . Then yes. I believe it is the work of the twitch. Are there any other injuries upon her?"

"No, ma'am. None that I can see. But . . . why would the twitch bother with Nusis?"

Ana cocked her head. "Can you confirm if her safe is still locked?"

I confirmed it was, the front sealed tight. "It is, ma'am."

"Is there any blood upon the safe?"

I studied it in the lamplight. "No, ma'am."

"Hm. Any aroma to it?"

I leaned close, sniffing the air. "There is, ma'am. Alcohol, I think. Just a hint of it."

"Good. We shall confirm more when the trackers arrive . . ."

"Trackers?"

Three Apoths then strode through the office door, their movements confident and assured. I recognized them immediately: Princeps Kitlan and the two trackers from the contagion crew that we'd ridden out with.

The three Apoths looked at the corpse with blank, hard eyes, then bowed to Ana. "You called for us, ma'am?" asked Kitlan.

"I did," said Ana. "This, obviously, is a death scene, Princeps, and we've need of your talents. I was wondering if you could catch any additional aromas about this place—and possibly remove the door to Nusis's safe. I believe you lot are in possession of some rather advanced corrosives . . ."

"We are, ma'am," said Kitlan. "Mostly for destroying contagion. But we'd be happy to comply here." She waved to her tracker, who moved to the door of the safe and slid his pack off his back.

He sniffed the door of the safe as he sat before it. "Smells of alcohol, ma'am. Grain, I think. Probably from the immunis's own stores. But . . . it also smells of blood."

"Blood?" asked Ana.

"Yes, ma'am." He nodded at Nusis. "Her blood."

"You're sure?"

"I am. I've enough here to sniff to make a match. It's the same. My guess is the safe was bloodied, and then cleaned with alcohols."

Ana steepled her fingers. "I see . . . Would it be safe to say, then, that the killer manipulated or touched the safe *after* killing Nusis? With bloodied hands? They likely did not kill her beforehand, since, well, Nusis couldn't open her safe if she was dead . . ."

The tracker shrugged. "Seems likely, ma'am."

"I see. Then please remove the door."

Kitlan and the tracker carefully applied drops of some smoking black reagent to the hinges of the safe. They did so in several rounds, tugging at the door after each application, until finally there was a groan, and the door fell away.

"Now, Din," said Ana. "Look. Remember. Has anything within the safe been stolen? Anything missing?"

I squatted to look, my eyes shivering as I summoned up my memories of the last time I'd glimpsed inside this safe. I saw the boxes of grafts, a handful of papers I had seen before; and there, in the corner, the reagents key I'd brought to her, the vial set in a little bronze disc. Everything was all still here—or so it seemed.

"The key, Din," said Ana. "Is the key there?"

I peered at the reagents key, then gestured to the tracker to hold the mai-lantern close.

"Well?" demanded Ana.

"There's . . . *a* key, ma'am," I said slowly.

"But?"

I peered closer at it. "But . . . it's not the key I got from Aristan's safe house, I think."

A thunderstruck silence.

"*What?*" said Ana.

I turned to the tracker. "Can I pick it up, you think?"

The tracker leaned forward and sniffed the safe. "Not catching scent of any graft trips . . . though the scent of blood and alcohol is much stronger in here."

"The killer cleaned the *interior* of the safe, you mean?" said Ana.

"Seems likely, ma'am. But it should be safe to review."

I lifted the reagents key, held it up next to the lantern, and studied it. I shook my head. "I'm sure, ma'am. It's not the same key. The bronze of the disc is discolored in the wrong places. And it's missing a few dents. There were four total, one big, three small. And the weight is wrong."

"You remember all that?" asked the tracker, surprised.

Kitlan snorted. "Boy's an engraver. That's what he's here for."

"You're sure about all this, Din?" asked Ana.

I felt the tickling in my eyes as I recalled it. "I'm sure of it, ma'am. This key is similar—but it's definitely different."

"Can we figure out what this new key *is*, then?" she asked.

The tracker took the key from me and sniffed it. "Well, it's . . . it's a reagents key, ma'am. I can smell it. Smelled 'em before. Dunno what kind, though, or what portal it opens, but . . . I do note it smells very, very strongly of blood as well, though it's also been cleaned."

"But you're *sure* it's a reagents key?" asked Ana. "An ordinary one? Nothing special about it?"

"Nothing that I can tell. A reagents key, ordinary enough."

Ana was silent for a long time.

"What's going on, ma'am?" I asked. "Why kill Nusis?"

She said softly, "Take me back to the Iudex tower, Din. Now. Quickly."

WE CROSSED THE CITY TOGETHER, the moon pale and sickly above us, the city full dark except for the lamp of the Legionnaire accompanying us several span ahead.

"What do you think happened back there, ma'am?" I asked.

"Evil," whispered Ana, "and trickery. I think the twitch came looking to steal the reagents key you found in Aristan's safe house. Yet they were in for a surprise . . . for after killing Nusis, they found that the key had *already been* stolen, with another key left behind—a fake. The one you just handled."

"What?" I said, stunned. "You think tha—"

"Keep your voice down!" she hissed. "It's now clear that there are many spies among the Iyalets here! I cannot give the game away just yet."

I whispered, "Do . . . do you really think so, ma'am? That there's a . . . what, a thief about?"

"I do. Someone must have learned what Nusis had in her safe, snuck in, opened her safe, and took it, leaving another key in its place. Then the twitch came, forced Nusis to open her safe, then killed her . . . yet when they seized their treasure, they realized it wasn't the *right key.* Someone had beaten them to it. The twitch then understood they were in a tricky spot—robbed of their prize, and now fearful we might now realize the true nature of the thing they sought. So they carefully shut the door and wiped it with alcohol, removing any blood, hoping we might not deduce what could have been worth murdering and robbing poor Nusis over."

I tried to think through this, my mind spinning. "What makes you so sure the twitch themselves didn't leave that key as a fake?"

"Because they went to the trouble of cleaning both the exterior *and* interior of the safe *after* they killed Nusis. The twitch is methodical, and careful—they don't normally make mistakes that require cleaning. So . . . why would someone so careful manipulate and clean a safe *after* they've already robbed it? Why create this mess for themselves? The easiest answer is that they did not get what they sought and wished to hide that they'd ever sought it at all."

"But . . . why would the Hazas risk so much over a reagents key, ma'am? And why would someone bother stealing it first?"

"Well, that assumes that the key you originally found actually *was* a reagents key," she said. "And I'm now convinced that it wasn't! I think it was something else entirely . . . Nusis herself was even puzzled by it. We asked her to identify what kind of key it was, and none of her tests could tell her—because it wasn't a key at all, you see."

"Then what was it?"

"The missing third you overheard Fayazi Haza discussing!" said Ana. "Something terribly important. The heart of all the sin that hangs over this canton, and perhaps the whole of the Empire. Now— get me to Vashta, quickly. For I know what we must do."

"And what's that?"

"Tell her that someone is going to try to kill Fayazi Haza," said Ana simply.

"A . . . A THREAT AGAINST FAYAZI HAZA'S *LIFE*?" said Vashta, horrified. "Again? Truly?"

"I'm afraid it is, ma'am," said Ana. "There is a third assassin, and they struck again tonight. I am convinced that they mean her ill."

Vashta paced the Iudex tower atrium, her face stricken, her black Legion's uniform tinkling softly as all her heralds clinked against one another. "And . . . and this is who killed poor Nusis?"

"I am still unsure of that, ma'am," said Ana. "But I think I can identify them. To do so, I will need to confer with Madam Haza, along with her engraver—for he has likely engraved many memories that may be useful to us in our search. Can we summon them here, to the Iudex tower, first thing tomorrow? The faster we move, the likelier we can ensure her safety."

"I . . . I can, certainly," said Vashta. "But, Dolabra, this is ill-timed . . . The leviathan approaches. The canton will likely devolve to chaos as it nears."

"And that would be the best time for an assassin to strike. We must resolve this quickly. And, if she does agree to come, I would recommend giving Madam Haza the utmost protection. Any Legion-naire you can spare must be present, ma'am, along with Captain Miljin."

"Of course. Yet is there no more you can tell me? I mean, who *is* this killer? And what is the nature of this threat against Fayazi Haza?"

"I cannot offer you anything of great certainty, ma'am. But I believe her engraver's testimony can illuminate that. Now, with your leave, ma'am, Din and I must prepare for our interview tomorrow."

She nodded. "Certainly. Certainly . . ."

I led Ana up the stairs, the whole of the tower creaking about us in the night wind.

"Just wish to comment, ma'am," I said, "that, ah, I've no idea at all what's going on anymore."

"We build a trap, Din," said Ana. "Vashta herself said that the only thing that would make Fayazi jump now would be if we said there was another threat to her life." She grinned. "And that is what I just told her."

"You lied to her, ma'am?"

"Oh, I did," said Ana. "But not about that. There *is* a threat to Fayazi's life—yet not the sort anyone expects."

"Then . . . what did you lie to her about?"

"Well, for starters, I *know* who the third poisoner is, Din. And I now know how those ten Engineers died. And I also know what that reagents key truly was—and where it is now. I do feel a bit bad for lying to Vashta about all that, but . . . well, there is so much corruption in this canton that I worry an errant word from her could ruin my plot."

We came to her door. I opened my mouth to say more, but she raised a finger.

"No time to explain, Din," she said. "I must prepare my rooms for tomorrow, for I worry that all this could very well go awry. But *listen*, boy . . ." She gripped my arm tight. "I am going through this door, and after that, you are to *never* open it again, understood? Not without my saying it's safe. Is that clear?"

"I . . . I don't understand, ma'am," I said, now thoroughly bewildered. "Why?"

"Do you understand that you shouldn't open this door unless I tell you, child?" she hissed. "Yes? Then do as I say! I'd tell you why, but I'm sure you'd just try and stop me, and that would imperil many lives."

"I'm your engraver," I said indignantly. "Shouldn't I be told of your schemes?"

"You're right—you are my *engraver*. You are here to look, and see. So be down in the atrium first thing tomorrow, and be ready to look and see! And bring your sword. For if my conjectures prove true, we shall unmask a murderer—and a great deal more than that. Or we shall get all our throats slit." She grinned again. "Now sleep, boy—if you can." Then she shut the door.

CHAPTER 37

|||

IT WAS DAWN WHEN I HEARD THE FIRST FOOTSTEPS from the tower entrance. I looked up from where I stood before the adjudication chamber, my hand resting on my sword, then relaxed when I saw Captain Miljin stumping up, his long scabbard swinging by his side.

He nodded to me. Then his eye danced down to my fingers, which still tarried near the grip of my weapon. "You're jumpy, Kol . . . What's all this about, then? Got a message from Vashta to be here. I thought it'd be about poor Nusis, but . . . something about an attempt on Fayazi Haza's life?"

"Or one that's coming, sir," I said. "Ana seemed sure of it. Fayazi Haza herself will be here shortly to be interviewed."

He gazed up the tower stairs. "But Ana's not here yet."

"Still in her rooms. Before you ask, no, I'm afraid she hasn't told me her plots, sir. I've no idea what she's playing at."

He snorted. "Perhaps today's the day she finally tells us what's been bubbling away in that brain of hers." He turned as six Legionnaires trooped into the atrium. He shook his head. "Just had to happen as the leviathan grows perilously close. Let us hope we all survive it."

We entered the adjudication chambers, the Legionnaires taking position at the doors and windows. We waited in silence, and then there came a rumbling of carriage wheels. Commander-Prificto

Vashta swept in, followed by Fayazi Haza, attired again in her silvery robes and delicate veil, and flanked by her engraver and her axiom. Fayazi looked nearly as shaken as she had when I'd seen her staring down on me as her carriage had taken me away. Her Sublimes, as always, were utterly inscrutable.

"Where's Dolabra?" Vashta demanded of me. "Is she not here yet? I thought she would be waiting!"

I opened my mouth to speak—but then I heard a door slam in the tower beyond, followed by small, careful footsteps. I bowed, excused myself, and exited to see Ana slowly, carefully descending the stairs, blindfolded as always, one hand trailing on the wall.

"They all there, Din?" she asked softly as she came to me. "Vashta, Fayazi, and her two Sublimes?"

"They are, ma'am."

"And how do they look?"

"Rather rattled, ma'am."

A grin. "Good. Let us rattle them more."

She took me by the arm. I glanced up the curling stairway, wondering what she had left behind in her room, and why I was not to enter it. Then I led her into the adjudication chambers.

The Legionnaires shut the door behind us and locked it. I glanced around, taking in their positions: two soldiers on either side of Fayazi, one at each of the two windows in this chamber, and two on either side of the door. Fayazi herself sat at the prosecutor's table, with her axiom on her left and her engraver on her right. Vashta had taken up her usual spot at the high table, and Miljin slouched on a bench behind Fayazi, hand on his sword. I led Ana to the first row of benches opposite Fayazi, who watched with narrowed eyes as she sat.

"So," said Fayazi. "We are here, as you have asked, Dolabra . . . You claim my life is being threatened, again?"

"So I have concluded, ma'am," said Ana. "And I thank you for being here to discuss this."

"I thought Jolgalgan was dead," said Fayazi. "And her crackler. That was the news being bandied about."

"They are. But the conspiracy against you goes beyond that, I am afraid. An immunis in the Apothetikals was murdered in her office last night. The threats continue."

"Immunis Dolabra," explained Vashta to Fayazi, "wishes only to interview you and your staff personally to attempt to identify the threat. It is purely a precautionary measure."

"Before I ask any questions, however," said Ana, "I would like to review all we know about the circumstances thus far—about the movements of Jolgalgan, your father, Kaygi Haza, and even Commander Blas—for I have had discovered many revelations in the past few days. Only once the nature of those crimes is established might the threat to you be made clear, madam. Would that be acceptable?"

Fayazi looked to her Sublimes. Both nodded.

"It is acceptable," said Fayazi.

Ana grinned. "Excellent. Let us begin."

"I WILL NOT bother any of you with reviewing the death of Commander Blas," Ana said. "I resolved that weeks ago, and we know now that the identity of the murderer was Captain Kiz Jolgalgan, of the Apoths, now dead. Instead I will move forward to the day of the party at the halls of the Hazas, for that concerns us most. Do we have any protest there?"

Again, Fayazi looked to her Sublimes. They shrugged. "We see no problems there," said Fayazi.

"Very good!" Ana stood up, hands clasped behind her back. "At that time, Jolgalgan was already on the Haza estate grounds. The crackler Ditelus had already lifted the trellis gate, allowing her to slip inside and secrete herself away in a small, shallow hole some several dozen span from the back patio of the house. She had the poison—this dappleglass—and she meant to use it. When she finally heard the sounds of the party, she rose, slipped out of the hole, replaced her cover, and joined the crowd, and no one was any the wiser." She raised a finger. "But here we come to the first unusual thing about

Jolgalgan—for she was already very familiar with the grounds, with the house, with the rooms and the halls. For she had *been there before.* Many times, in fact."

"Jolgalgan?" sniffed Fayazi. "At *our* house? I think that most unlikely . . ."

"I'm afraid it's not," said Ana. "I am *sure* that you were quite unaware of all this, Madam Haza, but your father practiced the very common and not at all unexceptional institution of *patronage*—the selection and encouragement of key officers in the Iyalets." Fayazi opened her mouth to object, but Ana thundered along: "This is, of course, not illegal. There are no laws forbidding it. And as I said, it is very common, especially here in Talagray. Why, I expect that even the commander-prificto has known the attentions of the gentry now and again . . ."

"I have known entreaties," said Vashta frostily, "but not for many years."

"Of course," said Ana, bowing. "Kaygi Haza was like many gentrymen in this fashion. He had a small circle of officers he met with, encouraged, and occasionally gave gifts to—and Jolgalgan was *also* one such officer. For how else could she have known of his bath? How else could she have so easily navigated the servants' passageways, and known which door to use? The answer is, Kaygi Haza had brought her there before himself, likely many times—as a friend." A languid wave of her hand, acknowledging her point. "Now that Jolgalgan was in the estate, she then used her knowledge and her altered vision to navigate the dark passageways without a light, ascending to the roof. And there, she delivered the killing blow, dropping the dappleglass into the boiler above the steam room. At that point, her goal here was accomplished. Jolgalgan rejoined the party and left with the throng. Kaygi Haza took his steams after the party—and then, sadly, he was to perish before the morning.

"*But!*" Ana said. "The story does not end there. For Kaygi Haza had other business that night—a *second*, smaller party. A private affair he intended to hold for the officers to whom he was extending

patronage—the same circle of officers that had once included Jolgal-
gan." She recited aloud: "That would be . . . Princeps Atha Lapfir, Sig-
num Misik Jilki, Princeps Keste Pisak, Captain Atos Koris, Captain
Kilem Terez, Princeps Donelek Sandik, Princeps Kise Sira, Princeps
Alaus Vanduo, Signum Suo Akmuo, and finally, Signum Ginklas
Loveh. The ten dead Engineers. All of them came to the halls of the
Hazas later to . . . taste the *delights* of the house. And the halls of the
Hazas, of course, offer delights beyond compare . . ."

Fayazi had gone very still. Her violet eyes flicked to me, then back
to Ana. I could see her wishing to object further but abstaining out of
fear of what Ana might say next; she surely did not wish to disclose
her own, very illegal courtesans before Vashta.

"That is a fascinating tale," Fayazi said finally. "But you have not
mentioned anything untoward or dangerous. You have given no indication, for example, of how the ten Engineers were also poisoned,
if they were even at my house—nor how any of this might threaten
me."

"I am *glad* you asked," said Ana, grinning. "For that question confounded me for a goodish bit. Yet then I realized . . . We already knew
that the poisoning of the Engineers was different from the deaths of
both Kaygi Haza and Commander Blas. They died much later, at ir-
regular times, and their blooms issued from different parts of their
bodies. This suggests they were *poisoned* differently, too." She turned
her blindfolded face to me. "Din saw the answer, of course. He just
didn't know."

Everyone looked at me. I simply frowned, for I had no idea at all
what she meant.

"Madam Haza," said Ana. "Am I correct in recalling that your father had a bejeweled ewer from which he enjoyed drinking wine?"

Fayazi reluctantly said, "He did. He had several, in fact."

"I see. And did he often enjoy drinking wine," asked Ana softly,
"while he took his *bath*?"

Lightning danced up my bones then, and the memory surfaced in my mind: there, in the old man's bath, a stone ledge; and all along it, many faded red rings from many past wine cups.

"He . . . he did . . ." said Fayazi.

"Then it's as I thought," said Ana. "On that very night, in his bath, Kaygi Haza enjoyed a cup of *wine* from his favorite ewer, right as the air was full of steam—and dappleglass spores. The ewer he drank from sat open to the air and was now tainted. And that same ewer was then used later at this secret meeting of Kaygi Haza's favored Engineers, to pour the wine for all those young people who had come to indulge themselves. And then they drank. They drank, unaware that whatever poured forth from such a vessel now carried death itself—inevitable, painful, and awful."

A HORRIFIED SILENCE hung over the courtroom.

"Truly?" asked Vashta, aghast. "Do you truly think *this* is how such a tragedy began?"

"I am almost completely certain," said Ana. "That would explain why it took so much longer for the infections to—what is the word— to *bloom*. For the Engineers had likely consumed fewer spores than Kaygi Haza himself, and those who drank more wine died fastest. But none had sat and soaked in the spores and breathed them in, like the elder Haza did. I also suspect the spores succeed more in the lungs than the stomach. But still they succeeded, eventually. And all ten perished."

Fayazi looked at her Sublimes, who stared back, speechless. The silence stretched on, and on; and Ana allowed it to swell, waiting for the perfect time to puncture it.

"And if things had gone just slightly differently," she said, "just ever so *slightly* differently, we'd simply have ten dead Engineers on our hands, and nothing more. A tragedy, surely, but not a catastrophe. Yet two of those Engineers just happened to work on the wrong strut within the walls at the wrong time . . . and thus, the breach, and countless casualties." She paused. "It really is unfortunate, isn't it, Madam Haza."

"What is?" said Fayazi.

"It is so *unfortunate* that you locked down your estate," said Ana, "and burned your father's corpse, and did not alert the Apoths to the contagion. For if you had, well . . . perhaps the past weeks might have gone differently."

The temperature in the room begin to change then.

I could see it in Vashta's face; the slow, boiling realization that this gentrywoman—powerful as she was—had perpetrated a conspiracy that had directly caused the breach; and I could see it in Fayazi Haza's posture: in the stiffening in her back, as she came to understand that the seneschal of the canton was now beginning to believe that her own personal deeds had caused the collapse of the sea walls, and brought about the dire situation of the Empire.

"I . . ." stammered Fayazi. "I thought this was an interview . . . I thought there were threats against me?"

"I am getting there," said Ana. "But to explain *that*, I must first explain Jolgalgan's most unusual method of murder, which I am sure must have puzzled all of us. Why bother with dappleglass at all? Why use the same contagion that had once killed her canton, her home? Dappleglass, after all, is difficult, temperamental, and—obviously—murderously uncontainable. It seemed a symbolic choice. Almost like a personal vendetta. It made no sense—until we discussed the history of Oypat with the late Immunis Nusis, who had personally served there during the canton's death.

"Nusis told us a most *curious* story," said Ana. "She told us of how the Apothetikal Iyalet successfully created an effective graft against the dappleglass—a cure, in other words—but that they were not able to put it into production. For when they tried to implement their plan to do so, too many cantons raised too many legal entreaties about growing too many new reagents—and by the time those complaints were resolved, the contagion had spread too far, and Oypat's fate was sealed. But . . . Nusis mentioned that there were *four cantons* in particular that were the most effective at blunting this plan to save Oypat. That would be the Juldiz, Bekinis, Qabirga, and Mitral cantons."

Vashta blinked, lost in the weeds. "Dolabra . . . what is the significance of this?"

"I wondered that myself," said Ana. "Especially when my assistant investigator collected evidence that Rona Aristan, Blas's secretary, had traveled extensively among those *same four cantons* in the past nine years—and had been carrying a fortune while doing so. And then I wondered it *again,* when Din reviewed the Haza rookery, and found that between the murder of Commander Blas and his own death, Kaygi Haza had sent scribe-hawks aloft to four destinations— the Juldiz, Bekinis, Qabirga, and Mitral cantons."

Fayazi's silver veil was fluttering very quickly now. She must have been breathing rather fast.

"I speculated on the meaning of all this," said Ana. "What could connect all this? The money, and Kaygi Haza and Commander Blas— who had been killed *by* Oypatis, in the *same manner* as Oypat—with these four cantons that had quibbled so much that Oypat itself had perished?" She paused. "But then I wondered . . . What if all this had happened before?"

"Happened before?" said Vashta. "What do you mean?"

"Well, Kaygi Haza, after all, had been a *very* old man when he died. Somewhere around a hundred and thirty, if I recall," said Ana. "What if, in his time, he had guided through several—how shall I put this—*graduation classes* of beneficiaries during his time here in Talagray, just like the ten dead Engineers? Several generations of Iyalet officers who had received his patronage, and been seeded all throughout the Empire—embedded to offer advice, information, or favors as needed?

"What if," Ana continued, "Commander Taqtasa Blas himself had been one such officer, once upon a time? What if he and a handful of compatriots had been members of one of Kaygi's clever little cabals, just like Jolgalgan had been? And what if some members of his group had eventually found their way to important stations in the Empire? Perhaps in the cantons of Juldiz, Bekinis, Qabirga, and Mitral?" She grinned that predatorial grin. "And . . . what if, eleven years ago, Kaygi Haza had requested a very, very *big* favor of Blas and his peers?"

Fayazi's engraver shot to his feet. "These are preposterous lies!" he snarled. "We came here after being told of threats, not to be . . . be tarred with such a poisonous brush! Commander-Prificto, I *must* tell you that I will no—"

Then Vashta said a single word—as cold, hard, and vicious as a stab from an icy blade: "*No.*"

Stunned, the engraver stared at her, then looked to Fayazi. "Madam, I . . . This is slanderous . . ."

Fayazi seemed to remember herself and leaned forward. "I beg your pardon, Commander-Prificto?" she said, affronted. "What did you say to my staff?"

"No," said Vashta. "I said *no*, Madam Haza. I am listening. And I am not *done* listening. Thus, we shall all sit, and not interrupt."

The engraver hesitated for a moment, then looked to the axiom, who was watching Ana with her cold, needle-like eyes.

"We are of the clan of the Hazas," said the axiom. "And we shall not be spoken to in such a manner by anyone."

Vashta leaned forward from the bench. "And I am the seneschal of Talagray," she said. "I hold in my hands the heart of the Empire, of which your clan is but a part. And if you wish to ever rejoin your clan, you will all be *quiet.*"

I could see Fayazi's mouth open beneath her veil, wishing to say something. Then she shut it, pursed her lips, and gestured to her engraver, who sat.

Vashta turned her furious face to Ana, and said, "Continue, Dolabra."

Ana cleared her throat, tried to wipe the smug grin off her face, and said, "This is the nebulous idea that crept into my mind—that eleven years ago, during the Oypat crisis, Kaygi Haza and Taqtasa Blas had gained knowledge about this cure for dappleglass. And then

Blas, well-acquainted with the many Preservation Boards through-out the Empire, had covertly directed his friends and allies to quietly *block* its use. This was the only thing that could explain the connec-tion between Kaygi Haza and Blas. It explained why Oypatis like Jol-galgan and Ditelus might wish this specific, poetic death upon the two men. And it *also* explained why Blas's secretary was traveling among those four cantons with a veritable fortune—making pay-ments to the collaborators, buying their silence. And it would explain why Kaygi Haza had hurried to send scribe-hawks to those four can-tons after the death of Commander Blas. He was *warning* his people there, you see. One member of their conspiracy had been murdered in a fashion that signaled that the murderer knew what sin they had committed. He was telling the others that their secret was known—and that this murderer might soon come for them as well.

"But . . . *why* would Blas and Haza do any of this in the first place?" continued Ana. "Why would these two men intentionally allow a whole canton to die? What could they gain from such death and destruction? Except, then I recalled . . . the Hazas' wealth comes from one very specific source. And that is *land*."

"Land?" echoed Vashta quietly.

"Yes, ma'am. Land," said Ana. "Land, and all that is grown upon it. All the reagents, all the agriculture, all the crops and feedstocks that spring forth from their earth—this is the source of all their riches." She sniffed. "So . . . what would happen to the value of their lands if a great chunk of fertile land they did *not* own suddenly van-ished?"

My head began to spin as I listened to all this. Although I'd begun to suspect many murderous things from the Hazas, it hadn't yet oc-curred to me that their involvement in such horrors might be moti-vated by something so simple, so bland, and so awful.

"They did it for *money*?" I exclaimed. "All for *money*, ma'am?"

"Quiet, Din!" snapped Ana. "I told you to watch, not to talk!"

"Yes, but . . . I echo the boy's comment," said Vashta faintly. "You . . . you're claiming the Hazas perpetrated this abominable scheme ... as some kind of *land valuation* plot, Dolabra? To gain a little *money*?"

"Not a little," said Ana. "A lot. An *inconceivable* amount. The death of Oypat allowed the Hazas to renegotiate countless contracts with the Empire, vastly increasing their wealth and influence—so much so that their wealth came to rival that of the emperor himself. It is, in its own strange way, the largest single land speculation scheme in memory. But if you would like hard numbers," she said, smiling like a loon, "I highly recommend *Summation of the Transfer of Landed Properties, Qabirga Canton, 1100–1120*. That's just one example. It's all written down right there, in the open. And it's fascinating reading, too."

"Speaking of *speculation*," cried the engraver, "this is all theorization and daydreams! We had nothing to do with Oypat, nor the increase in values of our lands! I have yet to hear of any evidence for this grand conspiracy beyond a few scribe-hawks our master had sent before his death! You have no real proof that he had any connection with Blas, or his secretary, or any ... any illicit payments made to people in these cantons!"

"But I do have proof," said Ana mildly.

The whole of the room seemed to freeze.

"You ... you what?" said the engraver.

"I do have proof. Because I have in my possession a *sample* of the cure for dappleglass—the very grafts that the Apoths produced ten years ago to save Oypat. The very one you stole."

A SILENCE SETTLED over the adjudication chamber. An errant cloud shifted in the sky, allowing a spear of dawn light to stab through the window.

"You have *what*, Dolabra?" said Vashta.

"Well, Immunis Nusis mentioned that those four cantons had seemed so curiously *informed* about the cure for dappleglass," Ana said. "But then she mentioned that the cure itself might never have worked—for though they had made twenty vials of grafts, they found that three had degraded to water. Yet I imagined . . . What if they hadn't degraded? What if someone had *stolen* three of the little vials to study and left simple water in their place? And that was what the Hazas did, you see. They bribed or paid their agents to steal the cure, so Commander Blas and his little gang could examine the sample, derive the reagents, and find a way to prevent the cure from ever being used. The solution was simpler than they'd ever dreamed— they found out where the reagents were grown and went to the Pres- ervation Boards. Ironic, for the Preservation Boards exist to protect the folk of the Empire—but in the hands of the wealthy and knowl- edgeable, they could easily be used as a weapon."

Ana wheeled to face Fayazi and her Sublimes. "But that's where things went awry, didn't they? For if you deal with corrupt people, inevitably they try to exploit you. And that's what Commander Blas did—for he *kept* one of those samples. One of three. A *third*."

The word sent lightning up my bones yet again. I remembered what I'd overheard Fayazi Haza saying: *A third? Third what? What are they to find? What do they seek?*

"Blas kept it as blackmail," Ana continued, "to ensure that the Haza clan never tried to eliminate him. He used it to extort more funds from you, which he and his secretary smuggled to his co- conspirators abroad. And for so long, it was easier to pay him rather than kill him. But then he *was* killed—not by you, but by Captain Kiz Jolgalgan, who'd discovered what you'd done. And then it became very, very important to find that sample. For if anyone else found it, and figured out what it truly was, then it would prove what you had done." She turned to me, smiling. "But despite all your searching, Din stumbled across it and picked it up. Very clever, to disguise it as a reagents key."

I felt faint, my eyes shimmering as I recalled that day in the empty little house. The feel of the bronze disc, the slosh of the fluid in the vial—to imagine now that it had been the very substance that could have saved thousands of lives . . .

And yet, I knew the key had been stolen from us. What secret game was Ana playing at now?

She pivoted on her heel to turn to Fayazi, leaning her blindfolded face forward. "You didn't know much of this, did you, madam," she said. "You couldn't have. This was all your father's doing. His schemes, his plots. And you weren't allowed knowledge of that. Why, you weren't even allowed in his rookery."

Fayazi's axiom gripped her mistress's arm again.

"I will say nothing to you," said Fayazi quietly.

"But when your father died, you had to take over his duties here. You sent word to the other prime sons of the lineage, asking for guidance—and they told you to burn the body and the evidence and suppress all knowledge, fearing anything that might connect your father's death to Commander Blas would reveal what they had done to Oypat. You did as they asked—and thus, you enabled the breach. And the deaths of all those soldiers and people now lie upon your head."

"No," whispered Fayazi.

"And then things got so much more dangerous . . . For then the clan sent their agent, didn't they? Someone *terrifying* to do their dirty work and clean up all this mess you'd made?"

Fayazi trembled under her veil, yet said nothing.

"They sent their twitch, of course," said Ana. "And all you could do was sit there. Sit there while the twitch went after Blas's secretary. And then that poor miller you'd hired for all that fernpaper—they killed him and left him to rot in a basement. And then poor Nusis."

"Dolabra!" said Vashta, alarmed. "What are you talking abou—"

"I wonder how many people your twitch has killed for your clan," Ana said. "Dozens? Hundreds? But you knew when they came, Madam Haza, that you might be the next one they killed. For you're distant from the elder sons. Vulnerable. Unimportant. The twitch was here to make sure you didn't step out of line . . . and if all their plans here in Talagray fell to pieces, it was *you* they intended to blame for it all and leave for the loop. Another tidy ending to a horrid little story."

Fayazi convulsed like she'd been slapped.

"Surely you've thought that," whispered Ana. "Surely you've known that's what they planned. But . . . why don't you ask her? Why don't you go ahead and ask your twitch *right now*?"

A loud, thundering silence.

"D-Dolabra?" said Vashta. "What are you . . . what . . ."

Ana turned her face to the axiom, who stared back at her with her cold, dark eyes.

"For it's you, isn't it?" said Ana. "You're no axiom. You're the twitch. And it is you who's here to threaten Madam Haza's life. And it's you who killed Immunis Nusis just last night."

ANOTHER STUNNED SILENCE.

The axiom smiled and laughed, a high, cold sound. "You're mad. She's mad. This woman is absolutely mad!"

"What's the square root of 21,316?" demanded Ana.

"Wh-what?" said the axiom, startled. "Why are you—"

"The answer is 146," said Ana. "What's 98 to the power of four?" The axiom was silent.

"The answer is 92,236,816," said Ana. "What about 92,236,816 divided by 21,316? Can you do that?"

Silence.

"Can you?" demanded Vashta. "Can you not?" She looked to Fayazi. "Why can she not?"

Fayazi began to shake but did not answer. The axiom's cold, dead stare grew even colder.

"I think the answer is a little over 4,327," said Ana. "But don't quote me." She grinned. "You bear the heralds of an axiom—but you can't do math at all, can you? You needed a reason to hang about Fayazi while Din talked to her, to make sure she said the right things.

And what gentrywoman goes anywhere without their Sublimes? You couldn't pose as an engraver—she already had one of those—but axiom, well . . . Why would anyone pose complex math problems to Fayazi Haza? I wouldn't have thought twice on it—but then Din asked a few very simple mathematical questions, and you said *nothing*. Nothing at all. And that was curious to me." Her smile faded. "It's you. You killed Aristan. And Suberek. And Nusis. It was all you."

The axiom was silent. Ana began moving back, but she started speaking louder so the whole room could hear.

"The Hazas sent you here to clean up," she said. "But the *real* mission was to get back that damn reagents key—the one filled with the cure for dappleglass. You learned from one of Kaygi's many dirty sources that Nusis just happened to have a reagents key that had been recovered from Rona Aristan. You knew right away what it was. And with the leviathan approaching, there was no time. You got desperate. You went to her office, forced her to open the safe, and killed her—unaware that she and I had *already* swapped out the keys, and I had the real one in the chest in my rooms. Right upstairs, right now."

I blinked at that, confused again. That couldn't be so. Yet Ana kept talking.

"Very gutsy, to come here," she said. "I wasn't sure if you'd do it. I made sure not to ask for you at all, worried I might spook you. But you're *very* loyal to the Haza clan. They told you to keep watch over their little sister, and that's what you're here to do."

Fayazi was trembling now. Miljin stood and drew his sword.

I shot to my feet and did the same. The Legionnaires about us took that as a sign and drew their own blades.

The twitch's cold, dark eyes flicked around the room, unnaturally quickly, counting us all.

"Fayazi?" said Ana. "You can move away now. Hurry, please."

With a strangled cry, Fayazi Haza shot to her feet, shook off the twitch's grip, and ran across the room. She pressed her back against the far wall and stared back at the twitch, sobbing hysterically.

Vashta looked on, stunned. Then she blinked and steeled herself. "Miljin?"

"Yes, ma'am?" said Miljin, his green blade raised.

"Arrest this person," said Vashta. "Bind her hands and feet. Immediately."

"Kol!" called Miljin. "Your engraver's bonds!"

My hands shaking, I unhooked them from my belt, then tossed them to Miljin. He and the Legionnaires advanced on the twitch, blades held high. She stayed seated behind the table with her hands in her lap, totally still except for her eyes, which kept darting about, reading the room.

"There's too many of us," said Miljin to her. He handed the bonds off to a Legionnaire, keeping his own blade pointed at the twitch. "Too many, even for you."

"I know," said the twitch quietly. She raised her hands.

"Good," said Miljin. He kept approaching, making sure his blade was angled toward her. "Keep raising them. Slowly now. Slowly. Slowly . . ."

I felt myself trembling. A fluttering to my eyes, and I recalled what Miljin had said: *You meet a twitch, there's no training I can offer that'd save you . . . They were supposed to be unbeatable in combat—for about a minute a day, mind. After that, their muscles wore out and they had to recover . . .*

Then came the awareness of all the folk that this person had killed: Aristan, and Suberek, and poor Nusis . . . And perhaps Ana's previous assistant as well, for all I knew.

"Slowly," said Miljin. "Slowly give me your hands . . ."

The twitch extended her arms. Miljin nodded to the Legionnaire on his right, who took her by the arm and snapped one end of the bonds about her wrist.

Then they all froze.

A sound from out the window, out in the city, starting low and then slowly growing.

Bells. First dozens of them, then hundreds of them, their high, raucous peals falling over the countryside like a storm.

"Tocsins," said Vashta hoarsely. "Tocsin bells. But we haven't yet seen ..."

We all looked to the window, and the east.

For a moment there was nothing but mottled clouds; but then a small, flittering green star rose in the distance; and it was joined by another and another, arcing into the darkness and leaving trails of smoke behind, until all the skies seemed swarming with bright, flickering green lights.

"Green flares," Vashta said quietly. "A leviathan is here."

The twitch moved.

CHAPTER 38

|||

I DID NOT REALLY SEE WHAT THE TWITCH DID. THE movement was so quick it was barely perceivable, like the flit of a moth's wing in the shadows. But then there was a scream, and when I whirled to see, there was blood.

The Legionnaire on the twitch's left was falling to the ground, blood pouring from her throat. The one on the twitch's right suddenly gasped and coughed, a dark splotch spreading on his chest, and collapsed to his knees. Through the spray of blood I saw her, this dark figure with cold eyes, my engraver's bonds swinging from one wrist and a long stiletto clutched in her hands, its blade so thin it seemed hardly more than a length of black hair. Where she had gotten her weapon from, I could not tell; she had moved too fast for me to see any of it.

Miljin brought his green blade down on the twitch, and the sword tore through the fretvine floor like it was made of straw. Yet the twitch was already gone, leaping away, her robes rippling as she moved like an acrobat. Then a flicker to her arms, and a third Legionnaire was collapsing, multiple perforations sprouting blood from her torso, like water from a decorative fountain. Fayazi's engraver was shrieking wildly, diving for cover with his hands clapped to his ears.

The remaining Legionnaires darted after the twitch, trying to encircle her. I saw her pause, her dark eyes flicking about, counting the swords before her.

"Trap her!" bellowed Miljin. "Pin her in! Keep her from moving!"

The twitch looked to the window.

Another volley of green flares arose in the distance. The bells screamed on.

"Strike her down!" shouted Miljin. "Now, now!"

But the twitch bent low, sprinted for the window, darted about the Legionnaires, slid between two of them—and leapt out.

We all stared at the empty window, flummoxed.

"Where did she go?" cried Vashta. "Where in hell . . ."

Miljin and I ran to the window, peering out into the courtyard. Though the yard was flooding with figures bound up in Iudex blue, the twitch was nowhere to be seen.

"What in hell?" said Miljin. "She vanished?"

"No," said Ana, standing slowly. "She did not run away, I believe. She went *up*, rather, climbing the tower."

"Up?" said Vashta. "What the hell did she climb the tower for?"

"To get into my rooms," said Ana. "The twitch is here for the re-agents key, after all. I said just now that it was in my chest, in my rooms—but this was a lie. What the twitch will instead find there should be greatly surprising to her."

"We must go up!" said Vashta. "We must go up and catch her!"

"No," said Ana. "She will come down, and soon. And then she will perish. Let us go the atrium to meet her. For though we might not survive the day, let us at least take comfort that the evil folk among us will not, either."

We exited the adjudication room in a dazed stagger, the bells ringing in our ears, Miljin leading the way with his sword drawn. Fayazi Haza began bawling that she wanted to go home, to go home, but Vashta told the Legionnaire to clap a hand on her arm and not let her go.

Then we heard a scream from high above us, and the slam of a door bursting open.

We looked up. A figure was staggering down the stairway, sobbing with rage.

"What..." choked the twitch's voice. "What have you *done* to me?"

Vashta drew her own blade and stood beside Miljin and the Legionnaires, waiting. I stood before Ana, my sword held high. Then another volley of flares rose, and the tower was filled with green light, and we saw her.

The twitch was descending, her nose and mouth pouring blood. She coughed, and yet more blood came, sloshing down her front.

"What did you do to me?" she spat. "What did you . . . what did you . . ."

Yet I recognized what I was now seeing. I had seen such a transmutation before, when Miljin and I had found Ditelus on the Plains of the Path.

"Dappleglass," I said softly.

"Yes," said Ana quietly. "I told you I was worried someone might try to poison me, Din. I took three of your hairs and stuck them to the lid of my teapot, just in case. Yesterday evening, while you were at the banquet, I found them gone—and a tiny leaf stuck to the interior of the teapot with resin. Dappleglass, of course."

The twitch stumbled down the last length of stairway, her eyes now leaking blood.

"Last night I lined my chest with leather, creating a seal," said Ana. "And then, this morning, I snipped off the tiniest bit of the leaf, placed it in my teapot, and started it boiling at a low heat in my chest, and shut it. Not much—but then, twitches don't need much. They're very vulnerable to contagion . . ."

The twitch staggered down the last span of steps, blood pouring from her face, her long, stiletto sword still raised.

"But she is not dead yet," Ana said, "and is still dangerous . . ."

"I tried to kill you before, you . . . you *bitch*," the twitch said savagely. Flecks of blood danced in the air with each word. "Got . . . got your little helper instead."

"So you think," said Ana with a sniff. "But then, you and your masters always were fools."

Her dark eyes glinted. "I'll kill you and . . . and your child now . . ." she spat. "Even . . . even if I should die doing it . . ."

Miljin and the Legionnaires made a line before us, swords raised in a wall of sharp steel. "Try it," he hissed at her. "Try it, and let me take vengeance for Nusi—"

Then the twitch leapt.

I had thought she'd been incapacitated by the dappleglass, but it seemed this was not so; for she managed to vault clear over Miljin and the Legionnaires, landed behind them, and sped straight for Ana and me.

I shoved Ana backward, putting myself in between her and the twitch. The twitch sped in at me, her eyes and nose and mouth now pouring blood.

Yet I noticed—my eyes could perceive her movements now.

She was moving slow. Too much movement, I guessed, for much too long.

I stepped forward, reading her stance, the angle of her shoulders, the bend of her wrist. She went in for the thrust, intending to spear me in my belly—yet I had expected this, for a thrust was all she could do with such a weapon.

My eyes fluttered. My muscles awoke and moved me, dancing me through one particular move . . .

The trick Miljin had taught me in the Iudex courtyard. His ugly little secret.

I angled my blade along her stiletto; then caught it, trapping it in my crossguard and shoving its point away, while keeping my own sword pointed at the twitch.

I saw her face change, shifting from savage joy to alarm. She was moving too fast. She could not change direction now.

My arm shook as her shoulder met the tip of my sword. She screamed, and I shoved forward, driving my blade through the flesh below her collarbone, severing the ligaments, rendering her left arm all but useless.

Her stiletto fell to the floor. She screamed aloud, shrieking, "You little son of a bitch! You little son of a *bi—*"

My body moved me again.

I pulled my sword from her shoulder, then raised it and hacked down at her.

My blow was clumsy. The edge did not slash open her throat as I'd intended, but instead smashed into the side of her skull, beside her temple and eye. Her bloody face changed to one of dull shock, the sword penetrating her eye socket and biting through the orb. I watched, mutely horrified, as her eye turned gelatinous and began to dribble down her cheek. She blinked once with her remaining eye, then tumbled forward, ripping my sword from my hand as she did so.

Fayazi started shrieking again, wild, hysterical screams. The tocsins rang and rang, screaming their warnings to us, to flee, to run, to panic, to pray. Vashta was shouting something, but I had no mind for it.

Then Ana's voice: "It's not done! Damn it, Din, the bloom's *not done!* Get away, get away!"

Miljin bounded forward, picked me and Ana up like we were but toys, and dragged us clear to the Iudex tower entrance.

Then came a familiar, horrid sound, akin to thick fabric ripping. I looked over my shoulder to see a green growth sprout from the base of the twitch's neck, then surge up about her, tearing her asunder in a burst of dark blood, and enveloping her in a veil of bloody, dark green leaves.

"Oh, Sanctum," whispered Vashta. "Oh, holy Sanctum . . ."

Fayazi Haza was screaming again. Her engraver tried to comfort her, but she was having none of it.

"By the titan's unholy taint," panted Miljin. "By the titan's unholy fucking taint . . ."

Vashta tore her face away from the body hanging in the trees. "We need to evacuate this tower, if your goddamn room's been poisoned, Dolabra!" she spat at her.

"I left the window open," Ana said. And the spores lose effectiveness quickly. "It should be vented clear and is now perfectly sa—"

"Shut up!" said Vashta. "For once, just *shut up*, woman! Miljin—I have a city to evacuate. I shall need your aid in that. But for now, you take that woman to the Legion tower!" she said, pointing at Fayazi. "And you *lock her up*, titan be damned! The rest of you Legionnaires, with me!"

Vashta and the Legionnaires sprinted off into the city, the sky still screaming with bells and the streets now coursing with folk trying to evacuate. Miljin grabbed Fayazi and the engraver, then turned to me and said, "Get Dolabra to the cart train! Now!"

I was still in shock from all I'd done and could barely make sense of him. "The . . . the cart train?" I said.

"Yes! To evacuate! Emperor's blood, there's a fucking titan making landfall! Go!"

CHAPTER 39

|||

THE EVACUATION OF THE CITY WAS, TO USE VASH-
ta's own words, nothing short of a fucking disaster.

Ana and I staggered out of the Iudex tower to find the city had
erupted into utter chaos. Every street was choked with carts, with
cargo, with people, with livestock, all jockeying for space on the lanes
leading west. People bellowed curses over the sound of the ringing
bells or cried out news that this or that distant street was clear. Only
the Iyalet cart trains presented any kind of order, lined with Legionnaires bearing tall black banners and stretching along the street before the Trifecta, waiting to bear senior officers out of the city.

But it was clear that even by cart train, leaving the city was going
to be impossible. There were simply too many people in the streets.
No one, it seemed, was willing to be taken by surprise by a breach
again, and all intended to flee.

I should have been terrified, but I was still too shocked to feel
much at all. I just mutely stared at the surging throngs of folk.

"I rather think, ma'am," I finally said to Ana, "that we aren't leaving soon. Nor doing much at all."

"No, Din," Ana said softly. "What a thing it is, to be reminded
that despite all the deeds and sorrows of the day, our work is small in
comparison to what occurs at the walls."

"Then . . . what are we to do?"

"Well. We could stay here, and vainly hope." She cocked her head.

"But . . . that feels like a waste of an opportunity. I've never seen a living leviathan, Din. I should like to do so, I think. Or have you look for me."

I stared at her blearily. "You what?"

"Why, it's the chance of a lifetime, Din! If we get to the right spot and snatch a spyglass from one of the Legionnaires here, we shall have the chance not only to see a titan on the shores of the Empire of Khanum, but behold the moment in which we learn if the Empire has a future at all. Who else could claim such a feat?" She took me by the arm. "Come. Let us go look and know if we shall survive the day together. And if not, then we will have time aplenty to make our peace with creation."

I FETCHED A SPYGLASS from a Legionnaire, and together we walked to the eastern part of the city, which was by now abandoned by the fleeing crowds. We came to a high earthworks rampart facing east, the noon sky yawning bright and clear and beautiful above, and in the distance rose the sea walls, just the barest thread of black running along the horizon.

"What do you see, Din?" Ana whispered.

I pressed the spyglass to my eye and peered out.

I saw the walls, tall and black and buffeted by earthworks. A whole landscape, it seemed, ripped from the earth and placed against the sea; and there, to the south, a narrow, ragged gap, and all about it lay broken stones and heaps of crumbled soil. Yet that was all I could see.

"It has not come yet, ma'am," I said.

"Hm . . . the waiting is the awful part," she said. "I've prepared to die many times in my life. I did last night, as I made my trap. I did this morn, as I poisoned my own rooms. Perhaps it is a wise thing, to prepare for death every day, just as the Empire prepares for death every wet season."

I glanced at her. "You could have told me she was a twitch, ma'am."

"I could have," Ana said. "But I didn't want you to try something gallant and stupid. Better to let the Legionnaires take her, I thought. There were enough of them. If only the bells had not rung, giving her a chance to escape . . ."

"And then," I said, "I had to go and do something gallant and stupid anyway."

"Yes. It shall take work to keep you alive, boy. A pity we might perish today, for you are an honorable officer, Dinios Kol. It would have been a fine thing, to rely on you further in my works. We could have done many great things together."

A rumbling in the east. The crackle of bombard fire.

A thought occurred to me. One I did not much like, but one I felt I had to obey.

I swallowed. "W-would you say, ma'am," I said softly, "that now would be the hour for honesty and confessions?"

"I . . . suppose?" she said. "What makes you say that?"

I was silent.

"*Do* you have something to confess, Din?" she asked.

"Yes, ma'am. I do."

"And what might that be?"

I swallowed again. "I confess I . . . I am no honorable officer, ma'am."

"How do you mean?"

I shut my eyes. "I should not be your assistant. For I . . . I did not achieve my scores on my Iudex exams honestly, ma'am. My scores were fraud."

Ana said nothing. The bombards crackled on.

"I had failed every other Iyalet application," I said. "I have great trouble reading and writing. And the position with you was the only one I could hope for. So I . . . I learned how to pick locks, ma'am. That was why I learned such a thing. I learned it to break into the Apoth's offices at night. I stole copies of the Iudex exams. All of them, for I didn't know which one I would be given. Once I had the chance to read them the . . . the way I do my reading, I saw that I knew the answers, but I had to practice writing them. So . . . I spent three days memorizing how to draw the letters. How to put the sentences to-gether. Remembering the movements. That was how I made such high scores, ma'am. My trainer knew and beat me for it. And I de-served it. And I have felt like a trespasser here every day, because . . . because I *am* a trespasser. I am no honorable officer, ma'am. And I am sorry for deceiving you. If we survive the day, I shall accept what pun-ishments you choose. For I tire of hiding my nature from you. I have no appetite for this sin."

I opened my eyes. Ana was staring at me, her blindfolded expres-sion torn between exasperation and bemusement.

"Well, now I do wonder if you should be my assistant," she snapped. "But not for your dishonesty, Din. Rather, because you ap-parently think me a *fucking idiot!*"

I stared. "I . . . I beg your par—"

"Ridiculous boy!" she cried. "Absurd child! Do you really not un-derstand that I *knew* you cheated? That I've known *all* this time?"

"You . . . What? Truly?"

"Din!" she said, incensed. "Is it not safe to say that you have *just* witnessed me formulating answers to some very complex problems? Ones far more complicated than the mystifying puzzle of 'How did this young man who was so shit at his exams suddenly score so well?' I mean, titan's taint! The only reason they didn't investigate further was that I selected you and told them to *forget* it!"

My mouth fell open. "So . . . wait. You did not choose me for my scores, ma'am?"

"God, no!" she cried. "Is it not obvious? I chose you *because* you cheated, Dinios Kol! I didn't quite know *how* you did it, no—not until you revealed your lockpicking skills. Then it was quite painfully obvious."

"You *selected* me for my dishonesty, ma'am?" I said, offended.

"No!" she said. Then: "Well, yes. Somewhat."

"What do you mean?" I demanded.

She thought about it. The guns crackled on.

"I chose you," she said finally, "because I needed an investigator who was resourceful, cunning, and willing to break the rules when necessary. I needed someone dedicated and determined! And you had not only broken into an Iyalet office and spent hours learning the answers to all the tests—you had somehow survived your engraver's training despite having tremendous issues reading and writing! That speaks to bloody-minded, grim determination if ever I've heard it!"

I grew faint. "W-wait. Wait. So you knew . . ."

"Am I to name every obvious thing I know, boy?"

"But, ma'am . . . I thought before now, I had been very . . ."

There was a limp silence, broken only by another crackle of bombards.

"I have good ears," she said. "I could hear you reading aloud to yourself. And I have seen your writing, of course. I thought it was obvious when you duplicated Sazi text that I was aware of your condition."

I felt myself blushing hugely. I felt a fool. What a fantasy it had been, to think my blatant weaknesses could go hidden.

"Why would you tolerate me so, ma'am?" I asked. "Why would you wish to . . . to have someone like me as your assistant?"

She laughed. It was a high, cruel sound. "Would you like to know what alterations *I* have, Din, that make me so averse to stimulation, and so reluctant to leave my residence?"

I looked at her, startled. To have her so cavalierly propose answering a question I'd debated for months was bewildering. "Well, I . . ."

"None," she said.

"What?"

"I have no augmentations that afflict me so. Rather, I have *always* been this way. This is my natural state."

There was a long silence.

"Truly?" I said.

"Truly," she said. "I have *never* liked the company of too many people, Din. I have *always* preferred patterns and the consumption of information to socializing. I have preferred and will *always* prefer staying in my residence and will avoid stimulation at all costs. This is simply who I am."

"But . . . but your abilities, the way you . . ."

"My situation," she continued, "made me amenable to an . . . experiment." She was silent for a bit, as if debating something, before finally saying, "An alteration. The nature of which should not bother you—for you would not be able to comprehend it. But if I hadn't been the person that I was, then the alterations would not have been a success. It was my choice. I changed and became. I self-assembled. Just as you have done." She leaned forward. "*Sen sez imperiya.* The Empire is strong because it recognizes the value in *all* our people. Including you, Dinios Kol. And when the Empire is weak, it is often because a powerful few have denied us the abundance of our people. That is exactly what has happened in Talagray. And I was assigned here specifically to amend that—and I mean to do so."

I leaned against the rampart, stunned. None of what she'd said had been a compliment, exactly, yet I struggled with emotion. I had never had anyone understand me for what I was and accept me—nor tell me that the Empire itself desired my services even so.

But then I realized the last thing she'd said.

"Wait," I said. "*Assigned* to be here? What? By who—"

Then another rumbling shook the earth, followed by a sharp crackle of bombard fire. A queer, horrid breeze swept over the landscape, and the fretvine towers of all the city creaked in a chorus.

"The time comes," said Ana. "Look! Look now, Din! Let us see if we shall survive the day!"

I put the spyglass to my eye and looked.

I SAW THE WALLS AGAIN, and the ragged gap of the breach.

I could see the sea beyond, I thought, the tides frothy and faint, the clouds above them soft and roiling; yet then something eclipsed it all, a shadow moving down from the north to block the gap, lumbering to fill the space between the walls.

The air there trembled, like a horrid fume caused the atmosphere to quake. It was difficult to see, but I thought I could make out . . .

Something. A form.

I stared, and stared, and stared.

It was far wider than it was tall, like a vast, plated, dripping dome, its surface gray and gleaming, and puckered here and there with growths and barnacles from deep-sea creatures that had made their home upon this colossus. The thing moved slowly, its uncountable legs picking their way across the coast in a fretful, nervous dance; yet as it moved I became aware that I was only seeing part of it through the gap, just the tiniest fraction of the vast, shambling beast emerging from the shores.

My skin began to crawl, unable to comprehend what I beheld. It was like looking up on an overcast day and seeing a gap in the clouds; and then watching, dumbfounded, as an eye peered through the hole, staring down at you.

Slowly, the leviathan came to the breach. Through the quaking air I spied some growth emerging from behind the broken walls, hanging from the bottom of the dome; and within this pendulous mass I thought I saw a pair of pale, luminous eyes shining in the fumes, and below them an open maw working stupidly, mindlessly, its dark lips trembling and convulsing as if trying to speak.

I started screaming then, the spyglass stuck to my eye, shrieking words as I tried to describe to Ana what I was witnessing. I was cut short as the horizon lit up with bombard fire, hundreds upon hundreds of artillery firing on the thing at once, and all was concealed with smoke; yet then at the very end of the volley came an immense, earth-shattering *crack*, a cannonry of a kind I had never heard before and could never imagine; and then a detonation, low and rumbling, one that seemed to go on forever.

The bombard, I thought. The titan-killer. But if it had slain the thing, I could not tell.

Then an enormous crash, like the very moon had fallen from the sky. Dust filled the air, rising in a rumbling wave. I wondered if the beast had pushed over the walls, topped them like a thrush digging through the mulch. I kept waiting, my heart hammering, my skin slick with sweat, the spyglass pressed to my eye so hard my brow began to hurt.

Then the smoke and dust were scraped thin by a breeze; and as it vanished I saw the walls, still standing; and there, before the breach, the form of the leviathan lying on the ground, its massive shell split asunder, and its abominable face lost in the sands.

The horizon lit up with flares, these a pale blue. I stared at them, my mind swimming.

"What color?" said Ana. "What color, Din?"

"Blue, ma'am. The flares are blue."

"It's done, then," whispered Ana. "The beast is dead. And the Empire persists."

CHAPTER 40

|||

I SAW ANA VERY LITTLE FOR THE NEXT TWO DAYS, for I and all the other minor officers were tasked with restoring the city to order. The panic and stampede had been almost as damaging as a leviathan's wrath, which frustrated and flummoxed many; for after all, the Legion had been quite clear that the titan was approaching. "People are often damned fools about what's before them," a Legion princeps commented as we tried to figure out how to move a slain horse from the streets. "And not much smarter regarding what's behind them, at that. It's amazing we ever get anything done."

At the end of the second day, an Iudex militis came calling for me, and I followed his summons to an office in the Legion tower.

I entered to find Vashta seated behind a long black desk with Ana and Uhad before her, listening as she spoke. "... seized all of their holdings here in the canton of Talagray," she was saying. "Fayazi and her entourage are being held for the time being. But greater progress will require greater labors ..." Her hard, dark gaze flicked up to me. "Ah. Kol. Please come in."

I did so, taking a station behind Ana and hoping I did not stink too heavily of horse.

"I suppose we ought to catch you up on what has happened, Signum," said Vashta. "But being as events are still happening, that may prove difficult. Scribe-hawks have been sent out across Khanum, reporting on both our victory over the leviathan and the sealing of the breach—and your investigation."

"The holdings of the Haza family have been seized in the third ring," Uhad explained to me. He was positively beaming. It was the first time I'd ever seen him smile so. "And work has begun on seizing their holdings in the second. I have delayed my retirement in order to assist in these noble labors."

"But this will take time, and will involve many legal and political battles," sighed Vashta. "But for now, it is very possible that all the elder sons of the Haza clan may find themselves dispossessed . . . and in reward for her cooperation, Fayazi Haza might take their place."

"Fayazi?" I said, surprised. "She'll be taking *over* for the Hazas?"

Vashta shrugged grimly. "She has given us all the communications her elders sent her, proving their guilt. And the Haza lands are invaluable. Someone must manage them. It might as well be someone we own. Time shall tell how all this goes. Needless to say, our victory at the breach has now changed to a much more protracted affair. A pity that we never found out who stole the real dappleglass cure. With it as proof, we could bring our enemies down all the faster. We shall look for it, but I am not optimistic."

"Yet there are rumblings from the emperor's Sanctum," said Uhad. "Signs he shall revoke some of the blessings and privileges bestowed to the Hazas—as well as possibly *all* the gentry."

I glanced at Ana. I noticed she had not spoken yet, but sat crooked in her chair, head bowed, face inscrutable.

"The institution of patronage shall be tricky to kill," said Vashta, "but kill it we shall, I think. There may be many more officers like Blas among us. As a sign of the emperor's devotion, I'm told an Iudexii conzulate will arrive in the canton shortly. It is the first time such a being has blessed the canton in nearly half a century. He has issued no orders yet, but the suggestion is that he intends to discover exactly how entrenched the Hazas were in the Iyalets."

I could not hide my surprise. Conzulates were akin to gods in the

Empire: as Fayazi had said to me, they never aged, but kept growing, until many were almost the size of giants, though their size made them incapable of movement. Some were hundreds of years old. The idea that one might be nearby was stupefying to me.

"You have done great works for the Empire, Kol," said Vashta. "As such, I declare your apprenticeship over. You may now formally consider yourself Assistant Investigator. You may bear your blade and heralds proudly, and your dispensation will be altered accordingly. Congratulations."

The enormity of it all was almost too much. I wondered how to react and settled on a bow. "Thank you, ma'am."

Vashta sighed. "Yes. Though I am unsure when you'll be able to return to your home, Signum, given that your immunis thinks there is still some third poisoner about. Unless you've changed your mind about that, Dolabra?"

"I have not, ma'am," said Ana.

"And I don't suppose you've had any revelations during all that chaos that could help us rest easier."

"Well . . ." Ana grinned. "Not during. But, rather, slightly *before*, ma'am."

There was a confused beat.

"What do you mean?" demanded Vashta.

"I have known the *true* identity of the dappleglass poisoner since Nusis's murder," said Ana mildly. "I know who it truly was who plotted and planned all the horrors of the past weeks."

"You . . . you aren't proposing that it was *not* Jolgalgan?" asked Vashta.

"Oh, Jolgalgan was guilty as sin, but she did not act alone," said Ana. "That's been obvious from the start. To begin with, she possessed an awareness of Commander Blas's movements that far surpassed anything a captain in the Apoths should have had. And then there is the more logistical issue of the blackperch mushrooms. Which I have already shared with you, ma'am."

"Yes . . ." said Vashta. "You told me you thought there had been another person at the Hazas' party—someone who had tossed the mushrooms into the fire, causing a distraction."

"Correct," said Ana. "I have felt for some time that there was a third person involved. But as the investigation has continued, I've begun to feel that this third person possessed a startling insight into Iyalet information. Then an attempt was made on my own life, in my own rooms, and I realized the third person had to be someone here in the Trifecta. A senior Iyalet officer."

"Is this true?" said Vashta, horrified. "Do you really think we have such a conspirator?"

"I do," said Ana. "And I think they are sitting directly next to me." She turned to Uhad. "For it was you, wasn't it, Tuwey Uhad? It's been you all along."

VASHTA AND I turned to stare at Immunis Uhad, who wasn't beaming anymore. Instead he gazed ahead with a curiously closed, serene expression on his face.

He cleared his throat and said, "I don't know what you mean, Ana."

"Don't be coy," said Ana. "I've known since Nusis's death. Her safe, as you know, is extremely complicated to open. Yet Din himself realized during that day he took his immunities from her . . ."

I felt my heart grow cold in my chest. "I told her I shouldn't watch," I said softly. "Because an engraver could memorize how to open it."

"Yes," said Ana. "Only an *engraver* could memorize how to manipulate her safe. And you told me yourself, Uhad, that you went to Nusis's offices frequently for grafts to manage your headaches. You had plenty of chances to watch and learn." She cocked her head. "And then there is the comment you made to Din at the banquet . . . that he and I should enjoy a cup of tea. Which would involve using my teapot. Which was, by then, poisoned."

I felt faintly ill. To realize that Immunis Uhad had tried not only to kill Ana, but me as well, was too gruesome for words.

"Why would I need the cure for dappleglass?" Uhad asked, his voice still calm and serene. "Even if I was this poisoner you've dreamed up."

"Because you aren't done," said Ana. "You're still retiring, yes? To the *first ring*. And who lives in the first ring? Why, the rest of the Haza clan, of course. You hate them, don't you? They've been flouting the law here in Talagray for nearly a century. Sabotage, corruption, black-mail, none of which you could ever do anything about. But then . . . you heard something from someone. A whisper about a greater crime. I'm guessing from Jolgalgan, yes?"

Uhad was silent.

"She became one of Kaygi Haza's chosen ones," said Ana. "And I'm guessing that during some party with him, she overheard him say . . . something. Maybe a comment about the cure. Some tossed-off remark that made her start digging in her Iyalet, asking questions, until she slowly put the pieces together. And then, well—she came to you. A crime had been committed, after all, and you're an Iyalet offi-cer. But . . . what could you do about it? Nothing. If you tried to bring a case about this, you'd likely get sidelined by the Hazas, or worse. But by then, Uhad, you were *old*. Beset with afflictions. Your days were short. How better to spend them than by eliminating the villains you'd watch carouse and kill and corrupt in your own canton?

"You plotted how to do it. You planned with Jolgalgan and re-cruited Ditelus—another Oypati. It was inconvenient that Jolgalgan insisted on a most poetic justice, killing them with the same conta-gion that killed Oypat, but . . . you made do. You used your sources and resources to track Blas, and you guided Jolgalgan into killing him. Kaygi Haza was trickier, of course, but you helped there, didn't you? On the day of the party, you attended very briefly—just long enough to toss a blackperch mushroom into the fire and give Jolgal-gan the cover she needed to slip inside and poison his bath."

Ana grinned madly. "But then came the breach. And the ten dead

Engineers. And you realized something had gone *terribly* wrong with your little plot. But then a stroke of mad luck—for you were appointed head of the investigation into your own crimes! How easy it was to send it looking anywhere except at you. Plots to breach the walls, to assassinate Engineers . . . anything that didn't lead to the halls of the Hazas, and your brief moment there."

Uhad exhaled very slightly. "But . . . but then you came," he whispered.

"Yes," said Ana. "You tried to slow me down. At first, I thought you were corrupt, you know. I even had Din test you, with the money. But you weren't corrupt at all. No, you were quite the other thing—righteous zealot, willing to both tolerate and inflict pain to achieve your ends. But still, I made you worried. You felt me getting close. So you went to Jolgalgan's little hut out in the Plains of the Path. You sabotaged her equipment. Then asked her to create more poison for you. And when she did so, she breathed in a lungful of contagion. You asked Ditelus to check in on her—and he was exposed to the same."

A fluttering in my eyes. I remembered Ditelus screaming just before he died: *You . . . you Iudex. You say you want justice. You always say that! You* always say that!

"You hoped the investigation was done then," said Ana. "But you were *committed* now, and your mission wasn't done. You still had dappleglass taken from Jolgalgan, and the elder Hazas had still escaped justice. All you had to do was get to the first ring and continue your murderous work—but then you heard of the reagents key in Nusis's safe. You realized what it *really* was. And you're no Apoth, like Jolgalgan was. You're no expert in dappleglass. An accidental infection was *very* possible. A cure for it would be most useful for your final days. You just had to make sure that I didn't catch you before you got away. Hence, the teapot."

Uhad closed his eyes. There was a long, unpleasant silence.

"Would you like to say something for yourself," said Ana, "or would you prefer to have Din go to your rooms, and find our missing cure, along with all your horrid poisons?"

"He didn't even try to hide it," Uhad whispered. "Can you believe that?"

"Who?" said Ana.

"Kaygi Haza. When . . . when Jolgalgan mentioned she was from Oypat, the old man, drunk, just said flat-out: 'Ah, Oypat. Well, Blas fucked that up, didn't he? Fucked it up for everyone, with the cure.' Then he forgot he ever said it. Because . . . it didn't matter to him, what he'd done. But it mattered to Jolgalgan. And it mattered to me."

There was a tense silence.

"Do you have any idea what it's like," Uhad said softly, "to have so many memories in my mind? So many eternal, endless, everlasting memories of . . . of corruption, of bribery, of exploitation? All while we imperial officers slaved and worked and died to keep horrors from our shores?"

Miljin's voice echoed in my ears as I gazed at Uhad: *Can't take too many wet seasons, the engravers. They don't age well.*

"I thought the walls kept the titans out," said Uhad wearily. "But the more I worked, the more I felt like they caged us *in*, with the gentry. And no one was going to fix it. It was all broken. Nobody cared. Nobody cared, so long as things kept going on as they were."

"So you tried yourself," said Ana. She trembled with rage. "You tried to fix it yourself—and you killed *hundreds of people doing it!*"

"I had to do something!" Uhad snarled. "I couldn't stand to just sit by and watch! The Empire was doing nothing, *nothing*! As was the Iudex! And *you* could do nothing, either, Ana! Hell, you'd tried to stop the Hazas, and you'd gotten banished to Daretana for it!"

At that, Ana stood up and bellowed, *"Are you so sure, Tuwey Uhad?"*

Uhad stared at her, bewildered. "Wh-what do you mean?"

"Don't you think it oddly *perfect*, Uhad," thundered Ana, "that I of all people was put on the doorstep of the Talagray canton? Don't you think it *very* convenient that of all the investigators in all the

Iudex, it was me who was placed directly next door to the canton with the *most* blatant gentry corruption of all?"

"You . . . you mean . . . You were sent to Daretana . . . to *watch* the Hazas?" he said, stunned.

"And I barely had to wait four months before they landed in my lap," she hissed. "But it was because of you. Because the Iyalets failed in their duty. Because *you* failed in *your* duty!"

"No, that's . . . that's impossible!" said Uhad. "They killed your assistant investigator! I know that! Even the Hazas know that!"

"Have *you* ever seen the body?" snapped Ana. She was shivering with rage now. "Have you ever considered that it was very convenient to let the Hazas *believe* that I had been neutralized, so that they could then do something very obvious and stupid? Something that would give the Iudex an *excuse* to bring them to heel? But then you had to make your play at justice. And countless people are dead because of it! What a fool you are, Uhad. What an utter, utter fool." She turned to me. "Din, get out your engraver's bonds. I am ordering you to arrest this man. You wanted justice, Tuwey Uhad, and it shall be given to you—by a rope and a scaffold, surely."

CHAPTER 41

|||

AS EVENING FELL WE GATHERED IN THE TRIFECTA, between the Legion and Engineering and the now-closed Iudex tower. They had built a bonfire there, a four-beamed structure with an ornate woven roof. In the center lay stacks of blackwood, soaked in oil, and atop the stacks rested four wooden figures, anointed in black, purple, red, and blue—a symbolic pyre, for each of the Iyalets that had lost officers.

As the sun set the holy men of the imperial cults lit their thuribles and bathed the pyre in holy smokes and sang of the Khanum, of the march to the sea, of the building of the walls, and of the Empire that awaited us on the other side of this life. When they finished a Legionnaire stepped forward, limping on a crutch, and lit a torch and placed it at the bottom of the pyre, and as the fires blossomed I stood among the weeping crowd and said my thanks to the officers who had fallen during these dark days—both those who had perished in the savagery at the walls, and those felled by the twitch, in this city we deemed civilized.

The crowd departed, yet I remained, my thoughts black and cloudy from all the suffering I'd witnessed, memories I'd never scrub from my soul. Then I saw I did not stand alone: the hulking figure of Captain Miljin stood at the edge of the pyre, staring into the flickering flames.

I approached until I stood beside him. The heat here was so great I felt the hairs upon my face curling. There was a distant, solemn look on the captain's face, and for a long while he did not notice me. Then he did a double take and stared, as if surprised to find me here, a glint of madness in his eyes.

"Oh," he said. "Kol."

"Evening, sir," I said. I bowed.

He did not answer but resumed staring at the fire. A long silence passed.

"How are you doing, sir?" I asked. An absurd question to ask, but it was all I could think to say.

"Tell me . . ." he said.

"Yes, sir?"

"Were you there, in the room, when she unmasked Uhad?"

I hesitated, then nodded. I did not tell him that it was I who'd laid bonds on the immunis and escorted him to the cells.

Miljin stared into the fire for a moment longer. "And . . . did you ever suspect?" he asked. His voice was terribly hoarse. "Did you ever know it was he who wove such evil about all our ears, all this time?"

"I didn't, sir. I had no idea. I don't think Ana truly knew until after Nusis was killed."

"Killed on my watch," he said. "In my city."

Another long moment passed. Ashes danced around us like pollen on a spring breeze.

"None of us knew," I said. "You couldn't have known, si—"

"Don't," he said sharply. "Don't bother."

I looked away, still bathed in the heat of the pyre, and held my tongue.

"But . . . I was right about one thing," he said. "The Empire has less need of brawn these days, and noble battlers, and more need of plotters and schemers. Like your Ana. And you, perhaps."

I did not know what to say to such a thing. I held my tongue.

"You're leaving soon—yes, Kol?" he said.

"Yes, sir. In a few days, I think."

He nodded. "Then will you do an old man a favor?"

"If I can, sir."

With a grunt, Miljin unbuckled his scabbard and gazed at it for a moment. Then he held it out to me. "Will you take this with you when you go?" he asked.

I stared at the scabbard, the mechanical hilt glinting in the dying light of the pyres.

"I'm not staying in the Iudex, Kol," said Miljin. "Not my place anymore. I'll return to the Legion, to what I know best. Walls and titans and bombards and the sea."

"Sir, I—"

"But it's as I told you—swords have little use against a leviathan. They're better applied against them's who make it difficult to *fight* leviathans. And this one will do more for the Empire to go with you, to wherever your path takes you, Kol."

I took the scabbard from him, bewildered. Again, I marveled at its lightness, its leather warm from the heat of the flames. "You mean back to Daretana, sir?" I asked.

Miljin finally smiled. "Ha! You think you're going back to Daretana, boy? How quaint."

I wondered what he meant by that, but then I heard a voice: "You're all right!"

I looked over my shoulder and saw the Legionnaire on the crutch approaching, his head haloed by the setting sun behind. It took me a moment to spy the shabby, earnest smile of Captain Kepheus Strovi within that shadowy face.

"You remember how to open it, Kol?" said Miljin beside me.

Distracted, I returned to him. I nodded. "I do, sir. But—"

"Good." He nodded to me. "Good luck in your travels, Signum. I wish you much honor, and great success."

Then he turned and marched away, stumping out of the Trifecta toward the east.

KEPHEUS AND I walked the lanes of Talagray, moving slowly as he was on a crutch—a memento he'd won when the titan-killer had been fired. "Blasted me clear off my platform," he said sheepishly. "Twisted my ankle. Medikkers should have me right in a day, but they've larger issues to deal with."

"I saw it from a distance," I said. "The thing, coming to the breach. I saw it . . . It had a face? And seemed to be trying to speak?"

"We killed it," he said gruffly. "And held it back. That's all's that needs to be said of it."

We did not talk any more of what we'd witnessed, he at the walls and I in the city. The things we'd seen and done now felt too big for words. Silence was a better language. Yet I did tell him of all that Captain Miljin had just said to me.

"Yes . . ." said Kepheus sadly. "It must be a hard thing, to go from the Legion to the Iudex."

"Why so?"

"Well, in the Legion, you know each wet season if you have won or lost. Yet in the Iudex, you can do all your duties aright, and catch every crooked soul—but at the end, there is no putting right what wrong was done."

I said nothing to that. I thought of Uhad, and how all his memories of so many injustices had changed him. I wondered, for the first time, if my own would do the same to me.

"You're leaving," he said finally. "Yes?"

"I . . . I think so," I admitted. "Our investigation is done. And you?"

"I shall stay here. My family has asked me to return home, but . . . There's more to do. And I mean to do it, until there is no more."

" 'The fulcrum on which the rest of the Empire pivots,' " I quoted.

"Ha! You remembered."

I gave him a look.

"Oh, right," he said. "I suppose that's not terribly surprising . . . But. Here. I've a gift for you, Dinios."

"Oh. Well. You didn't . . ."

He handed me a paper package. I did not need to untie it to know what it was: the scent of tobacco flowed from the paper the second I squeezed it.

"Pipes!" I said, laughing. "Shootstraw pipes. You'll bankrupt yourself, giving me these."

"I won't." He smiled at me. "I just hope they taste as good as the one we shared."

I smiled back. "I don't know how they could. That one had its own taste."

We fell silent, facing the east. Perhaps it was the sudden weight of so many memories I now had within me, but I felt tears in my eyes, and tried to wipe them from my face.

"I'm only here for a few days longer," I said. "It feels so little time."

He leaned forward and kissed me. He smelled of leather, and oil, and the frail curls of fretvine leaves.

"This is Talagray," he said. "Nothing is certain."

I took him by the hand, and together we returned to the city to find what sweetness we could in the few days we had.

CHAPTER 42

|||

I STARED BACKWARD AT THE TOWERS OF TALAGRAY
as our carriage rumbled along, the Plains of the Path and the massive
sea walls slowly retreating into the morning mist. I counted the remaining months of the wet season and grappled with the knowledge
that in a mere handful of months more another season would come.

"Will it hold?" asked Ana's voice softly.

I turned back around to her, sitting blindfolded in the seat across
from me, with her hands folded pleasantly in her lap.

"Pardon, ma'am?" I said.

"*Will it hold*—that's what you're thinking, yes?" she said.

"Do you read thoughts now, ma'am?"

"Oh, no. It is the obvious thought one might have upon leaving
Talagray—or coming to it. Will all those artifices and structures, built
from the blood and toil of so many and planned by so many brilliant
minds . . . will they hold in the face of what's coming?" She cocked
her head, grinning. "I wish I *could* read your thoughts, Din. Instead
I'm forced to ask you stupid questions."

"You've the rest of the trip to torment me, ma'am," I said wryly.
"No need to start early."

"Mm. But I'm curious about one particular question I have for
you."

"And what's that?"

"I'd like to ask you—what is the Empire, Din?"

I blinked as the carriage bounced along. "Ah . . . pardon, ma'am?"

"I've heard your reports, after all," she said. "I've noticed many people made claims to you that the Empire was this, or that, or functioned in this way . . . It's strange, isn't it? Perhaps the existential nature of the canton provokes it. But I am curious what your conclusions are. What *is* the Empire, Din? Can you describe it?"

"You don't really expect me to answer that, do you, ma'am?"

"I'm still your commanding officer. I could order you to do so. But that'd be rather boring."

I thought about it. "Well . . . before I came here, ma'am . . ."

"Yes?"

"I would have told you the Empire was might, and mass, and strength, and scale."

"And now?"

"Now . . . now it feels frail, and imperfect, and improvised, and . . . and coincidental, ma'am. The wrong wind might blow it all apart, should it go untended."

"Accurate. And I somewhat agree. But I have always rather thought the Empire was wrought in the image of that which it was made to fight."

"A . . . a titan, ma'am?"

"Oh, yes. For the Empire is huge. Complex. Often unwieldy and slow. And in many places, weak. A massive colossus, stretching out across the cantons, one in whose shadow we all live . . . and yet it is prone to wounds, infections, fevers, and ill humors. But its strangest feature is that the more its citizens feel it is broken, the more broken it *actually becomes*. Just look at Uhad. It must be tended to, as you said. For without this tending, the Empire shall fail. Yet it's rather tricky to tend to something from inside it, yes?"

I narrowed my eyes at her. "And . . . what is your role in tending to this colossus, ma'am?"

"Oh, I told you, Din," she said, smiling dreamily. "When we last rumbled down this very road. It's the *maintenance* folk who keep the Empire going. Someone, after all, must do the undignified labor to keep the grand works of our era from tumbling down. I simply perform maintenance, in my own little way. And you have ably assisted me in that, of course."

We rumbled on in silence for a moment.

I sucked my teeth, thinking. "You once said, ma'am, that there would be a time when you'd tell me many truths."

"That's so."

"Is now such a time?"

"Now?" She pressed a hand against the wall of the carriage, feeling its shuddering. "Now is the time for *some* truths, should you like to hear them, Din. We can then decide if you'd like to hear more after that."

"You are no ordinary Iudex Investigator. Are you?"

"That is true. I am not."

"Not if you were stationed in Daretana to watch the Hazas, as part of some giant plot."

"That is also true."

"Though I wonder what you're going to do in Daretana now, ma'am."

"Oh, I am not going back to Daretana, Din," she said. "The Iudex office there will now be closed. It was a very good place to be banished to, but it has served its purpose. Instead, this carriage shall first stop at a small town on the border of the Tala canton. There, I shall discuss the events of the past weeks with the conzulate, who waits for me now."

I stared at her. "The . . . the Iudex conzulate? He's waiting on *you*?"

"Has been for the past day. I am most eager to debrief him. It was his idea to invent the fiction of my banishment, after all."

"Wait. And your assistant? Did the twitch kill her, or is she truly alive? Was that all just a story you invented to deceive the Hazas?"

"You do not know her," sniffed Ana. "And her affairs are her own. I will not divulge her situation to you, as able and admirable as you are, Din."

I boggled at this for a moment. The idea that a conzulate—one of the giant, ageless beings who were second only to the emperor himself in the imperial hierarchy—was now waiting on Ana was impossible for me to comprehend.

"What will happen after you talk to the conzulate, ma'am?" I asked slowly.

"Well . . . he will likely give me a new assignment," she said. "For I *am* an investigator, but I serve in a very . . . special division. I am given issues that are either sensitive, inordinately difficult to make sense of, or both. In other words, I do what many folk do in the grand and heavenly Empire of Khanum—I keep things running, in hopes of keeping the walls up. Once I speak to the conzulate, I shall be off to my next task, I suspect. The next crime, the next murder, the next treachery."

I stared out the window, watching the countryside roll by.

"Yet before I go," she said, "the conzulate will also likely want to speak to *you*, Din."

I said nothing.

"For I will still be in need of an assistant investigator," she said. "And you did a decent job in Talagray." She thought for a moment. "Could have been cheerier and smiled a bit more, sure, but still, a good job. I would have you keep doing it, if you prefer."

My gaze stayed fixed on the countryside. The shimmering veil of the jungle had embraced us once again, and all was dark. I thought of muddy little Daretana, and what few opportunities would await there.

I glanced down at my boots, now worn and stained from all my travels. They didn't look quite so bad, I thought. Perhaps they would look even better with a bit more wear.

"I bought you something, ma'am," I said. "A gift."

"Really?" she said. "Why?"

I handed her a small wooden box. "Felt I owed it to you, after all this."

She opened the box and sniffed it, then sat up, her body thrumming with elation.

"Moodies!" she said, delighted. "Mood grafts! And are they . . ."

"The hallucinogenic ones," I said. "The ones you're always asking about. I had to visit a very dodgy shop in Talagray to get them. Just please don't consume one now, ma'am. I suspect that'd make this trip quite a bit less pleasant."

She cackled with glee. "No, no, and it'd be unwise to attend my debriefing mooded clean out of my skull, Din. Thank you. I do *very* much appreciate this."

I smiled wearily. "Perhaps an odd way to begin my duties as your formal assistant—breaking the law before I even start."

She stowed the little box away. "Is it?" Then she grinned her horrid, predatorial smile: too many teeth, and all too white. "I find it full of good portents, myself."

I pulled my straw cone hat down over my eyes, lay back with my sword at my side, and began to doze.

ACKNOWLEDGMENTS

|||

I would like to thank my editor, Julian Pavia, for helping me crunch this sucker out. I'd had the idea of writing a fun murder mystery novel for a while, and then I sat down and pumped out something that was very decisively not a murder mystery novel, and Julian helped me realize that. I then had to go through the rather tempestuous process of chucking it in the garbage and starting over. That is an odd psychological dance to do, but a necessary one—it is better to throw away words you did not want to write than keep them, even when their total is very high—and I appreciate him for sitting through it.

I would also like to thank my family, as I often do in my books, but especially for this one. Writing murder mysteries is largely a process of logistics, I think, ensuring that the timelines work and the right evidence gets in the right place at the right time. You essentially become the Jeff Bezos of killing dudes you just made up. This takes up a pretty large amount of brain space at any given moment, so I would like to apologize to my family for asking very stupid questions like "Which child is playing soccer today?" or "Which trip are we packing for, again?" or even "How old am I turning this year?" I would like to apologize further because I actually really enjoyed writing this one, and plan to write more murder mysteries, so I will probably continue being a very stupid man. Tough nuggets, suckers.

I would also like to thank my mom for giving me the Nero Wolfe books that inspired so much of Ana, even if I eventually decided she was more like Hannibal Lecter than Wolfe. I would also like to thank my grandmother Marilyn Shaw, whose laundry room was overflowing with old paperbacks, with many of them being murder mysteries I read. I like to think she would have enjoyed this one, though maybe not the language. Sorry, Nana.

Two other folks I'd like to thank are Jesse Jenkins and Jerusalem Demsas, who both spend what must be somewhat frustrating careers cataloging how America is now terrified of building stuff. Their work exploring this and lobbying for change—along with many, many others—inspired a great deal of the Preservation Boards in this story. Regulations have their uses, but we cannot allow them to form the jar that will eventually be used to trap us and pickle us in our own brine. I wanted to write about civil servants and bold builders for that exact purpose. Keep up the fight!

Yours,
Robert

ROBERT JACKSON BENNETT is the author, most recently, of the Founders Trilogy. Previous to this, he wrote the Divine Cities Trilogy, which was a 2018 Hugo Award finalist in the Best Series category. The first book in the series, *City of Stairs*, was also a finalist for the World Fantasy and Locus awards, and the second, *City of Blades*, was a finalist for the World Fantasy, Locus, and British Fantasy awards. His previous novels, which include *American Elsewhere* and *Mr. Shivers*, have received the Edgar Award, the Shirley Jackson Award, and the Philip K. Dick Citation of Excellence. He lives in Austin with his family.

robertjacksonbennett.com

X: @robertjbennett

ABOUT THE TYPE

|||

This book was set in Vendetta, a typeface designed by John Downer as an homage to the advertising signs painted on walls of old factories and warehouses of roadside America. Downer began his career as a journeyman sign painter, and Vendetta was inspired in part by the brushstrokes used in sign painting, which give this typeface its distinct angular character.